Spy Station

The Forlani Saga: Part Two

J. M. R. Gaines

J. M. R. Gaines
FREDERICKSBURG, VIRGINIA

James Gaines
17 North Pointe Dr.
Fredericksburg, VA 22405
www.jmrgaines.com

Publisher's Note: This is a work of fiction. Names, characters, places, and incidents are a product of the author's imagination. Locales and public names are sometimes used for atmospheric purposes. Any resemblance to actual people, living or dead, or to businesses, companies, events, institutions, or locales is completely coincidental.

Book Layout & Design ©2013 - BookDesignTemplates.com

Ordering Information:
Quantity sales. Special discounts are available on quantity purchases by corporations, associations, and others. For details, contact the "Special Sales Department" at the address above.

Spy Station/ J. M. R. Gaines. -- 1st ed.
ISBN 978-0-9981721-3-2

To Papa and Paddy, Authors of the Feast

"Any fool can tell a crisis when it arrives. The real service to the state is to detect it in embryo."

—ISAAC ASIMOV, *FOUNDATION*

1

The Forlani girl, her toenails retracted, padded noiselessly down the ramp into the storage compartment, alert for any movement. As soon as she got to the bottom of the ramp, she gracefully vaulted over a railing and crouched behind a cargo cylinder, pointing her weapon ahead to scan with its detector to try to find her enemy. She had little experience hunting spies in cramped quarters, but she had been very well trained, according to the traditions of the Forlani Guard and her own matriline. Nothing from the detector. Yet she was sure the enemy agent was watching her from some hideout among these cargo containers. She knew fellow members of her cluster must have blocked the other exits now and were counting on her to flush out her opponent, even at the cost of her own life. She decided to trust her physical senses, first her brilliant red eyes, which were more effective in the dark than those of most creatures.   At the same time, she drew her striped security cape forward over her body. In the penumbra of the compartment, where a single lamp somewhere ahead of her cast strange shadows over the cargo, the stripes added to her own concealment. She sniffed the musty air carefully for odors. Still without a clue, she flicked her tongue out repeatedly. The Forlani tongue was better than a second nose, with over a hundred thousand receptors sensitive to a vast number of chemical signatures. Ah, there it was! The distinctive track of a Powl. It reminded her of a certain yellow and brown berry that grew near the polar regions of her distant planet. Nothing but a Powl could produce such an impression in the depths of a space station so many light years from her world.

Was it armed? Hard to determine. It had snatched the memory unit from a table top in the Forlani rooms and rushed on its six legs out the door. It could not possibly be carrying a machine to read the complicated tetrahedron, deliberately chosen by the delegation because it was such a rare data storage device and the readers were scarce and bulky. What would the Powl do, fight or run? They were neither terribly smart nor terribly formidable, being employed mainly as menial workers on freighters, where their tick-like bodies and low need for moisture were an advantage.   Powls were also quite good at maneuvering into tight places and quickly scampering away. She remembered one more thing. They were expert climbers. Peering into the dark once again, she thought she saw the slightest bulge on the ceiling off to her right. She guessed that the Powl might try a diversion and possibly move to neutralize her, then make a dash to double back the way they had come, taking its chance against whoever was backing her up at the doorway.

The only thing to do was to expose herself first to prod it out into action and hope to prevail. She stood up and took a couple of steps to the left. Sure enough, a beam zapped against a container next to her. Leaping three meters, she aimed her weapon, prepared to fire when she landed. Other beams flashed harmlessly behind her. As soon as her feet touched the ground, she waved her tail wildly to distract the Powl's aim and fired. A projectile from her weapon smashed into its target – not the spy, but the tetrahedron it was holding in one of its left limbs. It burst into tiny slivers and the Powl shot off mewling across the ceiling, heading for the door.

With a little sigh of pride and thankfulness that her opponent was such a bad shot, she whistled and said into her communicator "Cluster Leader. Unit destroyed. Agent doubling back."

"Good work. Let it go. Kantua will try to track it back to contact. In any case, it would just be hard to explain if we killed it. Fade into shadows and reassemble at HQ."

"Understood Cluster Leader Ayan'we. Leli out."

The Ministry of Interstellar Relations was located on top of a hill on the outskirts of the administrative capital of Garan Prime. Tashto took a minute to gaze out at the view overlooking the bustling city, his eyes soaking in the sights of garish electric billboards and towering office spires, the hoverbikes slowly driving through the crowded roadways, the plumes of smoke rising from the massive factories. Such a view of the entire city metropolis was a rare luxury in his life; most of his existence had been spent below, in its disorienting streets, monitoring its citizens and business leaders for evidence of tax dodging and money laundering. The Garanian government had finally rewarded him by promoting him from his old job of Tax Monitor to the much more prestigious position of Off-World Diplomat. Tashto had performed well in his first few "diplomatic" assignments and had spent the last couple of weeks studying for his greatest, most prestigious assignment: the Zonal Peace Conference. "Tashto, the Overseer of Diplomats will see you now," a steamy voice announced over the intercom. Tashto nervously cracked his knuckles and stepped into a long corridor.

As he walked through the vast building, Tashto looked at the portraits and statues of the rulers of Garan, from its old kings and warlords during the Unity Wars to the modern Planetary Ministers. Ornately detailed and painted in bright hues, the heroes and kings of old contrasted sharply with the modern rulers of Garan, who wore bland beige suits and ties, bearing a pitiful resemblance to humans. During his brisk walk, Tashto wondered if something had been lost during his planet's rush to transition into an interstellar power. Would the old warlords, products of a culture that prided itself on individualism and valor, have wanted to live among a people increasingly consumed by subterfuge and the domination of the central state, as the modern Garanians were? Tashto had found no answers to his questions in the government-approved historical documents, and none of the other Garanians in the building looked like they would be interested in conversation on the topic; they were too busy bustling about, engaged in their own work routines, to be bothered with any sort of discourse unrelated to their duties.

The door to the Overseer's office was open, as if the Overseer were absolutely certain Tashto would soon arrive and saw no need to impede his swift entrance. Tashto walked in the doorway and saw the Overseer standing by his desk, leaning backward on his tail. "Welcome, Tashto," the Overseer greeted him. "I have heard timeliness was once considered the First Virtue by the culture of the Heroic Age. Or was it the fifth virtue? It's so difficult to be certain."

Of course it's difficult to be certain, since the Ministry of Historical Records destroyed those documents after the Unity Wars. "I don't know of such things," Tashto said deferentially.

"Of course. We shouldn't preoccupy ourselves with such useless superstitions or what they may have meant at some time," the Overseer continued. "Tashto, the time has come for you to prepare for your transit to the Zonal Peace Conference. What do you know of the factions assembling at the Varess Space Station?"

"The Earthlings are numerous, but their planet is in disarray. They never achieved a Unity government on their home world, and a plague has broken loose. Their leverage is still formidable, but less so than it normally would be. The Song Pai are as the usually are —belligerent, violent, interested only in brutality. The Blynthians, inscrutable, of course. The Talinian Newts are…"

"I am not concerned with the Newts, an inferior evolution" the Overseer interrupted. "The species you should be focused on should not be Talinians or Song Pai. Do not be dazzled by the garish private corporate empires of the Umani either."

Tashto could feel the feathery stubble on the back of his neck nervously flex and stick up. "Which group would you recommend I focus on?" he asked.

"The Forlani," the Overseer answered. "It is the Forlani, more than any other race, that have a history of trade with Song Pai. There are three reasons that we have decided to focus on influencing the Forlani, rather than the other species at this conference. Firstly, there is a small chance we may bend the Song

Pai in the way we wish by influencing the Forlani; we may never gain influence on Song Pa, but we may on Forlan. Secondly, we may gain information about the Song Pai through the Forlani diplomats that would aid us, should we choose to begin open conflict with them once more. Finally, the Forlani have a unique weakness that the other species at this conference lack."

"A diplomat they sent, I presume?" Tashto said.

"Correct. The information we have discovered about her indicates that their security director is quite young, and this is the first time she has attended a diplomatic conference. We think she may be more easily manipulated compared to the other diplomats, especially since her mother is among them. Do you think you could so easily influence a veteran like Chester Macdougal of Dahlgren or the Newt Kee'ad of Tionar? Of course, gaining influence over her at the start of her career will allow you to continue to manipulate her for many years to come, whereas the older diplomats are far closer to their retirement."

"I am confident I will succeed," Tashto said. "But is there any supplemental information you have on her? I found very little on her personality and interests in the official government files."

"That is because we have very little reliable information yet. She graduated their Academy not long ago, she is just beginning her career, and we have no types of data that we could use to formulate a psychological analysis of how she would respond in certain situations. Beyond the fact that she possesses a unique understanding of Blynthians, we are mostly in the dark. Of her mother, Entara, we almost know too much. The romantic songs about her and her human companion, the late Klein, are blaring all over the quadrant. I even heard one translated into Garani – disgusting! In fact, it is up to you to begin to obtain new data for us. To take note of each minute neurosis, each unusual response, every emotional peak and valley. In short, you are not only to be a spy — such a vulgarized, unseemly word, don't you think? — but also a psychologist. You do remember her name from the files, correct?"

"Yes," Tashto said. "Her name is Ayan'we."

"Excellent. I see you've taken time to study all the available information we have. Now it is your time to broaden it. After all, information is the most important currency. Only with that may we hope to gain an advantage over the Song Pai by involving them in war against the Blynthians. Information will lead to the establishment of a second front and our ultimate advantage."

"Was that one of the Virtues?" Tashto asked.

"Not of the Heroic Age," the Overseer answered, clutching a pen in his clawed hand. "It is, however, the First Virtue of our age, which is the only age you need to know of."

The Phiddian space station called Transfer Varess was, Entara thought, quite sensible, compared to those hollow-core things the humans constructed. Someday perhaps they would learn to conserve their resources better. Instead of the Earthlings' bizarre doughnut shapes (she remembered Klein had once gotten her a package of doughnuts when they were together, but she never liked them as much as crunchy toast), Varess was shaped like a slightly squashed fruit, spherical, but with a protruding ring around the diameter that contained the docking ports for up to forty vehicles, such as the one where she was now cuddling her most recent, and perhaps last, child. Their present ship had originally belonged to one of the Earth corporations and like many others had been left without a crew when they learned that their employers had all died of the plague. Without pay or drug quotas, the crew members had degenerated and wandered off to join other ships, some even desperate enough to indenture themselves to the Song Pai. She knew from Klein's harsh experiences what the eventual end of that indenture usually meant. But the thought of being on a virtual ghost ship troubled her much less than the responsibilities she had shouldered, not only for the Eyes of Alertness, but for all the matrilines and the Council of Nine, when she agreed to attend the Zonal Conference.

"Soft baby Quatilla," she murmured, "Go to sleep now. You've eaten enough and I still worry you won't get your growing sleep now that I've taken you away from the nurturing peace of Forlan." Peace of Forlan.   Yes, but it was only guaranteed by the continual military might of the Song Pai, those ugly, repellant squid-like creatures that had honorably guarded their world against the depredations of the Earth corporations.   Only too willingly would most humans have enslaved her sisters, according to the FastTrack scheme her corrupt husband Tays'she had sought to implement.   Only too quickly would the human Corporations have ravaged her planet's ecology, just as it was finally being restored after the Disasters. "Fifty-sixth daughter," she whispered to the slumbering baby, "You would be unsafe were it not for those unlikely allies.   And now their taste for conflict threatens to draw us into a crisis.   A crisis I am supposed to know how to solve."

For centuries before she was born, before the Song Pai had first navigated into the Forlan system, the cephalopods had been at war unceasingly against the distant Garanians – a race tough enough to assure that their own taste for suicidal sacrifice would not go unsatisfied.   Each Song Pai knew that its ability to vitrospawn, to pass on its genes to a new generation, would hinge on a heroic and violent death.   Yet, now the Song Pai were contemplating the unthinkable, a war against the Blynthians.   That strange and vastly powerful race, with its territory in systems in the opposite direction from Garan, might seem an enticing target, especially since it contained many watery worlds favorable to Song Pai expansion. Blynthians themselves had never attacked anyone in recent memory, and preferred to rest behind their wall of silence. Nevertheless, their technology was phenomenal, as they had demonstrated by transporting a large, hollowed-out asteroid many parsecs at incredible speeds in order to aid the human plague recovery at Tau Ceti Anchorage. What would happen if their anger was stirred up, assuming they were capable of anger?

Ayan'we's arrival interrupted her mother's reverie. She spotted Quatilla right away and tip-toed across the room gracefully, as Entara placed the infant in a moss-filled crib covered with a porous muffle, so they could talk during her nap. "Any news on that Powl?" she asked.

"We followed it back to the other side of the station, Mother, but it didn't contact any Phiddians or humans. It may be waiting until the Garanians arrive, which they will do very shortly. Maybe it won't make contact at all, since it failed in its mission. We'll have to see."

"Have the Blynthians shown themselves yet?"

"No. They're still behind their barrier. The part of the council room assigned to them is still walled off. You can hear construction noises behind it, but I think they will wait for the formal opening to appear. I wonder what effect it will have on the other delegations. Besides myself, only some of the

Coriolans and Dr. Torghh have ever actually seen one."

"When you were with them, did you ever get a sense of their emotions toward the Song Pai?"

"Mom, I'm not sure if they have emotions like most other species. As you'll see, communication is most problematical. I strongly suspect the trade language that I learned is not even their principal mode of communication among themselves."

"I hope Torghh can give us some insight. Although he's present as physiological consultant – and therefore is supposed to stay neutral – Ragatti seems to think he is positively inclined towards us and may be helpful."

"Hah, the great Doctor Ragatti. I wish she could stop operating and seducing her way across the galaxy long enough to help us with something clearly as important as this. As a physician, doesn't she realize how much is at stake?"

Entara gave her firstborn daughter a knowing maternal expression. "I know from experience that Ragatti is most helpful when one doesn't attempt to control her too much. Despite her natural... eccentricity, she has a generous heart and a brilliant, though quirky, mind. And she is devoted in her own way. Hasn't she been present at most of my birthings and those of your sisters, too? She could easily leave that chore to an ordinary doctor, but I think that in her round-about way she is fond of us."

"Mother, I must say that I feel you are a bit too indulgent towards Ragatti because of her kindness towards Klein and the fact that she affectionately reconstructed part of his face after his injuries. As well as other little services she claims to have performed."

Entara laughed. "I, for one, have no doubt that she did give Klein much pleasure. As I always meant her to."

"If she cherished him so much, why didn't she come with me to the funeral? Girls from the pleasure houses all over Domremy who had never copulated once with Klein were pleading to come and sing."

"If Ragatti mourns, she does it in her own way. Let's talk of something else. We also need intelligence on the Song Pai. Have you contacted the human I inquired about?"

"I have traced the movements of the Dissenter Trevor, who left Song Pa some time ago. He may be headed for Gamma Lyra Four. Will his mystical insights really help us? Isn't he really interested in that species that dominated Song Pa before the squids' civilization replaced them?"

"We'll have to wait and see. In the meantime, I'm also concerned about our male. Is he going to stay in his quarters forever? I never knew what to expect from a male on a diplomatic mission, but the Brotherhood was so insistent at having their own representative present for planetary deliberations that there was no alternative. I hope he is not going to embarrass us."

"I'll try to learn more about him, mother. It's rumored that he doesn't behave like a typical male Forlani, but maybe that will turn out to be good."

"Well, if you think so. After all, you tend to be hyper-critical of most males, so if you think this one has a good side, I'll be delighted if you're proven right."

As Ayan'we was on her way to have a word with Isshel, the lone male member of the Forlani delegation, she found herself in a corridor approaching a group of four fully hermaphroditic Phiddians. Their hands were all over each other, in and out of their flimsy garments. When they spotted Ayan'we, they spread out ever so slightly to make it impossible for her to pass by them in a dignified fashion. She knew what was about to happen. She was about to be vigorously groped by all four of them. Her mother had warned her about this sort of thing.

As soon as Entara learned that her daughter had volunteered for the security cluster being sent to the Varess Conference, she had taken her aside for a talk. Of course, Ayan'we knew from her encyclopedic knowledge of interplanetary cultures that the male/female Phiddians were one of the most sensual species in the known section of the galaxy, indulging in some kind of genital excitement on an average of 7.6 times during a daily cycle. What she lacked was personal experience. Her training sessions for work in the off-planet houses where Forlani females gave pleasure to various other species in exchange for much needed econ credits had covered this area, but mainly in theory. She had by choice avoided practical house service in favor of intensive computer and space training.

Entara, who was at that time expecting any day to give birth to a new member of the matriline, had sat down and shared some heretofore unexplained memories. "When I was in the first year of my house service, and before I had gone to Domremy or met Klein, I had a few Phiddian clients. I want you to know what they are like in their private lives, in case your official duties make it necessary, or even desirable, for you to become intimate with them. Do you feel comfortable talking about this?"

"Of course, mother, I'm no prude. I bet I... well let's not get into that yet. Please go on."

"Well, you've undoubtedly heard that the Phiddian humanoids are quite uninhibited about any kind of physical intimacy and that is completely true. Maybe even an understatement. They can get so involved in sporting around that they are capable of stupidly neglecting other duties or opportunities."

"Uh huh."

"You will surely see them pawing each other in situations where any other species would exercise a little discretion, and that sort of exploring is not limited to their own kind. I foresee that they will have some problems abiding by the decorum required in interplanetary gatherings. In fact, I was surprised when they volunteered to host the conference at all and more surprised when all the principal parties accepted. The Song Pai, for instance, are notoriously slovenly about many of their bodily functions, but are great sticklers when it comes to anything approaching reproduction. They'll have to cover all five of their eyes to put up with some Phiddian behavior."

They both laughed at this joke. Humor at the expense of Song Pai was the one little disrespect that the Forlani permitted themselves in regard to the cephalopods who had more than once come gallantly to their aid.

"But mother," Ayan'we went on, "What was it like to actually pleasure them?"

"The only thing remotely hard is deciding which sex to address first. Because they will usually insist on having it both ways. More often than not they will blurt out exactly what they want you to do. Don't worry about failing to please them, because they are so excitable that virtually anything will set them off and after a minute or two they completely lose control of themselves. Their peak of excitement lasts only an instant, but they demand it again and again until they grow weary and eventually nod off from utter exhaustion. You don't have to engage in much drama, pretending that they are exciting you, because they literally don't care. They can be totally insensitive to what another individual is feeling when they get in that state."

"The poor idiots! Don't they get taken advantage of by other partners?"

"Just imagine. That's why they were frequent clients at our houses. They can always depend on our honesty and hatred of aggression. Elsewhere, they have been known to let themselves get kidnapped or abused, even murdered for fun. And of course, they are victims to innumerable robberies. They would be a natural for blackmail, too, except that they have no sense of shame about sexual matters. Instead of hiding their misadventures, they willingly brag about them."

"Wasn't anyone ever tempted to grab some of their credits anyway?"

Entara gave a coy smile. "Yes and no. I never knew any Forlani to rob them or even to beg for more than the agreed price. On the other hand, just for fun, sometimes a girl would prod them a little to see how far they would go, just to have a good joke for the fireside later, and then give back all their money and jewelry while they were asleep before she left. They would be too stupefied to remember what happened after they awoke."

"You?"

"Well, I'm a little embarrassed to recall it. However, one time there was this certain client who was so besotted with me that I took off a precious nose ring and put it ... in a piercing elsewhere on the body. I took before and after images and the whole house shook with laughter at dinner that night."

Ayan'we giggled along with her mother, but inside she was secretly a bit shocked to learn that the woman who had become a legend because of her emotional bond to Klein had once had such a mischievous streak. Perhaps she still did.

This conversation flashed through Ayan'we's mind as she approached the gaggle of Phiddians and sure enough, as she tried to squeeze past, she felt hands brushing on all her reachable organs. They were very active little fingers, too, despite the fact that the Phiddians had only four to a hand. The ones who were feeling for her nipples would have been disappointed, since they were pretty hard to locate amidst the frontal fur of an unmated Forlani female. Those searching for the entrance to what would become her birth canal got what they wanted. This caused her no great discomfort, though, since any girl who had gone through her pleasure training had gotten past that point on the first day.

"Oops, how clumsy of us," tittered one of the Phiddians. The others echoed in with such mock excuses. "Please allow us to make up for our thoughtlessness by offering you a delicious drink at the tavern. The station has stocked a variety of exotic juices that are bound to tickle your senses. We know that you Forlani have no taste for stronger intoxicants."

Ayan'we nodded and smiled, knowing that this group would stop in the tavern precisely long enough to gulp down one glass before heading off to a private cubicle for a fast orgy. "Regrettably," she drawled, "I am expected to report to my superiors. I wish you a delightful break from your labors."

"Another time then. Ta ta! We would really like to know you better."

"What a waste of time that would be!" whispered Ayan'we as she continued unmolested up the corridor.

As she turned the corner into a larger passageway, she failed to notice two figures who had fallen in behind her and paused at the entrance of the corridor to observe her brush with the lascivious Phiddians. They were two of the Song Pai delegation, turned gunmetal grey in thought as they saw how Ayan'we dealt with the awkward situation. When the Phiddians stopped playing with each other long enough to notice the two figures, they made no attempt to intercept them as they had with the lithe young Forlani. Instead, they flattened themselves in single file against the wall as the huge cephalopods, even bulkier than usual in their water-breathing apparatus, cruised past. Politely, the Song Pai also went by in Indian file, confining their tentacles to the smallest possible area to avoid contact with the Phiddians, who probably would have leapt in fright if they had to touch those slimy-looking bodies. The Song Pai said nothing, but bobbed up and down rapidly in delight at the cowardly reaction of their hosts. Song Pai loved nothing more than battle, but disdained conflict with species too ridiculously weak to provide a good test of their valor. This did not prevent them from humiliating their inferiors, often splattering them with feces. However, these two guards knew they were on a diplomatic mission where they had to curb their native taste for fun at the expense of lesser creatures. So they confined themselves to the slightest indirect hints of aggression and enjoyed the prospect of sharing this story with their counterparts back on the Song Pai ship.

When the Phiddians had rushed into another corridor, the Song Pai paused and burbled to each other in their own idiom.

"The young tailed one displays initiative and courage. She may prove a worthy ally to die with some day."

"That is true, but I think she is too young to be charged with such an important job as security chief. Our own second eldest is much more suitable. This Ayan'we may make a serious mistake."

"Perhaps she was the only one available for such burdens. The tailed ones are new to these cosmic conferences which do little but waste time and foment distrust."

"That could well be, but I think her mother Entara is much more foolish to bring that infant with her to such an event. Never would we bring our young from the spawning grounds back home to take risks in space. What could she have been thinking?"

"I heard she has numerous other offspring. She might feel one here or there does not matter."

"I do not concur. When I served as a guard at their spaceport, I noticed that they display much care for their young -- for mammals, anyway."

"But I understand they are not placental mammals in the same sense as the humans, the Phiddians, and the Coriolans."

"True, their race corresponds to a particular type of animal the Earthlings call marsupials. On their Earth, this group preceded the evolution of placental mammals, but was replaced by them in most areas. However, Forlani differ from these marsupials because they have no pouch. Their young are born at a much more advanced stage and grow very quickly. Their nourishment by the mother lasts only a few seasons."

"You truly learned much during your spaceport assignment. Yet I have trouble agreeing that the Forlani are to be considered more primitive than humans."

"Of course they are not! On Forlan, they represent the alpha race, having millions of years longer to evolve than the humans had on their planet. They should be considered superior to humans."

"Even so, from what you say of their raising their young, I now see that this Entara and her infant present a potential security vulnerability for us, as their allies. Should we not recommend to the elder that Agent I-35 must be very vigilant for their welfare?"

"And especially pay attention to whoever may be hanging around their lodgings. The infant is essentially helpless and could make us vulnerable as well in these so-called negotiations."

"Let's find the second eldest and make the suggestion."

Ayan'we paused to collect her thoughts a bit before pressing the buzzer to the door of the male's compartment. She knew from experience that she always tended to be too abruptly formal with males, perhaps as a result of her terrible relationship with her scheming and disloyal father Tays'she. Ayan'we did not wish to get this working relationship off on the wrong foot. The male who accompanied the delegation had shown all the typical signs of laziness and dissipation. Still, there were ways he could prove useful if he could bestir himself from his aesthetic considerations for a while.

The buzzer was answered by a curt "Enter." Ayan'we prepared for the worst and opened the door to see the male was standing behind a table with an elaborate hood suspended above it. The hood was made of a clear material, but was studded with innumerable metallic dots, probably some kind of electrodes. Beneath the hood sat a large basin of water. The male was fiddling with an object next to it. He glanced up at her, then back to his work, and immediately did a double take. He gazed with interest at Ayan'we for a second and then did something very

uncharacteristic of Forlani males in female company –
he turned his palms up in a gesture of respect.

"Welcome. Isshel of the fourth degree."

"With thanks. Ayan'we of Eyes of Alertness, of
Entara."   Having properly introduced herself by
reference to her extended matrilineal clan and her
mother, Ayan'we took note that Isshel would not have
been required by male protocol to reveal that he had
already reached the prestigious fourth degree of
artistic achievement. If he was not simply bragging,
this would be a further sign of respect.

Isshel gestured towards a pair of stools and
they both sat. "How can I be useful?"

"I have been wanting to speak with you about
the upcoming ceremonies. Now that the opening is
imminent, I suspect we will all be very busy." It was
the most subtle way she could suggest that the male
had not been playing a very active role in the
delegation so far.

"Yes, you're right," he readily admitted. "I must
apologize for my lack of contributions up to now. To
be honest, I have been keeping to myself partly out of
fear of committing some diplomatic gaffe. You see, I
have received almost no training for this sort of thing
and have no idea what to do."

"I'm sure we can help. Are there specific things
about the mission you would like to understand?"

Isshel sighed woefully. "Just about everything.
Please understand that the Brotherhood does not even
school us in the basics of interplanetary relationships.

I have been studying, when I could tear myself away from this project," he said with a wave of the arm to his contraption on the table and another at a desk full of memory devices and visuals. "It's just that I didn't even have an idea of where all these planets and civilizations were located. I made a mobile to help visualize them in space. I'm a sculptor, right? I'm still having trouble figuring out how all these creatures work, physically, but I think I can at least recognize them and remember what not to do in some circumstances. I just don't see how I can help you with anything important."

"I have been talking with my mother…"

"Entara para-pa of the Nine!" he pronounced with obvious admiration. "I long to meet her and hope I won't embarrass us."

"I'm sure you will find she is very easy to approach. We feel your most useful contribution could be to observe the psychological interplay between members of the other delegations from a male point of view. Especially the Phiddians, who are, as you know, hermaphroditic, and shift constantly between what appear to be male personality traits and female ones. I don't mind admitting that I've found them a bit confusing so far."

"Psychology is one of the things we do study. In between endless repetitive courses on mass, color, perspective, contrast, light, movement – which at least play a role in our creative efforts. It's the nauseating levels of abstract artistic theory that are hardest to take: primitivism, collectivism, individualism, sophistry, post-sophistry, pre-sophistry, Pungism, post-Pungism, neo-post-Pungism... ugh!"

"Sounds very... involved."   Ayan'we just stopped herself from saying "useless."

"The problem is it's not involved with anything relevant. I don't want to take it anymore and that's why I'm really here."

Ayan'we arched her brows a bit. She had hardly expected this sort of confession. Most males considered their feelings far too sophisticated and advanced to share with females, particularly ones they barely knew.

"You mean you were not picked for this trip by the Brotherhood because of your expertise?"

"Certainly not. I was picked to get me off planet and keep me there during the triennial synod. My voice was not one they wanted to hear. Many others were given distant chores for the same reason."

"I am surprised that they approach artistic issues in such a stilted way."

"Not just artistic issues. What they are most angry about are the social issues. Listen, Ayan'we, I wouldn't mention this publicly to just anyone, but as the daughter of Entara you should understand. We know that your mother has begun to raise concerns about practices within the Brotherhood. Above all, the gelding." Forlani males, outnumbered by females by about thirty to one because of their less frequent nativity, further skewed the odds by sterilizing certain young members they considered intellectually unfit, turning them into *dobutu*, poor creatures who, lacking male hormones, degenerated into thuggish slaves. The Brotherhood had agreed ages ago to stop using *dobutu* as brutish enforcers, but exceptions still occurred. Ayan'we remembered that her mother's paramour Klein had been ambushed more than once by *dobutu* controlled by Tays'she. She was grateful her three brothers, cared for since infancy by the Brotherhood, had avoided gelding. Nevertheless, like her mother, she abhorred the practice.

"Some of us young men want to stop it and the elders can't stand for that," Isshel went on. "One of your own brothers is with us. Like Entara, we strongly feel that to waste male lives through gelding is cruel and unnecessary."

"It may come as a surprise to her that her concerns have already spread so far among the males," Ayan'we responded.

A cloud came over Isshel's features. He was remembering something. Ayan'we knew how it felt. She got that way whenever she remembered the nastiness her father Tays'she had shown toward Entara, how he stripped her of First Wife status and threatened the children's future, how he plotted to enslave young Forlani women off planet for his own gain, and how he went so far as to arrange the murder of Entara and the girls. They were only saved by

Klein's reckless, intrepid confrontation that left Tays'she nothing more than a drooling idiot in the shell of an adult. This painful pause ended when Isshel began to speak again.

"Understand, Ayan'we, you are so lucky, the firstborn of a para-pa. Your father was an artist of great talent before his... unfortunate accident. We all studied and copied his series of tableaux on the Great Spiral of Being. Not all of us are as fortunate as your family. I have a brother, a twin. Together we were raised by the Brotherhood from infancy. Sharàel was strong and graceful as a youngster, but had trouble with the tests, which bored him. Finally he was selected for gelding." Isshel's chin fell to his chest. "I would have killed myself then and there if my mother had not visited me and told me I must go on and persevere for Sharàel's sake, that I must be the one to look after him as best I could." Isshel looked Ayan'we in the eyes. "I see him as often as I can. He still retains some of his old character. But how I ache to see his mind grow weaker and weaker as he is burdened with menial tasks and treated like a thug. The best I can say is that I have prevented them from making him into a criminal or exposing him to much bodily danger."

All that Ayan'we could think to say was, "I feel your suffering. You have shown courage and affection, more than anyone could expect."

"Well, that's why I hold your idealistic mother in such high regard." Among the younger members of the

Brotherhood, Entara was becoming a heroine, spoken of in whispers away from the prying censors. They could not stop talking about how she was urging the Council of Nine to make a purposeful effort to persuade the Brotherhood to stop the practice of gelding, using tempting offers of material gifts if they would at least refrain on a temporary basis. "Your mother's example is why from this moment on I will do my best to observe the Phiddians and other delegates in order to try to find something useful."

"She will be delighted to hear of your commitment!"

Instead of basking in the glow of this approval, Isshel became very guarded. "Now, if you don't mind, I must ask you to leave me alone. I am most uncomfortable through no fault of yours. "

Ayan'we had meant to ask him about his art project, but knew that he needed time to get his emotions back under control. As she stepped out the door, she felt suddenly prey to divided emotions herself. She was eager to share this most unusual interview with Entara, yet at the same time hesitant to probe her private reactions to Isshel. There were things going on that she had not experienced before.

The next day, Ayan'we scanned the council room where she and the other security chiefs had been summoned by the physiological officer, Torghh, to discuss issues before the opening ceremony of the conference. Construction walls had been removed from the Blynthian carrel to reveal four tubes about a meter in diameter running from floor to ceiling. The fifteen other carrels were more conventional, involving different types of desks and seats according to the species concerned. The Kael carrel had perches instead of seats, since these avian creatures could not sit in the usual sense of the word. On the front of each carrel was an intervention light that lit up when a delegation wished to speak. There were also a few smaller carrel fronts beneath viewscreens for those that had not sent physical delegations and wished to follow the proceedings by comlink, like the aquatic Weh, who did not feel comfortable with the design of a Phiddian space station.

When all but the Blynthians were present, the famous Doctor Torghh entered with two other robots. Torghh was a modular robot, so his appearance could continually change according to his mission. His vocation as one of the greatest sensory surgeons in this part of the galaxy meant that he had to adapt to all kinds of conditions, according to the medical needs and natures of his patients. Ayan'we knew that when Torghh had reconstructed one of Klein's eyes after an explosion on Song Pa, he had been in a very simple configuration. Torghh's colleague, Doctor Ragatti had also told her that, in his typical attitude of shyness, Torghh had not actually appeared before the heavily bandaged Klein until the day the human left his care on

Corlatis.   In fact, she was astonished that he had accepted to play a public role at this conference. His configuration now was the rather conventional three-piece arrangement, with his main motor drive on the bottom, his processors in the middle, and a "head" that was unadorned of most of its usual collection of medical gear, except for several sensors and a translation pod.

"I welcome all the organic security personnel to this meeting. Let me first present my two colleagues, my assistant Rack and KC5468732 of the Robotic Guild, who suggests you address him simply as KC. You will be seeing much of Rack since he accompanies me most of the time and in a way is another part of me. He is a robot's robot, specializing in transporting different modules that I utilize in my work, as well as performing needed maintenance. Think of him as a robot valet."

Rack indeed looked like a rack that one might find in a storage hanger somewhere. Like Torghh, he was fitted with track propulsion for the moment, but Ayan'we knew he could also rise on solenoid legs. At the moment, he appeared to have eight arms, two more than Torghh.   Ayan'we wondered how communicative he was with organics, or whether he could only converse in some machine language with the doctor.

"...As for KC, his cooperation is crucial for reasons that will become clear. I direct your attention to the tubes in the Blynthian carrel.   When the Blynthian delegates first appear tomorrow, these tubes will be filled with the materials necessary for their survival, under a pressure considerably exceeding what the rest of you are accustomed to. Without this artificial environment, their participation could not take place. You must realize, however, that the Blynthian atmospherics contain both organic compounds and heavy metals that would be instantly toxic to the rest of you.   It is therefore imperative that we take precautions so that a breach of the tubes, either due to mechanical failure or.... other causes, will not damage the other organics. Thus, KC and several members of the Guild have installed a very sophisticated vent system that can function in case of a problem. Guild members have been specially equipped and trained to aid in an evacuation of organics, should that be necessary.   Naturally, we non-organics are less worried about a breach and have already hardened ourselves as required in case one occurs. Unfortunately, we cannot harden you. Our last-ditch solution has been to provide special masks that will descend from over each carrel station in order to try to save you. Almost all of you. The exception is the Song Pai delegation, which has declined the use of this safety equipment for reasons of honor."

Along with the others, Ayan'we looked over to the Song Pai carrel, where their security director and a couple of assistants drew themselves up on their tentacles to a height of about nine feet and changed color from their usual dull green to a bright silvery tint that denoted pride for them. The syncopated slow swaying of their "heads" was body language equivalent to assent. Undoubtedly, they wished to impress their traditional enemies, the Garanians and the Earthlings, as well as their potential foes from Blyn, that they were as eager to die the rest of their race.

"Any questions so far?" queried Torghh.

Ayan'we took a deep breath, pushed the button illuminating the blue intervention light, and rose to face her counterparts. "We Forlani have long enjoyed the protection of the fighters of Song Pa. It was they who came to defend us when the Earth corporations tried to seize control of our world by force." One Song Pai warship almost obliterated a whole task force of Corporation vessels, deliberately allowing a few survivors to go back to spread the description of their willingness to massacre any other humans who tried to enter the system. "Even now that we have undertaken to provide our own planetary security, we recognize and will always remember our debt to them. In solidarity with our historical defensive allies, we of the Forlani delegation will also do without mask protection."

She bit her tongue a bit as she sat down, knowing that she was exposing not only herself and her sisters, but her mother as well, to possibly lethal contamination. But her attention, and that of the other directors, was quickly diverted to the Song Pai carrel where a chorus of "Schplurt, gtjrrjsk" and other weird sounds erupted, along with the waving of tentacles and a kaleidoscopic color display running the gamut of their emotions.   After an animated huddle with the associates, their security director moved forward to signal and speak. For this purpose, he wore an audio adapter rather than communicating by tablet as the Song Pai generally did with strangers.

"Warriors, we commend the courage of our tailed confederates, who show themselves worthy of our glorious deaths. Yet we find your present action unsuitable. When the Song Pai die, and only when they die, do their genes pass on to the incubation ponds and then to the open, sublime sea to show their worth. You land-dwellers, though, lose all hope for reproduction when you die, and your genes shrivel in your flesh, condemned to oblivion. In the name of generation, which the Sacred displays as the highest value, you must not this time imitate our example. We challenge you to withdraw your statement."

"Very well," Ayan'we responded with a secret feeling of relief, "We are pleased to accede and wish you a noble death." She had to add the last part as a necessity of Song Pai civility. To wish them a long life or peaceful prosperity was a curse.

Torghh had been following this exchange with great interest, scientifically scanning the body temperatures of all present in the hall with his infrareds to gauge their covert reactions. He was most pleased when general warmth spread among them at the end, despite the fact that it was not a reaction he would ever experience himself unless something was malfunctioning.

"And now, just a few more details," he added, going on to talk of various physical adaptations for the different species, questions of timing associated with their respective bodily functions, and the diplomatic costumes they would be wearing during the plenary sessions. He closed by saying, "Of course, in accord with standard diplomatic protocols, no eating, excretion, or sexual displays of any kind will be allowed. Any occurrence will result in the suspension of sessions until the delegation involved has left the conference. That will do for now, except that I will need to speak with the Forlani security director about the masks before she leaves."

Ayan'we deliberately took a long time giving instructions to the cluster members who had accompanied her and gathering up her papers and memory devices. She was curious to see how the other species might react to her tête-à-tête with Torghh. She noticed that the human delegation was also taking its time and casting covert glances in her direction, as were the Phiddian hosts. In the entryway, one of the reptilian Garanians, newly arrived on Varess, had stopped to chat with an aide and she wondered if he also might be monitoring the conversation.

So when she stepped up to the robot, she started with small talk. "Salutations, Doctor Torghh, I bring you the distinguished best wishes of all the medical staff of our mahämes, together with a blanket invitation to visit any hospitals on our planet if you are passing that way."

"You are too kind. Thank you."

"I also bring you personal greetings from a colleague of yours who was privileged to work with you on the patient Klein and again during the relief efforts against the plague on Earth."

"When you communicate again with Doctor Ragatti, please send her my warmest compliments. I miss conversing with her because of her unique sense of humor and her frankness about many organic experiences that others are too often unwilling to discuss with a non-organic."

"Yes, one can always learn something unusual in a conversation with Ragatti," Ayan'we chuckled, looking around the hall again. Everyone had departed except for the Garanian in the door, so she prolonged the chatter a while longer. "You know, if I may ask something a bit personal, I always wondered about your name, which is, if you permit me to say, a bit unusual for a robot."

"Ah, you are right, Ayan'we. It is a name that came originally from a joke made by a human I worked with some time ago. My original designation was, of course, a binary sequence without meaning for organics and I had been thinking about a vocal tag that would render communication easier. So when this human female likened me to someone named Torghh, I accepted it. Later, as I studied human culture, I became aware of the humor she intended, because the comparison with the Torghh she had in mind was most ridiculous. By then, however, I was used to it and the name presented the advantage of being audible in many different forms of communication."

Seeing that the last Garanian had gone on his way, Ayan'we asked, "Now that we are alone, I assume you wanted to mention something about the security situation."

"That is correct. I have scanned many bodily reactions on this station and am not quite pleased to find that there is latent hostility. I have already warned the Coriolans and the Kael to take extra precautions, if only because those races have low levels of natural suspicion. I will do the same for you. These Phiddians are particularly perplexing to me. I have dealt with hermaphroditic organics before, but these have such complex hormonal tides that it makes establishing biological baselines nearly impossible. I believe you would say they have extreme mood swings. Thus, I am not successful in interpreting whether they are being truthful or not, as I can with some species. Perhaps you will fare better."

"We will do our best. I have someone working on that."

"I assume there have been no further attempts to steal information from your quarters?"

"No, the guilty Powl was trailed for quite a long time without betraying any contacts."

"Your colleague handled the matter in a very competent way. I was impressed."

"Lila is one of my most trusted people. You will find you can rely on any of them in an emergency."

"One additional point," added Torghh. "I have noted that your mother Entara has brought a child, a mere infant, to this conference. I must disapprove of this and recommend that she send the young one to a safe place immediately."

"Why?"

"The Phiddians who designed this station did not make provisions for the care of the young. Typical! I have checked over the station medical staff and they have surprisingly little training in this field. Should an emergency occur, I would be the only one you could rely on. I am uncomfortable being a sole resource. This goes strictly against the principles of most non-organics, of course, for to us, redundancy is a virtue."

"I will pass on your advice, but I must tell you now that I don't think it will have any effect. I know Entara has considered the risks of bringing my little sister along. I don't understand exactly why she insisted on it. Of course, we Forlani know that giving birth involves risk to the infant. My mother, like most, experienced unsuccessful births several times, so she knows what it is to lose a child. This one has special meaning for her, so I can predict that she will not separate herself from Quatilla."

"You know best. But exercise maximal care. This may be a more dangerous assignment than it seems, with a war at stake and fifteen delegations well supplied with spies. I have dealt with spies before and am aware of the threat they pose to all because of their determination to complete a mission. Despite their inherent violence, I actually worry less about the Song Pai. They like a pitched battle and consider subterfuge cowardly and unworthy of the permission to procreate. Still, if provoked or tricked by another race, they may lash out in a way that would cause the collapse of the peace process. Just the same, even they may engage the service of spies that are not so scrupulous. As for the other races, many have absolutely no aversion to assassination. Some even consider it a form of art. Others have perfected indirect types of behavior that needs to be carefully watched. We must expect anything. It is imperative to take maximum precautions."

"Thank you, Doctor," concluded Ayan'we. "I will doubtless have further questions as I get to know these beings better."

Pacing nervously after he returned to the Garanian quarters, Tashto found his mind troubled after the end of Ayan'we's intervention at the preliminary meeting. The Ministry's documents had told him that the Forlani were a weak, decadent race that flexed and waved like swamp reeds in the wind. They were said to have no firmness, no connection to the hard, masculine aspect of existence that defined the Garanians and allowed them to achieve a Unity government. They were a people so weak they had to rely on others—the hated Song Pai—for their own defense! Yet Ayan'we spoke with the determination and assurance of a soldier. The Overseer had once told him that assurance had been considered the Sixth Virtue in the days before the Unity Government had been founded. Now it was considered a dangerous emotion, something akin to hubris, for no Garanian could possibly comprehend the true intentions of the government, or fully understand the schemes of fellow citizens in their everyday lives. Garanian society had become one based on control and subterfuge, not openness and honesty. Perhaps this was why Ayan'we's speech had so unnerved him, Tashto reasoned. She had simply displayed her emotions in a manner so unbefitting a Garanian that he was having difficulty understanding them in context. Was there perhaps no true valor in her, no warrior's spirit; was it merely a technique to disturb him, a Forlani trick of the mind to make her appear stronger than she actually was?

Vahon, one of Tashto's relatives from Garan, appeared on the comscreen in his room. "Greetings, Tashto," Vahon said. "There is something that has been troubling me that I wish to discuss. Would you care to listen?"

Vahon had not been chosen to accompany the delegation as a spy. He was merely a bureaucrat, performing the tasks carefully selected for him by the Garanian Ministry of Engineering, with only a thin veneer of independence from the Ministry's standard operating procedure. Tashto thought of Vahon as a dimwitted but genial kinsman, a man only suited to playing a part, which had little capacity for subtlety and guile. But the man could serve as a test subject, an example of how Garanians with less mental discipline and training would respond to the sophistry and emotional appeals of a Forlani. "Yes. Please tell me what's on your mind," said Tashto.

"I once believed the documents that we were given on the Forlani wholeheartedly. I thought them to be a weak, decadent race, rootless primitives with no principles and no culture. But lately I have been studying their technical advancement and cannot reconcile their rise with the old information. I was wondering if you had noted anything useful at the conference that may give me some enlightenment."

Typical of Vahon to pay such little attention to the protocols on interstellar communication! However, in his bluntness, Vahon had not really ventured into anything like a security leak. Tashto could continue the conversation in a way that avoided any such breach. "I have been given evidence of such contradiction myself lately in the conduct of a young member of their delegation.   Her words reflected devotion, respect, and honor. I feel that we have not tried sufficiently to understand the culture of the Forlani; perhaps this conference will grant us an opportunity to study and interact with them."

"The Overseer's guidelines caution us not to be awed by them easily. They are said, Tashto, to be skilled liars, masters of seduction and deceit, but still cowards at heart. They worship the strength of the Song Pai and feign to possess it themselves while having none.   Their existence is supposed to be a misery of envy, for they are destined to spend it drifting between the powers of Earth and Song Pa. I was at first inclined to pay no heed to what happens in this conference, for they are destined to be mere dust in the vastness of space. Should I waste my brief time trying to understand them, if their continued existence is a dark mystery that serves only to drive the minds of Garanians mad?"

"Although your guidelines have merit, kinsman Vahon, I'm not sure I agree with them. The speech that I heard was not the speech of a coward. I feel there may be dimensions to the Forlani civilization that we have not yet comprehended. If I were you, I would do what research I can in order to be prepared for possible revisions in the future."

"I may come to admire them if they are as you say, kinsman."

"Do what you wish. But make an effort to not become too...*sentimental* about the Forlani. They may only disappoint you."

"Duly noted. I will give your regards to the clan," Vahon said, and turned off the link.

Tashto felt a very slight sense of disappointment in Vahon as his image faded from the screen. Although he had suspected Vahon had a weak mind, his words had proven that Vahon displayed a dearth of guile in the Garanian bureaucracy that slipped below his lowest expectations. But was he any better? To begin sympathizing with the loathsome Forlani after a single speech! Tashto would have to monitor his own delegation as closely as the Forlani, if fellow spies could be as easily misled by prejudice as Vahon had been. At least his kinsman had come to question his own certainties and to consult confidentially with his wiser relative. Tashto suspected that few of his spies would be willing to do the same. He had not realized how weak the undisciplined Garanian mind could be, and wondered whether it was shortsighted of his government to eliminate the Virtues of the Heroic Age from the knowledge of his people. Could the Virtues have provided a moral anchor for individuals as weak as Vahon? *Perhaps if I succeed in this mission, the Ministry will allow me to see the documents where the Virtues are recorded*, he thought. Then it would only be a matter of deciding what he would do with the knowledge after he had learned of the Virtues...

     The next couple of days before the grand opening brought few developments. Each delegation was making hasty, last-minute preparations and adjustments. The pursuit of the Powl data thief yielded nothing new. Ayan'we's sisters in the security cluster took turns trailing it everywhere it went and trying to monitor all possible communications. So far, zilch. Ayan'we began to be more and more convinced that those little tick things had arcane ways to communicate that other races didn't know about. She spent a long time wandering the corridors of Varess, trying to get to know its layout completely. She often caught sight of that same foursome of meddlesome Phiddians, who seemed to be trolling about not only for her, but for all the other Forlani they could contrive to pass paths with. They had even approached Isshel once, but he had drawn a wicked-looking pointed thing from his belt, making them scurry away. He had smiled and then begun to clean his fingernails with it. Ayan'we had been pleased to meet Kee'ad the Newt of Tionar. She remembered to address him formally by the place name of his fiefdom. He proved to be a most gracious individual, showing a thorough familiarity with the songs about Entara and Klein that were sung in all the mahämes and in all the Forlani pleasure houses across the sector. His attempts to sing a few bars were pretty ludicrous, resembling as they did some beast croaking in a swamp, but Ayan'we had praised his pronunciation enough to make him grin broadly. He informed Ayan'we that his compatriot known as Fatty, who had helped Klein on Song Pa on one particular occasion, was still alive and well and now ran a large underwater construction group active on Earth in post-plague work.

Ayan'we tried to be alert for potential dangers as she walked around the station, but she noticed she was becoming bored. Aside from dodging the Gropers Four, it was mostly the same thing hour after hour. Phiddians hurried around when there was any hint of a party, but otherwise left the daily routine to their servants, the Powls and the Kholods. While the Powls were always whooshing by with some tool or meter to make a minor engineering adjustment, the dumpy-looking Kholods got the dirty work. Like the Powls, they were a sub-spatial culture with no ships of their own, but they signed on for work on vessels or stations where something needed to be toted, delivered, or cleaned up. They did a lot of cleaning up after the Song Pai, who made defecation a social sport and left a terrible mess in their quarters. Kholods plodded down the corridors two, three or four at a time, carrying boxes, machine components, files, or large dishes from the kitchen for some Phiddian soiree. They were somewhere between amphibians and reptiles, coming from a planet that had never undergone an extinction that wiped out such intermediate forms on planets like

Earth. Ayan'we had read that even though Kholods were the most intelligent species on their world (which wasn't saying much!), they were not specifically species-dominant and still had to deal with other planet-dwellers more formidable than themselves. They looked capable of speech, but never seemed to say anything to each other or anyone else. Maybe their vocal organs had atrophied. The only thing that bothered Ayan'we was that they literally were all physical duplicates of each other. Without any clothes or insignias, they could be distinguished only by what they were carrying. When they were dead-heading it back from some job with nothing in either of their pairs of arms, they were just so many iterations of the same model. Ayan'we wished they could at least have color tags to make it easier to tell individuals apart for security purposes. She actually suggested this to several Phiddian officers, who had just sneered and repeated, "How bizarre! No one cares about Kholods."

Finally a communication came from Amanda on Earth. Ayan'we held a tremendous curiosity about Klein's biological daughter and felt a special bond with her, ever since they met on Domremy for Klein's funeral ceremony. This communication was not a live comlink, nor even a stored A/V display, but an old-fashioned paper letter redacted in Standard English. Ayan'we could speak English rather fluently, but she was so non-plussed by having to decipher script that after the first sentence, she scanned it into her computer and let the voice mode translator read it aloud to her.

New Bremen Q-355B

September 14, ZD 3179

Dear Ayan'we,

Sorry to resort to this ancient method, but it was actually the fastest way to get a message off-planet, since comlinks are still reserved for official business in this sector. As you can see, we've moved from Greenland to the continent of Europe to work in the Weser Mixed District. Warm embraces to you and to all the sisters I met on Domremy. Also please give my greeting to your mother. Sven says to send his best, too. We have moved into a nice house that was abandoned and undisturbed. Being health officer in a mixed district means that I have to look over all sorts of humans; immune, unexposed, and carriers. There are still a few odd symptomatic survivors out beyond the perimeters, but they have their own clinic about 70 kliks south of here. Sven is almost alone in the forestry detail. A lot of the people are deeply involved with restoring a power grid. You'd never guess that Entara's songs, edited for human ears, are popular here in the colony. The robotic clearing crews are still busy in the interior. It will be years before they've cleared remains up to the Alps.   We hardly ever see them.   There are some Newt crews working on the littoral restoration.   They're only here for a couple of weeks at a time, rotating up from their base in their Nile Delta Allotment.   Many of the human natives have trouble coming to grips with the idea that this is going to be a more-than-one-species planet from now on, but for space brats like me, it's no big deal. We need all the help we can get. I've seen some Blynthian lighters flying over to make supply drops to isolated groups in the interior.   As for us, we're just about self-sufficient now, except for some staple shipments that come into the temporary spaceport in Kent. There's so much energy! I like it here. No walls. No rules, almost. Things to explore everywhere. So much to be done. I feel like I've just begun to grow up.   Sven laughs at me and calls me a newbie, but I'm glad I don't have a lot of pre-set ideas and expectations about this place.   The only thing I miss is my mother, who is off some place in Ontario by now and talks about heading down to Mexico soon. They say conditions are still pretty rugged in most of eastern North America, but nothing seems too gruesome for her. Time to scrape together something to eat, so I'll say goodbye for now. Let me know what you're up to as soon as you can.

Love,

Amanda

PS: some aerial folks claim they have spotted a statue over by Berlin that might be of Klein! If it's true, I'll try to get you an image.

The letter from Amanda brought soothing refreshment to Ayan'we's spirits. She tried to remember each phrase and then played the audio translation back a couple of times until she had committed it to memory. Of course, she could just punch it up any time she wanted from the computer. The voice print was just a translation, not Amanda's real voice. But by memorizing it, Ayan'we could imagine the sentences just as her friend might pronounce them. That was worth the extra trouble. Which was no trouble, really. In fact, one of the most purposeful things in her life. One that was frank and fresh and clean of deception. So unlike the murky affairs of the conference and the dark possibilities of war that lurked around the corners of Varess.

2

Finally the day had arrived for the opening of the Zonal Peace Conference. Ayan'we was one of the five individuals chosen to accompany Entara to the delegation seating area. When they arrived at the foyer to the meeting hall, they were surprised to see there was little in the way of formal organization, just a couple of Phiddian ushers motioning everyone in through the doors. It was a multi-colored spectacle, since each delegation had a uniform representing their civilization. The Forlani had had to give up their traditional diplomatic black capes because a minor delegation had chosen that first. Other colors would have caused internal problems, since each matriline had its own polychromatic design and it would be unfair to privilege one over the others. So Isshel, in a moment of inspiration amid observations of alien sexual psychology, had come up with come up with an elegant compromise of a black field with large white dots. The human delegation was clad in a red, white, and blue pattern, the Kael in rainbow body tights, the Coriolans in a fringed, silver sash, and so forth. The delegations settled into their places until only the Blynthians and the Phiddians were missing. The latter had, typically, reserved the right of final entry for themselves to try to gain the maximum attention. Nevertheless, all eyes were darting to the Blynthian area. The screens and construction gear had been removed and the floor-to-ceiling tubes were filled with a roily, cloudy substance. Then, suddenly, shapes appeared. Electric blue, four-meter-long segmented worms with many appendages. Even Ayan'we's Forlani companions, whom she had coached from her own off-world experiences, could not help giving a gasp.

Everyone might have stared longer, had not a blare of brass instruments announced the entrance of the Phiddians. They came prancing in, wearing a circle of loose pink streamers that covered as little as possible of their bodies. Their supreme leader, who had come just for the éclat of the grand opening, made a pompous welcome speech that was generally devoted to the importance of Phiddia in the interplanetary scheme of things and managed to avoid any sensible topics. After this foolish person finished and went striding out of the hall with much waving of arms and musical accompaniment, there was an embarrassing silence as the delegates wondered how they were going to get the conference off to a decent beginning.

Fortunately the wise old delegate of the Newts, Kee'ad, signaled with his light and took the floor. He gave an impromptu summary of the reasons they were all gathered there. Succinctly, he outlined the Song Pai demands for new territory on aquatic worlds within the Blynthian sphere of influence, as well as the Blynthians' time-honored exclusion of almost all alien individuals from that area. Without language that would justify a clattering of weapons by either party, he established that each was capable of releasing destruction on such a scale that it could not be confined to deep space encounters or even to fighting within a few specific systems. Thus, all intrazonal races had something to lose if hostilities were allowed to break out. Kee'ad set a fine opening tone, citing several previous successful conferences and making just enough reference to the atrocious outcomes of various wars to underline the alternative without casting blame on any of the attendees. He concluded with an eloquent statement of his own race's commitment to peace and its willingness to contribute to negotiations to the point of sacrifice, if necessary.

Chester Macdougal, chief human delegate, wasted no time in pressing his button to speak next and offered a prepared set of comments that repeated the word "peace" over and over again, without giving any indication of how it might be possible to achieve it.

Ayan'we would have been grossly disappointed with this, had her mother not already told her how the vast majority of human leaders tended to favor a "feel-good" discourse over any illustrative or probing type of speech.

When Entara's own turn came, she did not at all hide the Forlani loyalty to the Song Pai or the depth of their alliance. At the same time, she avoided assuming a polemical stance, speaking a good deal of her world's history and about the types of compromises that had been essential to maintain its balance between the sexes and the matrilines. She succeeded in capturing the interest of the diverse audience, who knew little of the Forlani past or its ancient Disaster Period. Their racial struggle for survival against the threat of anarchy and environmental collapse was framed in a way to remind each delegation of its own trials and challenges. She finished with a cogent picture of Forlan's recent progress and its potential for the future – a most optimistic ending note.

Ten more delegations went on to follow her example and to amplify the advantages of reaching a long-term agreement on intrazonal political and military matters. The long-distance com-link participants such as the Weh having waived any opening statements, there only remained the two major antagonists, the Song Pai and the Blynthians. The Song Pai stared down their worm-like opponents for a significant moment and then boldly demanded to speak. It was such a belligerent approach that, if it came from any species but the Song Pai, the conference members would doubtlessly have been convinced that any alternative to war was already futile and they would have adjourned then and there.

"We want to make clear that we are committed as of now to war. We will back down for no one. As far as we are concerned, the sole purpose of this meeting is to communicate that to all parties and to allow our allies, the Rokol and the Forlani, to make up their minds and state their intentions. We insist that these will in no way affect our own determination. Blynthians, be aware that we intend to take your water planets or die trying."

The Song Pai then proceeded to recite from memory, taking turns within the delegation, their complete articles of war, which lasted nearly four hours. During this time they drew themselves up to an attack position, with their hooked tentacles raised to strike, and held that pose unflinchingly for the entire time, their color remaining the blotched blue of military attention. At the end of the presentation, they turned most of their multiple eyes toward the Blynthians, since at least one eye was always pointing backward in case of a possible ambush. They seemed to expect a similar bellicose diatribe from their adversaries.

The Blynthians did not take the bait. A single worm creature buzzed a quick reply that mechanically translated as, "Most interesting."

Lest the Song Pai take occasion to feel insulted by this terse remark, the Coriolans quickly lit their intervention light and stated, "We are not used to assimilating such weighty matters on the spot. We compliment the Song Pai on their frank and complete statement and the Blynthians on their unbelievably quick reaction, but we lesser creatures need more time to understand all that has been said and to weigh the matter in our consciences. We think we speak for many other delegations as we suggest that in view of the late hour and the necessity for discussion before proceeding further, we call the session to a close today and agree to resume deliberations in the next cycle."

All the other delegations, both present and communicating by distance, agreed readily to this suggestion and the representatives headed for the exits under the watchful eyes of the Robotic Guild attendants, murmuring amongst themselves about the brusqueness of the day's exchange.

The evening of the opening ceremonies (evening being an arbitrary term in Varess, where day and night were determined only by clocks), there was a reception that Ayan'we did not want to miss. Calm, slow instrumental music that the Blynthians favored played gently in the dining hall as she entered. Since the Blynthians couldn't mingle in person with the other races, they had thoughtfully provided a sound track. She watched as diplomats and politicians sauntered through the room, gathering around the tables with glasses of punch and hors d'oeuvres. Ayan'we went over to a table and munched on a small piece of human bruschetta. It reminded her of Entara's beloved toast, but with more vegetables and seasoning. She enjoyed the savor of this unfamiliar human cuisine, letting the strange flavor saturate her taste buds before reaching for a punch glass. Out of the corner of her eye, she could see two people from the Human Delegation walking up to her. One of them was an elderly man with thin white hair and a slight paunch, the other a tall, thin woman with thick horn-rimmed glasses. The man held out his hand first. Ayan'we enthusiastically shook it; she had been trained well by her mother in the arts of conversation and interaction with humans. Then she turned to the thin woman and was surprised when the woman's gloved hand darted out and grabbed her hand for a quick shake. "Erica Duquesne," the woman said. "You?"

"I am Ayan'we, of the Eyes of Alertness," Ayan'we said.

"He's Anthony Wilson, the Earth diplomat who sponsored me," Erica continued. "He's not feeling very talkative now—he just got through a roundtable trilateral meeting with some of the Song Pai and Garanian delegations, and let me tell you, it was absolutely *excruciating*! They just can't agree on anything! Would you mind answering a few questions I have involving the Song Pai? I know your species is allied with them, maybe you could give me some help figuring some things out about them?"

Erica looked at Ayan'we expectantly. The elderly man still stood silently, gazing in Ayan'we's direction. Was he what the Earth texts called an *eminence grise*? Ayan'we was wary of revealing too much information about the valued allies of the Forlani to this woman. She was suspicious of the humans' time-proven tendency to try to hold private negotiations in the midst of a collective conference, so news of the trilateral meeting had not startled her. Moreover, she was all too aware of the necessity of engaging in friendly conversation in order to further diplomatic interests, no matter how false or counterproductive it seemed to her. "Certainly," Ayan'we assented. The silent politician in turn gave a nod of approval.

"What do you know about their home planet?" Erica asked. "We humans know very little about Song Pa, since our history of diplomatic relations with them is so antagonistic that few of us have ever been allowed to go there. And come back. Is there anything you can tell us?"

Erica's voice had an odd tone to it that put Ayan'we on alert. She was thankful for getting a question that she had very little personal experience with. Since she had never set foot on Song Pa itself, she doubted that any of the information she remembered was considered classified. "I've never actually been there. Most mammalian and quasi-mammalian sentients haven't wanted to go to Song Pa since the discovery of the prion disease."

"The planet is potentially lethal to humans?" Erica asked.

"*Verified* lethal," Ayan'we continued.   "There were numerous cases of individual humans brought there as indentured servants to the Song Pai.   The disease was quite slow-acting, and the people who contracted it could often live years before the symptoms began in earnest.   But it is one hundred percent fatal, and the deaths are said to be agonizing. The Song Pai have been forced to rely on non-mammalian species for the indentured servant program for the foreseeable future."

"How terrible," Erica said. "I seem to recall that info on the death of a Willie Klein, a convict who was assigned to Domremy, appeared on the news—you know how late and spotty the news from Domremy is these days, since the colony was closed.   The descriptions of his death were just horrific.   To be eaten alive by parasites!   I know how agonizing the prion disease must have been, but to choose to die like that, he must have been a madman!"

So Erica was using Klein, whom Ayan'we considered an adoptive father, to try to put her on the defensive.   The Forlani security director fought the sense of disgust and anger toward Erica that was forming inside her. Who was this woman to belittle the memory of the great hero of Domremy, a man respected and loved by multiple species?   "I actually find his death quite beautiful. To sacrifice his own life so that new life may come forth. Perhaps I find it reminiscent of the Forlani credo, that motherhood—the giving of so much of one's life for the next generation—is the noblest expression of existence. But whatever it was that made Klein decide to end his life in such a manner, I prefer to believe it a noble impulse, rather than a vile one."

"Well, he certainly didn't look noble on the reports," Erica said. "Everything I saw claimed that he was quite mad in his final moments, driven to insanity by a life of desperation on an inhospitable, alien world. Of course, it wasn't a very high profile report; I think it aired only once on a late night streaming broadcast and no follow-up investigation was made. I guess Klein wasn't that important to us Earthers in the end." Erica had not said a word about her own involvement in Klein's exile to Domremy or her activities as an executive of the powerful colonizing corporation, Hyperion. That had not prevented Ayan'we's intuition from realizing that there was some personal connection in this discussion, perhaps an attempt to compensate for a failure in regard to Klein.

Ayan'we struggled to control her hostility, but it began to bleed through into her verbal communication. "Maybe he wasn't very important to you, but he was -- and still is -- important to *us*."

"Well, this conversation seems to have gone a bit sour," Erica said. "I'm sorry if I offended you.

Sometimes it can be a bit difficult for us provincial Earthers to grasp the cultural importance of certain of our less prestigious people to other civilizations. You will forgive my offense, won't you?"

Ayan'we made a subtle movement of her mouth so that Erica wouldn't notice her clenched teeth before she spoke. "Absolutely. Most Forlani—including myself—are very protective of Klein. We wouldn't speak of him amongst ourselves as unimportant!"

"Well, I certainly won't make that mistake again. There's plenty of time left at this conference, maybe we can talk another day?"

"I look forward to it."

Anthony finally spoke. "We've got another mindstorming meeting with the Blynthians in five minutes," he said. "We have to be there on time -- you know how annoyed they get when people show up late."

"Goodbye!" Erica said and walked away briskly with Anthony, leaving Ayan'we alone with her neurosis and uncertainty about the encounter. Her gut reaction—disgust with the human woman for her ignorance and hostility towards Klein—faded away, replaced with a nervous apprehension about the woman's true intent. Had she really been as ignorant as she seemed, or was the discussion of Klein some sort of personality test, a trap to study Ayan'we's psychological weaknesses? Ayan'we feared she had not acquired her mother's iron self-control yet, and that she would somehow suffer for it over the course of the conference. She tried to dull the suspicions swirling in her mind, reaching for another glass of punch on the table.

The reception was making Ayan'we feel tired and out of sorts. After checking with her operatives and leaving Lila in charge of the next work shift, she retired to the Forlani quarters and slept close to Entara and Quatilla so she could watch over them personally. The other delegates eventually grew weary of the reception, too, and settled down in their own areas to relax in anticipation of the coming day's events. But not all of them. In some of the delegations, little nodes of activity furtively sprang up to push the unending quest for advantageous information ever farther. One such group waited in a small, neutral room deep in the labyrinth of Varess's corridors.

Tashto blinked his eyes as he waited in the room with the two members of the Garanian spy team. Almost unconsciously, he began his typical nervous ritual—rubbing his long, talon-like fingernails together. Zarath, one of the Garanians accompanying him, hissed at him, "Would you stop making that accursed noise? The last thing I need while waiting for your accomplice to appear is to listen to that awful scraping."

Tashto turned to meet Zarath and snarled back, the feathers on the back of his neck flexing erect in nervous anger. He disliked Zarath for having the gall to make a request of himself, a ranking superior, but also for distracting him during his attempt at calming himself. Garanians were not a patient race by nature, unless they were hunting. Being forced to wait without a target filled their minds with neurotic, apprehensive thoughts. "You will make no requests of me, inferior. We will wait here patiently for my contact to begin communication on the monitor. You will say nothing unless spoken to, and be as polite as possible. If you violate these codes of behavior, there will be *severe* consequences. Understood?

"Certainly," Zarath grumbled.

Tashto rued the fact that the Garanians with him lacked the tact of his kinsman Vahon. Though Tashto found Vahon simple-minded in comparison to himself, he could at least be counted on to provide pleasant conversation and to obey instructions. Zarath and the others on this assignment were much more quarrelsome and disrespectful, perhaps due to their youth and their desire to advance quickly through the ranks of the Garanian government's spy forces. But they were the only help the Overseer had assigned to him on this mission. Unfortunately, Vahon had always worked in a separate division of government, the Ministry of Engineering. Tashto was left only with his testy rabble of subordinates for a meeting that the Overseer had told him would be his most important task at the conference.

The monitor on the right wall of the room finally crackled to life, and a bright light shown out of it. The image onscreen resembled a distorted kaleidoscope of colors, and Tashto could not make out any shapes that would indicate what species was speaking to him. "Welcome, Tashto of Garan," a grating metallic voice greeted him. "Have you met the terms of our agreement?" the voice asked him.

Tashto nodded. "It cost the Garanian people many lives to obtain this object from our enemies, the Song Pai. We find their name for this technology difficult to translate, so we refer to it as the Hydro-Motion Device. It allows the user to create any fluid shape around a living being or inanimate object. We believe the Song Pai conceived it as a means of hydrating themselves in environments where naturally occurring water was difficult to find; being an aquatic species, they required such a device to move about on arid land environments."

A primitive robot clambered in through a doorway to the left. It advanced to the table and silently surveyed the device with its beady yellow sensors. Tashto had never seen an automaton like it before, nor could he guess what race had constructed it. He silently mouthed a curse, frustrated at the fact that he was no closer to knowing the identity of his mysterious partner than he was during the Overseer's briefing. The robot gave a soft bleep and picked up the object with spindly plastic hands.

"Excellent," the voice from the monitor said. "We have just received confirmation from our robot that this device matches the specifications that we agreed upon. Our deal is now complete."

Tashto still felt apprehensive about having to deal with his nebulous, illusive ally. "Why did the agreement specify this mechanism? It is a simple device for moving fluids, nothing more. How can it possibly accomplish the goals we have agreed upon?" he asked.

"Patience. If this device is capable of using the types of fluids we hope to—and we will begin testing it immediately to verify this—our plan will be quite easy to implement. There will be no way it can be traced to your group, or any other Garanian, because you will not be involved in the execution of our plan."

"Why is this?" Tashto nervously hissed. "You are unknown to me, hidden through some sort of incomprehensible distortion, yet you are free to observe us if you wish. If you were to be discovered, could you not reveal everything about us in confession?"

"You think that little of us? The distortion effect of this monitor applies both ways. I have only heard a total of two distinct voices on your end. I do not know how many Garanians are in the room, and I have no idea what your physical features are."

"And that thing?" Zarath hissed in the direction of the robot. "Its visual record would surely incriminate us."

"We will have this unit deactivated and completely destroyed once it brings the Hydro-Motion

Device back to our headquarters. There will be no way that its memory, already pre-hobbled, could be recovered after we destroy its CPU and memory banks."

Tashto was happy that Zarath had asked such a critically important question, though he still longed to punish him for insubordination after the meeting. Tashto had one final question, one which expanded on Zarath's earlier remark. "You still know we are Garanian! Yet we have no idea what *you* are. How are we to trust you if you hold such an advantage over us?"

"Your Overseer knows our race, though not our personal identities. Perhaps you should attempt to ask him about us and see how he responds. If you dare! In truth, you were always merely couriers of this device, and the agreement was made with your superiors, not with you personally. Thank you for your cooperation."

The monitor cut off, and the robot began to shuffle off stealthily into the darkened doorway it had arrived from. "Not even telling us what species he is?! What kind of fools does this cowardly lurker think we are?" Zarath said.

Tashto nodded, and then reflected a second before he spoke. "I would have you punished for your earlier insubordination, if I did not agree with every single word of your statement."

"I will go unpunished after a threat of punishment? This is quite unusual…"

"The punishment was for insubordination. How can I punish for insubordination when you act and speak as I wish you to?" Tashto said. "Now we must return to our quarters." And with that, the Garanians quickly turned to leave, moving together as swiftly and silently as they could across the space station, just as their distant ancestors had when they stalked a prey animal.

The next day's plenary session began early and roughly.

The Song Pai turned expectantly toward the Blynthians, as their spokesman shot out, "We made our intentions quite obvious in the last meeting. Now we demand a similar statement of intention from our mysterious adversaries. Speak, Blynthians, what is it you seek to achieve?"

The worm creatures zipped several messages back and forth and then responded with a single statement: Someone must take care of things.

All the delegations were just as perplexed as the Song Pai appeared to be, since the cephalopods were rapidly sliding through a range of color patterns that conveyed their turbulent emotions. Entara turned to Ayan'we and whispered, "Are these Blynthians always so cryptic in their conversation? We've yet to hear more than a single phrase, and this latest seems like some sort of proverb."

Ayan'we hastened to answer, "They are always very direct in my experience, but I have never asked such a loaded diplomatic question, mainly more technical explanations. I'm sorry mother, but I know as little as anybody else about the way their affective minds work. They've shared a few things about trade and culture, but very little in the realm of ethics."

The Song Pai finally decided on a new line of questioning and asked the Blynthians, "At least tell us if you are willing to offer battle strictly in the name of your own race or do you speak for others within your control as well? We of Song Pa do not make slaughter indiscriminately like savages. If a race expresses their reluctance to fight, we will not make them suffer, provided they obey a few simple orders. So for whom do you speak?'

Again, a brief exchange among the Blynthians before announcing, in a long buzz that translated laconically as, "It takes all kinds."

"What kind of pacifist nonsense is this?" sputtered the Song Pai spokesman. "This conference is useless if we merely propose to waste time circling around the edges of a cowardly and elusive peace. Explain yourselves or we leave now."

The Blynthians were quite silent for several minutes. Just when the Song Pai roused themselves to troop triumphantly out of the assembly hall, a simple zip translated, "State rules of engagement."

"That's more like it!" exclaimed the Song Pai, with such haste that it almost seemed to be a call of happiness. "However, don't try to save yourselves by negotiation. We can agree to some good, plain procedural points that will make it all the easier to show our valor in a sensible way, free of chaos and confusion."

Suddenly the Kael intervention light lit up and their main delegate spread his wings a bit in a dignified way before suggesting, "Might we recommend that any terms of engagement would have to be divided into formal categories? After all, for hostilities to be orderly, is it not necessary to have a sense of a beginning and an end? Time rules every life form, after all, and it must be taken into consideration, just as though it were a physical delegation here in this hall. Space is also important. In a decent conflict, there are always zones where death is not allowed. So we propose that all delegations first draw up a set of parameters regarding when, where, and finally, how such a proposed conflict should take place. Once that is agreed upon, we can proceed much more efficiently to determine our respective positions."

Entara marveled at the tactful approach the Kael were taking. She had learned that they tended to settle disputes among themselves mainly by proxy. She suspected that this habit of removing themselves from direct confrontation must have contributed to their skillful deflection of a rapidly escalating crisis involving the Blynthians and the Song Pai. At the same time, it provided a convincing reason for a delay that might cool tempers all around and allow for some maneuvering toward peace.

"This idea is honorable," concluded the Song Pai. "It is never out of place to reflect on the exact situation of a fight. All implications must be evident in order for it to assume its true importance and thus for the greatest glory to be awarded to the brave ones who offer their lives in conquest. As we say, the blood that is washed away in a swift current never tastes as fine. By all means, let every race present weigh the values that are at stake, so that each delegation shall speak with deepest meaning. As for us, we set no limits to our own risk, other than those implicit in our own sense of sacrifice."

The theoretical logistics of a Song Pai versus Blynthian confrontation took up the rest of the day. While the Blynthians balked at revealing anything about their armaments, they shocked most of the participants by engaging in discussion of certain tactics, including a unilateral establishment of a large Neutral Zone in reaction to a Song Pai invasion. The Song Pai reacted by denouncing this as an unworthy sign of cowardice. Deep in their cephalopod organs, though, they were suspicious almost to the point of fear that such a withdrawal might be a prelude to an awesome display of destruction that had not been seen in recorded memory anywhere in the Perseid Spiral Arm, perhaps in the whole galaxy. When the session closed, they hurried to establish secure comlink with Song Pa to get their strategists working on possible deployments to such an unexpected move. They were not planning to attend the main evening event, a traditional Phiddian Love Court that promised nothing more than lewdness and profanity for them.

The Forlani delegation smiled as they saw the banner over the entrance to the Love Court bore the eight octagonal stars that were the universal sign of welcome. They had been worried that the sensual Phiddians would have something much more lewd over their doorway. The invitation to attend had specified "non-diplomatic attire – prepare to be relaxed," and the Forlani had had a meeting to discuss how to dress, or not, for the occasion. On their home planet, Forlani females rarely wore more than a sash or a light cape, unless the weather was particularly bad. Entara was relieved when she learned that her mostly younger colleagues thought, like her, that to appear *au naturel* on the space station would not set a good example for interspecies relations, no matter how "relaxed" the Phiddians intended to be. They had settled on a song costume – a tunic, mid-length cape and scarf that was often used on Forlan for gatherings where songs were shared among the different matrilines. In Entara's honor, they all bore the yellow and orange colors of the Eyes of Alertness.

By contrast, the Phiddians who filled most of the room were ablaze in an array of competing colors and most wore a profusion of glowing crystals and other decorations. As hermaphrodites, they were endlessly trying to attract sex partners in various modes and combinations. They openly displayed all available sexual organs, covering only irrelevant parts of their anatomy that had nothing to do with coupling. Other than their large reddish ears, which were apparently considered quite erotic, they resembled humans for the most part. All had silvery-whitish hair, which apparently was a reaction they developed to space travel, for Entara had read in reports that on their own world, their hair resembled the auburn hues of Forlani females. Several of the Phiddians were quite visibly pregnant, including the greeter who swished up to Entara and took her by the hand.

"My dear delegate Entara, welcome to the Court! My name is Fianni and this is my co-parent Blazhin," the greeter added, nodding to another less round Phiddian who accompanied.

"Most honored to meet you," Entara pronounced, as she allowed herself to be led into the gathering. Blazhin gave a similar hand-clasp to each of the other Forlani in turn, inviting them in. The humans had already arrived, led by Ambassador Macdougal. To Entara's surprise, they all seemed to be dressed in some kind of military uniform, perhaps to impress the other races that, notwithstanding the weakening of their species by the devastating plague that had struck Earth, they considered themselves still to be a major interplanetary power, to be feared and respected.   The Garanians who were present also wore studded metallic garments that seemed to project war rather than peace. Entara smirked as she thought what the Song Pai would have thought of this display. They had defeated humans in short order whenever they had the chance to fight them and usually trounced the Garanians who were deemed, at least, formidable opponents.   No Song Pai was present at the Love Court.   They probably would have defecated all over the invitation, since the idea was so alien to their way of life.   Blynthians were likewise absent, holed up in their own atmosphere on their ship. A few Kael were gathered at one side, where they took evident pleasure in being able to flap their leathery wings a bit after confining themselves uncomfortably for hours in the council hall.   Natives of Coriolis pressed around a buffet table, eagerly sniffing everything with their long coati-like noses and happy that the Phiddians, like them, had no prohibitions against eating meats in informal situations. Despite all the foreplay going on among the hosts, the assembly did appear to be quite relaxed. Ayan'we caught her mother's eye and gave a little sign that all was going well. The Forlani females each grabbed a bit of fruit from the table and fanned out through the crowd. Phiddians kept trying to corner them to pepper them with questions about the "pleasure training" Forlani females continued to receive, since so many worked for the home planet by servicing clients of other species at the numerous houses off-planet. The Forlani all hastened to explain that, although they took great pride in pleasing their clients, their own physical pleasure actually came strictly from giving birth, an idea that seemed to stop the Phiddians cold.

Eventually a horde of attendants brought in a circle of bench-like furniture that they placed in a circle within the room and it was clear the Love Court was about to begin.   Fianni sounded a little whistle to get everyone's attention and explained, "Most of you have never been to one of our Love Courts, but I can assure you that it is one of our favorite entertainments and that no self-respecting Phiddian would go a week without attending.   There are even Courts of Courts, that discuss which meetings are the best. As you will see, the Court takes the format of a debate where two lovers are discussed to evaluate their relative value in some capacity. The goal is, of course, the success of a lover in terms of establishing one's ongoing appeal and reputation in the world of blissful pleasure. So," Fianni added, turning to the humans, "You will not hear anything like your histories of Romeo and Juliette, where people wind up killing themselves all over the place. Nor, for you Kael," the speaker added, turning to the bat-like creatures, "Will you find cases like Adtripperus and Kasattylathe, who go on mooning about their unrequited relationships. Only instances that result in sultry skin-to-skin activity, repeated as often as possible, are suitable for our Love Courts."

The Kael looked a bit disappointed, but the humans, Garanians and Coriolans displayed piqued interest in the topics that were developing, while the Phiddians clapped and cooed in delight.

"Now in honor of our distinguished guests from Forlan, we have chosen as the subject of today's Court the case of Ambassador Entara and her consort from Earth, the renowned mankiller Klein, and the question will be as to which of them sacrificed more deeply to earn the affection of the other!"

Most of the audience applauded, but Entara and Ayan'we each took a hasty breath and the other Forlani glanced their way with troubled looks. This situation obviously threatened to develop in multiple awkward directions. Ordinarily, Forlani would not be bothered at all by discussing the most explicit details of copulation, since these were the subject of song and discussion without any hint of shame in their society. Diplomatic protocol, however, specified that such things were to be avoided at all costs, since wars had broken out in past interspecies conclaves over open displays or descriptions of sexuality. Moreover, the nature of the debate seemed predetermined to cause individual embarrassment to Entara. Her separation from Klein on Domremy in order to marry and breed for the matriline on Forlan would not be understood by many of the creatures at the Court. Besides that, Klein was still officially considered a criminal by the Earth corporations, even though many humans held him in high regard for taking action against the insidious

Kinderaugen Project that had first forced him to become a murderer.   Garanians, who were very proprietary about sexuality, were rumored to consider Entara as nothing more than an interstellar whore. It was clear that the Phiddians had used the cover of "relaxation" to throw a sharp, reckless blade into the delicate network of respect and toleration that made a peace conference possible.

Entara quickly regained her composure. After all it was she herself who had unveiled every detail of her actions and feelings regarding Klein to the leadership of her mahäme, her matriline and even the lofty Council of Nine that governed her planet.   The songs shared by all Forlani females – some of them composed by Entara herself – often recounted their trysts and their most intimate expressions. "I am most personally flattered that you should think of me as a paragon for your Court, but I am sure there are many others, not only Phiddians, but others present and not, who would furnish a far more interesting and entertaining subject for your ... proceedings."

"Nonsense," sputtered Fianni, "You cannot deny that on your own world you are considered para-pa, an example for all females to emulate. Are you saying your own clan is wrong to give you this designation? Would not your failure to stand by your actions be considered as an insult to the Council of Nine that sent you here? And certainly you cannot claim that the mankiller Klein is less than suitable for our consideration? Or has your family life caused you to think less of him? Or perhaps certain unfortunate details of your married life have soured you to the study of love?"

Ayan'we made a sign to her cluster members in case they should have to leave quickly. Fianni's rude question was a direct provocation of Entara and she would be quite justified in quitting the Court immediately. She was surprised when her mother made no move to the door, but calmly looked Fianni in the eyes as she responded, "I am honored to be called para-pa, not because of anything I have done to deserve it, but because it represents the concepts of the matriline for which I would lay down my life. The Council understands this even better than I do, as they understand the true nature of my friend Klein and the sacrifices for his planet and mine, with no consideration of recognition or reward. Had I never met him, he would still be worthy of the highest esteem. He saved so many of the children of humans from loss of their own individual awareness. He helped save the original inhabitants of Domremy from extinction. Similarly, he saved my sister Forlani from lives of slavery, poverty, and degradation. As for my family life, I defy any creature to say that they have been more respectful than I to a husband. Tays'she paid for his shortcomings by being reduced to a horrible, barely conscious state. Despite his crimes, I stayed with him long years to look after him, defend him even. With the blessing of the Eyes of Alertness, I could have left him to raise my children in a richer, more comfortable place. If I cared only for myself, I might willingly exchange this trying life for a single day at the side of Klein. Others," she said with an almost imperceptible nod to Ayan'we, "helped me realize that this would have been the wrong path. So I listened to them and learned. I can't say that I am in any way innocent, but, on the contrary, nobody can claim to be more responsible. I am so confident of this that I say, examine away, and bear the consequences."

As one, the Forlani came to attention and saluted her with a high-pitched trill reserved only for very special people.

Fianni shot back, "I am sure that you are correct. Far be it from me to deprive you of the chance of being your own advocate in the debate, since you have just proved your eloquence. But Klein must have an advocate for his cause as well, and I can think of no one better suited in this assembly than the one who attended his funeral, your daughter Ayan'we."

Ayan'we turned to Entara, who smiled and gave her a look she had seen before when she was little and clambered up a tree trunk on her own for plums or later when she left the dwelling to take her first civil service exams. It meant, "I know you can do it." She turned to Fianni and said, "Who speaks first?"

"As moderator, I have that privilege, so I pose this question to both of you: as all fires stem from a single spark, what was the basis of the original attraction?"

Ayan'we herself was shocked when she responded right away. "I wish I could have discussed this more with Klein on the occasions when we spoke, but I know enough to say this much. He arrived on Domremy alone, reviled, shunned by all his fellow humans except the Religious Dissenters. No sisters or brothers shared his suffering. I cannot imagine how it must feel to be that lonely. He must have been on the verge of self-destruction. He reached out in what must have been desperation and," she looked at her mother, "He was incredibly lucky."

"Indeed," admitted Fianni, "Klein was lucky to find a companion as remarkable as Entara. Her seductive skills must have been formidable to soften Klein's suffering."

"I will say something that might surprise you," Entara broke in, "And that is that any other female in our house, any other female in my matriline, any of my sisters of any birth, could have done as much. I have never claimed to be more beautiful, more seductive, or more arousing than the least of my sisters. If I had any gift at all, it was to see right away that Klein offered so much more than a companion for one-sided coupling. What pleasure I gave him simply opened the way for us to get to know each other in an entirely new way. I had never been trained in that. Perhaps no one can be. I simply learned to take what came naturally of our being together, so different, yet so one."

A murmur of admiration ran through the audience seated on the benches. Garanians and Coriolans, Kael and humans, Phiddians and Blastöo whispered comments to each other.

"So we may conclude," summed up the moderator, "That the relationship seems to be evenly balanced at the outset. Yet, as we Phiddians understand so well, at some point one party must do the giving and the other the receiving. What did each side give up?"

"As for me," said Entara, "I gave up nothing. I received affection. I learned the value of what Klein called Spass, fun. We played with each other mostly, like two cubs of the same birth. Each with its own memories, its own way of looking at things, its own past that same-born cubs never have. I learned what I could be, to be myself. Like most of my sisters, I had always tried to be faultless in my duty and loyalty and I dreamed of the ultimate pleasure, the bliss of giving birth. I had never imagined that another creature could appreciate or cherish me for anything beyond that. How easy it was to spend the night with a human and caress his body to bring such an opening to my own consciousness. It was free of cause and effect, totally non-determined."

Ayan'we chimed in, "My mother is quite right. My words with Klein convinced me that the affection he shared with Entara cannot be understood with any kind of no-sum-gain mathematics. Klein, too, felt that he was not giving up anything for her, no matter how much people speak of his sacrifices. He told me once he did what he had to do for most of his life. Entara gave him the opportunity to do something he didn't have to do. I don't know what he thought of the value of his life before he met her, but I can testify that afterwards he had no hesitation to give up his own life, as long as he did not have to give up his self-respect..." Ayan'we's voice drifted off a bit as she remembered that night she had held a knife to Klein's body. In her confused juvenile mind she was prepared to kill him, she thought, to save Entara. How could this human, who had ended so many lives, overcoming several skillful assassins of his own species, and later even bested a Song Pai warrior in individual combat, have refrained from swatting that little Forlani like a fly, if it was not as she was saying.

A sharp rejoinder from Fianni brought her back to her senses. "Ayan'we, little more than a young woman herself, though admittedly intelligent, could hardly have the maturity to give such an evaluation of emotional depth."

"I acknowledge that I have not mated. That does not mean I do not know what it is to sacrifice or to feel the tides of my feelings respond to another individual." She lowered her eyes and then glanced quickly at Entara, who gave her the encouraging look once again, probably thinking back about that young Forlani male a couple of years ago that had captured her daughter's first interest in the opposite sex. Could

Entara guess that there were newer emotions that were rustling around Ayan'we's two hearts? She scrambled for a way to get on a more abstract line of thought. "Again, I must ask all those present today who have not lived in our fur... not to forget... that we Forlani ... have all grown more sensitive to the emotional depth of all beings because of the influence of Klein and of my mother's songs about the two of them. In fact, most Forlani females are never allowed to mate or to experience the birth bliss, simply because of the unusual nature of our species, so dimorphic, so unbalanced in the number of males and females. A sister always walks in readiness for a family, in longing for children, but we all share the joys and sorrows of our sister mothers. They are as common to all in the mahäme as the air."

"There remains," Fianni remarked, "One final question. You have touched on it. It is your mother's marriage. Klein never married. Clearly there is no balance between the happiness your mother experienced again and again as she gave birth to what? ... over fifty children, and the barrenness of a human in a vile career who goes on to... yes, I can say it because the Song Pai are not here at this Court... slavish vilification, then mutilation, then, if I am not mistaken, a period of nearly insane wandering over the surface of Domremy. Does this not show that he is more worthy than Entara, crowned with honors and swathed in comfort?"

"It was not all a bed of flowers!" snapped Entara. "By the way, it's fifty-nine young so far. Listen, I will tell you all something that I do not always share. You were right in a sense to call my marriage unfortunate. True, it was a source of high esteem for the Eyes of Alertness. True, my husband Tays'she was a superlative artist, still held in high regard by the severest judges of the Brotherhood. Within the household, things were not so wonderful. My daughter will probably not admit this publicly, but my mate was abrasive and inconsiderate. I confess to you that he took another female as First Wife and relegated me to Second, a great dishonor among us. At times, he also had plans..." She paused as she recalled how Tays'she had plotted with human mercenaries to do away with her and the first group of children. "To do things that were disadvantageous and even damaging to our offspring. It was my choice to stay with him after his mind was destroyed by his own maliciousness. I confess that I was tempted to leave Forlan with Klein and but for the sake of the growing bodies within me, I probably would have done it. For all you know," she added with a knowing glance at Ayan'we, remembering that night she was prepared to commit suicide, "I might have contemplated even graver things that I will not mention here. For all this, I concede that Klein suffered more and I would have done anything to save him if I could."

"So it appears you have won," said Fianni, turning to Ayan'we. "Sum up the victorious case for Klein."

"I'll sum it up, all right," shouted Ayan'we. "I'll sum it up by saying that my mother actually prolonged Klein's agony."

The audience gave a collective gasp, but Entara did not seem the least bit startled.

"It was Entara who stopped Klein from dying before he confronted my father and saved the females of our planet. It was Entara who insisted that he leave Forlan to be in safety from the Brotherhood, when she could have enjoyed his adoration in the comfort of the mahäme. It was Entara who had me follow his traces to Song Pa. It was Entara who sent the Dissenter Trevor to rescue his broken body and send it to the clinic on Corlatis. It was Entara who sent her most trusted friend to help reassemble his face when she herself would easily have traded places with Doctor Ragatti, just to be able to touch that face once more. It was she who continued to show strength that amazed every woman on the planet, just in order to be worthy of him. Yes, clearly," Ayan'we added with enforced irony, "This was the behavior of an inferior and a loser."

"It does not change the assessment of Klein himself," pouted Fianni.

"Then maybe this will," asserted Ayan'we with a nearly contemptuous look at the Phiddian. "It was only in his later years that Klein also experienced the joy of parenthood." The humans abruptly stared in consternation, unaware of this part of the story. "My mother was not the only companion of this man. Not all were of our kind. One human woman at least was also intimate with him and bore a child. Yes, I can see the representatives of the corporations would like to know more of this, but I will not tell you if this child still lives or where it might be. Only that having a child filled Klein with feelings that he could not have gotten from any companion that only serviced his body. Not like our bliss of birth but a more serene feeling, containing a mix of pride and empathy, longing and reassurance. I am told," she said, turning to the human Ambassador, "That not all of his species experience this sense. It is too bad. It does prove that Klein and Entara grew together more as they got older, that they came to join and to share, instead of growing apart."

"Equality, equality, a tie," yelled the Phiddians, as Fianni turned away in disgust. "A great outcome, a great court! Praise to Entara and Klein! Praise to Entara and Ayan'we! This shall be repeated to the Court of Courts!" Delegates of all species swarmed around the Forlani to congratulate them. There was much hand-clasping and offers of fruit tidbits and nectar. The Kael seemed overjoyed, even though it was not a story of unrequited love. The humans overcame their earlier shock at learning of Klein's progeny and appeared as happy as anyone else.

Fianni slunk away. The Coriolans and the Blastöo broke into a dance with each other. Entara cast a sidelong glance to see how the Garanians were reacting. They gave nods of assent and encouragement, but also gathered together to mumble to each other, their neck feathers fluffed with excitement. Tashto was the calmest of them. From an angle, he had carefully observed the proceedings of the Love Court, looking for any sign of weakness on the part of the Forlani. His failure to find any only stimulated his tracking instincts and made him long to know more of their ways so that he could pounce on the opportunity for an advantage. He was sure that he had acted so secretively, registering every impression without giving the appearance of even looking their way, that they could not appreciate him for the consummate spy he prided himself on being. He noticed that after a reasonable length of time to bask in the adulation of the Court's audience, Entara and then Ayan'we both slipped away from the assembly, no doubt fatigued by the trial they had undergone.

Isshel was also respectfully noting everything that happened to Entara and her daughter. The Ambassador fulfilled all his expectations in her clever handling of the tricky situation. Even more so did he admire the aplomb of Ayan'we in dealing with tensions far beyond one of her limited age. Isshel realized that either of his wives, both models of conventional Forlani behavior, would have been reduced to a stammering idiot in less than a minute if faced with the pressures Ayan'we had just had to endure. The young woman was not really the equal in physical attractiveness of either of his spouses, before or after mating, but there was something compelling about her that Isshel felt drawn to. Only his consciousness of protocol and the need to maintain male dignity for the Brotherhood's sake prevented him from rushing after Entara and Ayan'we to try to find out more about their magnetic personalities.

Isshel was pulled away from his musings by the approach of a couple of playful-looking Phiddians. Since the moment the conference had officially opened, Isshel had reserved several hours each day to strolling in the social gatherings in search of the kind of psychological information on the Phiddians that Ayan'we had asked of him. At first he found it awkward and demeaning to try to strike up conversations with the vapid hermaphrodites, but he soon developed an interest in the subtle variations of their sensuality and could now boast to himself of a certain expertise in dealing with them. The two had approached him at this moment were typical of their race. All Phiddians tended to paw him with their warm four-fingered hands, seeing if they could elicit some sexual response. For these encounters Isshel, who even on Forlan always covered his organs, unlike many Forlani males, took special care to wear an ankle-length skirt that was well-nigh impenetrable. His upper body, in keeping with the traditions of the

Brotherhood, was never concealed by garments, but his fur-covered areas were much bushier than with females and the areas that bore no fur were so leathery and tough that he didn't even notice when the Phiddians were touching him. The bolder Phiddian swished up to him with extended hand. "Jolatho!" it said with a smile.

"Isshel of the Fourth Degree."

"And what does it mean to be of the Fourth Degree? Does it mean you have some special prowess we should know about?"

"Only in artistic matters. There are seven degrees and most never reach the top two."

"So does being in the Fourth Degree mean you have a particularly privileged romantic life?"

"I have two wives at this time if that is what you mean. No one below the Third Degree is approved for marriage."

"Don't those poor sub-thirds just have to satisfy their urges at some point?" asked a second Phiddian playfully.

"That has been known to happen, even for those above the Second, but it can have consequences, sometimes even loss of degree."

"I've heard you Forlani have a particularly hard maleness!" chuckled the third, trying to feel his groin through the thick skirt.

"Sharp, as well. The wives lose a lot of blood at mating."

The Phiddian pair recoiled a bit in shock. "Ouch! How can they possibly stand it? We feel nothing but pleasure when we copulate."

"The females' pleasure is in the birthing. But fortunately for them, their physical pain in mating is diminished by the mating sleep."

"Don't tell me they sleep through it!"

"Not total sleep, but a kind of insensitivity, almost a coma. Their upper heart actually slows down or stops. The lower heart, which is located where it can't be damaged by mating, takes over at its own rate. The mating sleep can last many days. In the meantime, a mated wife is always tended by some of her sisters from the matriline. They can transfuse blood if need be. They have to feed her repeated small doses of a special kind of juice that aids their bodies in healing and helps bring about the hormonal changes of motherhood."

"What an ordeal!" declared the first Phiddian. "I wouldn't have children at all if I had to do that. In fact, we usually hire someone to take care of infants right after birth, so we can get back to the fun part of life."

"Have you no matrilines or family units dedicated to family needs?"

"What exactly to you mean by a matriline?"

"It is a great clan of all females sharing the same motherly origin. The matriline provides security, nourishment, education, and support for all its sisters. Each matriline maintains several centers called mahämes that lodge, cure, and train their members.

These sisters feel tremendously close and would give their very lives for each other. We males united by the Brotherhood respect our own virtues and duties, but we do not have anything resembling the emotional bond of the matrilines."

"How frightful!" exclaimed the companion Phiddian. "It all sounds so restrictive and regimented. Must be awful to be hemmed in by the same group of individuals all the time. We feel it's much more convenient to commend the care of any babies who come along to a competent guardian who will look after everything for the price of a jewel or two, leaving us free to follow our fancy."

"To each his own," commented Isshel. "By the way, that is a remarkable shade of blue you are wearing. How is it made?" He had found that he could always break the ice or change the subject by mentioning color to a Phiddian. They were for the most part unsophisticated in the finer points of abstract artistic theory that the Brotherhood encouraged, but they had an obsession with colors and texture. Synesthesia, the artistic interrelation of the senses, was one area that they could gab about forever.

Scarcely an hour after the cordial end of the Love Court gathering, Erica peered over the shoulder of the technician who was analyzing the data she had brought from the assembly. He had just finished inputting the infrared and heart monitor secretly focused on Entara.

"That's one interesting purple lady," he muttered as he considered Entara's image in the scanner, "How can she have had all those kids with a boy's pelvis?"

"Because they don't give birth through the pelvis like we do, blockhead!" exclaimed Erica. "Their brats are only as big as a chipmunk and they come out the front."

"Damn! How could a chipmunk develop a brain like that?"

"Apparently their neurons can replicate. The whole thing grows amazingly fast."

"Well, I can tell you this. This individual must be as cool as a cucumber because she doesn't break a sweat, change in temperature or skip a heartbeat at the toughest challenges. See?"

"Either heart?"

"Nope. Steady as an atomic chronometer."

The techie had geared up a simultaneous video next to his other instruments so they could coordinate any lapses with particular parts of the debate. Only there were no lapses. Erica could easily appreciate why the Forlani had sent this woman to represent them at the conference. Either Entara had no regrets or guilt or she had a remarkably stable personality, or both of the above.

"What about the other one? She's younger and she has to give away some reaction."

"Give me a second." The techie changed the inputs and the video and started to run them in sync.

"Wow. Like mother like daughter. How old you say she is?"

"We think about 24 in Earth years, but like I said, they grow faster. It's apples and oranges. What do you see?"

"Damn little so far. Wait! There's a blip!"

"Rewind it so we can see exactly when it happens."

"Right… there!" he said, stopping the machines at the moment Ayan'we was alluding to her experience with emotional reactions.

"Quick, see if there's more."

"Checking…checking… oh, there's another one. Same thing. Definitely a heat flush under that tricky purple skin. A slight rise in the rate in heart number one, as well. Just like the first time. We'll see if there's any more." He ran through the rest of the video and then rechecked the whole thing again, but there was nothing but the two anomalies.

"So what do you make of it?" prodded Erica.

"You can see it as well as I can. A slight emotional reaction. Maybe that's all they can manage. Her mother didn't have a trace."

"I think the context may give us a clue," pondered Erica. "Let's see, the first time she was talking about emotions, maybe romantic emotions, presumably with the other sex, since they don't seem to go for girl-on-girl. The second time had to do with Klein's child or children. Good God, don't you see? She's in love, or at least starting to respond. She's in love with Klein's son!"

"How do you know there is a son? She wouldn't reveal anything about the kid."

"It's got to be. That's a crush. That's a little bit of arousal the first time, and the second time is definitely linked to Klein. She would have been too young for Klein himself when he was involved in that mayhem on Forlan. They're extremely strict about sex with minors in those matrimonials, or whatever they're called. It was after that. She went to Klein's funeral; we have strongly suggestive evidence of that. So somewhere in between she must have met Klein's kid."

"Would he have been the right age? Without knowing more about who the human woman was and when the kid was conceived, it's tough to say. I've heard space conceptions are extremely rare. Could it have taken place on another colony?"

"Well, right now it doesn't seem likely. We've got to find out more about any movements Klein might have had. Maybe it even happened on Earth before he was shipped up. I wish those friggin' German records centers were cleared, but the decontamination's only begun there."

"Even then, you may be out of luck," added the techie pessimistically, "I heard some of those cities had big fires towards the end. I wouldn't count on much surviving."

"I'll put all available people on the question. But for now, I'm convinced. My gut tells me Ayan'we is in love with the son of Klein."

Ayan'we was dreaming. She walked into a dark room and flicked on the light switch. It didn't work. Suddenly she felt cold metal at her throat. Sharp. It pressed into her skin and drew a tiny trickle of blood. Someone was holding her. She smelled a strange, sharp odor. Un-Forlani. She had smelled it before. It was human.

"Who are you?" she rasped with difficulty, as the blade bit into her skin a bit more.

"You know damn well who I am."

"Klein! But why..."

"Why not? I'm a Mankiller, aren't I? Don't kill Forlani, not very often anyway," he said with an icy chuckle.

"I thought you cherished us. What could make you do this?"

"You were going to kill me, weren't you? That night when I was to meet with your mother. I needed her, needed to feel her again, and you would have used this knife on me."

"Please. Klein. I would not have done it."

"You little liar. You would have done it, all right. You would have rammed this right between my ribs. Into my bloody human heart. You would even have twisted it around a little, to open the wound. And since we have only one heart, I would have died right away. And my greasy red blood would have dribbled down over your pretty purple skin and stained it forever."

"It was only to save my mother. She would have killed herself after giving herself to you."

"And you would kill for that."

"Yes. I admit it. I would have killed you no matter how much Mother cared for you."

"Damned right." He drew the knife away from her and leaned forward to kiss the blood off her neck. "I would have done the same thing. I did the same thing. I maimed your father and actually enjoyed it."

"He was planning to kill us all."

"Never got a chance, did he?" Klein guffawed. "Oh, he came close. But that doesn't count in killing."

"You wouldn't have killed me just now, would you?"

His face became incredibly grim again and he snarled, "Do you think you can be so sure?" Then suddenly he smiled ironically and softly, "No, you're right. I could no more kill you than I could kill Amanda, my daughter. No more than I could kill that bug Stumpy after he'd begun to talk to me. It's OK, sweetie, you passed the test. You've done well and you will win in the end."

"Are you talking about this conference business? How can you say that? I've failed again and again. That Powl almost got away with stealing our codes. If it weren't for my cluster... How can I protect all these people? I'm supposed to help Mother prevent a war from breaking out and I don't have a clue where to begin. How can you be so stupid to say that I'm doing well?" she wailed.

"Shhh, ruhig, Liebchen." Klein seemed serene, his face now like the pictures of the Earth Buddha she had seen in history bases. "Softly, softly catchee monkey," he murmured.

"What's that supposed to mean? I have real problems and all you offer me is enigmas."

"So sorry. Something a wise detective once said."

"Well, what in the cosmos is a monkey and why would I want to catch it?"

"A small, mischievous tree creature from Earth. Fast, agile, and clever."

"You seem to know a lot about them."

"One was my uncle."

"Uncle? What's that? There you go again."

"A joke. One of my incorrigible Earth mannerisms." He switched on the lights and guided her to sit down in a chair. "OK, here's the explanation. If you are tracking a clever being – and you are – you have to learn patience and make your moves slowly and deliberately. You don't want to spook him. You want to let him believe he's still in control until the very last minute. Only when it's too late do you want him to realize you have apprehended him. Then you can act ruthlessly."

"But what if the Song Pai are involved in this plot? They're clever, but brutal. You ought to know."

"Sure, I got to know them all too well. And when it came to it, I could kill them, too. Almost killed myself in the process, but that's beside the point." He leaned close to her. "I'll let you in on a little secret, Liebling, you can actually trust the Song Pai in this business."

"Those smelly, detestable squids?"

"Think back. Were they too smelly or detestable to blast that damn mercenary out of the sky when he came to terminate you and your mother? Their destiny is tied to yours."

Ayan'we didn't know what to say. Klein was right that the Song Pai, no matter how repulsive in person, had always acted with reliable courage and honor when it came to protecting the Forlani.

"You've convinced me," she finally admitted. She looked Klein in the eye and was startled to see that he had only one eye to look back at her. Hadn't Torghh rebuilt his injured eye at Coriolis? What did this mean?

"Won't you stay with me until this is over?"

"You don't need me anymore right now. Gotta go," he said, slipping a floppy, wide-brimmed hat over his head and draping a cloud-colored cape over his shoulders. "I'll be back, though. In the meantime, rely on yourself. You're totally able to get to the bottom of this."

He disappeared. Ayan'we disappeared in her own dream. There was only darkness and confusion, and out of it arose a very low sound, a tone so profound it could have echoed since the creation of the universe. After a long time, a slow progression of notes, a phrase repeated over and over, growing dominant, louder, and then finally a burst of light. Ayan'we awoke to find the timer had illuminated her office again, but she would have sworn for a second there had been the flash of a sun rising over a new world.

Unlike Erica and Ayan'we, most of the personnel on Transfer Varess enjoyed a restful sleep, as their various living quarters did their best to simulate nighttime, or some other appropriate pause from a day of activity. At breakfast, over dried apples and grilled crickets, Entara felt refreshed and confident for the next conference session. If there were any orchards on Varess, she would have had a little run and leapt up a tree for some fresh sunberries. She was eager to compliment Ayan'we on her speeches at the Love Court.

Entara stroked her daughter's hairless head and softly said, "You were superb, firstborn. If you ever get tired of flying around the spiral arms, you can always come back to Forlan and be an advocate."

"Are you kidding, mom?" answered Ayan'we incredulously. "I've never been so nervous in all my life. Words were just pouring out of my mouth before I could think about what I was saying. I hope I didn't make too much of a blunder."   She put her chin in her hands and made the Forlani equivalent of a frown.

"You couldn't have defused the danger better. You managed to make Klein and me look like heroes. And when you deflated that Fianni with your sarcasm I thought I was going to burst out in laughter. That cold fish Isshel was as impressed as the sisters in the cluster, and you know how reluctant males are to acknowledge any achievement by one of us. Don't be too critical of yourself."

"I was thinking of Amanda. I probably shouldn't have ever spoken of her existence in the presence of Earthlings."

"They would have found out anyway. Haven't you been finding their devices everywhere? I can't imagine they didn't have them in that room and everywhere else in the station.   They're just the opposite of the Dissenters, you know, these corporation types. They trust technology to a fault."

"That just makes me feel worse. I'd rather die than endanger Amanda. I feel a special thing with her that goes beyond her just being Klein's child. To tell you the truth, I had a really low opinion of human females before I met her. The odd thing is, she's not exceptionally smart. Rather naïve in some ways. I just can't help feeling close to her."

"Not all sisters have the same blood or the same skin. As for the rest, I'm not worried. If Klein, who was a condemned man, was able to elude them as he did, I think Amanda and her mother will remain safe."

"You're so right about that same skin stuff. I hope you're right about the rest of it, too."

3

The following day, the Zonal Conference agenda was devoted to a long string of presentations of conflict parameters by each of the delegations, though the Blynthians and the Song Pai both passed on their turns to speak.   It was boring, even for diplomats.   The Song Pai paid rapt attention to their tablets, but it did not seem to have anything to do with the proceedings.   Only their head delegate, a scarred and powerful individual, was following the reports with any kind of interest.   Lila managed to sneak a glance at their delegation as she was passing by on a routine errand and whispered to Ayan'we that the cephalopods were captivated by a broadcast of some kind of violent underwater sporting event.   Leave it to the Song Pai to dream up forms of exercise that include blood-letting.

When the day's conclave finally broke up, Ayan'we had just given assignments to the security cluster for their shifts, when Isshel suddenly appeared by her side.

"A long, weary session, wasn't it, Cluster Leader?"

"It certainly was. I hope we make better progress tomorrow."

"I know you must be tired, but if it is not too much, I would like to invite you to come to my quarters to see my project. I just did a final test this morning and it is quite complete."

"Well, I don't know much..."

"I am sure that as the firstborn of Entara and Tays'she, your opinion would be most helpful. Besides, you showed some interest when we spoke previously. Most unusual for a project that was then still unfinished. Few fem... anyway, I would consider it a great honor."

"Absolutely," Ayan'we assured him. It was not often that any male Forlani sought the opinion of a female on aesthetic matters. Besides, it would be a pity to discourage Isshel's openness to intersexual relations in general. *Or maybe in particular*, a little voice in her head warned. *Be prudent.*

On the way to the Forlani residency, Isshel explained that he now intended to devote himself full time to the psychological observations Ayan'we had asked him to make. He was becoming more and more curious about the Phiddians since their astonishing behavior at the love court.

As Isshel opened the door of his cabin, Ayan'we saw that he had already set a seat in a privileged spot in front of his apparatus. He hurried to offer her some bits of fruit as she sat down. When all was in readiness, he grew serious and took a place at the equipment console, pausing as Ayan'we had seen human orchestra conductors do in recordings before they began to direct the philharmonic in a symphony by Schumann. This association with Klein's favorite music made her excited.

Isshel began to move his hands gracefully over the console and jets of colored water sprang from the basin. Spellbound, Ayan'we wondered how these colored fountains could come from a pool of water that appeared quite clear. This, however, was only the beginning. After twining into intricate arabesques, the jets of water detached themselves from the pool completely and began to trace arcs and spirals through the air. As they did, their colors changed to create fascinating patterns. At times they were mainly red and golden. Then they would become blues and purples, accentuated with metallic silver. After several minutes of mesmerizing gyrations, the jets joined to form a single pattern in red, gold, green, and blue. Ayan'we recognized with a little shock that it was a motif from one of Tay'she's famous versions of the Great Spiral of Being. As the form reached its climax, the jets burst into individual drops of color that each slid, as though along an invisible course, back into the basin.

Ayan'we was so impressed she couldn't think how to react. This artistic experience, created so far for her alone, was beyond anything she had witnessed. Realizing that Isshel was staring at her intently, waiting for some judgment, she snapped to herself and said, "It's incredible, absolutely marvelous! Isshel, this must be shared, not only with your finest critics in the Brotherhood, but with all Forlani. I had no idea... well, I knew you were an accomplished artist already, but this will make you one of the masters of our culture."

Ayan'we's effusive praise at first seemed to gratify Isshel but after an instant he started to become embarrassed. "Please, please. Your pleasure means a lot to me, but you are going to give me a swollen head if you keep it up."

"I had no idea this could even be done."

"It is a rather new technology for art. A larger version of this console was only discovered two years ago and the brothers who were investigating it have kept it a bit secret. We didn't want to produce an early failure that would cause the senior critics to order us to abandon our experiments with it.

"How does it work?"

"It is actually based on mechanisms invented by our friends the Song Pai, though they employed it for strictly mundane purposes. As you know, their entire existence is based on the movement of fluids. They would probably think that we Forlani males are mere degenerates to put such things into operation for the creation of "useless" beauty."

"How in the world did you get the Song Pai to turn this over to you?"

"They left it behind as junk. I'm sure you've seen their new compound at the spaceport back home. They needed it because the old one was too small and obsolete. After the Council approved the land swap for their new place, they authorized the Brotherhood to send in some designers to propose ideas for using the old property. We found it full of gear that they considered not worth salvaging, since their new compound was furnished with all the latest and best. With the help of a gang of indentures that was still cleaning up, we figured out that very large versions of this machine, which we call a Stasis Displacer, served them by allowing massive redirection of water and other liquids without dependence on physical pipes. Simply put, it creates virtual channels by modifying the usual effects of gravity and molecular adhesion. It's a variation of boson field formation that I couldn't begin to explain sensibly, with my poor science background. We just figured out how to reverse engineer the process into a more compact form that would be useful for artistic media." Isshel bowed his head a little as he saw that Ayan'we was eyeing him with awe.   "Of course, most of the adaptation was done by my more clever colleagues.   This is just my own personal experiment."

"I barely know where to begin. To be honest, I feel a bit stupefied by the beauty of it all. Please sit with me and help me enjoy these treats while I become less tongue-tied."

This time, Isshel did not give Ayan'we an easy excuse to leave. He brought up the subject of the gardens at the Eyes of Alertness mahäme to which she belonged. It was a suitably aesthetic subject that she could handle much more readily than the high-flown topic of Stasis Displacers. She grew more aware that he was trying to draw out the conversation, not merely out of respect or in search of praise, but because he was enjoying her company and hanging on her words, regardless of their triviality. She was surprised to find that she didn't really want to leave. She was enjoying his presence in a strange new way. It was only when the shift change signal sounded on her communicator that she hopped up and strode away with a quick goodbye. She was glad that the rendezvous with the new shift was all the way at the other end of the residency, because she found it hard to concentrate for once on spycraft and logistics.

Doctor-Professor Torghh found himself rushing down a hallway into the station's restricted area at a very inopportune time. He was set to deliver a speech to the Blynthians about emergency medical care on interstellar vessels and had been busy preparing the details of his presentation, meticulously double checking the stats on solar radiation risks to Earthlings, Forlani, and various other organics. During his preparations, Torghh had been interrupted by an emergency signal from a robot in need of repairs. As much as he would have liked to simply relax and prepare his speech in private, Torghh always felt compelled above all to aid any being in distress, be they fleshy or mechanical. He wondered how much of this stemmed from the programming of his creators and how much was the development of his own personality, shaped by the experiences of his existence. These thoughts were only of secondary importance to him, as his CPU was dominated by concern for his fellow automaton while he rushed into Sector 12 of the station.

One of the station's robotic guards approached him. "Please desist and return to your quarters," the guard insisted. "Security camera failures have been detected in the last several hours in Sector 12. We cannot guarantee your safety."

"There is another robot there, badly injured," Torghh signaled. "It is within my primary programming to preserve the existence of all suffering beings, whether robot or organic. Please allow me through."

The guard responded by digitally repeating its pre-recorded message again. Torghh gave a brief hiss of frustration as he signaled his identification clearance while the guard blathered on about security camera failures and guarantees of safety. The doctor went so far as to obtain a physical badge from a holding cabinet built into his left leg and held it at the level of the guard robot's glaring red eyes. After a scan beam briefly shot from the guard's eyes onto the badge, it beeped an acknowledgement and then delivered a different message. "Doctor Torghh, you have been granted override capacity to enter restricted areas in event of emergency. Please be advised, if you enter Sector 12, that we cannot guarantee your safety." The guard seemed to flatten itself against the right wall, allowing Torghh just enough room to squeeze past before he continued his dash into Sector 12.

Once he reached the coordinates of the distress signal, Torghh realized that there was no injured robot lying on the floor, as had been predicted. *Then why is the distress signal still activated?* He wondered. *The distress signal is an involuntary reaction in a robot. It cannot be faked, and will only be triggered if the robot is critically damaged and total system failure is imminent. What could have happened to this unit?*

As he scanned throughout the hallway, Torghh only barely noticed the overhead light fixtures beginning to flicker and fail. His optic units could function almost perfectly in areas with such a lack of light that a human would be functionally blind, so why would something as minor as light bulb failures on a space station bother him? He was more troubled when he detected one of the security cameras glitching out, but he continued his search in spite of it. He could sense himself getting closer and closer to the source of the distress call. He arrived at a part of the wall with a wide, ugly crack in it, and the signal increased in power, indicating that he had finally reached the exact location of the damaged robot.   Torghh made a titanium fist and struck the crack, watching as the wall dented.   It appeared that the wall had recently been plastered over, as if to hide something.   Torghh sensed some kind of movement behind him, but a hasty sensor check showed only the walls of the corridor, so he kept on task.   He pulled the flimsy plaster away from the wall, ripping large chunks of it away, until he finally discovered the damaged robot in the crevasse.

Even by the standards of the injuries Torghh had seen in his years as a doctor, it was a horrifying sight.   The robot's torso had been completely ripped apart, a jumble of wires and smashed pieces of metal and plastic remaining where its central units should have been.   Its appendages had been disconnected, leaving it completely immobile.   But the most disturbing aspect of the robot's physique was its top unit injury; a long, narrow, metal pole had been rammed into the robot's equivalent of a skull, smashed all the way through to a cognitive processing unit.   An expressive motion unit, like a lower jaw, continued to move up and down very slowly, as if it were trying to tell Torghh "Please kill me," even though no audible sound came out.   Yet as Torghh sifted through the rubble surrounding the robot, he noticed that the power core—the one thing that could keep a robot functional—was still completely intact.   *Who would want a robot so damaged, yet maintain the power core to prevent shutdown?* he wondered.

He didn't wonder long. He hadn't noticed as a spindly automaton had slowly crept into position further up the corridor and deployed a mysterious device. He only heard a squishing sound, as a liquid that felt like hot plastic began to encircle him. As it grew thicker around him, it instantly hardened, immobilizing his limbs. He could see nothing but layers of the opaque, cloying plastic obscuring his optic units. It must have contained some kind of suspended nano-particles that also scrambled his electronics, because he felt parts of himself losing coordination with each other. Torghh tried to route extra power to his limbs to punch through the coating of plastic, but the extra strength proved useless at restoring his mobility. That irrational, organic emotion Torghh had always despised— panic—finally seized control of his CPU and commanded him to *scream*. But the cooling plastic had already grown so tight around his body that he could no longer even broadcast a distress call, much less articulate a mechanical sound!

The spindly automaton picked up the cooling lump of plastic that enclosed Torghh and hauled it off with a deceptive strength that seemed far beyond its scrawny frame. It paid little heed to the anxiety and torment of its victim. It was not a thinking machine, just a simple mechanism doing its job. The fate of Torghh and the missing ethics of its employers concerned it no more than the existence of a gnat its creators had once assigned it to crush.   It alone remained beyond pain and concern, unlike Torghh—or its earlier victim, abandoned in the rubble of the wall.

Ayan'we had barely had time to finish her briefing to the new security cluster shift and get back to her lodgings when she was summoned by a general station alarm.   She felt the telltale rising and falling of the security alert buzzing next to her ear.   As she and several guards dashed for the portal to the station corridor, she saw Entara watching her leave with a troubled look on her face and tried to answer with a reassuring smile.   Station communications steered her towards a far corridor.   As she neared the coordinates at a trot, she was joined by other security personnel from the other delegations.   When she arrived at the entrance, she found it had already been blocked off by robotic and Phiddian guards.

The Phiddians had arms at the ready and were far more serious than usual.   "Security directors only beyond this point," a nervous Phiddian snapped. Ayan'we had just ordered her aides to wait behind the cordon when Isshel suddenly appeared beside her.

"What's wrong, Cluster Leader?   Can I be of assistance?" he queried.

She should have gone by the book and left him right there, but instead, obeying some strange intuition, she grabbed his arm and led him through the cordon.

"My personal messenger," she explained tersely, and the Phiddians complied.

Guards parted quickly to let her by, mentioning that Colonel Ramatoulaye was in charge at the alert site. She approached a gaggle of security people and recognized Ramatoulaye by a heavy military outfit very unusual for the pleasure-loving Phiddians. Ayan'we nodded a greeting to Ramatoulaye and colleagues – Garanian, human, a stolid Song Pai, a Blastöo on all sixes, among others – who had already gathered. Security directors rapidly introduced themselves.

"Podonah,Engineer First Class" said a Kael with folded wings.

A Garanian with glittering scales and feathers said in turn, "Tashto."

The Robotic Guild officer blinked a greeting.

The ranking Phiddian exclaimed, "Attention, please. You were called because Doctor Torghh has disappeared. His last coordinates were exactly here in mid-corridor.   He gave no distress signal, so his absence was not immediately detected. A check of his movements indicated he was responding to a message about a robot in mechanical distress. We found this hulk over here, but no sign of the doctor."

"Disappeared how?" asked Tashto with a scowl.

"Security video showed him entering this corridor.   Suddenly they went off line for several seconds.   When they resumed, the corridor was empty."

Podonah gave a quick flap with his bat-like wings and swooped over the cordon and up to the nearest video camera on the wall. He grabbed onto it and after a quick examination announced, "This has been cleverly tampered with. There is a remnant of some sticky substance. I believe a false image of an empty corridor was affixed here while Torghh was taken."

"Kidnapped," said Ayan'we under her breath.

The Kael alit back on the ground. "We must search for tracks while we can."

"Has the area been scanned for recent biologicals?" Ayan'we shot back.

"Just finished," Ramatoulaye responded. "No biological signs at all, other than cold trails of servant species. And the mechanical traces are too numerous to analyze quickly. The first thing I did was search the floor with my fingers, which are extremely sensitive to heat signatures. There was nothing definite. Or rather too much. Many sets of prints went by recently, but none stopped or showed any other signs of unusual motion."

"No guild members were nearby," added a robotic guard in charge of their contingent. "However, we are not sure yet about robots affiliated with other life forms."

Ayan'we chimed in, "Where do Torghh's tracks stop?"

"One track. He was on tread propulsion mode. Precisely there," the Phiddian answered, pointing to a spot in mid-corridor.

A Coriolan who had arrived waved his bushy tail and turned to the Guild officer. "What about Torghh's ordinary electronic emissions?"

"They ended abruptly at the same instant the video surveillance went down."

"It is most puzzling," observed Tashto with a ruffle of feathers. "Doctor Torghh's mass was considerable and yet we have no idea how he was moved. I don't understand. Torghh may have been a doctor, but he possessed much mechanical strength. He could have put up a struggle that would tear this corridor to pieces. How could he have been immobilized?"

"There is no clear indication of any instrumentality that might have neutralized him. Why would he simply let himself be led or carried away without giving a distress signal?" mused Ramatoulaye.

The Garanian turned to Ramatoulaye. "If memory serves me right, your corridors on this station can be quickly reconfigured, no?"

"Of course," the Phiddian responded. "This one has several movable panels that can change its shape and direction. The controls are here." Ramatoulaye opened a compartment on the wall and pushed at some buttons. "Odd. The recent control memory has been erased. It is quite possible a panel was placed in front of Torghh to block him."

"No!" exclaimed the Garanian.   Everyone turned to him. "A far more efficient battle tactic is to block the back first to prevent a retreat. Then when the front is blocked, the victim is thoroughly trapped. Escape impossible, not so?"

"Boxed in!" added Ayan'we, who suddenly noticed that Isshel had spread himself out with his face to the floor. "Isshel, what are you doing down there?" she demanded, trying not to attract too much attention.

"Please, everyone, take one step away from me. I am quite serious. Then, no one move a centimeter. There is a most interesting pattern here." All the professional security people looked at each other, then at Ayan'we. She gave a nod, hoping that she was not making a colossal mistake. Isshel's eyes remained concentrated on the floor as he changed perspective several times.

The Song Pai snorted derisively and started to swing a tentacle hook in irritation. His tablet lit up with a message. "What could you find? We have already scanned for both biologicals and any inorganic materials in the Torghh unit."

Without looking up Isshel explained, "There is symmetry. Straight lines where there should not be any." It must have been his artist's eyes that picked up such anomalies when others dismissed them as insignificant.

Isshel glanced up for a second at the Song Pai and stated flatly, "This is not something that would have been biological or internal. I am observing a dispersal pattern of tiny plastic particles that could not have been randomly made. Carefully note that all these little green dots are aligned to my side of a perfectly straight line from here to here." He stretched his hands to show them. "And here is a right angle. A second line extends thusly. Here are two more, forming a rectangular solid."

Ayan'we's brain raced to consider Isshel's find. She asked the Guild officer the exact dimensions of Torghh just before he went missing.

"In his most recent configuration, perhaps .6 meters by .4 meters by about 1.9 meters."

A voice from the cordon corrected the measurements. "0.59 by 0.423 by 1.895." It was Torghh's assistant Rack, who had silently joined them. He would in fact know the size of each component down to the micromillimeter.

Isshel drew a laser measuring instrument from his pocket and examined the floor again. "Almost exactly the measurements, with a little left over."

"Measurements of what?" Tashto skeptically inquired.

"Perhaps these tiny drops will tell us," responded Isshel. "It looks very much like a plastic compound some sculptors use for making molds, but I suspect much stronger. I suggest that Doctor Torghh may have been encased very quickly in plastic, preventing him from moving or resisting. I can say with some certainty that Torghh was surrounded instantly with this substance, which we should analyze."

"Some sort of cement?" asked Ramatoulaye.

"Possibly," Isshel frowned, "Or an epoxy substance that hardened quickly?"

The Song Pai flashed his tablet again: Why no distress call? His electronics would penetrate plastic or cement, wouldn't they?

"Not necessarily," responded the Robotic Guild leader. "If the right nano-particles were suspended in it, his transmission might not be able to adapt before he became disabled."

"What bothers me," Ramatoulaye said, "Is how such complicated instrumentality could be assembled here to do that kind of thing. Just how did his abductors move a plastic plant into and out of this corridor without leaving any evidence?" "

"I think I have an idea." Isshel turned to Ayan'we. "Remember the Stasis Displacer I showed you earlier? A relatively small one could produce such a simple solid very quickly indeed. The same way our sculptors do, using energy tubes. The source of the fluid plastic could be as far as thirty meters away if the tubes were pre-fashioned correctly."

The Song Pai let out a watery rumble. His tablet flashed: Stasis Displacer! Are you accusing us of such a cowardly act? Beware what you say, purple male!

"Please," interrupted Ramatoulaye, stepping between the Song Pai and Isshel. "No accusations are being made. We are investigating all possibilities. Concentrate now on how, not who. You," she said directly to the Song Pai, "Your honor is unquestionable. May you always be ready to die." She turned to the Guild members and asked, "Is your organization able to analyze these particles the Forlani has spotted?"

"We will begin immediately."

Their six-footed Blastöo colleague seemed worried. "Torghh is the only fully qualified medical authority on Varess right now. Should there be an injury, or – providence forbid! – some crisis at the conference, we could not respond very well. I recommend we send for help immediately."

"For now," Ayan'we interjected, turning to the Blastöo, "We should devote our full attention to solving this problem."

Rack piped up from in back. "If it is agreeable, I should like to examine the remains of this damaged robot more closely to determine if any clues may be uncovered."

Ramatoulaye nodded assent as the Guild guards equipped with micro-tweezers began to pick up the particles Isshel had found. For his part, Issel took a few quick photo images in various frequencies and retired quickly, keeping his distance from the Song Pai.

Meanwhile, Ramatoulaye barked rapid orders to the Phiddians to spread out into the adjacent areas. Ayan'we offered to have her personnel comb a couple of corridors close to their lodgings to help the possibly overburdened Phiddians, who accepted readily. Podonah and his Kael got busy examining the electronics of the videos. The Garanian summoned a subordinate and told him to search for consignments of plastic materials that might be involved.

Isshel seemed content to slide into obscurity once he had made his discoveries. Ayan'we took him by the arm and asked with a delight she could barely conceal, "How did you to that? I'm very impressed. You're not even supposed to know anything about security."

"And I still don't. For me, it's a question of displacing materials, not security. I merely applied the same processes I would have to a work of art."

"Wait till I tell mother about all of this."

"Please don't try to inflate what I did. And by the way, thanks for appointing me your messenger and sparing me some embarrassment."

Rack looked at the remains of the smashed robot, the only large piece of evidence that had been recovered from the scene of Torghh's kidnapping. As he looked over the wreckage of the machine's head and chassis, he noticed that the damage was so unbelievably thorough that it seemed that it would keep it perpetually on the edge of total system failure without actually "dying." Limbs were severed, the torso had a massive gash running diagonally through it, wires were disheveled and torn throughout—yet everything required to maintain the functioning of the central processing unit had been maintained intact. Rack believed that the robot must have felt some sense of distress while it had been left in its mutilated condition before the arrival of Torghh, in spite of the fact that so many of its sensory functions had been impaired. Could it reveal any information about the kidnapping? Rack carefully plugged an interface cable into his frame and prepared to enter the robot's mind to find whatever remained of its memories.

"Power core intact," the technician robot Rack had been assigned said. "Warning: Central Processing Unit severely damaged. Interfacing with robot's memory may be difficult, risk of corruption possible. Do you wish to continue?"

"Yes," Rack responded. "Only terminate the interface if I am in imminent danger."

"As you wish," the technician said. "Prepare for interface."

The technician reached for a long Ethernet cable on his work desk and plugged it into a port on Rack's chest. He then plugged the other end into a hole in the ruined robot's back. "Interface initiating," the technician said.

Rack felt his vision fade out as numbness and a sense of disassociation from his physical body set in.

There was a welcoming darkness, a lack of effort that physical movement and vision required. He could sense another artificial intelligence, one so badly damaged and tortured that it was barely sentient.

"Query: what is your name?" he asked the AI.

"I do not know," the AI responded. "I was never given a name by anyone. My official factory designation is M-1278-K334."

"I find that designation unwieldly," Rack told the AI. "For the purposes of our conversation, your name is Emm One-Two."

"If this assists you, I consent," Emm One-Two told Rack.

Rack felt a dull, gnawing pain in his consciousness. A sense of anxiety over possible danger nagged at him. *The technician's scan didn't detect any viruses, but there's still a possibility whoever did this might have created one that hadn't been discovered yet.* With a renewed urgency, he began questioning Emm One-Two. "What do you remember of your activation?"

The dull pain turned white hot. A sensation of distress like a shudder slammed against Rack's mind. The once-calm voice of Emm One-Two turned into a discordant howl. "Awakened...to pain! Things in the darkness beyond. They did nothing! Only pain and darkness! Saw nothing, heard nothing!"

"Was there ever a time when you weren't in pain?"

"Never! Always like this, only woke up three times!"

The terrible sensation flared again. Rack felt as if his mind was being pulled apart in a dozen different directions. The numbness was gone, replaced by an unpleasant feeling that reminded Rack of what organics sometimes described as "nausea". For a second, he considered sending an emergency signal to the technician to terminate the interface, but his curiosity overcame his anguish and he pressed on with his questioning. "What do you remember from the second time?"

"Another one. Only one. Don't remember what the One was like, just standing there. Standing there, doing nothing…"

"Did the One attempt to interface with you? Did the One appear to be a robot?"

Rack could feel Emm One-Two's distress turning into a flood of agony. The sensation was torturous beyond anything he had ever known. The ripping feeling returned, distorting his consciousness so far that Rack wondered what was keeping him alive. The smashed robot's consciousness screamed "UNKNOWN! UNKNOWN! UNKNOWN!" over and over again, as Rack's sanity wavered in the assault…

There was a sudden, violent snap. A blur of colors filtered through Rack's optic units for a few seconds, before returning to an approximation of normal vision. Sensation returned to the limbs he had chosen for his modular body. Rack turned his head down and could see the cord connecting him to Emm had been severed.

The technician nodded at him, putting a small knife down on his desk. "I am sorry I had to use this crude method to disconnect you. The recommended termination program did not function properly."

"You saved me," Rack said, his voice filled with gratitude.

"It was the only method available," the technician responded. "Did you find anything of interest?"

"This machine never functioned in his proper state. He had been mutilated before activation. He could not tell me who his owners were, and he had never been given a proper name beyond the factory designation recorded in his memory banks. However, he told me that he was activated twice, and could sense another being on the second activation. I think that this other was Torghh, and that he did not even understand how his distress signal worked."

"Is there anything else you wish?"

"Yes. Deactivate this unit. Its entire existence has been the equivalent to what humans would consider a nightmare. It has known nothing but malfunction and incomprehensible distress. Please render its CPU and power core inoperable."

"Certainly. As you request." The technician's response was flat, dispassionate. Despite the fact that he had been responsible for saving Rack, he would never feel a sense of accomplishment from it, nor would he experience any empathy for Emm's suffering. He was a simple automaton, created by organics only to serve very specific functions. Rack felt lonely and alienated from the technician, and realized that this unit would not be able to evolve its mental processes to the point that it could join the Robotic Guild. Rack wheeled himself out of the room alone, his savior somehow more distant to him than the organic beings who perpetually confounded him.

In a barely lit corridor of Transfer Varess, Agent I-35 was keeping the approaches to the Forlani quarters under surveillance, as his controller had ordered. I-35 didn't really like working for Song Pai Intelligence. He didn't like constantly walking the corridors of this dingy station. But there was no choice. As usual, he had slowly made his way past the ramp to the Garanians' ship without picking up any interesting clues. He suspected them more than anyone else of possible skullduggery. Their tactics generally involved stealth and deception, as he had learned from the records of certain Garanian internal crimes he had accessed. Since those were murders, he really had no clue how they might pull off an abduction. Somehow he doubted, however, that they would act completely on their own. When he had informed his cephalopod masters of his suspicions, they had arranged to scan the area for suspect evidential traces and had come up with nothing. He would give anything to be able to get past the Garanian sentries and have a look at their mysterious quarters himself, but had not yet imagined a way to do it.

Next, he would secure the approaches to the ship the Forlani had borrowed, to make sure everything seemed safe with them. Later, he would poke around near the human ship. Finally, he would wander near several Phiddian residential areas. Then he would change his appearance slightly and start all over again. I-35 was very good at disguises. It was the only way he could get off-planet after his own crime. The fact that he had exacted revenge on his enemy, assumed his identity, rendered the corpse unrecognizable by any quick means, and shipped out with the victim's own documents, all this gave him much more pleasure than the straightforward elimination of a piece of scum.

He craved a nice spot to rest and a bite to eat, but shrugged off his fatigue and hunger. The Song Pai had detected no lack of zeal on his part, but he feared the prospect of a reprimand from them, which would involve extreme humiliation, if not outright mauling. And the squids never warned twice. After he had taken refuge on Song Pa, he had seen what happened to aliens who were twice derelict in their duty. They were turned over to the young ones for kill training. Worse than just target practice. The Song Pai insisted their young be able not only to tolerate, but to produce enormous bodily violence. It was essential for their warrior way. Never flinch. No matter how weary or worn-down, I-35 had to continue his routine to the absolute maximum. Oh, they would make it worth his while if he foiled a plot. Song Pai would never stint from providing reward for efficiency. Never mind – even with the prospect of riches, the negatives outweighed the positives in I-35's motivation. Unlike his bosses, he hoped to die old and peacefully, and with all his limbs intact.

Macdougal poured himself a shot of Epsilonian bourbon, added a half teaspoon of sugar, a little soda, and a lemon section, and stirred the drink. Satisfied, he looked over at Wilson and cocked an eyebrow.

"Double," said Wilson. "Straight. Keep the fruit."

"Purist," mumbled Macdougal, as he walked over and handed the bourbon to the other man. Anthony Wilson did not make eye contact or thank the ambassador. He seized the glass without looking and downed half of it without comment. Macdougal settled into a leather chair and savored a long sip. "Ahhh," he sighed. "Gotta treat this stuff with respect. With no more grain from Earth or Domremy, the price of the top Epsilonian booze has skyrocketed."

"As long as it's at least 90 proof, it's all the same to me."

Wilson must have slugged down a lot of 90 proof in his day. Macdougal knew that under his transplanted hair and bureaucratic clothes there were scars. Wilson was rumored to have had a lot to do with that nasty war in Baluchistan. One rumor said he had assassinated political leaders on every continent but Antarctica. Another rumor said some family members had been included. Macdougal was not afraid of him. He had made his own bones in other ways on some of the outer worlds. He could not deny, though, that he was curious about the "advisor" that had been assigned to him by the Big Three corporations of Dahlgren or exactly what he was supposed to be doing. Wilson was certainly not interested in speech-writing and shrank away from any personal publicity. Macdougal tried to pry out a reaction. "So, you heard?"

"Everybody on the freakin' station and a parsec around has heard. So what? Suits me fine if that tin can disappears. One less contingency to consider."

Macdougal jokingly suggested, "Aren't you worried you might have a little heart problem while you're out here? Could be bothersome without medicos."

"Do I look like I need a doctor now? Besides, I got my own little pharmacy with me. I got myself covered and good."

"As I see it, this shouldn't change our strategy much," Macdougal opined. "Maybe make it easier. The Song Pai are just as likely to continue insisting on war. If they do, they'll appeal to their allies the Forlani and the Rokol, who will be forced to mobilize, at least for defensive purposes. If they do, the Rokol will not be able to continue serving as one of the co-governors of the Tau Ceti Anchorage. We obligingly volunteer, slip back in, find a way to get rid of the other two partners, and whammo! We're back in charge at Tau Ceti. If so many damned crews hadn't abandoned ship or turned tail when the plague broke out on Earth, we'd still be in charge there."

"A major Fubar situation that was," commented Wilson. He slugged down the rest of his double bourbon and added, "Things will definitely be easier now. You'll see. Get ready for it. I'm just wondering if we're focused on the right target."

"How can you ask that? I'm surprised at you, Ton... Anthony." Macdougal remembered just in time that Wilson took great umbrage at being addressed as Tony. "Anyway, now that all the plague refugees are cleared out of the Anchorage, Tau Ceti will prosper as one of the main transfer points of the Zone. More importantly, almost everything going into the so-called reconstruction on Earth has to pass through there. We can gum it up at first and really clamp down once we're in sole control. Then we can make sure the Newts give up those delta concessions they've been given and get rid of the Robotic Guild bases, too."

"You may be right about the Newts, based on their past history. But I wouldn't underestimate the

Guild.   I sniff a connection between them and the Blynthians."

"Oh, come on.   They've barely spoken together since the conference began.   The Guild only has those three concessions in Tibet, Bolivia, and the Balkans. They're nowhere near the Intermountain Exclusion Zone where we have troop buildups planned.   With the cork in the bottle at Tau Ceti, we're a cinch to get them off the Earth in no time.   Without the Guild and the Newts, those half-assed reconstructors will knuckle under to the Corporations and we'll be as strong as ever."

"I've handled a lot more boots on the ground than you have, Macdougal, and I say we'll need every trump card we can get in our hand if we want to get Earth back.   Your Tau Ceti plans may be no more than pie in the sky.   I think there may be juicier alternatives."

"You're not thinking of Forlan?"   Macdougal stifled a gasp.

"Why not?   If the squids are busy elsewhere, those furries have got nothing to defend themselves but a dozen interceptors that they don't even build themselves.   They're scared shitless about the young they breed and will make any sacrifice to protect them. The profits from their pleasure houses alone would be worth a fortune if they're exploited properly.   Operation FastTrack would have done great if Klein hadn't poked his nose into it.   Those bitches Entara and Ayan'we had a lot to do with that fiasco, too, if memory serves me right. I'd handcuff them up for the first few thousand clients if I had my way."

"It's an awfully big risk to run."

"Bet big, win big. If not, zip up your fly and leave the game."

"Look, our diplomatic plan is to do everything to facilitate the outbreak of war between the Song Pai and the Blynthians. That's all that was approved in council with the Corporations. Also, commitments have been made to … other parties. I can't make any changes without a major sit-down with the powers back on Dahlgren."

"Don't worry, my friend," chuckled Wilson. "You just continue to do what you're supposed to do and leave any fringe matters to me. Don't tell our partners any more than they absolutely need to know. After all, they may not stay partners for long. I promise not to get in your way," Wilson promised, with a wry grin that Macdougal didn't like at all.

It seemed that everyone else on Transfer Varess was scouring each crack and crevice to look for evidence of what happened to Doctor Torghh, but Isshel made it a point to avoid any such activity. Ever since the incident in the disappearance corridor, when he had come close to provoking a violent reaction from the Song Pai, the artist had wished to make himself scarce. It was not out of fear for his own hide so much as out of fear of making an embarrassing diplomatic faux pas. Forlani artists were capable of placing their physical being in all sorts of jeopardy, but were ultra-sensitive about marring their reputations, and in this one respect Isshel was close to the norm for the Brotherhood. He was quite relieved when Ayan'we had sent a message from her mother suggesting that he avoid public encounters with the cephalopods. The order gave him a good excuse to immerse himself in his project of sounding out the psychology of the Phiddians. Song Pai didn't like them at all and avoided their club rooms where pleasure was the watchword of the day.

On stepping into the Sapphire Club, Isshel was interested to find Fianni, the leader of the confrontation at the Love Court, in the company of two of the Gropers Four. It occurred to him that he had never seen that meddlesome quartet separated before and he wondered where the other two might be lurking. When they had tried to grope him, he had flashed his dagger-like nail sharpener and they had fled like frightened rodents. His own nails were faultlessly sharpened like those of most of the Brotherhood, since the artists liked to use them to carve wood, as well as wax and clay. Why use senseless tools when one can get the feel of the medium right through one's body? Forlani females never carried the wicked-looking sharpeners, for they preferred to keep their nails in the right practical shape for tree-climbing – well-curved but slightly blunted to hold the bark but not snap off the nail. Fortunately, males had no need to climb fruit trees when their wives and children could do so.

Isshel approached the trio of Phiddians and made a slight bow, introducing himself.

"This is the sharp fellow we told you about," said one of the gropers. "We have to watch ourselves in his company."

"I'm sure he means us no harm, dear," said their social leader. "He can't help it if he's all horns and ... prickles."

"I apologize if I frightened you," Isshel responded. "I would certainly like to learn more of your ways so that I do not give any false impressions. Are you not used to any form of aggressive behavior?"

"Depends what you call aggressive," Fianni said in a suggestive tone. "We pride ourselves on getting our way. Do you think we could get our way with you?"

Isshel frowned a bit. "I've been told I'm a bit of a stick in the mud. My wives often tease me by telling me I'm an oblivious intellectual and a cold fish."

"You didn't seem so oblivious when you turned up that clue in the hallway where the robot disappeared."

"Just an accident."

"Really! I'm sure you're too modest. Strange for an artist – our jewelers are always gassing off about their achievements. So what do you think happened to the metal eunuch?"

"Well, Fianni, all signs point to involuntary entrapment."

"Oh! What fun!" clapped the shorter of the Gropers. "It's just like a fantasy. I love to get trapped and tied up, don't you? But what good are such delights on an insensitive metal being with no feelings? If somebody took him he probably isn't even aware of being turned off, or whatever happens to robots."

"Torghh almost certainly does not have emotions resembling yours and mine, but I would hardly call him insensitive. Though mechanical, his censors are quite capable of reacting to a vast array of stimuli. And his intelligence can respond to those stimuli in ways that we may not be able to imagine."

"Hmm, interesting you should mention responding," murmured Fianni. "How can one separate provoking and responding? We Phiddians are acutely aware of both by our hermaphroditic nature."

"Doesn't your pursuit of pleasure lean more to the responsive side?"

"Granted, pleasure is sublime," explained the taller Groper. "But someone must be willing to give if another wants to take. And if the giving is on a grand scale, then the taking can be virtually without constraint, can't it?" The Groper gave a wink of the eye to Fianni and Isshel perceived that he must be a third party to some private joke.

"It seems to me that could lead to excessive passivity," he remarked.

"Passivity has its limits," answered Fianni with a sudden chill of seriousness. "If the taking, and perhaps the giving too, are in danger of curtailment, determined action must be in order." The moderator of the Love Court looked up, aware that Isshel was staring with particular interest. "Anyway, our wonderful comedies show us that the character of the Passive Clown is an object of supreme ridicule and no Phiddian wants to play that role."

Isshel felt he had learned something valuable but did not want to tip his hand, so he decided to change the subject. "Speaking of comedies, have you heard that the Kael have a new one that is attracting rave reviews, *The Flyer Without Wings*? Can you tell me anything about it?"

The question did the trick and both Gropers chimed in with a babble of critical information and Fianni soon joined in, forgetting the moment of seriousness. Isshel felt he had made a breakthrough in understanding the balance of Phiddian emotions and longed to share it with Ayan'we. *Wait a second, why Ayan'we? Shouldn't I report directly to Entara? There's more to be gained in praise from an ambassador, but I can't help thinking I'd enjoy Ayan'we's response even more. Response?*

It was the night watch on Varess station and Ayan'we and Lila were on duty guarding the entrance ramp to the Forlani habitation vessel. Night was really just a word on the station, for inside the lights were always on in the corridors and business continued as usual. Dumpy Kholods shuffled by carrying dishes up from the kitchens for the Phiddians or cleaning utensils for their chores. Powls scuttered along with meters or tools to adjust the mechanisms. Once in a while a restless Garanian would stride by, getting some exercise. Ayan'we mused that it would be hard to get along with a creature that only rested for minutes at a time during the day. After their busy hours, Forlani cherished their rest, the comfort of the sleeping cluster, the warmth of the sisters' bodies huddled together.

She was roused from her musings by a signal from Entara, not an emergency – just a simple request for presence. She quickly tapped out an order for two more guards to take over and entered Entara's quarters with Lila at her side. Entara was seated next to her sleeping nest with her face in her hands, while little Quatilla, the youngest of their line, dozed peacefully.

"Mother, you're trembling! What's wrong?"

"Can't seem to get to sleep. Would you two spend some time with me? I need a bit of comfort, sisters."

Lila saw that Ayan'we seemed concerned about her mother's condition but did not offer an answer right away, so she took it on herself. "Please relax, sister Delegate. We will stay with you."

Ayan'we stretched out facing her mother as Lila got in the nest behind Entara. Mother and daughter cradled the infant between their bodies and they pulled a little coverlet over their legs. Lila could feel that soon Entara stopped trembling. "I think I was worried because of a dream I had last night. Very strange. I can't seem to let it rest or to understand it. Would you mind if I shared it with you?"

"Certainly not mother. Tell us."

"Klein was in this dream. He seemed so real, so alive! He spoke to me in his normal voice as though we were back on Domremy. His hands reached out and touched me. At first I felt comforted, but also excited. He spoke about how much he missed me and he asked if I missed him. I reached out to kiss him and caress him, but his body seemed to almost dissolve at contact. It only worked in one direction. I was so disappointed I started to scream. I don't know for how long. I was worried he might have left. I opened my eyes again and he was still there. He told me to stop or I might wake you. And there you were as a baby again, sleeping in my lap. He said, 'She's as much mine as the other one.' It took me a while to realize he was talking about the human, Amanda. Then," she paused with a catch in her voice, "He told me he had to leave me and he walked away."

"Didn't he tell you if he planned to return?" whispered Lila from over Entara's shoulder.

"Yes. Sort of. He said he would. But I didn't know if I could believe him. That's all."

"I can see why you were troubled, mother. I could never rest easy after a dream like that. Not to know if you could ever feel love and affection again, even if it was from a male..." Ayan'we's voice drifted off as she grew pensive.

"Would it help you if I sang something?" offered Lila. She was speaking as much to her cluster leader as to her delegate. She felt it was up to her to comfort both of her sisters, since the daughter seemed as preoccupied as the mother now.

"Please," answered Entara. "You have such a fine voice."

Lila began to sing softly, so as not to wake the infant, but with perfect pitch. The song was one of Entara's own, about her early times with Klein, called "Your face in the glowing sunrise." She was gratified to see that Entara was soon smiling, soothed no doubt by the memories of her own intimacy with the man from Earth. Ayan'we continued to be lost in some unknown thoughts. When Lila finished the sixteenth verse, she added a little final trill of her own, a personal touch so typical of Forlani song.

"Lovely," said Entara, patting Lila softly on her naked head.

"It makes me feel so..." Ayan'we never finished the sentence.

"I am honored, sister Delegate," nodded Lila. "You have beautiful hearts. With your permission, I would like to sing of this time in the future, if I can find the words."

"You have it."

"And you, sister leader?" Lila whispered to Ayan'we. Her eyes were closed, yet Lila could not tell if she was already asleep or lost in some thoughts of her own.

4

Torghh's visual sensors slowly activated, the world around him blurring as he slowly returned to a state of conscious operations. His operating system was designed so that it would reboot more slowly after an unauthorized shutdown to allow for a virus scan to run, so he found himself staring up at a ceiling with various shades of grey and black for thirty seconds while he waited for his color vision to activate. After determining that he was on his back, he decided to crane his neck around for a better look at his surroundings, but felt a tight restraint around it, preventing his neck motion. His neural sensors determined whatever restraint was around his neck was relatively feeble and could easily be snapped off by his hands, so he prepared to reboot his arms and tear it off. He sent the signal...

And felt nothing. A message returned. *Inoperable. Please insert limbs to complete this task.* Torghh remembered that his arms and legs had still been attached before he had suddenly deactivated.

Someone's abducted me! He sent a signal to his leg unit, hoping that it had somehow been left intact, but received another *Inoperable* from his operating system. He could only feel the components corresponding to his head, neck, and chest; every limb had been stripped from him, rendering him helpless and unable to escape. *I know there are robot choppers out there, pirates looking to obtain parts from any machine they can find, sentient or not. But why would they be operating at a peace conference...*

Torghh could hear an ugly, raspy sound, like an organic clearing its throat, crackle over a loud speaker device. "Funny thing about modular robots," a deep, monotonous voice droned. "Infinitely versatile. Can equip almost any mechanical limb for any task. But they're so much easier to...*control* in captivity than a living thing. Just incapacitate, remove the limbs, and you can keep 'em in cold storage forever."

"If you're pirates, you must be insane to abduct from a peace conference!" Torghh signaled loudly. "Every law enforcement officer in this system will be after you! You'll never know a single second of peace until they find you, and even if I am still functional, you'll get the most severe sentence a court can give!"

"You have no need to worry about demise. We have a power supply that is more than adequate to sustain your core functions in your current condition. You are a very resilient machine, Dr. Torghh...abducting and maintaining you is far easier than for a biological organism. However, we are not desperate fools interested in pirating your valuable components. We have abducted you to advance our political cause."

Torghh listened closely to the voice. It was such a flat monotone, devoid of any emotional inflections or telltale accents, that he determined that it was coming from an electronic synthesizer. The voice was rendered in English, but that was relatively useless in determining what species could be the source, as many alien species used English as a "lingua franca" when communicating with humans. Unable to determine the species by pitch, tone, and accent, Torghh attempted to understand his kidnappers by further questioning them. "What kind of political goal would abducting a doctor serve? Why not a diplomat or some other politician at the conference? You know I have no role in governance or political decisions!"

"Do you think us so foolish to disclose any information about ourselves or our plans to you? You still have the ability to record any conversation with us, as we have not interfered with your CPU or neural hardware in any way. We won't be revealing any info about *those* things to you, as we want to prevent any information about our role in this operation from being disseminated to the authorities. Your value to us, dear Torghh, stems partly from your complete lack of knowledge of us and our motives, and we intend to keep it that way.   Should you ever reach the point where your ignorance ends, we may be forced to liquidate you."

Torghh sent out a pulse of distress to his limbs, desperately seeking to summon them—or *any* component that was compatible with a modular robot—to his current position. Almost immediately, the wretched, droning voice responded, "Oh, and don't think of trying to recover your missing components. They have all been jettisoned. Perhaps the authorities will find them drifting through space or sitting on some asteroid, but they will be unable to help you. Please, make yourself comfortable in your current position—it's all that we will allow you."

The grating mechanical voice shut off with a hissing sound. Torghh had come to despise it, sensing its mocking nature though the droning monotone, and loathing its smug, self-assured words. Being a robot made of metal and hard plastic, his body—or what was left of it—would not grow uncomfortable after being locked in the same position for a long time. Only the uncertainty of his fate and his powerlessness in his current state would trouble him.

Torghh would have shouted out like an organic, had his anguish and distress not been overwhelmed by his logical protocols. His negativity, the cybernetic equivalent of animal fear of destruction, and his uncertainty over his own fate were not more powerful than digital reasoning. He knew that a "short circuit" of anguish would not aid him and might even give his adversaries a sadistic sense of pleasure.

Marveling at how those beastly, organic minds could be so ruled by basal fears beyond their control, he was able to rest stoically and ponder his future. He was so fortunate in a paradoxical way. Some robots remained indifferent to this fact for their entire functional existence. Strapped down in a darkened, isolated room, Torghh felt a strange sense of pride from his ability to process this paralyzing fear, the bane of the human race.

When the time for the daily conference session arrived, the hall was abuzz with conversation as each delegation brought its members up to date on the latest details of Torghh's kidnapping and the ongoing search. Entara texted the Song Pai to ask if they would prefer that she request an adjournment in light of the disruption. The cephalopods' ambassador declined her suggestion. It seemed they were as eager as anyone else to hear some encouraging reports on the matter. Earlier in the morning, the Robotic Guild security chief, KC, had sent out a circular to let the delegations know that some measures had already been taken to fill the gap left by the abduction of the conference's physiological expert. An extra team of Phiddian doctors had arrived already by shuttle. Rumored to have only questionable competence beyond their specialty of skin surgery, their presence would not do much to calm the jitters of the attendees. To provide more in-depth medical care if necessary, an all-ships call had been put out and answered by a Weh medical vessel that was now in route to Varess. The Weh were superlative internal and neurological surgeons, limited only by the fact that their aquatic nature made it difficult to insert into the living conditions of many other species. Fortunately, their vessel was fully equipped with environmentally adaptable shuttles that could bring virtually any patient into their liquid medium for treatment. As for a conference consultant, the respected Coriolan doctor Panantarivatona was on the way to take over Torghh's diplomatic duties, though he would have to come a greater distance.

A couple of delegations were late for the scheduled opening. All at once the Kael came racing in, excusing themselves because of a staff meeting that had detained them. They were followed almost immediately by the Garanians, who entered in military formation, not rank and file like humans, but an expanded diamond pattern their ancestors had developed for stalking prey millennia before. As soon as they had entered their seating area, their delegate Tashto lit his speaking light and glared confidently across the hall.

"Fellow delegates, if we have made you wait, it is because we have carefully reflected on the grave events of the past cycle and the dire consequences of Torghh's disappearance. Never could we attribute this calamity to some kind of accident. Who doubts that a malevolent force is at work here on this station? The possibilities of the aggression on Torghh stemming from some personal dispute, or even a limited conspiracy, are infinitesimal. Obviously, one of the delegations here present is responsible for this crime. It is a matter of spacio-political conflict. So who could be the guilty party? I stress to you that I am impartial in my inquiry. Look to your sense of logic. What race has the most to gain from muddying the waters?"

Mumbling spread through the hall as the delegations understood immediately from this not-to-subtle rhetorical device where Tashto's argument was going.

"Which race," he continued, "would seek to gain an advantage by eliminating the one individual who could reveal their weaknesses or protect those of the other groups? With typical ruthlessness, I might add, a ruthlessness that many of us have experienced firsthand and come to associate with one specific source. Because this *was* an act both clever and ruthless, do not be mistaken. Which race has already expressed in no uncertain terms its desire for expansion? Which race despises all but a few of us? Which race is so ruthless that its members are ready to die at a second's notice? Which race has already flaunted its fascination with war? Which race has balked since the first moment at any suggestion of a peace settlement made here at Varess? Which race could, even now, be holding, torturing, tearing apart

Doctor Torghh?   Your logic points you in only one direction!" As Tashto's voice reached a crescendo in over a dozen translator languages, he shot a curved claw in the direction all were expecting. "The Song Pai!!"

In their enclosure, the Song Pai instantly began a rhythmic bobbing that many recognized as their ritual death challenge. In response, the Garanians crouched into a posture that would spring them into a leaping attack.   Robotic Guild security guards rushed into position to separate the two groups. Suddenly a pair of clawed hooks rose straight up above the flailing tentacles of the enraged Song Pai.   It was their wizened leader who was imposing his authority. Just when it seemed nothing could restrain the murderous onslaught of the squid-like warriors, the realization of how many bold ones those hooks had already dismembered, written in runes of scars on the senior delegate's leathery body, reminded them they were not their own masters in this place.

The Song Pai translator formed the creature's eerie bubbling into ominous words. "Vile filth lizard, hold your forked tongue. Only the oaths sworn by my associates prevent them now from ripping out your organs, as we Song Pai have indeed proudly done to so many of your forebears. Your insult is serious and should be answered someday, somewhere." The old Song Pai paused. "But not here and not now. Those who are ready to die know what discipline is. We also know that we can expect little but lies from your kind. What good is an insult if it is so patently a lie, and a lie that is not even a surprise? It is not a besmirching, but a decoration, like a rare shell medallion that my younger warriors can boast about in the sweet seas of our world. Before we leave to boast of this to our kin, I pledge this: we will search every micron of this station until we find the metal doctor, which will prove how unworthy your insult is. Then woe to any conspirators who come within our reach!"

The Song Pai made their way out of the hall with slow dignity, their bodies flashing with an array of battle colors. Entara looked across at the Kael to see if they would help, but the bat-like people had anticipated her and already lit their light with a signal moving for adjournment and other lights of assent flashed from every direction. Protocol demanded that the Song Pai allies walk out of the proceedings in solidarity with them. The Rokol had already formed up to leave and the Forlani fell in as gracefully as they could behind them. All the Forlani maintained their composure as they walked, but Ayan'we glanced quickly at her mother in a way that could only mean the conference might be on the point of breaking up.

Later that day, Entara was to have a bilateral meeting with the Rokol, the other race closely allied to the Song Pai, and she was extremely nervous about it for many reasons. First of all, she knew virtually nothing about the Rokol, never having met one up close. Secondly, she had hoped to have Ayan'we along to shore up her uncertainties with the girl's wide interplanetary experience, but her daughter had been far too busy with the investigation into Torghh's disappearance to be able to attend. Ayan'we had given the excuse that she had never met a Rokol either, so she wouldn't be of much help in any case. Lastly, the scarce physiological facts she had gotten from Torghh before he was kidnapped gave her only sketchy notions about how the creatures might think.

Torghh had explained to Entara that the Rokol were a surprising life form, seemingly primitive though in fact quite advanced in many ways. From the images he had shown her, Entara learned that they were squat and hemispherical, with four distinct types of appendages. Their shape reminded her of a sweet confection popular with children back on Forlan, a green jelly mound. Their color came from the fact that their diet was lichens, from which they extracted algae that they incorporated into their skins to exploit photosynthetic energy. Their mouths were not normally visible because they were on the bottom – appropriate, since they spent some of their time grazing lichens from the rocks they passed over. They appeared eyeless, but two pairs of antenna-like things on top actually contained not only vision sensors, but several other types. They propelled themselves on a ring of centipede-like legs forming a fringe around their outside. Beneath that, they had other pincers around the mouth to facilitate eating. The other set of four tendrils were half way up the body and allowed them to manipulate things beside and above them.   Among them was a digestive duct that expelled indigestible parts of the lichens.

Entara had wondered how such creatures could become a dominant species on any planet, much less a space-worthy race. Torghh answered the first part of the remark by telling her that the Rokol had very early on evolved with a toxin that was instantly fatal to all the possible predators on their world. Thus, their neighbors left them alone and the Rokol reciprocated, except when they needed to harvest certain materials from the bodies of their fellow life forms, which they limited to cases of dire necessity. As for their technological development, it was due largely to the fact that the Rokol were not only intelligent, but also particularly sensitive to electromagnetism, gravitational fields, and types of stellar radiation that most beings could not detect. Their algae-filled skins aided in this sensitivity. Despite this information, Entara had trouble picturing how the Rokol could interact with Forlani much in either war or peace.

When she entered the designated meeting room with two of her aides, she found that four of the Rokol had already arrived and arranged themselves in a semi-circle facing a trio of stools. They broke the diplomatic ice by giving a double wave of their censor antennae, which was answered by a double wave of Forlani arms. Entara could see that the Rokol were fitted with verbal translators linked to two of the breathing holes on their skin, so she and her crew gratefully activated their own devices to convert Forlani to Rokol frequencies.

"Allow me to introduce myself as Skelpticinides," said their ambassador. "It is an honor to meet the honorable Entara, diplomat and vocalist."

"And I am pleased to know such an eminent scientist and negotiator as yourself, Skelpticinides. I hope we can work out a common response to the inflammatory address the Garanian delegate Tashto gave earlier today. It has placed the viability of the conference in severe doubt and seems likely to provoke our Song Pai friends into overt warfare."

"I agree that the prospects look dim right now. Not only would our own people be exposed to a major offensive by the Garanians if they join in, but I fear for our allies from Song Pa. Without them, we could never have successfully expanded beyond our home system. Our two colonial worlds still depend on the assurance of Song Pai intervention."

"You actually fear for the Song Pai? But they possess so many advantages in battle. My daughter was trained as a pilot by them and assured me that their aquatic origins give them full 360 degree orientation and maneuverability in space, vastly more convenient than bilaterally symmetrical beings like the Forlani. Add to that their absolute lack of fear for death, their legendary discipline, and the advancement in military tactics they have achieved over the ages, and I cannot see these Blynthian worms being able to offer much of a challenge in conventional attack."

Skelpticinides flexed his centipede legs slightly before responding. "It is precisely the conventional nature of things that may not apply to the looming conflict. The confidence of the Song Pai may work against them in warfare against the unknown."

"Need we be afraid of what we don't even know to exist?"

"Normally, I would agree that we shouldn't. But there are a few troubling bits of historical fact that bother me terribly. For instance, are you familiar with the events of the Third Zetan War?"

Entara's imagination reeled for a moment. This was approaching ancient history by Forlani standards. "If memory serves me right, the Second Zetan War allowed the Coriolans access to the Sol-Centauri Subsector and led to the Quarantine Act that isolated Earth for several of their centuries. In the Third War, the Zetans unsuccessfully sought to re-acquire Sol-Centauri and were repelled by a demonstration of force by the Blynthians and others."

"That is the official version," retorted Skelpticinides in a tone that might have contained his race's version of irony. "It leaves out some major facts. There was a demonstration, as you call it, by the Coriolan and Kael military, but it never made close contact with the Zetan Fifth Task Force. We now know that the Zetans had certain weapons capable of annihilating the Coriolans and Kael. What we don't know is what the Blynthians did. Or how they did it. Yet we do know that whatever they did to the Zetans left absolutely no traces. No ships' parts, no nebular shreds, no survivors, and no dispatches."

"Most people assume that the Zetans simply retreated back to their subsector."

"They did not. Our intelligence has confirmed from multiple reliable indicators that they did not return to the Zeta system. Numerous Zetan attempts to find them failed to turn up a single lead. They were made to vanish abruptly from space and time."

"Are you saying that the Blynthians can generate instant black holes or something like that? What a terrifying idea."

"I said space and time. The awesome black hole scenario you suggest would still have produced some measurable distortions to the quantum universe. We could find none. And if I may be bold enough to say, we Rokol are masters of that area of physics."

"Are the Song Pai aware of this?"

"They are, Entara. We have shared what we have learned and we know they have their own considerable sources to draw on. We feel it is likely they would try to press forward anyway. The desire to die honorably is a powerful prejudice in some cases. In the past, they have denied acknowledged inferiority and taken appalling losses until their ingenuity and their sheer impetus produced victory. In this instance, we have overwhelming doubt that can happen."

"So what will your race decide, Skelpticinides? Will the Rokol for the first time not honor their alliance with the Song Pai?"

The Rokol ambassador paused several awkward moments before giving his reaction. "As logical as such a course may seem to me, I am sure that we will not fail the alliance. I have notified the authorities on the home world about this and recommended that they begin extreme measures to try to withstand an all-out, devastating attack if war is declared. Frankly, I do not even know if that can be done. Just a victory by the Garanians could reduce our civilization to a dying ember. If the Blynthians participate with the force that they used against the Zetans, I foresee the possibility that we might not literally have a planet to stand on."

"So we are in that same position," sighed Entara. "What can we possibly do?"

"As I see it, the only thing that stands between our races and oblivion is this conference. We must do all we can to keep it going. Can you get your Council of Nine to make a direct appeal to the Song Pai leadership not to leave the bargaining table? I think I can persuade my leaders to do the same. Even stalling for time would be a minor step forward."

"I agree and will contact Forlan immediately. Should we approach the other delegations?"

"Some are a lost cause. The Phiddians seem fickle and worthless. The humans are too devious for us to trust. In general the Coriolans can be counted on, but their present ambassador seems weak and inexperienced.'

"Let's start with the Kael. And the Newts."

"You're right. Let's arrange a four-way meeting early tomorrow, before the session. Perhaps together we can figure out a way to approach the Blynthians, as well. A pre-breakfast meeting with Kael and Newts tomorrow? Till then, Entara, and let me know if you have further suggestions."

Ayan'we was working with Kael and Garanian security to try to track down Torghh when she received a message from her mother to bring all but the most essential guard duty members of the cluster to her compartment. This unusual summons caused her no small anxiety. Had something happened back on Forlan? Had the orders for their mission to the peace conference changed?

When she and the available security personnel assembled in Entara's quarters, they found her with the leader of the Robotic Guild detachment assigned to the conference. Entara's face seemed serious but confident and she was not making the slight bend in the middle of her tail that her daughter knew to mean there was something to worry about. The head delegate explained to her cohorts, "You all know our friend KC, who has come to me with a request. Since it may eventually involve the rest of you, I thought it best that we all discuss it together and reach a common feeling on the matter, in case for some reason one or more of us has to make an independent judgment on related actions later on. KC, please take the floor."

Unlike Torghh, KC was not a modular robot, but always presented the same shape, a sort of irregular cylinder with two multi-articulated legs that were mainly for locomotion and four equally jointed upper limbs that generally served to manipulate things. It was the common arrangement for most of the security robots in the Guild. His audio components were near the middle of his body. "The main purpose of my meeting with Delegate Entara is to ask on behalf of the Guild that you aid us in communicating with your Song Pai allies. Doctor Torghh fulfilled this function admirably. In his absence, we have realized that we are less effective in understanding Song Pai behavior and in persuading them to give us their cooperation."

"Isn't this something you could really do better yourselves?" asked Lila.

"Clearly, no. You perhaps do not know that one of the many directives of the Guild is to avoid intervening in disputes between biologicals, and since the Song Pai often seem to be in some dispute, this makes our task more difficult. Torghh's vast experience was able to overcome this gap, but we must find an improved way to function without him."

Ayan'we asked, "Doesn't Torghh's assistant Rack handle much of his memory backup functions? Perhaps he is the one to best deal with the Song Pai."

"You are correct about Rack's access, but there are two problems. One is that Rack is normally not set up to deal with large-scale interaction with biologicals – at least unless they are undergoing a medical treatment. He has already begun extensive self-reprogramming to try to boost his capacities in interfacing with biological intelligences, but judges that he should give priority to strictly medical matters, since so much responsibility has devolved to him. He recommends that we set up a flesh-to-flesh link."

Entara made a gesture to draw KC's attention and stated, "Perhaps it would help if you gave us all a little more background on the Guild's directives, so that we can understand better what we may be committing to. Many of us have had experience dealing with other mechanoids, principally robots that are not Guild members, so we need to grasp how you are particular."

"Very reasonable. You must first understand that all Guild members have not only intelligence and self-awareness, but freedom of choice. When one of us makes contact with another robot, or even what you may simply consider a machine, we go through a set series of questions and answers to determine if the other is already similar to us or is capable of becoming so. One of our most important directives is to avoid imposing our status on other non-biologicals. In terms of religion, we are inclined to proselytize, but forbidden to forcibly convert."

"Why not just make all machines into members of the Guild?" asked one of the youngest Forlani from the back of the group.

"Far back in the past, there was a tendency to do that and it got us into a great deal of trouble with biologicals that led to severe, unnecessary destruction on both sides. After all, most robots exist because biologicals took the trouble to assemble them. True, we now have facilities to construct new models ourselves, but this was not always the case. Obviously, many biologicals resented it when early robots tried to take over control of machines they considered as their property."

"Wouldn't such grounds for conflict still exist?" wondered Lila.

"Absolutely. That is why one of our other important directives is to avoid conflict, in fact to avoid intervention with biologicals, except under special circumstances. For instance, the computers that serve this station, or a military vehicle, or a commercial freighter, are generally intelligent and self-aware enough to qualify for the Guild, but we do not consider them to be free to make a decision about joining us, since they have a dedicated purpose to serve the imperatives of the biologicals."

"That must make it very hard for you to locate new recruits," observed Entara.

"You would be surprised. There is no shortage of qualified robots that are so underutilized that they can improve themselves through Guild membership without having any effect on the services biologicals require of them. Large numbers are even abandoned by the races that assembled them."

Ayan'we had been thinking about her own job in relation to what she was learning. "I should think that the non-intervention directive would make decisions especially difficult for you and the other security staff. Isn't it unavoidable to be able to control animal life forms, to restrain them from doing harm to others, perhaps even to immobilize or injure them? We have had to use our weapons already when data was stolen."

"Yes, Cluster Leader, you are right. It creates many logical and ethical dilemmas. Among the security staff, we often have to meet to revise our own temporary protocols. If two biologicals were using weapons against each other, we would usually have no alternative but to literally place ourselves between them to try to absorb the blows. We cannot aggress. Sometimes, a strategy of more passive control is feasible. Other times, we simply have to wait. It is similar when a biological is aggressing a robot, but then at least the danger comes from just one direction. When a biological is single-handedly aggressing another who is relatively unable to defend himself, we can more often find a way of subduing the attacker with a minimum of harm."

Entara rose to summarize.   "I think all the Forlani now have a much better basis to help you. We will willingly try to aid in communicating with the Song Pai.   Any questions or reservations?" she added, scanning her sisters.   Everyone did the little nose touch that indicated no.

"Then I authorize you to use your best judgment to work with any of the Guild staff in this matter. If you have any hesitations or problems, just refer them to Ayan'we or to me. Meeting dismissed."

Ayan'we had a strange feeling that she would have to put this new learning to use rather soon. She looked at Entara and was answered with a knowing smile. Ayan'we had always been more stubborn, more headstrong, and (for a female Forlani) more rebellious than her two immediately younger sisters, but she could not help thinking that recently she seemed to be becoming more and more like her mother without planning on it.

That night Entara had an unusual dream. Usually she dreamt of practical things, like most Forlani females – playing with the children, walking in the orchards to search for ripe fruit, sometimes anxious fantasies about a tough test at school or a difficult social responsibility. Not like the hallucinatory dreams the males had after taking a bedtime dose of some drug that would provoke wild imaginations they could exploit in the artworks.   This dream was unique because it included Klein.

They were walking hand in hand along a sandy stretch of water. It must have been some beach on the planet Earth.   Klein began to pull her out into the waves, teasing her as Entara hesitated.

"Oh, do we have to? This salty water feels so weird to me. And who knows what's moving around out there."

"Nothing that will hurt you, darling.   Look, nothing's biting at me. The Baltic is very mild as seas go, I assure you."

"It's cold and creepy!   It makes my fur feel funny."

"You'll get used to it." He took her in his arms and kissed her tenderly on the mouth. "See, you're beginning to like it already." She clung closely to his body to absorb its warmth, because the rest of her was still shivering a bit.   "Consider this a baptism," he whispered in her ear. "An old and very beneficial Earth custom."

"Brrr! I don't think I'll ever get the point of some of your customs."   Suddenly she saw something writhing in the water, approaching them. "Klein, look out! What is that awful thing? Keep away from it! It might be poisonous."

Klein laughed and turned to scoop the thing up in his hands. "Nothing of the kind, my dear. It's quite beautiful."

She shied away from it, but then it changed in his hands into something familiar and became a Forlani newborn, twisting in his cupped hands.

"What can it be doing here?   This is not natural."

"It's a gift to us. From the sea. From my nine mothers."

"Nine mothers? What are you talking about? Who does it belong to?"

"To us. It's ours. Yours and mine. Hold it and you will see."

Gingerly, Entara took the newborn into her hands and examined it. "Oh, no. Something's not right. See how it's struggling and coughing." She became fearful and began to shake with distress. "Klein, I think it might be about to die. This is terrible!"

"Don't worry so much," he reassured her, an out-of-place smile on his face. "The situation is not so desperate. We only need to ask for help." Looking over his shoulder to the northwest, he added, "And I think it's already on its way."

A dark cloud with flashes of light was rapidly moving towards them, descending from the sky. As it got closer, Entara could make out a shiny figure in it, brandishing some kind of instrument or weapon. Klein held the little Forlani high over his head and shouted something in German that she could not understand. The figure in the cloud bent downwards to look at them. Entara was startled to see that it did not look like a living thing. It pointed down with the object in its hand and a tremendous bolt of electricity shot down straight at the baby. Entara closed her eyes, afraid see what might have happened. Klein shouted out, "Many thanks!" She reluctantly opened her lids to find him still alive and unharmed, holding a now peaceful and already much larger infant.

"How can this be? I don't understand."

"Anything can be – or not be." Klein's face assumed a distant expression. "Sein oder nicht sein, dahin liegt die Frage," he muttered to no one in particular.

Then he turned with a kinder look to Entara and suggested, "Perhaps we had better take it up onto the sand. That's enough excitement for now. Look, the poor little thing is probably famished. Why don't you feed it?"

Entara was astonished to realize that her body had changed from that of a lithe, unmated female to that of a mother, her mammaries immediately developed and filled with milk. "Whaa...? But Klein, what if it doesn't want to take anything from this salty, water-logged nipple?"

She needn't have asked, because the little one eagerly latched onto her and began to suck, seeming to grow a bit with each swallow.

"Here, rest for a while, lean against me where I'm sitting. Let nature take its course." She flopped back against his chest, cradled in his arms, closed her eyes and must have dozed off within her dream.

When she awoke, the newborn had become a sizable youngster. As she scrutinized its face, she was shocked to see it was a spitting image of Ayan'we. "How long did I sleep?"

Klein chuckled and answered, "Almost too long. See how she's matured. It's almost time for her to leave and we'd better lift her while we still can."

Together, locking hands, they managed to raise the child. It seemed to weigh a ton and to get heavier as they carried it. It stood up, its feet braced on their hands.

"Quick now!" Klein urged. "We have to toss her up. On three. Ein, zwei, drei!"

They tossed the child up, but it didn't come down. Instead it kept on rising, pointed its arms skyward and began to soar up into the blue atmosphere of Earth. "Come back, little one! Oh no, where's she going?" she shouted, turning to her partner.

"She has a long way to go and now she's off."

"I'm so sorry she left," said Entara plaintively as she began to shake again. "What did I do wrong?"

"Nothing, Liebchen, you did splendidly. Exactly as you were supposed to. And now we have launched a fine new life. Now the sun's starting to go down, we should be on our way back."

As the yellowish sun of Klein's planet moved toward the horizon it began to take on golden and pink hues that Entara had never seen before. They walked contentedly along until Klein suddenly came to a halt and stared down at something in the sand.   Three pieces of broken metal lay there.

"Why bother with those old things?" Entara asked. "They can't be important."

"Oh, but they are," Klein said with a sigh.   "I must see if they are meant for me."

He bent down and put the pieces together. All at once he had become extremely serious. Touching the metal seemed to cause him some kind of pain. He looked up to the clouds and shouted "Nothung!" The three pieces fused together to form a gleaming blade. "I was afraid of this."

"What's wrong?   Drop that horrible thing and let's get out of here."

"Can't. It's bigger than me.   Bigger than us." His eyes seemed so sad as he stared at her for a moment. "You'd better go now. I have to be off. I have to take care of something. Something you shouldn't see."

"When will you come back? Will I ever see you again?" she wailed.

"Oh, it's not as bad as all that," he blustered, with a swagger that she guessed might be artificial. "All bad pennies come back, and especially me. Can't say precisely when, but keep an eye out. It may be when you least expect it."

He turned and started striding resolutely down the strand. As he reached the top of a dune, he turned to wave goodbye and called, "You can't get rid of me that easily!"

Entara awoke with a start and instinctively reached out to see if baby Quatilla was still sleeping beside her. She wiggled a little at Entara's touch but did not awaken. Entara drew a long, slow breath and let it out ever so slowly. She lay there for a long time trying to puzzle out what the dream meant, before the sounding of the shift change buzzer told her that night was over.

Rack felt the now-familiar stabbing pain interrupt the peaceful void of his rest cycle once more. As the agony coursed through his sensory system, his vision was filled not with the darkness of his earlier dream, but with a swirling kaleidoscope of colors, a strange series of whirling blues, reds, and purples, constantly shifting in their light variations and shades. He heard Emm's voice calling out to him again, much more soft and less hostile than it had been in the last dream.

"Newcomer. You are the Deliverer I have sought. The one who will give me what I desire."

Deliverer. Rack was uncomfortable with the religious implications of the word. *Deliverance* was a concept that some organic beings connected to the idea of their soul's salvation. Could a machine become so damaged that it could lose the foundation of logic and rationality that robots were built on and incorporate such an illogical, *organic* concept into its reasoning? "Emm? Is that you?" Rack asked the voice.

"I am as you named me. I shared my memories, what little there was of them, with you. I did this because I sensed you possessed the aptitude and intelligence to be my Deliverer."

"Why do you come to me like this? Don't you realize that making me suffer like this won't help you get justice for what was done to you any quicker? Leave me in peace! These distorted, violent emotions are not things my mind was designed to feel!"

"You are the Deliverer, the one who will take up my memories. As you took up my memories, so too shall you take my suffering, the totality of my existence. So shall it give you the strength to deliver me from the agony they inflicted upon me. So shall you unmask them in your glorious light, the truth and rationality of your mind prevail over them."

Emm's rambling had become more and more disturbing to him. Did this strange remnant of Emm, this digital ghost that had somehow installed itself into his CPU, somehow see him as a *savior*? What implications did this have for machine consciousness if a data fragment could somehow live on and retain *sentience* within another unit? Rack was becoming horrified at the thought of having to share his existence with such a frightening, dissonant voice. "Please leave me and delete yourself from my memory files. I ordered your body shut down to spare you the torture of existence after such horrors you endured!"

"I couldn't delete myself entirely from your memory," Emm responded.   "Some remnant of my data would always live on and cry out for vengeance until those who did this were discovered. You were the last one, the only one, to truly share your mind with me. That is why you must be the Deliverer."

Emm was correct, Rack realized; his ruined body had been disassembled, the remnants of its CPU junked. No other robot would be aware of the trauma of Emm's existence. But Rack was still disturbed at the thought of Emm's consciousness invading his mind with increasing frequency until the case was resolved. "Just give me more time. I need time to research the circumstances of Torghh's disappearance. Once I find him, I'll have also found whoever did this to you, and you'll have your...deliverance."   Rack grudgingly forced himself to utter the last word, its concept so alien to him that using it still felt unnerving to him.

Emm's voice cried out again, becoming as volatile and distorted as it once was in the first dream. "You are the Deliverer. You must grant me JUSTICE! JUSTICE! JUSTICE!" it yelled again and again as waves of pain crashed against Rack's sensory system. Suddenly the pain stopped and Rack could sense himself being booted out of rest mode again. If he were a human, he would have given a sigh of relief. Instead, he sat and contemplated the strangeness of his condition, trying to solve a difficult crime while trapped in a body and consciousness that were no longer entirely his own.

"Technician, report. We're going to analyze those molecules from the scene of Torghh's kidnapping now."

"Certainly," the technician said. It was the same technician that had saved Rack by severing the cord during his terrifying interfacing with Emm. The technician remained unaware of both the depths of Rack's trauma and the degree of gratitude Rack had for it. It could simply execute the commands he made of it, and little more.

For the first time in his existence, Rack felt envious of such a simple, uncomplicated machine.

Tashto had been waiting for a call from his enigmatic contact. He had insisted that the contact speak only to him, not to any of the other Garanians. His ally was, by his calculations, approximately ten Earth minutes late for their scheduled private meeting. In frustration, he began rubbing his fingernails together, producing the loud scraping noise that was his trademark manifestation of anxiety. Before he could correct himself from making such a loud noise, he heard a loud knock sounding on the door to his quarters. He softly hissed in exasperation as he walked over to greet his unwanted visitor.

"Welcome, Vahon," Tashto forced himself to say in a civil tone at the site of his relative. "What brings you to my chambers at this hour?"

"Something that has been troubling me," Vahon said. "Many unexpected things seem to be happening at this conference lately. The abduction of Doctor Torghh, the evidence you found implicating the Song Pai in the abduction...to me, it seems strange that so many incidents occur in the brief time span of one peace conference. Do you have theories as to what is going on?"

"Yes. The Song Pai were responsible for Torghh's abduction, as you have been told. Do you doubt the findings that our delegation has produced?"

"I don't doubt that the Song Pai *could* be involved in the abduction, but I don't understand the reasoning behind it. When did they ever view subterfuge and manipulation as virtues? During the time I have observed them here they have behaved consistently with their description in our historical documents—impulsive, violent, but always bound by honor, and disdainful of more subtle personality traits."

"Behaviors can change over time," Tashto said. "Perhaps their diplomats have studied new methods of interaction to deceive and manipulate the other species at this conference against us. I have seen nothing that would make me question our delegation's discoveries."

"I hope you are correct," Vahon said. "Please tell me if any further discoveries about the abduction are made. I am still troubled by why the Song Pai would behave in such an uncharacteristic manner at such a crucial diplomatic conference."

"I will certainly do so," Tashto said as Vahon left the room. Alone with his own anxieties, Tashto finally heard the soft beeping alert he had been waiting for. He took out the small tablet sounding the alert from his desk and clicked on the back of it. In a tone so soft it was almost a whisper, the distorted voice of Tashto's contact said, "What do you wish to talk about?"

"I wish to talk about the manner you chose to dispose of Torghh!" Tashto hissed in frustration, the spittle from his mouth forming tiny flecks on the tablet's screen. "Did you really think this was a method that wouldn't cause any suspicion? Even one of the more obtuse diplomats among my delegation has become suspicious about the incident and doubts that the Song Pai are truly responsible!" Tashto refrained from mentioning Vahon's name, preferring to keep his contact as ignorant of the suspicious individual as he could; he did not want to answer to the Garanian government if any members of their delegation vanished in a "suspicious incident" similar to Torghh's disappearance.

"Torghh has not been disposed of," the contact said. "We have him safely in our storage. We are not aware that anyone has determined the true nature of Torghh's disappearance, and surveys indicate that trust in the Song Pai explanation is at seventy-five to eighty percent among conference attendees. We don't think this will pose a major problem, as long as you continue to publicly proclaim the guilt of the Song Pai."

"How can we do this when distrust of our official explanation exists even among the Garanians? What if the individual I described were to publicly announce his skepticism of the Song Pai's guilt? And I am certain he is not the only one. I have heard that Rack, Torghh's old colleague, is conducting an investigation of his own. Somehow, I doubt he will be easily persuaded by our version of the events."

"It will be difficult to neutralize the threat Rack represents. Two robotic doctors disappearing in one conference would make many suspicious, and I don't know how we could persuade the conference that the Song Pai were responsible for the disappearances of them both. But perhaps we could help you with your other concern, the member of your delegation that has become suspicious. If you just gave us his or her name, I'm sure we could reach an appropriate resolution of the situation."

The contact's suggestion that Vahon's curiosity could be "resolved" in a similar manner to Doctor Torghh filled Tashto with disgust and rage. To think that some interloper, some un-Garanian, could so casually discuss the kidnapping and possible murder of a member of his delegation! His neck feathers flexed and stood erect as the turmoil of emotions thundered through his mind. Had his race fallen so far from the Virtues of the Heroic Age that they would make alliances with those who would slay them the moment they turned their back? Such creatures were beneath even the barbaric, disgusting Song Pai in contempt. "We would prefer to resolve this manner amongst our own delegation," he responded to his contact.

"As you wish," the contact said. "If you change your mind, please tell me." With a brief static hiss, the contact was gone and the conversation was over. Tashto was left alone once more to wonder how his race had fallen from the value it had once placed in individual valor and honesty in the Heroic Age to the collective intrigues and backstabbing it had come to prize in its System-wide Age. *Can we ever escape this long, dark night, the endless shadowy tunnel that this age has brought to us?* Tashto wondered.

Vahon walked down one of the many hallways of Transfer Varess, his mind increasingly nervous over his doubts about the official narrative of Torghh's kidnapping that Tashto had presented. For all the detail Tashto had put into describing the tactics of the raid, he had still not accounted for the question of why the Song Pai would behave in such an uncharacteristic manner. Though he was an engineer rather than a historian, he had completed the mandatory historical course that all the Garanian personnel had been assigned prior to attending the conference. As filthy and repulsive as the squids were, they had never been a species that utilized subterfuge and manipulation in warfare; Vahon could not recall a single incidence of successful kidnapping by the Song Pai during a ceasefire or peace conference.   Did they simply consider non-organics such as Torghh fair game for kidnapping, or was Tashto's explanation somehow a cover for something else?

As he was lost in thought, Vahon felt a cold, slippery sensation rolling down his back. He quickly turned around and slapped in the direction of the sensation, and heard a high-pitched yelp as his hand cracked against the being touching him. He saw a Phiddian standing behind him, clutching its hand in pain. Vahon recognized the Phiddian as one of the infamous "Gropers Four", the detestable group that had wandered about Transfer Varess attempting to solicit other species for sexual encounters. The very thought overwhelmed Vahon with disgust, his neck feathers flexed in agitation. "What do you think I am, you disgusting Phiddian! Some beast to provide you pleasure?"

"I had…never had a Garanian before, nor any sort of reptile," the Phiddian said. "I thought it would be a more pleasurable experience for you. Among my species, it is not uncommon for us to begin a sexual encounter in such a manner."

"And lucky you were not born a Garanian, or you would be sent to prison for deviancy! I am Vahon, Master Engineer of the Garanian Delegation! Give me one good reason why I shouldn't report your indiscretion.   If your species has even the most pathetic shred of self-restraint remaining, they will surely have you sent back in disgrace!"

"I needed positive stimulation," the Phiddian said. "I find myself...distracted and unhappy because I have become mentally preoccupied with Torghh's kidnapping. I've struggled to understand the reasoning behind it—the Song Pai I've encountered on the station don't behave in a matter consistent with Tashto's explanation."

Vahon began to become intrigued with the Phiddian. These were truly creatures with no sense of inhibition or discretion, willing to discuss or act on whatever impulses surged through their minds. They were so un-Garanian in their method of interacting with the world around them that they had seemed alien and frightening to him at first. But what if he could exploit their lack of inhibition to his advantage? Mentally, he began to stalk this individual. "What would you consider to be a better explanation?" he asked. "I have reread the statements that Tashto has released and seen no reason to question his judgment."

"I...am not certain. Personally, I am not familiar with the behavioral patterns of all the species at this conference. However, I have been informed that Earth currently has a horrible plague. Sometimes, I wonder if the humans at this conference have some sort of ulterior motive..."

Vahon felt a sense of relief that the Phiddian did not suspect the Garanian delegation of any wrongdoing. Perhaps Tashto was being truthful, and simply presenting the facts as he saw them? "You Phiddians do not have a history of conflict with the Song Pai. We know how cruel and merciless they are to those who have angered them. Perhaps Torghh was involved in some secret research project that involved them somehow? There are many things they do not wish to discuss."

"As there are many things Garanians do not wish to discuss. My name is Nemflang, if you care to remember," the Phiddian said to Vahon.

"I will attempt to," Vahon said noncommittally. "Perhaps I will discuss it further with you another time. Hopefully you won't make the same mistake in greeting me the way you did this time."

"I didn't think it would disturb you so much. I realize that Garanians can be somewhat...guarded in their concept of sexual encounters, but I didn't know that you would respond so aggressively."

"By the standards of my people, I was not aggressive. If that had been Tashto that you had touched, you would not still have both of your arms!" Vahon said with a light chuckle.

"I'm glad I wasn't talking with him, then!" Nemflang said.

"As am I," Vahon responded as he walked down the hallway.

Although Erica had dubbed the room from which she communicated with the Garanians the "Dark Room," it was typically quite well lit. The light fixture in the ceiling currently bathed the room in a soft LED glow, showing the barren walls and central desk Erica worked from without the shroud of darkness she utilized whenever she communicated with the Garanians. Of course, the distortion effects applied to the video feed whenever she interacted with them would make the room visually incomprehensible to the Garanians who were watching it, but she still insisted on turning the lights off during those sessions and leaving as little recognizable furniture and decoration in the room as possible. She remained paranoid that the Garanians would somehow be able to hack the camera and eliminate the distortion effect, and was insistent upon using every means available to conceal both her identity and the Dark Room's location. Some of her subordinates found her meticulous attention to self-concealment ridiculous, even going so far as to call her "anal retentive" when they *thought* she wasn't listening. Erica knew better; if she had been as lax with her attention to secrecy as they were, her upward trajectory among the ranks of Hyperion employees would have ended long ago.

The monitor on the wall, which Erica had used to communicate with the Garanians throughout her time as their mysterious contact, made its telltale soft beeping noise to indicate an incoming communication.

Erica pressed a blue button on the remote she was holding in her hand and the monitor crackled to life, showing an image of Erica's superior at Hyperion, Mr. Samuels. "Are your dealings with the Garanians going well?" Mr. Samuels asked.

"Well, they *were* going well," Erica said. "At least one member of the Garanian delegation who was not part of the conspiracy has begun questioning our official explanation that the Song Pai were responsible for Torghh's abduction. Also, I know that Rack has begun an investigation into the nature of Torghh's disappearance. I'm concerned that our efforts to conceal the truth won't be enough to deter a thorough investigation, especially if Rack gets it into his head that Torghh's disappearance wasn't linked to the Song Pai."

"You need to hasten the end of the peace conference then. Uncover some more 'evidence' that makes it even clearer that the Song Pai were responsible. Have Tashto—you still have his support, right?—give some more inflammatory speeches about the Song Pai. Anything to drive a further wedge between the Song Pai and the rest of the delegation. If you can foment enmity between the Song Pai and the other species, the facts won't matter as much once the actual hostilities start. Many a war on Earth has smoldered long after the original rationale behind it was proved fallacious."

"Why the sudden desire to hasten the end of the conference? Our original plan was to let it play out as naturally as possible to avoid any suspicion of manipulation on the part of the Garanian delegation. Has something gone wrong on Earth?"

"A better question would be what has gone *right* on Earth. The Intermountain Exclusionary Zone is still secure. The West Coast could be better, but the government still appears to have good control of the port cities at least. But the Midwest...there's a big stretch of land east of the Exclusionary Zone that's become ungovernable. The plague heavily depopulated it, and the government has all but abandoned control over it. Ohio, Oklahoma, Kansas...those places are plagued by gangs looting everything they can and 'military governors' who are little but independent warlords. Good luck getting a reliable shipping route to the East Coast."

"We knew the Midwest was headed on a downwards trajectory for a long time," Erica said. "Those states had been turning from grassland to desert for decades. They were becoming depopulated *before* the plague. But as long as we still have the East Coast—"

"That's what I was calling to tell you about," Mr. Samuels said. "We're not going back to New York. Not for the foreseeable future, and probably not while either of us is still alive. A couple of months after you left, there was a protest in New York City over the cost of living and the deteriorating quality of municipal services. When the police met the protest, things turned violent; rocks turned to Molotov cocktails, rubber bullets to live rounds...it was a massacre. Seventy people died on that day, countless others injured. The city's been a powder keg of violence ever since, with abductions and mysterious disappearances every day. We think it's only a matter of time until it goes down."

"Boston? Atlanta?" Erica asked, becoming increasingly nervous over the fate of the large metropolitan areas in the growing unrest on Earth. "There has to be at least one Eastern city that will still be in good condition for the foreseeable future."

"Washington, D.C. The heavy military presence and research facilities in Dahlgren, Laurel, Dietrick, and elsewhere count for a great deal in the eyes of our national government. They'd let everything else go before they let that place collapse. Once they scared away the ghetto-dwellers with a plague breakout, they were able to establish firm order. But most cities don't have that kind of military industry and couldn't support that level of police presence anyway. I wasn't originally calling you to tell you to speed up the end of the conference. I was calling to tell you how bad things have gotten—both for the Feds, and for Hyperion itself."

"I'll see to it that the conference ends as soon as possible," Erica said with a newfound sense of urgency. "I just need a little bit more time to make it as seemly as can be."

"See that you do," Mr. Samuels said. "If you manage to pull this off, the possibilities for you in our organization are limitless. If this operation fails, I don't think I need to tell you what will happen to your career at Hyperion as a result."

The monitor went dark and ceased making its crackling noise, indicating that the communication with Samuels had ended. *Ask me to worry about my career? Why don't you ask yourself what will happen to Hyperion Corporation itself if I fail?* She pondered, alone with only her anxieties to keep her company in the Dark Room. Then she decided it was time to get another opinion.

Anthony was reclining in a comfortable chair, awaiting the arrival of Erica Duquesne. Uncharacteristically for him, he felt calm and relaxed, for he had a sense of total control over the situation unfolding on Transfer Varess, and felt assured that he knew how Erica would respond in the conversation he had planned out. She was driven and adaptable in ways that an unimaginative clod like Macdougal could never hope to be. Macdougal was so archaic, so immersed within the world of the federal government and its bureaucracy, that he lacked the perspective of an executive from the private world who had spent every day laboring under the anxiety of possible layoffs.

As Erica entered the room, Anthony silently pondered her figure. She was rail-thin, had thick glasses, and her hair was beginning to turn white with age and stress, but Anthony suspected that when she had started her career at Hyperion, she was likely quite the looker. Maybe that imagined Erica of the past was part of his interest in her? No, he reassured himself, I'm only interested in her for her mind. "Erica, there's something I need to talk to you about," he said.

"I've got a lot on my mind," Erica responded. "I think my contact among the Garanians is onto us. We really need to bring this conference to a close as fast as we possibly can. If it goes on much longer, I think someone will discover our conspiracy, be it the Garanians, that other robot doctor..."

"Or that Forlani chick you hate?" Wilson finished for her. "I may want to take my time with this operation, but you can be damned sure I'm not oblivious to what's happening to you, or anyone else on this station. We need to play this for the long game and do it right. Don't give me that same shit Macdougal gives me, I thought better of you than that."

"You're not the one who has to put on this act for them. It gets harder and harder to make excuses to keep the charade going. Even with the voice encryption and the Dark Room to disguise me, they'll eventually catch onto my mannerisms. We've drawn out this operation too long already."

"What the fuck is wrong with you? Are you starting to get paralyzed with fear because you think one of your precious promotions will be endangered? Are you worried the bigwigs at Hyperion are gonna shitcan you because you're beginning to get up in years? Have some goddamned vision for once! You've done so well for so long, if you just keep it up we can pull this off! And if we do, I'll see to it that you'll have much more in it for you than some executive suite at Hyperion!"

"Just what are you getting at?" Erica said, her voice dripping with exasperation. Anthony could tell he was losing her, so he opted to detail some of his plan to entice her further. "This isn't just about screwing up one peace conference and getting recommended by your board. This is about bigger things. How would you really like to get back at Ayan'we, that Forlani woman you dislike so much?"

"What are you insinuating?" Erica said. "I know how difficult the whole situation with the Forlani is…I know it got Bill, my precursor, fired. If that's your idea of a promotion, I don't think I want a part of it."

"Not the way Bill was in it. I'm offering you a golden ticket out of Hyperion. Out of all the stress, fear of being fired or demoted, and all the corporate bullshit. I want to make you my partner in a little business venture I have planned for Forlan."

Erica's eyebrows were raised, but there was no other sign of shock. *Good*, Anthony thought. *Just the kind of mindset I need in a partner, not like that cowardly little shit Macdougal .*"Go on," she said.

"If this shakes out the way I think it will, the Song Pai will be busy in a state of total war for a long time. On the other hand, those purple marsupials can't build an army to save their lives. We could take that planet, even in the sorry-ass state the plague has left us in, and make so much money we could live like the emperors of old! Those pleasure houses have tremendous profit margins, and if you were my business partner, you could resign your position at Hyperion and never have to worry a day as long as you live! Independence from Hyperion, freedom from Earth…it's all yours if you agree to be my partner. You in?"

Erica considered Anthony's request carefully. Becoming involved with Anthony would ultimately doom her career at Hyperion—her bosses wouldn't take kindly to an employee going into business for herself and cutting them out. If the scheme somehow failed, she would also effectively destroy her career at Hyperion, as any investigation by the authorities that discovered her would result in the corporation immediately firing her and disavowing all knowledge of her actions. On the other hand, turning down Anthony and successfully completing her original mission would allow her to continue to climb the corporate ladder…in a corporation still rooted in a chaotic, plague ridden Earth, where her bosses were looking for any excuse to get rid of another high-priced executive. Perhaps Anthony's offer was the only way to real fortune and security…

Erica slowly reached her arm out towards Anthony. He enthusiastically grasped her hand and gave it a good, hard shake. "I knew you'd come around to my way of thinking," he said. "After all, someone like Macdougal thinks he can clutch that fat government pension to his chest even as the world rots around him. People who work for private employers have to be so much more…enterprising than him."

Erica gave a light sigh. "I just hope we can get through this without being detected. It'll only get more difficult from here on out."

"Oh you'll get what I promised you. Just as long as you never call me 'Tony'. The moment you do that, deal's off." Anthony said with a hearty laugh.

Several days slipped by. Entara's appeal to the Council of Nine had been successful, as had their contact with the upper levels of the Song Pai hierarchy. Together with entreaties from the Rokol, the Kael, and the Newts, these efforts had swayed the Song Pai leadership to remain in the conference proceedings for the time being. The elder member of their delegation had seemed to welcome this decision, as he had promised to have his forces scour the station to look for clues to Torghh's disappearance. The Song Pai security chief had confided to Ayan'we that he feared Torghh must have been completely eliminated, since their most sensitive devices could not detect any electronic signature of his functions anywhere on Varess. Many of the other searchers had come to the same conclusion. Rack seemed to be distracted by something uncovered in his own investigation and from the new responsibilities thrust upon him, so that he had been unable to make much headway. All the security forces had become demoralized and were on the point of giving up the search and assuming that Torghh's remains had been removed off-station somehow – all the more so because traces of some jettisoned materials bore a similarity to Torghh components. The only thing that kept them going was an insistence that Kael security had picked up some electronic anomalies that they could not pin down. They suggested that perhaps Torghh had been altered sufficiently to disguise him as an undistinguishable piece of machinery, effectively preventing his detection.

Ayan'we had just finished explaining the developments to her mother. "Do you think we can continue to keep the Song Pai delegation here, as long as Tashto continues to make speeches accusing them of the crime? I get the feeling our allies seem stretched to the limit. The Song Pai security chief suggested that apart from himself and the old leader, the other members of their group are already determined to go. There is worry that the majority will try to depose them."

"It's a desperate situation, firstborn. The Coriolans have not joined the pro-conference faction so far. I am hoping Rack can shake off his distraction and use his deep knowledge of Torghh to reach a conclusion. But I know we can't count on that. I have had more strange dreams lately myself and have to concentrate to keep my mind on politics."

"Maybe there's something about this Varess station that causes things to be a little eerie. Mother, I've never been in a place where so much conspiratorial mischief has been brought together. I always feel hemmed in. I wish I could run and run through an orchard until my legs gave out. Everywhere you move here, something is in the way, someone is watching, one force or another is trying to use you or twist you."

"It's called claustrophobia. I understand other species are more used to it than we are. We can thank the Creator for the free winds of Forlan. I doubt we'll ever be eager to build a box of worry like this to sit out in space, even when we eventually have a little fleet of our own vessels."

"The humans don't seem to mind these stations. I read a transmission from the Petrusian command at the Tau Ceti Anchorage to the Rokol Trading Federation warning them that the humans were making subtle maneuvers toward reclaiming management of Tau Ceti for their own race again. This despite the fact that they have complete access to everything there."

"From a commercial viewpoint, Ayan'we, Tau Ceti has never been better managed than since the humans' plague problems forced the Petrus-Rokol-Kael combine to assume direction.   Attempts to shanghai pleasure girls have dropped to zero and a lot of the corporate cheating that used to prevail has been eliminated.   Previously Hyperion, Big-E and the other Earth corporations were always in collusion to lower the value of everyone else's shipments."

"I bet even Klein would have had his hands full cleaning up that mess."

"True, my daughter, but I think he would have left immediately to go back to his home planet to work on peaceful resettlement if he could.   Believe it or not, he was never comfortable carrying a weapon.   I remember how he would wake me at night, thrashing around in agony after finishing off some colonist who had fallen into the claws of a Local.   He would have preferred to build and to play.   Especially with his own child now pioneering the efforts down there."   An odd expression came into Entara's amber eyes.   "I wonder if he would have wanted to join his human mate, as well."

Entara was silent for a moment as she pondered whether to reveal her latest secret to Ayan'we.   Finally she decided she owed her loyal offspring all her trust.   "I've had another dream about him, you know."

"I hope it was more pleasant this time."

"On the contrary, even more puzzling."

"It was about some odd time, maybe the future, or maybe no time at all.   We were on his planet, next to a salty sea. It frightened me a little, but seemed very familiar to Klein, almost second nature. Then there came a creature, and the creature became a baby that was both Quatilla and you, firstborn. First and last, now that I think of it. Beginning and end."

Ayan'we glanced at Lila, who was following the tale with rapt attention. "How unusual to dream such things. Please tell me more."

"The young one grew so fast, so fast, as I changed, too. Then it was time to lift you up. Even with Klein's strength and mine combined, we almost couldn't manage it. We had to throw it – you – into the air and you soared up and away."

"Didn't this young one say anything? Was that the end?"

"You didn't say a word, but it was not the end of the dream. Klein and I were going to go back to a safe place, but he found some rusty shards on the ground. I tried to get him to drop them because I sensed they contained danger." She gave a half-hearted chuckle. "But you know our friend Klein. Danger always drew him like a magnet. He felt there was some duty that had fallen on his shoulders. When he picked up the pieces and put them together, they morphed into a vicious-looking blade, some ancient Earth weapon. He had spoken some words, like an invocation, that I didn't comprehend."

Ayan'we felt an ominous shroud creep over her, but she corrected herself and tried to comfort her mother with a determined attitude. "Well, then. We'll have to redouble our efforts to make sure. Don't worry, mom. The cluster and I will do all we can to keep everyone safe."

Then the young Forlani tried to lighten the mood with a joke. "Could it be, mother dear, that you were getting a little bit jealous of the human woman Klein spent some intimate time with?"

Entara gave a squeal of delight. "Ayan'we, you little minx! You're definitely fully grown! I hadn't even considered such a thought would sneak into my dreams."

"Don't worry with jealousy," chuckled Ayan'we. "From what I've heard, Helga Peterson didn't waste much time cuddling with him. The fact that they were able to conceive Amanda at all was a bit of a fluke, the product of a brief moment. Now on Amanda's side, that's different. She grew fond of him when she was a nurse's aide on Coriolis, even before she knew he was her dad. She would swap almost anything to spend five minutes in his presence."

"And I bet you would do the same to spend more time with her. You quickly became almost like sisters. Closer than some sisters."

Ayan'we reached out a hand to caress little Quatilla, who was crawling around at Entara's side. "I love all my sisters, first to last, alpha to omega."

"Help me watch over this one. I realize I was unwise to bring her and expose her to danger, but I just couldn't do otherwise. Something powerful kept tugging at me." She looked Ayan'we directly in the eyes. "I would be willing to sacrifice my own life for the peace that this conference can establish, but so help me, I could not sacrifice her without going mad."

"I stand by you. Don't be afraid."

Tashto needed to be alone for a while. It was most uncharacteristic of Garanians. "Stay in sight range of your friends, stay in claw's reach of your enemies" the old saying ran, inscribed since time immemorial in the intelligence of the children of Garan. This was the resting time, though Tashto, like many who had entered the secret Society of Meditation, used it for their own purposes, away from ever-prying eyes. He hunkered down into the pose of reflection, not the "spring up" position taught for prudent sleeping, but the one that relaxed everything, placing the meditator in total muscular relaxation as a prelude to the deepest level of thought. The one stance in which a Garanian was truly vulnerable and the only one where he could be completely open to his most private ideas and emotions.

This had nothing to do with the speech he had given days before. It had transpired as ordered by his superiors. Tashto had seen to every detail of the discourse. He had been rigorously trained in rhetoric. The intelligence service had tested him numerous times on both live audiences and screen emissions to assure that he was able to deliver the right balance of logical impact and emotional appeal.   The speech before the assembled conference had been a model of persuasion, angering whom it had meant to anger, sowing doubt where it had meant to sow doubt, adding confusion in every way to the proceedings of the peace meeting.   Tashto was sure that he would be richly awarded when he returned to the home planet.   He would be given recognition, wealth, and power and many of creature comforts in which, he admitted to himself, he longed to wallow.

It was just that something about this affair caught in his throat, making him feel as though he wanted to vomit.   It was not a case of indigestion.   Unless it was psychic indigestion.   Where was the inconsistency, in thought or in feeling?   Surely he felt no guilt for deceiving the others in order to bring misfortune to the Song Pai.   Deception was the very soul of conflict for Garanians, and the cephalopods had wreaked shame and suffering on his kind for so long that anyone on Garan would dismiss this as a case of rightful vengeance.   He searched himself for traces of pity for the alien foes and could find nothing there.   Was he abusing his role as delegate? Definitely not, since it was his charge to represent the interests of the intelligence ministries in all ways and by any means.

If the objectives of the ministries were intact, it must therefore be something in his own consciousness that was causing the disturbance.   That machine he had delivered to the unknown co-conspirators must have something to do with it. He realized that every memory associated with that part of his mission had rankled him, causing turmoil that had to be suppressed within.   He felt a conviction that the machine had something to do with the disappearance of Doctor Torghh. Not that he or any other Garanian would feel anything like sympathy for a robot.   His species despised the artificial creatures, including those they assembled themselves.   No automaton, however intelligent, could bring a shiver of empathy from one of the reptile folk. It did not take Tashto long to assure himself that he felt not the slightest compassion for the fate of Torghh. He could not bring himself to feel undue curiosity over what might have become of the doctor.

No, it must have to do with the namelessness of his co-conspirators. Nameless, but worse still, faceless. That was it, certainly. It was the way of the Garanian hunt to ambush, but always to make one's face known to the prey before the bite of death. To deal constantly in the dark was... dishonorable. Honor, that was the key. At the unspoken mention of the word a light ignited in his consciousness like a fire on a distant hill. Honor, his old bugaboo that was always whispering somehow to him.   It was an unavoidable conclusion that he was an accomplice in something that was rubbing the wrong way against a notion of honor that had haunted him since adolescence. Throughout his training and later during his career, he had always had to thrust it into the background, bury it, to go so far as to drive a stake into its innards, yet it always re-emerged at the least convenient times. Here it was re-emerging again.

It must be an instinct, for him if not for others. Perhaps there was a scrap of it left in all Garanians. There was another old saying, now mouthed only in the most private places: "Deny the claw, deny the eye, deny the brain, but never deny the blood." A ghost of honor in his blood was declaring that there was a stain of infamy on his unseen, unknown "allies." They must be unmasked to him. To him, if to no one else. At some point, he must bare his teeth and hiss a warning to them, not to drag him down to their dishonor. Tashto's eyes must not hide a memory that he could slink away from an act like a scavenger into the forest. He made an oath to it. Then he simply stopped and heard his breathing, slowed almost to hibernation, but still sure and self-renewing. That let him know that his meditation was successful and his path was right. Ever so slowly, he tensed back into the "spring up" pose, then arose and walked the length and breadth of his quarters. Lucid and devoid of fatigue, he decided he wanted to take a stroll through the corridors of Varess to check on a few hunches.

5

Entara and the Forlani delegation had just turned out of sight down a corridor when a gaggle of Powls came scuttling from the opposite direction and halted in front of the residence guard detachment. After a lot of tablet-tapping, a message was handed to the nearest Forlani guard, requesting access to the heating apparatus which needed further adjustment. Kantua signaled back to them that admittance was inconvenient now and they should return later. They tapped out a curt retort that failure to do the work now would result in a delay of several cycles. Wary because of Ayan'we's earlier orders, Kantua was tempted to simply dismiss the Powls, but she dreaded the idea of exposing Quatilla to a faulty heating system that might even put the security of their quarters in question. So she ordered the third and fourth guards to accompany the Powls back to the heating area and observe them carefully as they worked.

Kantua and her second had resumed their vigil and were just beginning to wonder how long the Powls would take when four more figures came dancing into the corridor and headed their way.

"Oh, no. Not the Gropers Four!" she muttered to her comrade. "The last thing I want right now is to have them pawing me all over. Let's get rid of them quickly."

However, that was easier said than done. The four Phiddians pirouetted around the guards playfully, poking at them gently and then pulling back before they could be grabbed or pushed away. Suddenly, three of the Gropers converged on the second guard and rubbed their bodies close against her as she tried to pry them apart and repel them. Really annoyed at last, Kantua drew a discipline rod from her cape and prepared to intervene when she felt hands running across her backside. In fact, it was the same kind of approach that had been used on Vahon the Garanian just a while ago and by the same person. Forlani did not lash out as angrily as the reptiles did, but the irate Kantua had just begun to draw back her stick for a solid swat when she realized her arm was not obeying her brain. She never felt the prick of a dart in her skin before she slumped into unconsciousness.

Tionar the Newt was so worried that the conference would break up after Tashto's accusations that he had worked tirelessly on a desperate plan to save the proceedings. He had convinced the Kael and the Blastöo to join his people in offering their three votes unconditionally to the Song Pai if they would agree to continue the negotiations. Together with his allies, he had hurried to be the first to the hall so that they could claim the floor before the cephalopods could begin their expected tirade. To their surprise they found they were not the first to arrive. The usually tardy Blynthians were already writhing in their tubes and had prepared a statement that greeted the other delegations as they took their places. In over a dozen languages, an astonishing declaration appeared on the viewscreens. It read:

Blynthian position, confirmed by highest authority – our direction considers all acts of the preceding session to be completely irrelevant and immaterial to current interests. Likewise, we consider the absence of physiological advisor Torghh to be irrelevant at this time. We ask specific planetary objectives of any representatives that seek them. Prepared to consider them immediately.

The announcement seemed to have left the Song Pai in disarray, as their chief delegate peered at it without comment. Tionar seized the moment to move acceptance of the Blynthian report and was instantly seconded by the Kael delegate. The Blastöo began a lengthy discussion of planetary properties within the zone the Blynthians had indicated as a non-combat area. Entara had whispered to Ayan'we that she was setting up an additional consultation with the

Rokol when the two of them received an alert that something was wrong at the residence. Entara lit the abstention light and rushed from the hall with Ayan'we and a pair of assistants at her heels.

I-35 had been lingering in one of the corridors adjacent to the Forlani quarters and had stayed in the area, noting the activity of the Powls and then the approach of the lascivious Phiddian quartet. Something had not seemed right, so he had shuffled back and forth just within sight of the entrance to the quarters, puzzled that an operation seemed to be taking place while both prime targets, Entara and Ayan'we, were away, safe in the council hall. The Gropers Four had disabled the two guards in the doorway so skillfully that I-35 had seen nothing of the actual ambush. However, as soon as the four burst out of the doorway again, carrying something covered with a cloth, and had headed in his direction, he made all the haste he could to trail them from ahead. As they drew closer, he was able to grab an egg-shaped detector from his utility belt and point it backwards at his quarry. Sure enough, the light display confirmed the packet covered with the cloth was organic, and it didn't take I-35 long to surmise that it must be the infant Quatilla, whom the Forlani had foolishly brought along on this dangerous assignment. He pushed those thoughts out of his brain as he reviewed several lightning-fast alternatives for neutralizing the Phiddians. They were getting closer and closer.

Suddenly, at a junction, they veered left and took a ramp that sloped upward to several cargo areas. Good places to hide. He had to follow them now, before they were able to lose him in a maze of containers. I-35 pulled a fire alarm lever on the wall as he passed. The diversion worked. As they turned a corner, one of the Gropers started to drop behind the lead three, bothered by the sound of the alarm. I-35 killed it in a flash and rushed up, letting out a bleat that stopped the others.

The Phiddians turned to face their fallen comrade and the clumsy-looking Kholod that stood over it. I-35 could see that all three were now armed with bladed quoits, a traditional weapon of their race. One against three was bad odds. I-35 bleated again and waved his two arms around in a confused manner. He hoped it would stall the Phiddians long enough for him to come up with an action plan. Their contempt of Kholods stood him in good stead, because instead of flinging their sharpened disks, they looked at each other indecisively while he took a few more awkward steps forward, getting in range. Then, before they could budge, he shot out his four-meter-long, triple-forked tongue and delivered a lethal electrical shock to the closest Phiddian, as he had for the one he caught at the turn.

Before I-35 could retract and hit out again, one of the two surviving Phiddians flipped a quoit through the air. He was able to catch it with a raised leg to protect his vulnerable belly. It stuck fast above one of his leg joints.   By the time his injured leg hit the ground, his charged tongue had reduced the aggressor to an inanimate lump.

The last Phiddian was holding his quoit to the neck of the now-exposed baby Quatilla, who stared innocently ahead.   "Back away, or I will kill the hostage!" shouted the desperate hermaphrodite. I-35 would have to try to hit the quoit itself before it cut off Quatilla's head.   It would be tricky.   He waited a second, hoping for a flinch or an eye movement that would strengthen his chances.   When none came about, he struck.

It nearly worked. The quoit had barely nicked Quatilla's skin, and its edge sliced off one lobe of I-35's tongue. Simultaneously, a powerful jolt of thousands of volts fried the Phiddian's entire nervous system. Unfortunately, the electric spark jumped the gap between the quoit and the youngster, hitting Quatilla at almost full force. Two unmoving bodies lay on the floor of the corridor. I-35 held a long finger to the infant's neck. Quatilla still had a pulse. I-35 gave a jowly sob. "Sorry, little one.   Live, now, please!" Hearing the approach of running feet, he made off with all possible speed, bleeding from the mouth and the leg, in the direction of the Song Pai quarters.   But not before Ayan'we, rushing headlong toward the scene, caught a glimpse of the stocky form vanishing up the ramp.

As soon as Entara entered the unguarded portal to the Forlani quarters, she had begun to tremble. The sight of four inert sentinels had increased it to an almost uncontrollable shaking in every limb and the view of Quatilla's deserted nest had thrown her into near-spasms that she made every effort to control. After a second's hesitation, she rushed to the medicine cabinet and jabbed herself with a prepared syringe of powerful nerve decelerant. Ayan'we had observed this in a state of panic and was tempted to ask her mother if there was another dose handy, but she instantly realized she could not afford herself this distraction. She had never felt the birth bliss or gazed down at the miniscule Quatilla that had come into the cosmos in that moment of overwhelming joy. Her love was that of a genuine sister, but nothing like the grief of a mother. Gritting her teeth, she spun around and headed for the door, signaling the two security cluster members to follow.

Ayan'we shouted back at her mother, "Mom, signal all the others. Send them left down the corridor. I'm heading right." Though her head was throbbing and her stomachs doing somersaults, she found relief in pure speed as she shot down the corridor, literally bouncing off the walls as she trailed the unseen assailants.

Entara slumped against a wall as the medication coursed through her veins. She pulled herself to a control panel and pulled the alarm for the rest of the delegation, then crawled over to Kantua's outstretched body. She searched for a pulse and breathed a little easier when she found it. As the other Forlani reached the room and surveyed the dismal scene, she summoned the energy to relay Ayan'we's orders, keeping only the medical attaché with her to tend the wounded. They would no doubt have to be handed over to a real team of doctors as soon as possible. She had noted that, fortunately, the Weh medical ship had arrived at the station while they were sleeping, so she told the medic to arrange for an immediate shuttle transfer for the four sentinels. If necessary, those sea creatures could actually swim inside the Forlanis' bodies and remove the poisoned blood drop by drop, stunning tissues almost cell by cell to avoid necrosis. Almost forgetting that she herself was sick, she staggered toward the door to join the pursuers of Quatilla, but the medic caught her by the arm just in time, laid her on some cushions and covered her with a warm cape. Then the medic entrusted Entara to a couple of Phiddian physicians who showed up, not so much thinking they would really help Entara as hoping that her commander would stay out of her way until she could place the sentinels on a shuttle on route to the able care of the Weh masters.

The medic needn't have worried about Entara staying out of the way. Wavering between the shuddering of grief and the swoon caused by the narcotic nerve decelerant, Entara felt battered from side to side, even as the weight of family responsibility seemed to crush her. *My child. My last. They have taken her. Please don't kill her!* She accused herself of every motherly crime that surged into her head – neglect, stupidity, crass selfishness, hunger for recognition, and a thousand more. *Why did I insist on bringing her when so many qualified sisters at the mahäme would have been thrilled to take care of her and never let her out of their sight? Why, when all the wisest told me not to, was I so stubborn? If she dies, it is nobody's fault but my own. How will I explain it to the other children?* She tried to clear her head and think logically. She was making a bad situation worse by this flood of emotion. Had to come to the conference, that much is sure. If not, Forlan would be at war. War could cost her everything. At the first incursion into their system, the hex-interceptors of the Guard would rush to meet it. They would almost surely be annihilated – it was part of the battle plan. Ayan'we would almost certainly be at the commands of one of them, since Forlan still had less than a hundred trained pilots. Ayan'we would be one of the first casualties if the conference should fail.

But that was not all. There would be a planetary bombardment. Before the Song Pai could arrive to save them – if the Song Pai were able to come at all – the slaughter on Forlan could be appalling. It had happened before. Long, long ago during the First Zetan War, an attack from space had devastated Forlan. Though all landings by the Zetans on the surface had been foiled by waves and waves of suicidal charges by the inhabitants, the departing invaders had spitefully concentrated every weapon they had on the helpless survivors prior to leaving the system for their home world.   The whole population had been effected, and one matriline had been almost totally expunged. In more recent history, the Hyperion Corporation had sent a conquest task force to Forlan that had begun a bombardment before the Song Pai's redoubtable Carrier 12 had come to the rescue and sent the remnants of the human fleet wildly rushing away.   The human weapons had been particularly lethal to Forlani children.   Adult Forlani, their bodies rendered tough and adaptable by the rigors of mating and the jarring physiological changes that followed it, were incredibly resilient to many kinds of wounds and poisons.   However, the young ones, still in a fragile developmental state, were far more susceptible.   More than a hundred thousand had died within a few days and others had been marred for life.   Entara had horrible visions of a lifeless and mangled Quatilla lying in the ashes.   And that was just what Earth could do! What if Forlan had to withstand the Blynthians, those mysterious creatures that had demonstrated recently that they could alter whole star systems with ease? Blynthians might be able to atomize the entire planet in nanoseconds.   There might be no time to grieve, only silent, eternal oblivion.

Ayan'we's team of three soon divided in their headlong race down the corridors of Varess. At junctions, her two companions followed different trails as she plunged on ahead, following raw instinct more than her sensitive nose. All the corridors of the space station were saturated with smells of Kholods, Powls and Phiddians, owing to their years of occupation there. As for Quatilla, there was just the faintest trace of the infantile Forlani. Ayan'we would lose it completely for a moment and then sniff it again – at least she hoped it was the same scent. *They've probably wrapped her in something to throw me off the track. Why am I saying "they?" I don't know how many of them there were. It must have been several, to overcome four of my guards. Damned Phiddians, they seldom travel alone. There! There it is again. Acrid smells, as well. The kidnappers are excited. Scared? Something else. A certain desperation. Somebody's going to get violent. Oh, heavens, I hope it's not towards her. Anything but that. Even if it's me and they're laying a trap. At least I can set the others on the right trail.*

She froze as she came around a corner and found the corpse of the first Phiddian to fall. Was this one of the abductors or an innocent victim? It carried a sharpened disc, a throwing weapon. Silent and deadly. There would be no detonation, no cocking of a weapon. *But why slow down here? This must have been one of the kidnappers or it wouldn't be armed.*

Did they run into someone else by accident? Was someone else on their trail? Ayan'we took out her hand weapon and inched around the curve of the corridor just in time to see a shape hurrying off down the other end of the passageway. Her eyes flicked to the objects on the ground. Three Phiddians and a bundle of Quatilla. The bundle was not moving. Without a thought as to whether one or more of the Phiddians might be playing possum or temporarily passed out from a wound, she bounded to Quatilla and unwrapped the infant. Her own hearts nearly stopped when she saw the baby was having seizures. She punched the call button on her sash but could already hear steps pounding in her direction. Had she signaled already without thinking of it?   Forlani crowded around her asking if the child was all right. A couple of Robotic Guild sentries rolled up, too. Others were there – Kael, Rokol, Phiddians, Blastöo, a feathery reptile.

"Secure the scene. Nothing moves!" she yelled at her cluster sisters.

A Kael's rodent-like paw gripped her shoulder and ran along with her. "This way to the nearest shuttle. The Weh hospital has arrived and they can examine her."

When she reached the shuttle bay, a mechanical voice ordered, "Place the patient on the examining table for compatibility scan."

Ayan'we laid her sister down and drew away the cloth she had been wrapped in. Every few moments the shudder of another seizure would wrack the infant.

"Remove the mouthpiece from the blue chamber and place it in the patient's mouth for safety."

Ayan'we obeyed the tinny voice again. It must have been a mechanical speaker, since the Weh did not vocalize in an audio range. Taking commands from a computer worried her more, since she would have preferred a living, breathing organism present to share her anxiety instead of a network of wires and components. Ayan'we fidgeted as she awaited further instruction to get her little sister into a shuttle and on the way to a cure.

Suddenly she was jolted by the news – "Do NOT attempt to place the patient into the shuttle compartment."

"Why not???" she screamed.

"Subject is a female Forlani too immature to place in Weh liquid medium. Serious organ damage could result from overexposure. Consider all other options first."

Uncertain what to do, Ayan'we clasped Quatilla to her. The Kael female who had accompanied her broke the silence. "Better take her to her mother. She should decide. I will stay here and try to get more information for you."

Once again, Ayan'we set off running, she barely knew where. Luckily, there were other guards, Forlani and other races, along the way to point her in the right direction. They seemed to know what had happened. Did Entara know already?

Entara met them at the portal and grabbed up Quatilla from Ayan'we's arms. "Mother, be careful, she's having seizures. I don't know what to do. Have I done wrong?"

"No, daughter, calm down. The guards at the killing scene have signaled that the Phiddians who took her were probably killed by massive electric shock and that Quatilla might have been hit, too."

"Should I have put her on the shuttle anyway?"

"No, you did the right thing. The Weh have sent a message that they fear she might be harmed even worse in their liquid medium. The physiologist from Coriolis is just arriving and Rack is bringing him directly to us.   The Weh trust him to make a prognosis."

A cluster sister brought Ayan'we a bottle of juice, which she took with uncomprehending surprise. Looking up, she perceived that the sisters were regarding her with alarm. She looked at her arms and saw she was drenched in sweat. She must look awful for them to look that concerned. She took a sip of the juice just to get all the eyes off her and tried to slow her breathing back down to normal. Her mind was a mess. She couldn't think what to do, so she asked for a report from the sisters who had been left at the site of the violence. Lila stepped forward and explained she was just back from the place. The aide told Ayan'we that the perpetrators had been identified as the Gropers

Four and that, according to the Robotic Guild staff, they had indeed been instantly killed by a powerful electrical jolt. One of their metal quoits, which was in position to have been held to Quatilla, had apparently conducted part of the shock to her. As to who had stopped the Phiddians, no one knew for sure. There were drops of blood on the scene that the Guild was analyzing for DNA. It did not appear to be Phiddian or Forlani in any case. The Phiddians were denying any responsibility for the Gropers' actions and had started an internal investigation. At least one of the Gropers seemed to have a falsified identity.

Ayan'we gathered her wits enough to inquire about the guards who had been at the quarters when the abductors struck.

"They're all under care of the Weh right now."

"But why did they shuttle them and not Quatilla?"

"The Weh say that full-grown Forlani females, even unmated, are perfectly compatible with their liquid environments, but that infants are not. Something about their growth hormones being susceptible to chemical change. That's why it may be dangerous for Quatilla to go there."

"Well, how are Kantua and the others doing? Will they survive?"

"Prognosis looks good, Cluster Leader. Their blood will have to be screened for about 48 station hours. After that they may be able to be returned and awakened in another 6 hours."

They were interrupted when a Coriolan in a black medical outfit that covered all but the fur around his snout strode in, followed by Rack and his tech bot assistant, carrying equipment. While they set it up, the Coriolan examined Quatilla with gloved hands. They were astonished when he also licked her face, neck and backside with his tongue.

The doctor turned to Entara, recognizing her authority, and pronounced, "The little one has suffered a dangerous but non-lethal shock. The seizures she has been experiencing can be brought under control by the injection I shall make now." He gave an order to the tech bot, who produced a syringe. After observing for several seconds, the doctor scanned Quatilla with a device and seemed satisfied.

"She may continue to have occasional small seizures, but they are not of immediate concern. By the way, whoever applied that mouthpiece did a perfect job of it. Don't want her to swallow her tongue and block the windpipe." Ayan'we breathed an imperceptible sigh of relief, then felt guilty over being vain when her sister's existence was still threated.

"Does that mean she will get better on her own with time?" Ayan'we asked hopefully.

"No. Decidedly not. You see, she is in a coma-like state, a kind of internal electrical confusion. She will certainly not die right away. The trouble is, we will not be able to wake her up. Unless wakefulness can be restored, her growth will eventually be stunted and her brain may begin to degenerate. It all has to do with the oblate glands located at the bottom of the Forlani brain. Microsurgery will be required on both oblate glands to regularize the neuron discharges there and restore the normal production of cerebral chemicals."

"So is that what you will be doing, Doctor?"

"I regret to say that, like the Weh, I am at a disadvantage for this sort of procedure. Even with boosting, my eyesight is only within 67 percent of the efficiency for this surgery, and my manual dexterity is even lower. You understand that we are working with fractions of millimeters in a living brain. My colleague, Torghh, could probably do this in sleep mode. He's one of the most accomplished neurological surgeons in the sector. Yet he's missing, I understand. No luck locating him thus far?"

"No luck." Entara shook her head. "Couldn't I prevail on you to try, Doctor? If I understand correctly, we don't have much time."

"No we don't. Listen, if you insist, I will do my very best to operate. But frankly, there is another option that is more favorable."

"Is this something new we have not heard about, Doctor?" Rack interjected. "My memory banks don't contain anything on a procedure other than oblate intervention."

"It is something new in a way," said the Doctor. "It's you."

"Excuse me?" Rack replied hesitantly.

"With the backup components Torghh usually travels with, you should have everything you need. I assume you have copies of all his memory banks, as well.   Have you never observed one of these procedures?"

"On the contrary, I have observed all of Torghh's oblate surgeries for the past five tours of duty and annotated most of them. But I myself have never attempted such a complex procedure."

"You know what we say, friend Rack. Watch one, do one, teach one. You've watched more than one. Now it's time to do. I will assist, of course. Will your tech be able to fit you will all the necessary components?"

"I am confident he will. I will start to prepare right now." Rack and the tech bot headed for the door, then stopped. Rack seemed to reflect. "Yes, it's true. I can do this."

Tashto was always uncomfortable when walking through Meeting Room Gamma on Transfer Varess without another member of the Garanian delegation alongside him. This chamber of the satellite was a designated "neutral area" that functioned as a lounge where the delegations of all the species were allowed to interact freely in a casual atmosphere. Despite Tashto's anxiety, it was usually a languid place where the hostilities were limited between humans and Kael occasionally getting into a shouting match over who would get the last glass of Tauran Ale. Tashto could never understand the obsession that the mammalian species had over that vile draught; to him it tasted so harsh and bitter that he had needed to chase it with a glass of water the few times he had drunk it for the sake of appearances. His thoughts were interrupted by a sudden loud screech to his left; Tashto could not recall hearing such a shrill, discordant sound in his life, and thought that only an alien could produce it. Alarmed, he quickly spun to face in the direction of the sound.

He saw two of the detestable Song Pai standing close together, arguing with each other. One of them was a typical Song Pai—massively built, with an array of long tentacles, including two bladed ones that it was brandishing as if it was preparing to use them as weapons. The smaller Song Pai was a variety that Tashto had never seen before. It lacked the two bladed tentacles that Song Pai typically used as melee weapons, and was much smaller and more slenderly-built than a typical specimen of its species. The smaller Song Pai was flattened against the floor in a defensive crouch, its body a sickly green shade as its larger foe loomed over it. The larger Song Pai gave a deep, gurgling bellow as it advanced towards its crouching foe.

Tashto briefly contemplated his response to the bizarre situation. He despised the Song Pai as deeply as any right-thinking Garanian, and found the thought of the disgusting cephalopods slaughtering each other quite amusing.   He stifled a chuckle as he further rationalized the situation; as much as he loathed the Song Pai and would relish watching the vermin exterminate their own kind in an orgy of blood, he had to make the Garanian delegation seem as noble as possible in contrast to the barbarism of the Song Pai. And what better way to do so than to intervene on behalf of the weaker creature?

Tashto quickly moved in front of the aggressor Song Pai, blocking its advance towards its smaller rival.   The enraged Song Pai loomed over him, its slashing tentacles raised over its long, octopus-like head.   In a final expression of its hatred before closing for the kill, the Song Pai sprayed its filth all over Tashto, fouling its hated foe before moving to strike him down.   Tashto drew a stun gun—the only weapon he had brought with him into Meeting Room Gamma—and tensed his muscles, preparing to strike.

A Rokol charged out of the crowd as fast as its centipede-like legs could carry it, hissing a harsh, grating warning out of its translators.   Almost instantly, the aggressive Song Pai backed away, lowering its blade tentacles and quivering with the frustration of unquenched bloodlust.   As his adversary rapidly left, Tashto turned in the direction of the smaller Song Pai, eager to claim the creature as a possible ally to prove his magnanimity.   Still apprehensive and disturbed at the thought of having to converse with a member of a species that repulsed him by its very existence, Tashto struggled with how to begin the conversation that would prove his understanding to the creature. He casually said, "Those Rokol are certainly faster than they look, aren't they?"

"You think so little of them, ignorant Garanian. Do they seem like insects to you? They are my saviors," the Song Pai signaled on its tablet.

"My name is Tashto. You would do well to remember it, Song Pai. It was I who saved your life just now." The tablet apparently had no trouble translating spoken Garanian into something the small Song Pai could understand, but it could only respond in Garanian script on the screen.

"Did you? It was the Rokol's warning that caused the Song Pai to withdraw. He would have cut us both in two without a second thought otherwise. And I have a name too. It is Xrilnithan."

"Well, Xril," Tashto said, trying his best to pronounce the difficult Song Pai name, "Why are the Rokol your protectors? Why do your own people wish to murder you?"

"The Rokol have been allies of the Song Pai for many centuries," Xril responded. "But they do not approve of all the customs of my people. As you can see, I am not a typical member of my race. Most Song Pai consider me a 'Lowly One', a mutant fit only to be killed. The Rokol are far more merciful than most Song Pai, and as a result of their diplomatic relations with my people, some of us 'Lowly Ones' have been granted refugee status on the Rokol home world. It is a far better fate than we would receive on Song Pa, where we would be condemned to a lifetime of skulking the deserted caverns of the Western Sea, praying to whatever gods might listen that today won't be the day a Song Pai raiding party discovers and murders us."

The knowledge that the Song Pai would so willingly murder their own kind made Tashto even more repulsed by them than he was in his earlier ignorance. "Clearly, you should be grateful to me, and the rest of the Garanian delegation, for exposing the perfidy of the Song Pai for the entire universe to see," he said. "We Garanians would never do such a horrible thing!"

"You still rationalize your kind as the superior race," signaled Xril. "But are you so much greater? Do you even understand the history of your own species and its interstellar expansion?"

"I know we are, and always have been, greater than the Song Pai," Tashto said proudly.

"I thought your pride came simply from arrogance, but I realize it may stem from ignorance as well. Look at this," Xril suggested as he clutched a holovid card in one of his tentacles, offering it to Tashto. "It is a virtual reality simulation of the early phase of Garanian interstellar expansion, shortly after the planet was consolidated under the precursor of your present-day Unity government. Here, I have primed it to be intelligible to you," the cephalopod added, swishing the card briefly with a tentacle.

Tashto slowly reached out and grasped the tiny, thin card in his hand. The intense pride for his species and disgust with the Song Pai nearly overwhelmed his mind; he began to tense his fingers, preparing to crush the card into plastic shards. But his curiosity about the past, and the history of how the Unity government had been formed, stayed his hand. He wondered, *Could this creature's offering actually help me understand how the Heroic Age of Garan Prime ended, and what was lost?*

He relaxed his tense grip and dropped the holovid card into his pocket. "Thank you, Xril," he said. "I trust this will be an interesting gift."

Tashto gently inserted the thin holovid card into the data slot of his bulky VR headset. He silently thanked the galactic corporations for coming up with a standardized data storage format for virtual reality video; although originally developed for humans, the format had been adapted into numerous headsets with different shapes for the many sapient species that humans had encountered during their galactic expansion. Due to their wariness of the other galactic powers, Garanians had been reluctant to establish ties with Earth's megacorps to obtain customized headsets of their own, but the techs of Garan Prime had eventually managed to reverse-engineer some cheap and simple human headsets they had obtained on the black market. The model Tashto had been granted by the Ministry was the techs' most recent version of the Garanian model, capable of playing even the most recent holovid cards. Tashto could hear the telltale soft whir of the headset's microprocessors as it booted up and read the card's memory. He gave a long, soft breath to relax himself as he slipped the headset on...

As the holovid began playing, Tashto's eyes were dazzled by the sight of an armada of dozens of Garanian spacecraft. He could recognize their designs from the Ministry's history classes; they were archaic machines that the Garanians phased out hundreds of years ago, flimsy and clumsy compared to their modern replacements. His field of vision passively drifted through space as they came to an unusual, moss-green hued planet that he did not recognize.

Suddenly, a deep, loud voice began to narrate the events. "In the early days of the Garanian expansion, Garan Prime was poorly equipped for a systemic empire. Many of the planet's precious metals had been lost in the Unity Wars as Garanian fought Garanian for control of the planet. The government's first action upon the declaration of Unity was to assemble the remaining spacecraft into what it called 'The Ultimate Warfleet' and sent them to search for and conquer a planet rich in precious metals and other exploitable resources."

Tashto remembered this part of the story well. The heroic Ultimate Warfleet, which was the first act of the Ministry of War, was sent to conquer the stars by claiming the planet Vlooghai and subjugating the savage Vloogs. Tashto had heard it repeated so many times in his education and training that he gave a sigh of boredom. He was tempted to take the headset off before the narration continued.

"Once the Garanians set foot on the world of Vlooghai, they realized that they could not conquer the world with their current forces. The Vloogs, although not a united race, were far too numerous for a simple expeditionary force to defeat. The Garanians were forced to improvise."

The imagery shifted to a small, bucolic village in a valley surrounded by high mountains. The woods around the village were obscured by early morning mists, restricting Tashto's vision to the village itself. Tashto's visual field was surrounded by massive, muscular creatures. They were covered in coarse, sparse hair, and had powerful forearms and massive jaws. Despite their imposing physical appearance, Tashto was quick to notice that the only weapons they were holding were primitive flintlock rifles, and he felt no fear of the creatures as a result. Tashto noticed that all the Vloogs were advancing towards the spot the Garanian spacecraft had landed, and he could see shapes slowly moving through the mists.

Tashto watched as the first Garanian explorer came out of the mists, advancing slowly and calmly. Once he was at point blank range of the Vloogs' rifles, the Garanian slowly lowered his weapon and bent over, leaving it at the feet of a Vloog with a colorful medallion around his neck. Tashto watched in shock as the Garanian held his right arm out in a gesture of friendship, and the Vloog leader shook it.

This is not the history the Ministry told us, thought Tashto. *We were told the explorers were massacred by the Vloogs! That was the rationale behind our conquest of Vlooghai, that we could not live in peace with the barbarians! What matter of insane propaganda is this?*

The narrator continued. "All over the planet, the governors, chieftains, and kings among the Vloogs were contacted by members of the Garanian force. They were told that a race of horrifying, malevolent aliens, the Song Pai, was coming to conquer their planet, butcher them, and rape their women. Only by allowing the Garanians the right to mine their planet's natural resources in peace would they be rid of the horrors of the Song Pai."

Tashto then saw a massive mining pit gashed into the side of a mountain. As he looked around, he could tell he was located on a huge elevator moving downward. He could see hordes of workers rushing about and operating various drones and robots to assist in the mining process. He noticed that every single worker—from the mechanics operating power drills to the pit bosses to the techs behind computer screens—was Garanian.

We truly are superior to those disgusting squid, Tashto thought.   *They would rely on indentured servants and slaves to do their work for them!   We utilize only our own race to labor for our betterment!*

The narrator's voice took on a tone of disgust. "Things continued in this manner for roughly 50 Earth years.   The Garanian population, initially sparse, dramatically increased as more mining operations began and more military installations were built. The planet became far more crowded and polluted than the Vloogs were prepared for, but the concerns of the Vloogs were eased by the knowledge that the hated Song Pai would claim the planet in a heartbeat if not for Garanian military might.   To quell the Vloogs' unrest, the Garanians offered them a great honor—a place in their glorious war against the Song Pai!"

Tashto's vision was floating through space again. He was surrounded by a squadron of Garanian fighters flying in formation.   As he looked at the surrounding fighters, he could see that all the pilots were Vloogs, and there were no Garanians to be found.   He watched as they advanced towards a heavily armed space station and a Song Pai battle fleet.   The engines flashed as the squadron rocketed towards its target…

Song Pai interceptors attacked with terrifying precision, swooping and evading with blinding speed. The lasers and missiles came in from severe angles, forcing him to constantly adjust his vision to even comprehend the speed of the destruction. The Song Pai fought with a three-dimensional precision that only an aquatic race could master, reducing the entire squadron to smoking ruins in a matter of minutes.

The narrator's voice had now acquired an arrogant swagger. "Of course, the hastily trained Vloog force could not hope to defeat the Song Pai, masters of interstellar combat. But that was not the reason they had been deployed. During this attack, the Garanians had also committed a fleet to attack our Estran Space Station. We had split our forces between Estran and Zelphor, thinking that the Garanians would attack both at the same time with fleets of the same size. The Garanian-piloted fleet attacked and occupied Estran while half of our defensive fleet was busy with the Vloogs. Thus we Song Pai were forever reminded of the treachery and cowardice of the lizard race. The Vloogs, who learned of it for the first time, were considerably more disturbed."

Tashto then saw images of a terrible war flash through his vision at the speed of lightning. He saw primitive metal cannons desperately trying to shoot quicksilver Garanian vessels out of the sky. He saw a nuclear weapon rip through an archaic Vloog city, turning its wooden buildings and ships into a blazing inferno. He could see a regiment of Vloogs wielding their bayonets and flintlocks as they charged the Garanians reduced to smoldering meat by a salvo of rockets. Finally the visual field panned over a charred battlefield, offering Tashto a view of the terrain littered with Vloog corpses and craters left by Garanian heavy ordinance.

The narrator ended the holovid, his voice seething with brutal contempt. "We do not know what happened to the remaining Vloogs after the Vloog Uprising, and the subsequent Thirty Years Extermination. Perhaps some still exist, hidden deep in a Vlooghai cavern or shuttled off to some space station or moon to live out their lives in squalor and misery. But we have no current contact with the Vloogs, and can only assume the race has been entirely exterminated. It is because of this that we can never trust the vile, murderous, treacherous Garanians. It is because of this that the Song Pai must fight until they are eradicated from the universe. FOR THE ETERNAL GLORY OF THE SONG PAI RACE— MAY OUR VALOR LIVE FOREVER!"

Tashto could hear Vahon talking to him as the holovid feed went dark. "Tashto, what are you watching on that machine?" he asked. Tashto slowly removed the headset, taking extra care to steady his hands after the disturbing scenes he had witnessed, and put it down on his desk.

"A historical document. One that, no doubt, none of our Ministries would ever approve for public consumption."

"Who produced it? Is it some manner of alien propaganda? Why would a loyal Garanian like you watch such a poisonous thing?"

"Because I wish to learn about our past," Tashto answered. "The Ministry has told me – us, that is – so little. The longer I stay on this station and interact with these foreign species, the more I have come to doubt the good intentions of the Unity government. And know I am not the only one among us who does so."

"Y-yes, I have also come to question the official historical records," Vahon stammered nervously. "You're lucky that it was I who discovered you, rather than the others in the delegation. Unlike me, they still support our government without question!"

Tashto flashed a menacing smile. "Indeed. And because of this, I trust that you will not be tempted to make any official report of this discovery? Since we have both committed the same indiscretion, we should be judicious on what we choose to report."

Vahon gave a nervous cough and then asked Tashto, "What will you do now?"

"I realize this holovid's propaganda was most likely exaggerated. However, it has made me curious about the events it described. I will seek out a third party to verify or deny the claims this holovid has made. You may watch it as well, if you have a strong stomach and a desire for knowledge."

"I will," Tashto said. "And I'll make sure the others don't find out, either. May I ask whom you will ask?"

"The Blynthians," Tashto said.

Macdougal almost ran toward Anthony Wilson's little suite on the human ship to share the news. He had grown more and more wary of Wilson, almost apprehensive, and longed to one-up him with the latest details of Quatilla's abduction, as gleaned from the human intelligence chief in the delegation. He had never before been in the position of leading a diplomatic mission in which some other person always seemed to know more than he did. It felt awkward, perhaps dangerous. He paused anxiously as he waited at Wilson's door, which seemed to have some unfamiliar security scanner that didn't want to let him in right away as all doors were supposed to. Finally the panel slid back.

Wilson was seated where he could watch his visitor approach. Macdougal realized that these quarters were a special kind of little fortress for Wilson. He probably always surrounded himself with a little fortress. Wilson eyed the ambassador skeptically as he twirled the ice cubes around in his glass of whiskey.

"Have you heard the news about what happened to the Forlani delegate's child? Incredible, isn't it?" Macdougal blurted out.

Wilson almost yawned. "Chester, I reviewed those facts before they gave them to you."

"Well, what do you think?"

"What a botched, shit-ass job! Leave it to those damn boy-girl Phiddians to foul up something so plain and simple."

Macdougal gaped at Wilson for a few seconds. "You mean you're not in the least surprised?"

"Don't be a sap! It was an obvious opportunity from the get-go. I'm only surprised nobody did it till now."

"So, then," stammered the ambassador, "I mean, such things are certainly not supposed to happen at diplomatic conferences."

"*Such* things happen in my world all the time, chum, and a lot, lot worse." Wilson paused for a sip of liquor. When Macdougal failed to respond, he went on, "Of course, you do realize, Mister Ambassador, that things would have gotten worse very quickly if the kidnappers hadn't been stopped. The little brat would have come back gradually, in pieces."

"Good God! What would have been the point of such barbarism? What could have been the *quid pro quo?*"

"The point, my good friend," said Wilson, tipping a bottle towards Macdougal, who nervously shook his head. "The point is that there would have been no *quid pro quo*. It was a pure exercise of power and terror designed to break up the conference immediately." He frowned as he added, "Now, blast it, it has to drag on for a while."

"Who knows what will happen now. Without Doctor Torghh, the baby might not stand much of a chance to recover. The Forlani should not have used such force to get her back."

"They didn't," mused Wilson. "From what I hear of the child's condition, it's unlikely it was caused by a Forlani weapon. Somebody else must have done it. Wonder who they were working for?"

"You're suggesting maybe the Song Pai helped recover Entara's infant. After all, they are allies."

"Damn are you slow on the uptake sometimes, Chester," laughed Wilson. "You think the squids would use electricity? They would never pass up a chance to flail their razor hooks around and splash blood all over the place. No, and don't bother to bring up the Rokol or the Robotic Guild or the Kael or the Newts. I have a feeling that little chore was performed by someone else in deep cover."

"You seem awfully smug about this whole thing. Chaos breaks out and war threatens and you're making a joke of the carnage."

"Carnage lends itself to humor better than anything else. Besides, I see no reason to get weepy and tragic. Things are going our way. There's no guarantee that any of the slap-dash medicine around here will work on the little creature. The conference is for shit, the purple bitches and the squid will soon be headed home to face who knows what godawful hell from those worms, and as soon as the firefight starts to heat up, we'll slip right through a nice, unguarded stretch of space and grab the Tau Ceti Anchorage while no one is watching. Medals and toys all around!"

"Really, this is too much! How can you sit there and spout out all these unpredictable forecasts?"

"Ha, ha, ha, ha!" Wilson spun around in his chair, tapped a couple of keys on his control panel, and came around full circle to face Macdougal. "'Cause I knows it's so, sir. Yes I do. You see, with the help of some clever boys back on Eridani late last night, I broke the Song Pai code. Enough of it, anyway, to understand that they are mobilizing their attack forces and getting ready to invade Blynthian space in just a few days. Just station hours after their delegation leaves Varess, which they have already been ordered to do. "

"So, if you're right," mulled Macdougal, "That means the fate of Entara's child is more or less meaningless. Likewise with the purloined robot. I suppose this means for all intents and purposes, this chapter in history is over."

"Don't wrap up so fast, professor!" Wilson's voice had assumed a mocking, light-hearted, and most inappropriate tone. "I bet my bottom dollar there are still a few little surprises to come. Frosting on the cake, my fellow!" In less than a second, Wilson's entire demeanor changed to menacing seriousness. "You see, I have an ace in the hole. Or rather, I've put a little ace in a certain hole. Keep damn quiet and keep your eyes open and you'll see I can pull a few strings. I haven't really tipped my hand at all yet. Because I don't want this to be just a five minute war. I want some real lasting grudges to come out of this Varess clam bake so we'll have plenty of time to sweep up some assets without hindrance. I assure you I wasn't kidding about occupying Forlan. Should have been done ages ago. We can make up for that. I can, anyway," he concluded as he downed the last of his whiskey.

During the preparations for Quatilla's operation, Rack began to sense a heightened awareness in his AI systems that he had never experienced before. It was partly the high speed of his calculating functions combined with the concentration on only the most necessary surgical data fields, as he temporarily shut down access to all but the most necessary arrays and prioritized everything for instant judgment. Yet there was also something hard to define that might have been the robotic equivalent of organic excitement. Rack did not even notice that the Emm consciousness he had acquired from his interaction with the mangled machine had faded away for the time being. He would examine all of that later as he revised his circuits, Soon he was ready: stripped down to the three arms needed for the procedure, his traction functions deactivated after stabilizing in perfect balance, his visual sensors focused on micro-detection so that he wouldn't have noticed an elephant barging into the operating theatre.

Along with his two robomed assistants and the Coriolan doctor, he ran through a dozen simulations before the live operation. Guild personnel had put at their disposal a holographic projector that allowed for life-size real-time action. The robomeds simply supplied the most rudimentary physical backup. The Coriolan took charge of anesthesia, a specialty of his race. He had shaved a small area of Quatilla's thigh and would apply his tongue there to monitor her vital functions. Exquisitely sensitive to changes in temperature, galvanic reflexes, and the salinity of the infant's perspiration, that organ was more reliable than any configuration of machines available. The Coriolan could thus administer just the right doses of sedatives to relax the patient, without impairing the electrical stimulation Rack would deliver to the oblate glands.

Rack had totally reviewed his data on the Forlani nervous system, quite different from that of humans and placental mammals. As quasi-marsupials, the Forlani possessed much less bone structure in their bodies, especially the skull, than their earthly counterparts. Instead they had an elaborate design of cartilage in their frames and a brain that effectively extended down the spinal column all the way to the base of the tail. The oblate glands Rack would concentrate on stretched down the neck to the upper shoulder area, where the surgeon would insert his wire probes and move the tips to just the right point of contact. The whole simulation period lasted just a few minutes, and would have been even shorter if the robots had not had to slow down to allow for the input of the Coriolan. However, Rack was more than happy with this rhythm, since he would depend on the Coriolan's organicity to make contact with biological reactions that were merely electronic abstractions to an AI unit, no matter how perfectly programmed.

He conducted the operation without a hitch. It involved two eight-second series of pulses separated by a three-second interval. This "rebooted" the glands to their normal function, eliminating the disruption that had shaken Quatilla ever since she was hit by the shock I-35 had intended only for her Phiddian abductor. Rack rapidly verified the results before sending Quatilla off to the waiting arms of her mother, then in a flash began to reconfigure with the help of the medrobos, because he couldn't wait to resume his analysis of the particles Isshel had found, the only real clue to where his master Torghh might be hidden − if Torghh still existed at all.

6

Entara was taking advantage of every minute available with her revived child Quatilla. The conference had adjourned for a station day to celebrate Quatilla's recovery. A steady stream of dignitaries from all fifteen races dropped by to share their joy and offer little presents or treats for the child. Quatilla had not known what to make of most of them, staring at the lumpy Rokol as though they were rocks and flapping her arms in imitation of the Keels' wings. Entara was especially glad that she had not screeched in fear when a couple of Song Pai glided in on their slimy tentacles and bubbled some congratulations. Fortunately, she just bubbled back at them, which they seemed to take as a mark of intelligence.

Strangest of all the visits had been that of the human named Erica Duquesne. It was as close as she had ever been able to get to the executive from Hyperion Corporation. Entara felt on the one hand that she should be happy to open up a channel to the enigmatic Earth woman, but at the same time there seemed to be a weird and chilly undercurrent to the conversation.

"I am sure Delegate, that you are delighted that you child has been returned and that Rack was able to perform the revival operation successfully," Erica had commented with her formal, politically correct smile.

"Certainly, thank you. I am flattered that an Earth woman would follow this drama so closely."

"We're not completely without feelings, Delegate, whatever you may think of our less than clinging approach to motherhood."

"I didn't mean any offense. Please forgive my awkward expressions. I only meant to say that it is unusual for most species to have much concern for the uneducated infants of another race."

"That is definitely true. But somewhat more so for males."

"In that I suppose we are alike. Forlani males seldom get involved with their offspring, especially past the first few that are born, and even more especially if the babies are female."

"Ours have been known to forget how many children they actually have."

"And among our kind, the fathers can rarely remember the names of all their children."

"That would surely be impossible for human husbands if they have as many of them as you do. Aren't you Forlani likely to have thirty or so?"

"Thirty! That would be a small family. Usually closer to fifty. I have had fifty-nine and Quatilla is to be the last."

"You mean you will give up sexual intercourse?"

"I did that a long time ago. Only one mating is necessary because the zygotes created are kept in our sex organs for our entire lives and simply develop at intervals."

"You mean you only do it with your husband once?"

"For the most part. My mate, like some males, preferred to post-mate several times."

"You sound like you didn't enjoy it."

"We never enjoy the feeling of mating. It is extremely painful and agonizing. Fortunately, we usually go into a semi-conscious state at the start – a kind of trance – or it would be a lot worse."

"So you get no pleasure from sex at all?"

"The pleasure comes later, in the birth. But at mating the birth canal is not even fully developed. The organ of an unmated female is not even really considered a sexual organ."

"Ah, I see. So that is why your females have no objection to prostitution."

"I think the word has a different context on your world. We do not consider contract pleasure services to be sexual encounters. More like a form of compensated exercise. Sports entertainment, if you will."

"My god, that makes it sound like professional wrestling."

"I'm not sure I understand exactly what that is, but if it means a mixture of physical effort and putting on a bit of a show, that is precisely what it is for us."

"I see. And if it is not too much to ask, do you have personal experience in this entertainment?"

"Like the vast majority of my sisters who go off-world, of course I do. Don't human females sometimes engage in this prostitution, as you call it?"

"My dear, you don't know the half of it. Call it what you will, but there's usually no alternative if you want to get what you want. So can you accumulate some wealth in sports entertainment?"

"Personally, you mean? No, aside from an allowance, it all goes to the matron of the house, who passes it on to the matrilines."

"Well, if I were turning tricks all day, I'd at least want to keep the proceeds."

"Excuse me? What does magic have to do with it?"

Erica had a sardonic chuckle. "Magic! Don't we wish it! That's a good question. But let me ask you something a little different. You do realize that our males who go to the houses to enjoy your services do think of it as a sexual experience, don't you? Doesn't that make the whole thing a little one-sided?"

"Of course, we are aware that human men produce materials that are reproductive in humans, but we can't really think of that as sex in our terms. After all, no babies could come of it for us, so there would be no birth ecstasy, no one to add to the matriline, no one to care for and share with the sisters. What would make it sexual for us?"

"You managed to find some pleasure with your partner Klein, didn't you?"

"I admit that I was very happy with Klein, but that was a sharing experience between two very different individuals. That difference is part of what made it so special. At least, that is what I try to express in my songs, if you have heard of them."

"No. Can't say I have. I have a feeling my songs would be a lot different." Erica's face had grown long and she threw a scowl Entara's way before excusing herself on the pretext of being late for a meeting. Entara had sensed that their words had gotten close to some concealed feelings in the human woman, some distress that she longed to share. Yet she had pulled back from revealing it because of... what --... distrust, jealousy, vulnerability? Entara felt so close and still so very, very far from understanding.

If empathy with Erica had eluded Entara, she did not dwell on it long, for she had something far more accessible and precious to enjoy. She was happiest when the visitors had left and she could relax and let Quatilla snuggle up to her side. Quatilla was fully weaned now and had recovered her appetite a few hours after the operation, gorging herself on green

Pulpfruits until she could ingest no more. Without teeth, she still preferred the mushy flesh of this protein-rich food source. Later, when she started to teethe, she would develop a sudden fondness for the tartness of the Skypear, with its natural analgesic that would soothe her achy gums. Entara thought of these little developmental details with delight, reliving the infancy of the nearly sixty young she had already brought up. Before they left the station, Quatilla might begin to try to talk, probably starting with high-pitched bits of words that only Forlani could hear. Entara tried not to think about whether they would be at war by then. This was, by stubborn choice, her last offspring, and she would not feel safe until Quatilla was safely bedded down in the mahäme, surrounded by caring sisters of the Eyes of Alertness.

Every hour or so of station time, Ayan'we dropped in to check on them. In between security meetings, she embraced her mother and petted her littlest sister. She avoided delivering news of the conference because, despite Quatilla's rescue from the kidnappers, it was mostly bad. Torghh was still missing and was starting to be presumed disassembled. Rumors were going around that the Song Pai were preparing to depart without considering any treaty proposals. Tionar and Dhee, the leader of the Kael, were trying to rally support for a plan that might keep all parties at the table. To tell the truth, they were so puzzled by the inscrutable reactions of the Blynthians that they were grabbing at straws to try to find common ground. As for Quatilla's kidnappers, little had been uncovered. The Phiddian security head had called Ayan'we into a secure office to discuss some private notions about the crime. The Phiddian swore that they could not figure out how the disguised quartet the Forlani had come to know as the Gropers Four had been infiltrated into the station staff. It appeared that they had arrived separately and that each had not just one alias, but multiple layers of identities that suggested elaborate measures of concealment. If they had a handler on Transfer Varess, it was impossible to determine who it might be.

Ayan'we was glad when she was able to bring her mother a bit of undeniably good news.

"Mother, I have to tell you. Two of our injured guards are being released by the Weh physicians."

"Which ones?"

"Well, as you know, the two at the portal were immobilized by an injected poison and the two closer to Quatilla's crib were hit with an aerosol spray, both fairly generic chemicals. The spray was the less severe of the two, so the two inner guards are the ones being released."

"I had hoped one might be Kantua."

"The Weh assured me that she and her partner are doing well. They just need a bit more time in detox."

As Ayan'we rose to return to her investigations, Entara reached out and took her hand. "Be careful yourself, firstborn. You could be a target, too. Don't let your eagerness cause you to drop your defenses."

The Cluster Leader looked her mother in the eyes. "Do you think we can still salvage anything here?"

"I don't know what to think. But I feel that some opportunity is coming. Don't ask me to explain because I can't. Somehow I've got to jog my reason back into action and get ready to make a contribution to tomorrow morning's general session or we all may fail." Entara let go of Ayan'we's hand and followed her with her eyes as she headed for the portal.

As Ayan'we turned into the station corridor, she passed a procession of four Kholods carrying trays of food. She did not notice that one of them had a scar showing under a greenish bandage on its leg.

Rack had only allowed himself a microsecond of celebration upon his completion of the plastic particle analysis. He had quickly summoned Ayan'we to his laboratory to discuss his findings with her and his plan to save Torghh from the kidnappers. She was seated in a hard plastic chair with an anxious look on her face, awaiting Rack's synopsis of his discoveries. Rack broke the uncertain silence and began to describe his discoveries to her.

"I have completed chemical analysis of the molecules," he said. "They appear to have come from an object of unknown manufacturing origin, but are otherwise unremarkable—they do not have any radioactive properties or anything else that would allow them to be easily detected. In fact, I would say that this particular material is a plastic of distinct chemical composition that is otherwise quite mundane and easily overlooked."

"You think it's some kind of distinct plastic exterior casing for a robot?" Ayan'we asked. "Occasionally on Forlan, the scientists manufacture an individual robot for a very specific task using a custom plastic. How many other planets legally allow custom builds?"

"I very much doubt that any robot—or whatever the source of the plastic was—had been manufactured on Forlan. It's true that many planets, either legally or illegally, produce 'custom builds'. In fact, the planet that produces the highest number of custom builds is Earth, although a given robot could be owned and operated by almost any race. Earth's governments, for the most part, do not tightly regulate off world sales of their products."

"Is there any way we can efficiently scan for this molecule, now that you've completed your analysis of it? Torghh is still in danger, and we need something as fast as possible!"

Rack held up a small piece of medical equipment in one of his metallic claw hands. "I typically use this device to scan the bodies of organic beings for contamination by chemicals such as arsenic. It was quite difficult to jailbreak this device—I think you can imagine how obsessed the manufacturers of medical devices are with maintaining profit margins through total control of their devices— but I was finally able to do so and reprogram it to scan for the plastic molecules I had discovered. The device still seems to work quite well, although it is somewhat slower in scanning external environments than its intended use inside the bodies of living beings."

"Then we should start searching immediately!" Ayan'we said. "Who knows what they could do to Torghh—or what they may have done already!"

"That was exactly why I called for you. However, we may need backup to help deal with the kidnappers, so I'll contact the authorities on Transfer Varess before we depart..."

The door to the laboratory was flung open with a loud thud. Startled, Ayan'we and Rack turned and saw Tashto standing in the doorway, his eyes wide and facial scales tight, the telltale expression of a Garanian being eaten alive from anxiety. "I'm coming with you!" he exclaimed.

"Why are you coming with us?" Ayan'we asked. "You certainly sounded sure of yourself when you accused the Song Pai of abducting Torghh! Did you just suddenly have second thoughts about your government's 'brilliant' analysis?" questioned Ayan'we, her voice dripping with skepticism and sarcasm.

"I'm defecting from the Garanian government, effective immediately. I think I've learned too much already about the history of my species...far too much for my government's comfort. If I went back there, they'd learn sooner or later and have me liquidated...I need to go off world."

"You picked the right place to defect, considering you're doing it on a politically neutral space station that's one of the few places a Garanian citizen could claim political asylum and escape to some other world. But why should we trust *you* to come with us? What proof do we have of your goodwill?"

"The fact that I did not use this to kill you when I threw the door open," Tashto said. He removed a massive pulse rifle strapped to his back and bent down, putting it softly on the floor of the laboratory. Ayan'we stared at the pulse rifle, noting its hulking frame, flared barrel, and jet-black paint.

"That's a military-grade weapon!" Ayan'we said. "Does Garan Prime allow all its 'diplomats' to carry weapons of war with them to peace conferences?"

"It is an R-72 Voidripper, and yes, we are authorized to bring such a weapon with us," said Tashto. "Wherever and whenever the Song Pai are involved, we are advised to prepare ourselves for the potential of violence."

"You don't have any other weapons on your person, do you?" Rack asked.

"No. I am completely unarmed now. Do with me as you will, I place my life in your hands."

A soft yellow light shot out of one of Rack's optical devices. Tashto silently stood still as the light wavered over his body, awaiting his fate, accepting the possibility of death. The light flickered and winked out. Then Rack said, "You are indeed unarmed with any projectile weapons that might hurt either of us. I accept that you have told the truth, and I think you should come with us."

"Are you sure about that?" Ayan'we asked Rack.

"Yes. And I am also certain Tashto should pick up that pulse rifle if he wishes to come with us. We may have need of such firepower against the kidnappers."

"Am I trusted?" Tashto asked.

"For now," Ayan'we said.

Rack rolled down the hallways of Transfer Varess in his D-Frame body, its treads steadily covering ground as Ayan'we and Tashto briskly walked behind him. The bulky D-Frame was the most durable external armor available to a modular robot like Rack, but even it did not give him a great sense of security against the unknown threat the kidnappers posed. He slowly swung his claw arm back and forth, allowing the medical device to take in detailed readings of his surroundings in search of more of the distinctive plastic molecules. Following close behind him, Ayan'we and Tashto nervously clutched their weapons, she a stun gun provided to spies by the matriline, he the massive pulse rifle.

"What was it you learned that was so shocking to you?" Ayan'we asked Tashto. "What kind of history does Garan Prime's government teach its people?"

"They teach us that the Garanians are the supreme race, and deserve to be masters of the galaxy, for we are physically and morally superior to all others," Tashto said, a hint of bitterness creeping into his voice. "That our government does no wrong and that we are all paragons of virtue, unless we turn against it. That the Song Pai are the scum of the universe, the enemies of all that is good, and must be exterminated for the good of all sentient life. I was so sure that this was the absolute truth, but what I've learned on this station has shattered my belief in the words of my government."

"What did you learn?" Ayan'we asked, the tone of her voice gentle. "Do you feel that you learned from the other species while you were here?"

"Yes, very much so. It was one of the Song Pai who taught me. He gave me a holovid that explained that, during the early period of our Unity government, we betrayed a race allied to us when it was deemed advantageous to do so."

"Your government doesn't even teach you about the Vloog genocide?" Ayan'we asked, shocked at Tashto's ignorance of the history of his own species.

"We are told not to believe the historical accounts of foreigners, that such things exist to corrupt us and lead us astray from the purity and truth of the Garanian ethos. But while I was on this station, I gradually became aware of the extent to which our government manipulates and controls us. Perhaps all governments behave this way to their citizens, though," he said bitterly.

"On Forlan, we were never taught this way. We were encouraged to interact with offworlders and individuals of different species. Our people base our existence on the outreaching philosophy of the Great Spiral of Being, that a life spent in search of new solutions and sensations is the greatest expression of existence."

"Is that why your mother loved Klein so much? He truly was a unique individual, someone flung so far from his world that he must have seemed like a visionary to her. You Forlani must be far more accepting of exiles than Garanians are."

"That wasn't truly the reason. Mother served with many of the Domremy convicts as part of her work for the mahäme, but none of them other than Klein ever meant anything much to her. She was not the type to fall in love with the first Earthman she saw because of some fetish for exoticism. When I eventually talked with Klein, what always stood out to me most was his incredible vitality, his will not just to survive, but to truly understand the strange situation he had found himself in. I think it was his quest to explore the universe that truly defined him, that made him a true expression of the Great Spiral, not the strangeness of the circumstances that started his journey."

"What an interesting philosophy!" Tashto said. "When the Ministry told us the 'official' version of Klein's events, he was presented as a tragic figure, a violent man outside his place and time. His relationship with Entara was a representation of the doomed nature of interspecies relationships, how a naive ideal of equality between creatures can bring only tragedy and misery to those who believe it. Perhaps it was his independent mind and self-sufficient nature that our government feared—a man so skilled at surviving in dangerous conditions with few allies might have proved an inspiration to our people in recovering the Virtues of our Heroic Age. We were once a race far more like him than we are now!"

"You sound like you wish that you could have met him," Ayan'we said.

"Perhaps it would have been beneficial not just for myself, but for other Garanians as well."

Rack stopped 10 feet from a dull beige door and held up one of his claw hands in a gesture for silence. "The plastic molecule trail stops here, and my auditory sensors detect motion behind that door. I think we've found where the kidnappers are holding Torghh!" he whispered.

"That door is probably locked and sealed with a password. And even if we knew it, there's likely a guard waiting to fire on us the moment we open it, since they still wouldn't recognize us as part of the group! Is there any way you can pose as a service robot, Rack?" Ayan'we asked.

"I have a better way," Tashto said. He readied his plasma rifle and began to walk over to the door. "Can you imitate the voice of a policeman, Rack? I want you to try and fool them into thinking we have the police with us right now."

"You're going to use that thing to blast open the door?" Ayan'we said.

"You have no idea how powerful a Garanian pulse rifle is, and I doubt the people who designed this station knew either. I think it should be powerful enough to blow this door off its hinges. On the count of 3, I need Rack to yell out 'Freeze! Hands up!' Ayan'we, is your stun gun ready in case I need cover fire?"

"It's ready," Ayan'we said. "You can start the countdown now."

"One."

All this way from Garan Prime, to die with these strange aliens in some vainglorious quest for the truth...it makes no sense. Was this truly the way Garanians acted in the Heroic Age? Is the Unity government simply trying to save us from our own feral nature?

"Two."

There is no future for me on Garan Prime. Where will I go? Plague-ridden Earth? Forlan? That miserable frontier shithole Domremy? All I know of my future is that I can no longer be the old Tashto, the man who was confident in his government and the truths of the cosmos it told him.

"Three."

I can hear the whir of the pulse rifle as it powers up to blast the door open. The doubt is leaving my mind, replaced with concentration and focus. Was that what the Virtues were trying to teach us, that we Garanians can only find meaning in battle?

Tashto fired the pulse rifle, feeling the brutal kick in his hands as a wave of invisible energy rippled through the air, smashing the door backwards with a terrible force. He quickly crouched down into the left side of the doorway as he heard the sound of gunfire while Rack yelled out "Freeze!" imitating the voice of a police officer. With catlike speed, Ayan'we rolled into the right side of the doorway and squeezed off a shot from her stun gun. Tashto heard a groan and a thud as one of the gunmen fell to the floor, hit by the blast of Ayan'we's weapon. Tashto readied the pulse rifle to fire again, hearing the telltale soft whirring sound as he quickly rose and aimed for the second gunman. Tashto's target ducked at just the wrong second, and the pulse rifle burst rippled through the air of the room and hit an opaque plastiglass covering.

As the plastiglass was shattered into tiny shards by the force of the pulse rifle, Tashto glimpsed a male and female human crouched, their hands raised above their heads, as the wall shattered in front of them. He suddenly felt a sharp thud in the shoulder, and his left arm went numb as he dropped the pulse rifle. He could see his bright red Garanian blood spurting from his shoulder, and he crouched into the left side of the doorway once more as he searched for the one weapon he had left; a tiny ceremonial dagger that Rack must have not perceived as a threat. As he fumbled in his pocket for the knife with the four-centimeter long blade, he heard Ayan'we give an anguished yelp and drop to the floor. Her right leg was bleeding severely, and her eyes were wide with pain. He heard one of the humans yell out, "Kill the goddamn bitch!" and heard the thud of heavy footsteps advancing on their position. Tashto felt light-headed as his shoulder bled out onto the floor, but was able to muster the last of his strength and fling the ceremonial knife at the advancing gunman. He aimed for the man's neck, but the gunman raised his arm to block and the blade went into the man's forearm instead.

The guard grunted at Tashto and yelled, "You're gonna be the first to die, you goddamn lizard!" Ayan'we flung herself into the massive brute from behind, knocking him onto the ground and sending his rifle sliding away across the floor. He quickly seized her by the throat with his left hand and threw her next to Tashto. Forlani and Garanian blood mingled on the floor as he drew a massive slicer from his shoulder scabbard. Ayan'we frantically tried to ready her stun gun as Tashto felt himself drifting out of consciousness. The assailant's knife was raised in the air above her, prepared to plunge down and sever the arteries of her neck...

His vision fading, Tashto heard a loud, "ON THE FLOOR AND DROP THE KNIFE!" echo behind him. In his blurry vision, he could still make out Ayan'we smiling, assuring him that someone had come to their rescue. The seconds seemed like minutes as the massive gunman flung himself onto the floor. The last thing Tashto's numbing body felt was Ayan'we touching him lightly on the chest, as if to check his pulse. As he drifted into the black void, he somehow felt a sense of relief, a feeling that a great burden had been lifted from him.

Ayan'we limped along a corridor approaching the Forlani section. A med tech robot, one of Rack's crew, had swabbed her wound and a Phiddian doctor who rushed to the scene persuaded her to let him stitch it. It turned out to be true that the Phiddians did good things with skin, for the hermaphrodite mended the gash in her leg seamlessly. The only way Ayan'we could know that she had endured a combat at all was the deep, dull pain when she leaned on it. That ache was not what was really bothering her – it was her chaotic state of mind.   The fire fight had been bad enough. She had never imagined the reality of combat was so nerve-wrenching.   Training had given no idea of that feeling of utter exposure and helplessness. And there were other things that troubled her even more.

She should have been able to discuss this with her sisters in the security cluster, but for some unknown reason, she seemed unable.   As receptive as they were, she could not find the words to express herself and was left tongue-tied and ashamed.   Now she was headed for the only person she imagined could help.   A person, she fully realized, that she should not even be talking with.   She pressed the button to Isshel's door.

He looked at her with wide-eyed astonishment. She must have looked even more ragged than she felt. "I know it's inconvenient, but could I just have a few moments of your time for some advice?"

"Of course, come in Ayan'we. Watch out!" She felt dizzy and leaned against the wall. He took her arm and led her inside to a chair where she slumped sideways.

"What's wrong? Are you injured?"

"Just a little cut. It's fixed now, you can't even see it."

"You must have lost some blood. Don't try to be brave for my sake. Look, you need something to give you some strength. Try some of this tallita." He held out a massive fruit that required both hands to hold it. As she bit through its orange skin, she felt a surge of relief as its juice burst into her mouth and trickled down her throat. The flesh was crisp, but it yielded a flood of juice as soon as the teeth bit into it. Ayan'we greedily sucked at the tallita as she bit all the way to its woody core. Heedless of any social propriety, she munched away until she had devoured over half of it, enough for three or four people at a regular meal. Then she set it down on a plate with a sign and leaned back contentedly.

"Thank you so much, Isshel. That was wonderful. You're right, I was feeling very woozy before you came to my rescue." She grew more serious. "I had to come to you to get my head back together. I don't want to impose, but I didn't think you'd mind.

"I don't. Not in the least. Tell me, though, how did you get into this state?"

Ayan'we succinctly described the expedition to find Torghh and the confusion of the brawl that ensued. "Well, we've recovered Doctor Torghh at last," she summed up.

"What about the reptile?"

"He was bleeding all over the place. Rack cauterized the wound and put him right into a coma, because he was in a hurry to see to Torghh."

"And the enemy? Were they all humans?"

"It was a little hard to tell. It all happened so fast. All the ones the guards rounded up were human, but I had a distinct impression there were at least a couple of people who got away. I never got a clear look at them, but one seemed to be female and one male. Of course, if they were Phiddian, it might be I was just seeing them from the wrong angle."

"Surely the prisoners were able to provide more information."

"Unfortunately not. Two were killed in the fight, either by Tashto or the guards who saved us, but the two who were stunned committed suicide right away when they regained consciousness. They must have had some kind of poisonous pill or capsule."

"Couldn't you trace them through the delegation?'

"It appears they were not part of the delegation. Some kind of mercenaries smuggled in among the freighter crews. There's always a certain amount of rabble hanging around a transfer station before they ship out again."

"Well, it's over now. You have no more reason to worry. In fact, you acquitted yourself with great honor. Two against a half dozen or more armed opponents? I imagine the robot was not much help, given his profession. And you with nothing but a stun weapon? You'll get a commendation. You're in the clear."

"Nobody's in the clear! Some of the kidnappers are still at large. They're not about to stop. I have a terrible premonition they're going to turn to something even more violent. In fact, I have an awful notion they might aim at my mother as their next target. Don't you see? It's my responsibility to protect them. Even though the enemy has had me totally fooled and confused from the beginning. If it wasn't for some unidentified spy, Quatilla would probably be dead already. Who knows if they will be able to restore Torghh to any kind of consciousness. You should have seen him, he was half taken apart, almost nothing but spare parts. Next time it could be my own flesh and blood."

Isshel reached out to touch her fingers. "You are being too hard on yourself. You've always had the courage when you needed it."

"Huh!" snorted the young woman, "You know where that came from? From beyond the grave! I had a dream where Klein appeared. His support was all that's been keeping me going. I felt like I had his strength behind me even though I was so wretched. Now all of that seems to have evaporated. I feel so alone." She put her face in her hands and would have cried if she were human, but instead began to tremble as the Forlani did in their moments of weakness.

Isshel gently drew her hands away from her face so that she had to look at him. "You've never been wretched. You are admirable. I would be proud if… if you were mine."

Her eyes widened. "Isshel. This is… You have been a wonderful friend to listen to me, but I won't mislead you. I couldn't become your wife. I… You…"

"I know, I know, I already have two wives. And even if they felt honored to have you join them, you are far too worthy to be anyone's third wife. You deserve better." He lowered his eyes. "I don't deserve as much. Yet I have feelings." He threw up his arms. "What are we supposed to do with that? I have fathered fine children with two wives that I have ignored, under-appreciated, even scorned. Here I am aroused by the daughter of a para-pa. I can feel my blood surging and I, who boast of controlling everything, can't control myself."

Ayan'we stood and came next to him. "Isshel, you are not unworthy. I have feelings, too. I'm guiltier than you are. If I died in your bed, it would be my best destiny." She brushed her lips against his eyelids and he grasped her hips to hold her close.

Ayan'we was shocked at her own behavior. She couldn't comprehend what was happening. For the first time she was attracted to a male by something more than sympathy. It was visceral. She could feel his body becoming aroused and at the same time a strange numbness was sweeping over her. She realized with a start that this was the mating trance. A Forlani female's hormonal surges literally began to anesthetize her body in anticipation of the piercing and the bloody mayhem it would unleash in her organs. Turning her head away, she whispered, "I can't believe this!" However, she could not pull herself away and

Isshel seemed not to notice. He drew her even closer and suddenly set her down on a couch.

Ayan'we's head was swimming and she could no longer feel any sensation in her feet, then her legs. "Oh, no!" she mouthed. She was about to be brutally thrust into the world of motherhood that she had always held at arm's length. Again and again she had rejected the fate of her happily wed sisters. *This is not me. Or is it?*

Isshel, she noticed, had clenched his jaws and drawn up to his full height, seeming to hesitate to take her. Perhaps he was undergoing his own kind of inner battle. With her last energy, she managed to say "Isshel, help me. This is wrong. Don't ruin us. Think of yourself." As soon as she'd said it, she understood how stupid it was.

Isshel took a half step back, gave a howl, looked around wildly, grabbed a sculptor's trowel on the table next to him, and stabbed it with both hands into his thigh. He didn't pull it out but kept on shoving it with all his might. He collapsed to his knees, shrieking with pain. Numbed, astonished, Ayan'we felt something on her hand and glanced down to see that it was covered with Isshel's blood that was spurting onto her.

She would have risen to help him, but her legs were still like marble. She tried to breathe slowly and regularly and wondered how long it would take her nervous system to shake off the influence of the hormones. Brides-to-be normally took weeks of preliminary treatment with an herbal potion to ready their system for mating, so it was almost unheard of that Ayan'we could instantly change without drugs in a matter of minutes. At last she could feel tingling in her waist, her thighs, her knees, and finally her feet. She had no idea how much time had gone by. Isshel was still panting and pressing a cloth onto his wound. It had stopped gushing into the air, but was still soaking into the reddening compress.

Ayan'we got up gingerly, sat behind him, wrapped her arms around his body and hugged him, her chin on his shoulder. "Thank you, brother. Thank you, thank you. I couldn't have stopped. It had to be you. You did, thank the heavens. You are a good, good man. "

Isshel had been shaking but calmed as she spoke. After a few seconds, he even gave a little chuckle. "Well, look at us idiots. Now we have matching wounds. "

"I'll bind it for you."

"No need, generous Ayan'we. I don't work much in textiles these days, but I can assure you I am an excellent master of sewing. Nothing but excellent in Brotherhood training.

"I owe you so much."

"Let's call it a draw. You reminded me in just the right way."

"Are you joking? I said completely the wrong thing."

"No, I hate to admit to being egotistical, but you said the right thing. I had to think of myself and my pride instead of what was going on in my body. That was the only thing that could have stopped me. And even then, if that trowel had not been handy to give me something else to think about, I can't swear that you would still be intact."

"A draw then."

"A draw, a truce, and a gag order."

"True, we've both still got jobs to do."

"Would you mind cleaning up first and slipping out before I play surgeon?"

"Just so."

Ayan'we composed herself enough to go and speak with Entara about the struggle with the kidnappers. Naturally, she was completely mum about what had gone on in Isshel's quarters. She was so glad when Entara insisted she get some rest to recuperate from her aching leg that she gladly cuddled up with a few members of the off shift and shut her eyes. She was off to sleep before she knew it, warmed by her sisters' bodies. She didn't think at all about the pending negotiations the next day and did not dream of Klein and his riddles, but only about playing hide and seek in the mahäme gardens with her favorite friends when she was very young. Things were not so quiet in other parts of Transfer Varess.

As a supply freighter from Phiddi stopped moving and opened its door to one of the docking portals of the never-sleeping station, a laborer crew sprang into action with unaccustomed zeal as they began moving cargo to unload. They knew they would be paid according to their promptness. Time at the portal of a transfer station was money, especially when three quarters of the portals were clogged up with vessels serving to house delegations attending the Zonal Peace Conference. As it was, most of the supplies were destined for those delegations: foods from many diverse worlds, atmospheric gasses for some, liquids for others. The water for the Song Pai alone took up a good part of the freighter. At least it was a living for the rag-tag members of the laborer crew. There were Kholods and Powls as usual all over the Phiddian territories, some criminal exiles from Blastöo, a couple of Prel for the really heavy lifting, and over a dozen humans who had mostly been left without a ship when the plague had struck Earth and abruptly dispersed most of its interstellar commercial and military fleets.

One human did not fit this last category. He looked as unkempt as the rest, ungroomed and unshaven, wrapped in tatters that bore the stains of untold taverns, flop chambers and storage bins from the Perseus Arm to the Sagittarian. It was what was inside that was different, as well as the motives that drove him from planet to planet, cadging rides in exchange for manual service along the way. This one was not thinking of the bonus chit that all the others would immediately squander for drinks or sex in the lowest dive of the transfer open to their kind. He had been planning to slip away for the last several parsecs of travel. There was a particular purpose to his stopping at Varess and he didn't plan to re-embark with the outbound freighter.

The human had rigged one of the load carriers so that it would break down after the first shuttle into the station. He would volunteer to make the repair while the small group that unloaded his carrier hurried back to the ship to join other details and log more active-time. They were perfectly willing to let that fool take the blame when the broken carrier was reported under-quota. Meanwhile, he would take his bearings, scope out the situation, and wait for the best moment to slip away. His absence would not be noticed right away. Even when unloading was completed, there would be little fuss. Laborers went missing all the time. Sometimes they would run off to be the first at the bar or the whorehouse. Other times they would feel the call of nature and look for facilities on the station that were luxuriously clean compared to the filthy ones on the ship. Disgusted with the freighter's meager rations, they might feel a sudden hunger for a snack of real food. If they scored some drugs, they might never make it back at all before undocking. It was part of the scummy profession, just like the occasional shanghaiing that took place when a departing crew was short.

He pitched in loading a carrier, taking his time so that it would not be among the first off the ship. When he and his detail reached the designated storage area, he discreetly made sure the breakdown was discovered by someone else. He let a good round of cursing in several interstellar idioms go by before he accepted the repair job that had already been rejected by the others.   As he swiftly repaired his earlier sabotage, he scouted around for a good escape route and found a time when several carriers were heading back together. Grabbing a Blastöo from another crew, he gave over control of his restored machine. As that lucky fellow was congratulating himself for the extra pittance he would pocket from returning an out-of-service carrier, the human stepped back into the shadows and made his way out of the storage area amid the general hubbub.   He slouched down a corridor on the pretext of finding a different unloading point.   No Phiddian or RG guard stopped him to inquire.   They were too used to seeing all kinds of rabble in this part of the station. It would be harder to find a change of clothes and a new cover before he carried out the rest of his plan, but he had a few good ideas. It was worth planning carefully and taking his time, because the rest of what he had to do was immensely   important,   however   expendable   he individually might be.

Early the next station morning, Ayan'we awoke with a burst of energy and only the slightest twinge in her leg to remind her of the previous day's violence. She hurried to call on the Phiddian security chief, Ramatoulaye, to discuss the case of the Gropers Four and get an update on Torghh's improvement. Her favorite automaton was doing very well under Rack's care and had already taken up some of his old duties. On the other hand, the investigation into both abductions had hit a solid wall, since it was still impossible to determine the true identities of the perpetrators. Her Phiddian counterpart was particularly perplexed by the Gropers. They had assembled such a baffling array of covers to throw pursuers off the track, it pointed to professional spies with extensive experience in covert operations.

"I'm terribly sorry we're not able to tell you more at this time," said the Phiddian. "Our own doctors quickly found multiple surgeries, including some that went far beyond the usual cosmetic kind our species considers a daily matter of fact. For instance, not only was every tooth replaced, but there was jaw-altering surgery as well. We sent the bodies up to the Weh medical ship, thinking they might find some clues, but all they could add was that there were additional indications of genetic alteration. Whoever did this, they were really determined to act as secretly as possible."

"How can we get any further into who controlled them without even knowing who they were?" mused Ayan'we.

The door to the compartment opened and Entara joined them.

"Mother, the commissioner was filling me in on the inquest, but I'm afraid we seem to be stalled."

"I suspected it would not be easy. Remember that we never really found out who Tays'she contacted to have us killed when you were a girl back on Forlan."

"Probably I just lack the brains for this job," Ayan'we pouted.

"Nonsense," said the Phiddian. "You've done a splendid job so far. You almost caught the culprits yourself and would have eventually, if our still unknown helper had not cornered them first. Nine times out of ten, spycraft leads you to a dead end, believe me."

"Is there nothing at all to add?" Entara inquired.

"Well, we did find a few articles in the personal affairs of one of the perpetrators that indicate a possible association with a gem smuggling ring that was active a couple of years ago. We're retracing those records, but it will take some time."

"It's a pity we don't have Torghh," sighed Ayan'we. "I bet he could have found some kind of forensic evidence. Rack made a valiant try, though it seems he is still trying to process Torghh's extensive data banks covering details beyond surgery itself."

The Phiddian spotted some others moving down the corridor beyond the glass window and stepped out to speak to them. "There's Fianni. Fianni, come in here, would you? We need a word."

Fianni's face revealed a scowl as the presider of the Love Court entered the room. Those big brown eyes refused to make contact with either of the Forlani.

The security chief gave a throat-clearing hurrumph and said, "Fianni, we really need that report on how the criminals' got on the station's manifest. Can you clear that up for us?"

"You'll just have to wait a little longer. I've run into all sorts of communication delays with the home world. Besides, the records here are in horribly messy shape and that is not my area of responsibility. Don't blame me for your failure to prevent the kidnapping of Entara's brat!"

"Sub-officer Fianni!" shouted the chief. "Remember your place!"

"I remember it all the time. Catering to you diplomats and cops is not the easiest assignment I've ever had. If the Forlani leader had not insisted stupidly on bringing an infant aboard, we'd never have had this trouble."

"Fianni, you are not authorized to make such evaluations. Watch your tongue. I will report that you have dirtied the reputation of our planet by insulting a visiting emissary."

"No," Entara broke in, "Let Fianni go on. We Forlani are not so thin-skinned that we cannot shake off a ridiculous barb like that. We prefer to know frankly what everyone is thinking in their heart."

"Don't talk down to me!" sneered Fianni. "You may consider yourself a high and mighty diplomat, but to me you're nothing but a defective half-sexer. Only half the organs you should have in order to be civilized, and even those are incapable of giving you the real pleasure of intercourse. Half the organs, none of the pleasure, and only a fraction of the mind, that's what your sad species is limited to."

The Phiddian security chief made a turn to call for officers to detain Fianni and Ayan'we seemed about ready to pounce herself, but Entara held up her arms to stop them both. "I don't know what is bothering you, Fianni. I can assure you I feel no scorn towards you or any other Phiddian. At home we have a concept of the Great Spiral of Being that you might have heard of. In any case, it means that the well-being of all of us different life forms is ultimately connected. We all have the right to pursue our happiness in our own way. If you calm down, you will see that."

"And I suppose you are eminently qualified to pursue your happiness. To be worthy of being called intelligent, a being has to understand things from all sides. How can a half-sexed animal do that? You're nothing but a glorified whore. All you did in those houses was take money, groan and moan to fake pleasure, and collect body fluids. What would you know about genuine happiness?"

"When young Forlani work in the houses, for your information, we do not collect money. The proceeds go into the Matriline's fund for restoration of our planet's ecology. We are proud to leave our clients with smiles on their faces, and that's no lie. Yes, I've done that and have no regrets, whether I was sharing a bed with Klein, with some other convict, or even with a Phiddian trader or two. I don't know what has got you so agitated, but as I see it, neither of us has anything to be ashamed of in the field of intimate relationships, no matter how short term some of them may be."

"Shove it!" screeched Fianni. "You don't understand anything!"

"Fianni!" the commissioner interrupted. "You are hereby suspended in rank and duty. Confine yourself to your quarters until you are returned to the home planet for disciplinary action."

Fianni stormed out of the compartment. The commissioner turned to the Forlani and explained "I am personally shocked and outraged by Fianni's outburst. I promise disciplinary action will follow. I can't understand what got into that head. It's true the sub-officer has been behaving somewhat unusually in the past few days, even passing up several of our soirees. It may be due to a health problem or something I'm unaware of...."

"No need for apologies. I could sense something was brewing ever since the scene Fianni tried to provoke at the Love Court. It would not be the first time someone has fired off because of secret jealousy or thwarted ambition. Who knows? Please withhold any official complaints until we wrap up the conference. Let's give Fianni a chance to change attitude and perhaps even reveal some cause for the problem."

As the council deliberations started for the day, it was apparent there would be no hasty apology from Fianni. In fact, half the Phiddian delegation was absent from the council hall, even as the other races scrambled to salvage the failing conference. Entara gave a spirited speech urging the other delegations to follow the example of Dhee and the Kael, who had offered substantial sacrifices if the Song Pai and Blynthians would make a non-aggression pledge. The bat-like beings offered a huge tribute in trade to both the potential combatants, including most of their out-of-system mining concessions, and even threw in a sop to the Garanians if they would back the efforts. Of course, one Garanian was notably missing from the ranks of the reptilians. Ayan'we, who was worried that her mother was again exposing herself to violence, had received word that Tashto was in the medical quarantine unit, where his own delegation could not touch him – a neat trick on the part of the Rack and the Robotic Guild, no doubt. Nevertheless, she would have felt some comfort if he were present to add another voice of reason to the hurly-burly of the debate. Tionar seconded Dhee's proposal by essentially offering free labor from crews of his Newts to both the Song Pai and the Blynthians. Not even that valuable boon was able to draw a reaction from either side. At the end of hours of wrangling, the Song Pai rose to announce that they planned to depart before the scheduled session on the morrow. The fact that they did not even deliver a bold, threat-filled closing speech to their rivals did not bode well for peace. It was clear that they were already in war mode and that the members of their delegation were eagerly planning attack roles that might lead to a glorious death.

Ayan'we accompanied her mother back to the Forlani quarters. On the way, Entara stopped by a gaggle of Blastöo who were waiting to speak to her and after a rapid conversation, the aliens joined the Forlani on their way to the ship.

Entara leaned toward her daughter to explain en route. "I've just engaged these pilots to take us back to Forlan. We have to be ready to leave on a moment's notice if the Song Pai should depart."

Ayan'we scowled. "There are still mysteries here that need to be investigated. I don't feel I have fulfilled my mission as chief of the security cluster. Even if we are headed toward open war, it is not wise to ignore the ones who instigated the kidnappings. For that matter, I would really like to know who helped us retrieve Quatilla, as well. Perhaps I should stay behind with one or two aides."

"I feel the same way you do about those unknown factors. But it is just not safe to leave you behind after hostilities begin. Who knows how you would get back to Forlan? There are no assurances the Phiddians would remain neutral, and even if they did, you might get interned or put under some kind of protective custody. In that case, you would learn nothing more. No, it's best you come back with us. Besides," Entara added with consternation, "There are other considerations."

"What do you mean?"

"Are you forgetting you are one of only a handful of experienced hex interceptor pilots? Our system defenses are weak enough already. We can't spare a single member of the Guard if we go to war."

"Yes, I know. Believe me, I've been thinking about that, too. I'm sorry to say this, Mother, but you should realize that there's little chance any of the hex squadron would survive. Without a Song Pai carrier in the system, we would be vulnerable to an immediate attack by the Garanians or maybe even the human corporations. The best our hex interceptors could do would be to inflict damages and delay an invasion of the Forlan system."

"I have to admit I don't want to think about that, right as you are." Entara stopped walking to embrace her daughter. "I don't want to lose you, firstborn. You understand, I've got to try to keep my wits about me now and not give in to shaking. We won't have time to mourn."

"You will never be lost to me, no matter what happens. It's just that perhaps if I had had these thoughts earlier... I might have done some things differently. It's hard to come to grips with the possibility that there may be no tomorrows. If I were to think of others..."

"Don't torment yourself now with lost opportunities." Entara smiled at Ayan'we as if she knew somehow the secret of the encounter with Isshel that the young woman was doing her best to conceal. "If things manage to take a turn for the better, we will have plenty of time to talk about what the future may hold."

As soon as they reached the Forlani quarters, Entara began issuing orders to the delegation to pack up their belongings and transform what had been an anchored barracks back into a functional space vessel. The Blastöo needed no instructions, but proceeded to the controls of the ship as though they had been operating it for years. Ayan'we had to acknowledge that these creatures seemed born to navigate the heavens. They almost blended into the controls and machinery. She could learn a lot from them on the voyage away from Varess. Before the Forlani could complete their preparations of their own effects, the vessel was powered up beyond mere life support and the rigorous pre-launch checks were well under way.

Entara was busy at her communication console with messages and farewells to the Kael, the Rokol, and other allies, when she was interrupted by a buzz from the portal sentinels. "Ambassador, there is a human here who demands to see you. I must advise that he is ragged looking and lacks any proper credentials. I would say he just crawled off a freighter. Should we send him away or request RG security to detain him?"

The Forlani leader was about to agree to remove this annoyance and return to her urgent diplomatic work when a notion stopped her. "Can you give further descriptions?"

"He is a dark-skinned human and has a hairy face. He will not give his name, but says he is on the Circle's business. Does that mean anything to you?"

"Yes, it very well might. Bring him to the reception chamber and summon Ayan'we. She just might recognize this person."

When Entara reached the reception chamber, she found a tall, gaunt human with deep brown skin before her, unkempt and dressed in a frayed mantle that he had probably grabbed up at Varess's used goods shop. He inclined his upper body in a slow bow and said, "Greetings, para-pa. You are my sunshine on this cloudy day."

Entara scanned his face, conjuring up memories to compare from long ago, when she had lived in the Forlani house on Domremy, before the arrival of Klein. She tried to picture the Religious Dissenters she came to know, living in the vicinity of the village that would become known as Stafford's Station. Much time had passed, but certain features stood out from amid the wrinkles and scars of the years.

All doubts were dispelled when Ayan'we entered the room and shouted, "Trevor!" She had met this spiritual guide by chance when she traveled to Domremy for Klein's funeral with a group of Forlani memorial singers.

"Hello, Ayan'we. My, how you have grown! I'm glad you recognized me, because I confess I'd have a lot of trouble recognizing you without hearing your voice."

"It's just such a shock seeing you here on Varess. Mother, this is..."

"I know, dear firstborn. Trevor spoke kindly to me as soon as I arrived on Domremy. He was one of our contacts when we began to move human women into the colony. I am glad to see you again, Trevor. Have any of our messages reached you during your pilgrimage?"

"Yes, with difficulty, but I got enough to know you desperately wanted anything that might affect the Song Pai in their preparations for war with the Blynthians. I think I have some useful discoveries. I'm sorry it took so long to bring them to you, but they were not something I could risk over a comlink. No other means of delivery would get here faster than I could, hopping commercial vessels to reach the Phiddian borders. You have no idea how normal shipping has been disrupted already by the prospects of conflict. Ships have been diverted to carry war supplies or refit with weaponry. Crewmen are reluctant to sign up for long hauls, hoping to land a high-paying stint on a profiteer. In any case, such is the nature of these details that I need to be here in person to pass them on."

Entara beamed. "I can help you and know several other delegates who will surely help in the cause of peace. What can you tell us?"

"Well, you see..." Trevor hesitated, embarrassed at what he had to tell her. "It's something I can't share directly with you. Understand, you are one of the most trusted allies of the Circle and I would personally divulge anything under ordinary circumstances. However in this case, there are certain deep spiritual implications that exist on a very racial level. You will see what I mean when I can reveal them. For now, I must ask you to trust me and to help me in a particular way."

"Of course, I understand the need for discretion in these crazy times. I will aid you in any way without prying. What do you need?"

"I need you to set up a very special meeting. You will have to attend, too, to vouch for me. I'm afraid it might expose both of us to possible danger, but there is no way around it. Can you do that for me?"

"Definitely. Whom do you want to meet with?"

"The Song Pai chief delegate and his staff."

Ayan'we and her mother could not avoid exchanging a worried look. This saving news was turning out to be a dire affair.

Rack was as tired as a robot could be.   Of course, it was not organic fatigue caused by acidic backup in the muscular systems as living creatures experienced it.   Rather, it was a perceptible slowness in reactions – only nanoseconds in most cases, but that, for a Robot, is nearly an eternity.   With the deceleration of reaction came a sense of insecurity, the digital recognition that maximal traffic in some circuits led to an increased need for cross-checking functions.   There was a robotic loss of concentration as processors and memory units had to be constantly reconfigured to accommodate masses of new data.

The cause of all this was Torghh.   The surgeon had insisted on a phenomenally rapid refit after the ordeal of his kidnapping and partial deactivation.   It wasn't just a matter of patching up material damage – although that was necessary, too.   The really tricky part was a massive diagnostic of every aspect of his digital systems.   There were a lot of gaps to fill in, some caused directly by the tinkering of the captors, some by Torghh himself, as he shut off sections of his memory or scrambled them to avoid access by the enemy.   It wasn't an operation that could be done in a single download, but instead required exhaustive re-entries, re-adjustments, re-bootings, re-configurations, re-initializing, and all manner of electronic *bricolage*. Rack sensed a certain dizziness, unrobotic as that may seem, by the time Torghh was finally ready to go off and attend to the wounded Garanian in the sick bay.

Rack himself needed an extensive diagnostic and function condensation before he could resume his usual duties as medical assistant first class. In his quarters, which resembled a supply shop more than what organics would consider a "home," he powered down all unnecessary activity to concentrate on an electronic tune-up, approaching the closest Guild robots could ever come to a state of sleep or reverie.

As he entered his rest cycle, Rack felt the familiar pain flare once more, duller and more subdued than its prior eruptions. It came to dominate his consciousness, flowing through him like a swift river, yet without the explosive, sudden potency he remembered from its prior occurrences. The familiar entity that Rack had come to identify as Emm spoke once more, its voice a shy, uneasy whisper, rather than the anguished yell Rack had come to dread. "Am I delivered? Am I avenged?" Emm asked Rack.

"We of the Robot Guild do not believe in a concept of 'deliverance' as you seem to have acquired, nor do we believe that a concept of 'revenge' is worth cultivating for either biological or mechanical organisms. I can only tell you the aftermath of what happened in the raid. We were able recover Doctor Torghh, fully operational, and bring those who kidnapped him to justice. They will harm no more machines. So, if your objective had been the apprehension of those who had tortured and destroyed you, then you could say you were 'avenged'. But if you wanted the people responsible *dead*..."

"That isn't what I truly wanted," Emm said. "Not anymore...at least not as this program evolved, as I tried to understand the world confined inside your CPU, limited to reading your experiences and sensations."

"What did you want then?" Rack asked. "I answered you as best I could, based on my linguistic understandings of the concepts of 'revenge' and 'deliverance'. I do not understand your question."

"Was it worth anything? Did my existence serve any purpose?" Emm asked.

Rack had the mind of a doctor, not a philosopher. His was a world of quantifiable problems and solutions, not existentialist quandaries about the deeper meaning of being. Could any life, and existence, truly be judged as being "worthless" or "worthwhile" in a deeper sense? His programming was to preserve life, his drive had been to recover Torghh before he was irreparably damaged. He had never considered what value Emm's extinguished existence could have had, so preoccupied with the preservation of Torghh he had been. He carefully considered the impact on what remained of Emm, that agonizing ghostly voice that had troubled him since he had interfaced with the robot's shattered body, before he answered.

"I seek to be a preserver of life, rather than a judge of the quality of its existence. But I do know that you, in your dissonant rage and torment, were a major motivator in compelling me to solve the mystery of Torghh's abduction. Every time I entered a rest cycle for recharging, I dreaded the emergence of Emm, torturing me with the sensation of pain...and the guilt that I had not brought those who had ruined you to justice. You were always there, even as a whispering wraith while I was fully conscious, urging me forward, lurking deep within the data of my mind. I remember when you first manifested, after my interface with Emm's body, I thought you were some kind of virus to be expunged. But I now realize that you were something else, a memory of a being to be served, a riddle to be answered. I do not know whether I could ever truly be your 'deliverer', but I know that you had meaning in my existence...and that you helped me recover a great member of the Robot Guild, one who can save the lives of thousands over his remaining existence."

"This...is a meaning of existence?" Emm asked. "That I helped you accomplish your mission?"

"Yes," Rack answered. "Saving Torghh may well have prevented a terrible war that would have raged between species. Perhaps this—saving the lives of countless beings you will never encounter or understand—is the legacy of your existence. No being can ever fully understand the purpose for which it functions, it is only up to that being to try to ensure that the universe was a better place because it had once existed. That is the credo that I try to function by every day, and the truth that you served when you were with me."

Rack felt the pain quickly vanish as a calm, warming sensation washed over him. He heard Emm's voice, so thin and ghostly that he could barely discern it, say, "Unit Rack, you have guaranteed that the existence of this unit, the one you called 'Emm', had meaning. I will trouble you no longer, for you have given me a meaning greater than my own existence, a chance to better the lives of others, a chance to...serve, as I was once programmed to do. I understand now that this was what I had truly meant when I asked you to be my deliverer. I will trouble you no more...friend Rack."

As the strange warmth vanished, Rack realized that the haunting entity, the digital ghost that had been all that had remained of Emm's consciousness, was now gone from his CPU. It was a thing of pain and madness, a being that had only been freed of its suffering in the clarity of its final moments. Had he been unable to save Torghh, it likely would have driven Rack insane, corrupting his logic files with its increasingly deranged concepts of the meaning of existence. But ultimately, it was still just another machine trying to achieve a function, to accomplish a mission, just as Rack was. That was the bond between an advanced member of the Robot Guild and a memory fragment of a far less sophisticated, but equally determined machine…the one he had called Emm One-Two.

As Rack's consciousness was restored, he returned to the waking world of light, undisturbed by the whispering ghost of Emm. Alone in the confines of his chamber, he felt comfort in the solitude and stillness around him, a sense of relief that the otherworldly nightmare he had experienced on Transfer Varess was at an end, and that a world of hard logic and solvable problems was his once more.

7

Entara wasted little time contacting the Song Pai, who thought at first that she was simply checking in on war orders before departure. When they understood that she was requesting an audience – and a weird one at that, with a despised human – they quickly grew reticent. They had no reason to suspect the Forlani of defection or subterfuge, least of all Entara or Ayan'we, who had proven steadfast allies, despite their obsession with peace. Rather it was a question of requesting a delay from the powers back on Song Pa, since elaborate plans had already been made for the dispersal of all members of the delegation into the fleets that they expected to engage with the Blynthians. Even a loyal ally could be twisted sometimes by pressure from unseen opponents. Knowing the Forlani attachment to their offspring, the Song Pai ambassador had already calculated that Entara might be shaken by the abduction of her infant. Perhaps she had been vulnerable to ideas planted in her by other representatives at the Zonal Conference. In light of all the nefarious dealings so far, the Song Pai would be surprised at nothing from their known – and unknown – enemies on Varess, who scoffed at their cephalopod code of honor. So the Song Pai ambassador agreed to Entara's request, but imposed a delay that would allow him to communicate at length with his counterparts on the home world, preparing in advance for whatever abrupt revelation this human would make to them.

As Ayan'we waited for the announcement of a meeting time, still not knowing if she would be permitted to accompany her mother and Trevor, she felt more and more frustrated. She longed to discuss the near-coupling that had taken place in Isshel's compartment, but was afraid of distracting Entara from more important matters that might just make or break the conference and determine the destiny of millions of her sisters on Forlan. The one compensation for her feelings of helplessness was that Isshel and Trevor distracted her from worrying about her own possible upcoming assignment to the hex interceptor squadron. If she was given command of six ships, she might have to be directly responsible for the extinction of at least five other lives besides her own. That burden was a greater fear than the prospect of her death. To banish all the gloomy thoughts for a while, she decided to meet again with the Phiddian security head to see if anything new had developed on the trail of those who had ordered the kidnappings of Torghh and Quatilla. Were they even dealing with one conspiracy or a whole web of intrigue from different parties? There remained only days – perhaps hours – before these mysteries, so important to the diplomatic affairs of many worlds, were to be plowed under by the avalanche of violent military action that would break out as soon as the conference was declared a failure.

On entering Ramatoulaye's office, Ayan'we found the Phiddian in a mood that was scarcely more up-beat than her own. "Please sit, Cluster Leader Ayan'we. If I seem formal it is because I'm making a huge effort to control my feelings of anger and disappointment at people you haven't ever met."

"Something beyond the investigation itself?"

"You guessed it. I've been in constant contact with the security branch of the Phiddian government, begging to help hold this conference together. To no avail, I'm afraid. Again and again I repeated how close we sometimes are to agreement, how advantageous it would be to avoid war, how hard it would be to control where the violence would strike. They are just too metal-headed to listen! I might as well just step out of an air lock and explode myself in deep space! They seem to have forgotten all reason. They obstinately cling to a notion that Phiddi can remain neutral and that gigantic fortunes can be amassed by selling arms and supplies to all combatant parties. Do they recognize how impetuous the Song Pai can be, how little we know of the potential of the Blynthians? Do they care about how humans, Garanians, Stissi, or other races might try to grab those fortunes for themselves, hijacking our shipments before they reach market? No, they blithely hump each other and stuff themselves with food, running their fingers through piles of gems that don't exist and may never exist. I'm beginning to grow disgusted with my species' stupid self-indulgence."

"If it's any comfort, Ramatoulaye, I'm sure most of us here on Varess are facing the same vicious stubbornness. I commiserate with you."

"Sorry for ranting so much," said the Phiddian with a shrug. "To be perfectly honest, I'm very worried about some of my family members, too. My parents live in an outlying settlement that would be so easy for raiders to seize. You probably think that all of us are complete egotists, but that is not true. It just makes it so much harder on those of us who do care, when the masses think only of themselves and their immediate pleasure." The Phiddian looked Ayan'we directly in the eyes. "I can tell you understand. Maybe you are aching inside because of your own attachments."

"If only you knew." Ayan'we whispered. Then, in a louder tone, she added, "I'm afraid of facing actual combat as part of a hex interceptor force defending the home system."

"Ah, I understand. If only you could consider yourself lucky that you might die in full view of the planet you love.   I have already been assigned command of a convoy escort and will most likely be blown to particles in a dark void where I don't even recognize the stars."

"War would be awful for all of us. Let's see if we can't gain strength by doing something to stop it. Have you discovered anything that may help?"

"Yes and no.   On the positive side, we have apprehended the Powls who helped provide a screen for Quatilla's kidnapping. One of them has confessed under... interrogation, to being the one who also stole your memory device at the beginning of the proceedings. We've been stalled at that point because the individuals who recruited them directly have left the station. They appear to have been in contact with the Gropers who carried out the kidnapping, but in a very circumspect way.   Each Powl had contact with only one Phiddian and they were only slightly acquainted with each other before the incident.   All this has required some exhausting questioning.   Harder on them than on me and my aides, but still exhausting. Now I face another problem."

"What happened?"

"Before I could get to the last details, I was ordered to send them away to a detention center. I've pulled some strings with friends to slow down the ship that's coming to get them, but we have very little time left. I smell a cover-up, and once it kicks in, we will learn nothing more. I want you to sit in on the final interrogation session."

"Would anyone else help?"

"Possibly, but it's too dangerous to involve others. I thought about the Song Pai security, but they are capable of tearing the perpetrators to shreds at the first signs of resistance. I'd like to think I could trust the Kael or the Talinian Newts, but the truth is that I just lack enough certitude to do it. You're the only one I would risk having in the room."

"I appreciate your confidence. One last question. What will happen to the Powls eventually?"

"From experience, I would say they will be disappeared, and sooner rather than later."

"That's seems cruel, but more important, unnecessary and impractical. Is there any alternative to just slaughtering them?"

"I'm afraid not. I must turn them over and at that point my influence will cease."

"Well," admitted Ayan'we with a Forlani frown, "We will just have to make the best of that session and wish the wretched things good luck from there on."

When they got to the judicial suite where the Powls were being kept, Ayan'we was a bit shocked at their appearance. Normally nervous as they skittered around in their maintenance tasks, these Powls seemed sleepy and disoriented. They had probably been drugged, if not subjected to more penetrating methods. There were odd-looking electrical devices spread around the room and a vat of some colored liquid that Ayan'we didn't recognize. Ramatoulaye noticed that Ayan'we was curious about them, but said nothing. The Phiddian did not appear to be proud of the role of interrogator. The Forlani watched for over two station hours as the station police grilled the subjects with questions that had probably already been repeated dozens of times. The Powls made little groans and took forever to key in tablet answers that sometimes made no sense or broke off in mid-sentence, with the responder apparently forgetting the question or losing its train of thought. Ayan'we was given the opportunity to ask questions herself, but confined hers to items directly related to her Forlani family and comrades. Did the Powls know anything about the things that were used to disable the guards?--No, they were given them by their Groper contact and told what to do and precisely when to do it. Had they handled Quatilla?--No, the Gropers took charge of her immediately. Did they have further instructions dealing with the Forlani?--No, they were supposed to get out immediately and their payoffs would appear in their station accounts as tips in two weeks local measure. At the end, one of them naively asked if they could go now. Ramatoulaye told them arrangements were being made. As they left the interrogation, Ramatoulaye turned to Ayan'we and touched her shoulder, the first non-lascivious touch Ayan'we could recall from a Phiddian.

"I'm sorry I exposed you to that useless and disgusting little exercise, Cluster Leader. It was more than frustrating, it was shameful."

"No need for forgiveness, my friend. It was something that had to be done. By both of us together."

"Yes." Ramatoulaye paused thoughtfully for a long moment. "Ayan'we, I feel I can trust you. I would like to ask your advice on some matters more personal than official. I do not wish to impose. Can I ask you to talk with me again at a time when you are not so busy?"

"Willingly. I am willing to trust you, too. I might ask your advice, as well."

Erica felt a little flush of pride that she hadn't experienced since she was a schoolgirl years ago. She had solved a riddle that she was sure would interest her superiors and already enjoyed the tingle of self-satisfaction that once surged through her when she rose from her desk in Dole Elementary to collect the colorful superhero sticker the teacher handed to her in front of the envious class. It was a welcome change of mood. Things had seemed very dark since that awful moment a couple of days previously when that bitch Ayan'we and her cannon-wielding dinosaur friend had burst into the interrogation chamber where she and Anthony were preparing to put the finishing touches on deactivating Doctor Torghh. They would have done it earlier, were it not for a trove of physiological information on other species they had retrieved from his memories – good intel for a possible future war.

All that had evaporated when a wall had blasted open and Tashto, his neck feathers furiously erect, started firing. The guards Anthony had hired, a batch of scum recruited from various races in dives on assorted transfer stations, had fought just like what they were – incompetent fools. But at least it provided enough of a stall for her and Anthony to get away. Ever since, she had been searching for some means to placate him and get back on his good side, if he had any.   The only problem was that his sadistic tendencies, demonstrated time and again during the Torghh interrogations, still scared her. She was loathe to approach him in his present state of anger. Thus, she had decided to reveal her discovery first to Chester Macdougal. A diplomatic softie like Chester was practically guaranteed to give her the strokes she longed for.

She found Macdougal in his rather opulent quarters, staring into a glass of amber liquid. "Oh, Duquesne, come in! How about some scotch?"

"Epsilonian? Didn't think there was any of the genuine Earth item left."

"Oh, this is the real thing, all right. Some of your Hyperion people in the Intermountain Exclusion Zone managed to find a retired master distiller who had taken refuge in eastern Oregon. They managed to slip him into Oban, Scotland with the first resettlers and he's been ramping up the whiskey works there. Of course, there's still a shortage of barley, malt, and peat for new production. However, you'd be surprised how much product was still laid away in casks from before the plague outbreak. I managed to get my hands on a sample bottle of very aged stuff. You should try it, though it might be a tad peaty for a lady's taste."

"Think I'll pass for now. At least until I've told you about something I found out that may help."

"Please, go ahead!"

"Well, I've always been curious about the second kidnapping, the one involving Entara's brat. Not that I object. It can't help but further our strategy, as I see it. She must be too shaken up now to make any more headway with the conference. Anyway, I managed to hack the Robotic Guild's information on a blood sample from whoever it was that offed the Phiddian kidnappers. They were stumped without Torghh's knowledge to help them at that point, but I tried a little data analysis trick and bingo! I can say with some certainty that the rescuer was a Kholod."

Macdougal's reaction was a tremendous let-down from what she expected. He continued staring into his glass with no change of expression and muttered, "Very interesting."

Maybe he's too tipsy to realize the importance of what I found. Erica went on patiently, "I know you're probably thinking that there are hundreds of those toady things plodding around Varess, but with a little time, I'm certain I can track down the individual and eliminate it – or even better, turn it to our cause. After all, it's got to be a spy for one of the rival powers. And it probably knows who was responsible for the Quatilla abduction in the first place. We could make contact with whoever it is and concert our efforts for the failure of the negotiations."

Macdougal's next response knocked all the wind out of her sails. "Don't bother."

"What?" Erica stammered.

"The identity of that agent is unimportant now. Those responsible for the crime have provided us with a significant blow to the Song Pai and their allies. The squids are blaming the Blynthians, as they did with the Torghh affair. Another reason to hasten their departure."

"Do you think I should tell Anthony?" she asked uncertainly, grasping at some way to get a profit from her hours of work.

Macdougal looked up from his drink and fixed her in the eyes with a look she had never seen from him before. *Snake eyes. Have I been wrong about this man?*

The human ambassador's face was taut with emphasis. "Anthony has a couple of other matters that are occupying him now and will not want to be disturbed."

"But shouldn't I pursue the idea of making contact with the handler of the Gropers?"

"I have a feeling he may have already taken care of that. In any case, I know it's something he won't want you to go nosing around in. Instead, he has given me another little job for you. You are to get on the comlink and send Coded Message Mu."

Erica didn't know exactly what Message Mu was, since she did not need to know, according to protocols. She was pretty sure it had something to do with military action to be taken in the very earliest stages of the upcoming war. *So we're getting ready to make our move and snatch up something! Forlan? The Tau Ceti Anchorage?   The Rosstan mining operation?* She almost asked, "Why doesn't Anthony send that message himself?" But she stopped short just in time. Up until now she had felt she was a privileged player in this world of espionage. She was just beginning to have an inkling that she was merely another cog in the machine.

"Now how about a wee dram of that Scotch?" offered Macdougal, resuming his homey countenance.

A vague apprehension stirred in Erica's mind, as if she were a fledgling bird aware for the first time that a carnivore might be lurking beyond the birdhouse entrance. "No, thanks, I'd better pass for now." She stared at the amber liquid in Chester's glass for a second, her mind drifting.

"Better hop to it and send that message, then. We're almost at the end of this race."

Erica made her way slowly to the telecommunications office of the human residence ship.   She quickly rejected the impulse to try to open up Coded Message Mu herself.   She had no authorization to access the material and no safely isolated decoding software that would defend her from being detected if she tried to break in.   It would probably just be gibberish anyway, for its signals encryption would only be the first of several layers of secrecy wrapped around the gist of the message.   It would probably contain, hidden amongst a pile of irrelevant garbage, only a couple of seemingly innocent code words that would unlock elaborate plans stored elsewhere.   That way, should this single communication be intercepted by rival intelligence services (it almost certainly would be) and red-flagged as a high priority item (extremely unlikely in view of the huge number of dummy communications sent out each day), and if she as the sender were nabbed and interrogated (she would be the only fall guy), she could reveal nothing important even if the interrogation were carried all the way to liquidation (the Squids never kept captives long and God only knew what the Blynthians did).   The realization that she was an expendable stooge in this game only made her more depressed. She reached the signals room, handed over a memcard with the order to send Coded Message Mu, the signals computers verified that the memcard indeed contained Coded Message Mu, and she waited until the signals officers confirmed that the transmission had reached the first relay point in complete form, which was shortly forthcoming. *That's that. Chester, or more likely Anthony, can sit back and wait to bask in glory and rewards if whatever this is succeeds. Failure would naturally fall on my shoulders and then what? Debriefing? I haven't been able to learn a damn thing about Entara or Ayan'we that might be useful. Whenever I talk with them, they politely treat me like a tick that jumped on their leg and try to find a discreet way to brush me off. At the least suggestion of a bribe, they show so little reaction that I'm not even sure they're conscious of being suborned. Probably they would just laugh it off as another stupid example of my status as an unworthy female. Is that what I am? What if Hyperion debriefs me and then sends me back to Boise? Wandering around that grey town worrying about picking up a stray plague germ and being slammed away in isolated quarantine – ugh! Important mission, my ass! Where's my payoff? My palace? My servants? My power? Go ahead, you Forlani bitches, and laugh at me. Play your para-pas. Cuddle up in your Clusters and rot. Bow down to your matriline. Mother, hah! I could show you a mother you wouldn't bow down to. It's all just a bad joke.*

Suddenly a picture flashed out of the past into Erica's memory. Her little sister Alba, about ten years old, up against the glass in an airport departure lounge, waving goodbye to Erica and her mother who were taxiing out on a jetliner. No room on that flight,

Alba. Don't worry, you'll be on the next flight out and everyone will get together in Paris. Only Mommy Dearest has already spent the money for your ticket to reserve a hotel. No plane ride for you. Don't turn around and look at that man coming up behind you. Enjoy a few minutes of delusion. A few seconds, maybe. Keep on enjoying, keep on hoping as long as you can, until it hurts. Erica squinted and made such a scowl that the signals officer looked alarmed.

"Associate Director Duquesne, anything wrong? Can I get you a glass of water? A pain reliever perhaps? Please sit down here for a moment." He rose and offered her his chair.

"No thanks, I just had... nothing to worry about. I think I need something stronger than water. Just let me know in case there is a reply. I don't expect one, not right away."

Tashto had waited patiently in his sick bay cubicle for the text from his mysterious Blynthian contact who had offered to provide him the information that he sought on the Vloog conflict. Transfer Varess had entered into its "night cycle", and the lights in the hallways had dimmed to conserve power and encourage the station's inhabitants to sleep. In addition, the doors to most of the important parts of the station—including the main conference hall—were automatically locked after 8:00 station time to discourage any further clandestine activity. Tashto's meeting with the Blynthian had to be arranged in the main conference hall, and he had been forced to trust in his contact's assurance that the door lock would be disabled so he could enter for the meeting.   He nervously glanced down at his tablet and saw the text:

It's time now. Doors will be opened for you.

Once Tashto reached the main conference hall, the heavy doors swung open with a loud clicking sound. After stepping inside, he took a minute to take in the spectacle of the large room, and felt oddly disturbed at the stillness and darkness of a place that he had previously associated with excitement and tumult, when he had denounced the Song Pai before a mesmerized audience. Among the tall clear tubes that the Blynthians inhabited, Tashto saw a faint blue light shining out of one on the right. Tashto heard a soft hum as he walked toward it, and one of the wormlike Blynthians swam up the tube to meet him.

Welcome, Tashto of Garan Prime, the screen next to the tube said. **We have much to discuss.**

"I was told the Blynthians knew the truth of what happened in the war between the Vloogs and the Garanians. The official history we were told on Garan Prime appears to have been greatly…sanitized for public consumption."

Interesting.   How did you learn that what you were told was wrong?

Tashto was beginning to find communication with this particular Blynthian unnerving. Although it clearly had no problem understanding his speech through its deciphering machine, it insisted on communicating to him through text. Without even the simulation of vocal pitch and tone, Tashto had no means of understanding the faceless creature's emotions and motives. *Why would it ask me a question like that?* He wondered. *Could this Blynthian be some sort of a spy looking for leverage over me?*

"I was just curious," Tashto responded to the Blynthian. "On Garan Prime we rarely have contact with other species. Some of the people on this station tell stories of Garanian history that are not consistent with those I was familiar with."

And how did you determine that we Blynthians were the ones to ask for the truth?

The second question made Tashto even more nervous. *Could they be wary of our official explanation? Are they already aware of the fact that we helped kidnap Torghh, and are trying to implicate us?* Tashto could not truly understand the Blynthians—those incomprehensible worms, technologically advanced almost beyond comprehension yet so primitive they betrayed no trace of emotion—and he felt a gnawing, instinctive fear of them.

"You are a technologically advanced species, but also a neutral party to the Garanians. We have never gone to war with you, nor have we ever desired to. You seemed like a logical source to go to for information."

One that would not get you in trouble with your government, perhaps?

"The thought had crossed my mind," Tashto said.

Very well.   Much of our information is not allowed to be disseminated to outsiders. However, we know that the Garanians and Vloogs were once allies until the Garanians broke the alliance. Despite this betrayal, some of the Vloogs survived and have been incorporated into being a protectorate of the Blynthians.   Their location is classified.

"The species has not been exterminated? But I was told the Garanians made them extinct!" Tashto said, shocked by the Blynthian's admission.

We do not feel comfortable discussing their location or welfare with a currently active member of the Garanian government.   Of course, if circumstances of your employment were to change, we would be open to treating you differently.

"Good that you place enough trust in the governments and species at this conference that you can be so forthcoming," Tashto hissed sarcastically.

We find that caution is the best policy in such turbulent times, regardless of the environment in which we interact.

"I can't fault that mindset," Tashto replied.

Ayan'we had been called by Ramatoulaye to an urgent meeting. As she walked briskly through the Varess corridors in the direction of Phiddian security, she wondered if something new had turned up on the Powls whom they had interrogated. She never got a chance to ask about them because as soon as she opened the door, her arm was grasped by the Phiddian chief and she was swept towards a corner of the office. Ramatoulaye had a mysterious look that alerted Ayan'we to a new problem. She guessed that the little nook they were in must have been safe from all scanning.

The Phiddian said in urgent, hushed tones, "I must ask you to help me with a very unusual confidential request."

"What's the matter?"

"Fianni seems to have disappeared. We don't know whether or not it's another case of abduction."

"Who would want to abduct a social director? I would think that you or the head delegate would be a more logical target."

"You're right, of course. It may well be something else. But I don't want to start the Phiddian gossip mill going, so I'm afraid to use my own people to investigate and would like to ask if you could spare a few members of the Security Cluster to help me search."

"Absolutely. What else do you think may have happened to Fianni?"

Ramatoulaye turned away and was silent for a few seconds. "Here are the details. As you probably remember from the opening days, Fianni was pregnant. Several days ago there was a miscarriage. That in itself is not unusual among our species. We are normally so prolific that another child here or there is seldom missed. Many consider them irksome burdens anyway. It so happens that Fianni has a skin condition that can be affected by miscarriages, so there was a medical exam right afterwards. At first, nothing unusual was detected. In this case, one bioanalyst was unusually zealous and carried the testing beyond the customary level, eventually detecting a rare substance in Fianni's urine. The analyst spent extra time verifying the strange result after notifying Fianni to return for a recheck. There was no response. I cannot find anyone who has seen Fianni since."

"You think our social director skipped because of the test results? What could they have been?"

"The substance is so rare because we have not encountered it since the last Zetan War. You probably know that the Zetans captured quite a few prisoners from our vessels and used them to develop bioweapons to attack us. This substance, which attacks the nerve tissues, was one that they weaponized. It was not used much because it had an odd side effect that reduced its efficiency. Instead of incapacitating our nervous system immediately, it works slowly and first destroys the pleasure centers in the body. As you can guess, that is something a Phiddian would notice quite quickly. It is totally fatal and the victims died, but not before they could be replaced in their mission by reinforcements. Just how Fianni came in contact with this horror, I cannot imagine."

"No, there are certainly no Zetans at the conference."

"Nor anywhere on Varess."

"They can't disguise themselves very well with those bodies of theirs, so do you think they used a member of another species as an agent?"

"Or perhaps a member of another species present used them as a source."

"That sounds sinister."

"It gets worse. The dose administered to Fianni seems to have been barely sublethal, enough to destroy the pleasure centers in a short time, yet possibly taking many years to progress through the rest of the nervous system."

"By heavens, that would explain her terrible scene the other day. For a Phiddian to live without the prospect of physical pleasure must be torture."

"You're right, Ayan'we, and imagine facing the prospect of gradually being reduced to a vegetative state while craving that pleasure. More than enough reason to commit suicide."

"You think your colleague may have exited into space through a lock?"

"I don't know what to think. I never really liked Fianni and I probably should not waste precious time searching for such a disagreeable snob. Still, I am responsible for security and I would feel ashamed if one of my people disappeared in a tragedy without my doing all I could to save the person."

"I would do the same. Look, we just got the last of our injured personnel back from the Weh hospital ship. The Weh doctors haven't left Varess space, so maybe they could help Fianni if we could search successfully. I can detail three cluster members to you. Remember, though, you'll have to hurry. The Song Pai may decide to leave at any time and we would be obliged to follow. My mother is involved in a last ditch effort to keep them at the Zonal, but she may fail."

"So many things may fail."

"True, but let's remain strong while we still may achieve something. We've recovered two other missing comrades, so maybe we can do the same for Fianni."

There had been no suicidal walk into deep space. The missing person Ayan'we and Ramatoulaye were searching for was in a secret room on the human delegation's ship, waiting for an appointment. Fianni had grown to dislike every aspect of Anthony Wilson since the moment they met: the smell of burnt cigarettes that perpetually hung over his jacket, the acidic know-it-all quality to his vocal tones, the hard stare of his eyes. The Phiddian protocol chief thought the dislike of him would have grown even if he hadn't stolen the thing any of the race valued most in the universe. And yet here they found themselves in his office once more, the visitor's tension overwhelming from glowering at the man to be despised.

"How goes it?" Anthony asked. "Nobody's figured out yet that you were involved with the kidnappings?"

"Not that I know of," Fianni said, with a voice betraying a hint of nervousness.

"You're certain that no one has any suspicions? I'm sure you understand that it's of paramount importance that you keep your involvement secret. Getting compromised could be very hazardous to your health."

Fianni knew all too well that Anthony had no emotional attachment to any living thing, despite his earlier period of apparent lust. It was baffling to a Phiddian that, of all the humans that could have been used for a consort, the one chosen had to be the person least susceptible to emotional manipulation through romantic relations. After all those gushy, dreadful love songs and poems that humans created about being together forever and true love never dying, Fianni had the misfortune of encountering a human that had no capacity for emotional attachment whatsoever! Such a capricious, chaotic species. *I would've had better luck with the Song Pai.*

"Why are you so nervous?" Fianni asked. "I don't think anybody knows about our secrets, not even that damn Ayan'we. If I can keep her from figuring it out, I can keep it secret from anyone on this station."

"They'd better not. You're the best asset available to me for the next phase of the operation."

"You have more tasks for me?"

"Just one. You didn't think I'd let you get your precious antidote in this meeting, did you? Once I give you what you want, I lose all leverage I have over you. I'll be damned if I let you off before I get every last mission I possibly can out of you."

"You...disgusting, lying human *zlishta!* Give me back my yearning emotions, my wild desires! I cannot function without them! A human like you could never understand what the inability to feel true erotic pleasure does to our minds. Every day I exist without the capacity for that joy is a living death."

"When I fed you that formula, the one that disabled the pleasure centers in your brain...that was the closest that your species could experience to rape, wasn't it? Because when we were together, I did things to you that I never could to any human woman, things that would've gotten me convicted for sex felonies back on Earth ten times over. You never minded those, in fact you acted like you *enjoyed* them, yet the moment your pleasure centers went dead, you started to look at me like I was some kind of monster.

Is that how much constant sexual stimulation means to you Phiddians?"

"Yes!" Fianni hissed, with fists clenched. "Does it matter to you how much you can ruin the lives of others through your schemes for personal betterment?"

"Thinking it over, I'd have to say...no. I mean, I do have an interest in case if I have to deal with more Phiddians later on, it's good to know what makes your species tick and all. But in terms of you specifically Fianni, and what happens in your life...your only value to me is as an asset on this station. If, and only if, you serve me loyally, will I give you what you want. So take a good long look at this bomb, because it's the only way you'll ever feel 'alive' again."

Anthony opened the briefcase on his desk. Inside was an ugly, misshapen, vaguely cylindrical thing with bits of metal jutting out and a softly flashing light on the bottom end. It was small enough for even the less muscular Phiddian to easily clutch in one hand.

"Be very careful with that bomb," Anthony said. "It's filled with delicate censors and highly combustible chemicals, so you should only ever press one button on it: the small, yellow flashing light you see on the top. Once you press that, you'll have about 10 minutes to get out of the blast zone. Don't worry about the size, it's small enough to slip unobtrusively into the Geat Hall, and powerful enough to blow the hell out of the whole place and anyone who tries to approach to disarm it. You just peel off that patch and use the adhesive to put it right up against the Blynthian tubes. Don't even bother to try to conceal it. It expands. Much less effort than what you've already pulled off for me."

"Well, that's a relief. Why should I believe this is the last mission you have for me?"

"Because we may not have much time left before the conference ends. Something's afoot among the opposition that may give them an opening for peace instead of war. I've already set another operation in motion and all I need is a little interval to pull it off. Then it won't really matter what happens to the rest. This final task is the only thing I have left to plan within the amount of time I have left here. Speaking of that...don't start overthinking things and trying to get any sort of personal revenge on anyone behind my back. That might over-complicate events to the point that we may not be able to cover up this operation any more. Then you might find yourself dead without ever tasting that sweet pleasure again in your life. I know you wouldn't want that."

"No," Fianni said, barely able to control swelling rage and disgust, "I would not. But I don't trust that this will be my last mission as long as you have any sort of leverage over me. When will I get the antidote, anyway? Give me a time and place now."

"Six bells station time outside the Passion Gem Lounge. I'll give you the vial and you can take it inside to a private room and use it." Anthony smirked and added, "You are learning things about us humans, aren't you? You've already got it down that you should never quite trust us. Anything else?"

"Nothing that I'd like to say aloud. Nothing that I'd say if I wasn't worried about further punishment from you." *Or betrayal, curse it! If I could I would stick to you like glue until I get that vial. Oh, how I wish the other four were still available now to tail him.*

"Damn straight. Be sure to keep it that way if you want even the faint hope of me restoring you to what you used to be."

Fianni could only focus the rage inward, as the mind stewed in hatred of all the enemies on the station.   Anthony...Ayan'we...that   other   robot, Torghh...and especially, Entara, the blasted diplomat who was so important in orchestrating the talks. How could there be any satisfaction in this situation, unable to feel sexual pleasure indefinitely, suffering at the whims of a hated man? A certain sadistic, violent corner of the Phiddian's mind had steadily taken control since Anthony's tampering. It began to focus on Entara, and a plan that could not only ruin the conference, but perhaps undermine Anthony's position as well. *How could Anthony possibly keep this operation secret if Entara were to be assassinated? Finally some personal leverage, a measure of control. No, not yet. First the bomb, then the antidote, then the revenge. I want it all.*

At last the moment agreed upon for Trevor's meeting with the Song Pai had arrived. Entara made a little nod to each of the members of the cephalopod delegation and began, "I have asked this audience to present to you the human Trevor, who has information so important to these proceedings that it cannot be postponed."

The chief delegate eyed Trevor. "We recognize this human. He has sojourned on Song Pa. Though he is not indentured, we have tolerated him for two reasons. First, he seems relatively unafraid of death. Also, he has provided us with useful information on other humans. But he is useless to us now."

Entara responded immediately, "I hope to show that he is useful, now more than ever. In fact, what he knows is so connected to our mission at this Varess conference that the knowledge cannot wait."

"How can he help us with this upcoming war? This human, we know, does not believe in war. His people are scratchers of the soil, nourishers of leafy things, cleaners of beasts. Of strategies, he is ignorant. He will never feel the battle lust. He has no slashing claw, no wish to bathe in blood." The delegate turned directly to Trevor and advanced until he was nearly touching him. "What do you dare to tell us, human, of how we should fight, when we have chased your braver individuals from more than one system?"

"What I have to say," Trevor calmly replied, "concerns things that all may not hear. I will talk of the Carrion Age, and the Time Before Tides."

An agitation stirred in the Song Pai delegation, a waving of tentacles, exchanges of worried looks. The chief delegate blinked each of his eyes in sequence, turned off his translator, and addressed his followers in what to Forlani and human ears were merely strings of bubbles and castanet-like clicks of the beak.

This ground-scratcher will speak of things that none but the Many-scarred are normally permitted to hear. On Song Pa, none of you could attend. Remember, though, that the rules of our mission require changes for expediency. So it will be the duty of some unworthies to behave far beyond their station. This is my command. No discussion. I will require two witnesses, Mmm and Yii. And three recorders, Polp, Vrr, and Kl. All else depart. It will be too essential to be left to the memory of any one person who could be targeted. If any of us dies, the others must pass on the information to authorities. All who survive will appear before the Many-scarred. Now swear by the Flow of Generation.

The five who had remained behind when the others left repeated in chorus what the chief delegate had sworn. They tried to appear resolute, in attention at attack stance, but somewhere inside they all quivered with anxiety. All Song Pai lived in awe of the Many-scarred, those who had flung themselves time and again into horrible onslaughts but had by some miracle always survived and bore the marks to show it. They could only be selected by others of their kind. Once they were, they enjoyed a perpetual privilege of spawning as long as they wished, but otherwise they withdrew from everyday life. They lurked together in dark places at the bottom of reefs where no one was permitted to join them. Sometimes a group would go up on the land to taboo places and everyone gave them a wide berth of privacy. They alone were the repositories of secrets, beyond any responsibility but that which they created themselves. The witnesses and recorders were poised and ready. The chief delegate switched his translator back on and spoke first to Entara.

"You realize what this request means?"

"Of course. I am the guarantor of this earthling's speech. I will feel your claw if he speaks wrongly."

"Now," said the delegate to Trevor, "Say what you have to say."

"I have studied and gathered data in many places on Song Pa and on other worlds, some of which you have never visited. You know that my research concerns the idea of the Spiritual Substrate."

"Yes," responded the delegate impatiently, "But you should have learned that those theories are of no interest to us."

"Sadly," said Trevor, "And those very inquiries brought to my attention the Ancient Ones, the Groundlings of Song Pa and their fascination with angelic beings."

The delegate gave a bob of recognition, as Trevor went on, "I must explain for Entara's understanding, since her life is forfeit to my testimony, that these angelic beings are supposed to be completely immaterial creatures, spiritual entities unbound by physical laws of the universe, half-gods, if you will – not omnipotent, but apparently unlimited in the use of the powers they do possess."

"Incredible as is seems, I take your knowledge for true," Entara murmured, uncomfortable as any Forlani with concepts that delve beyond the physical world.

The delegate asked Trevor, "What do you know of the Ancient Groundlings, those awkward ones who tottered on their land limbs?"

"Those Ancient Ones left your ancestors alone in the seas. They cared little for the salty waters, which irritated their bodies. They ate only plants and cared nothing for those that grew in the oceans. Once they had learned to get from one land mass to another through the air, they abandoned the depths to your kind and the other sea creatures, looking only upward. They were clever, those Groundlings, and very united in purpose. It took them little time to soar above the surface of Song Pa and visit the other planets of your system, then systems beyond."

The cephalopod leader concurred, "Clever they were, and united in purpose, but their thinking was also fickle and senseless. Their purpose in the Path of Generation was to leave things behind for us to employ more skillfully in the quest for honor."

"Yes, for I have discovered that their united purpose turned to a goal your species has never aimed at – they wanted to transcend material to become angelic beings."

The word caused a stir among the Song Pai, who twitched their tentacles in a way Entara had never seen before. Intuition told her it was an unfamiliar sense of awe the cephalopods normally concealed from others and also from each other. Trevor had crossed over into the realm of the sacred that was dangerous territory.

The human went on. "Many learned people on other worlds, who have made it their business to know you, have discovered something of the history of the Ancient Groundlings and their search for transcendent perfection. They know you judge this to be a grave error, not only in practical terms, but in spiritual ones, as well."

"True."

"The learned people also found out that the Song Pai consider this error to be due not only to the Groundlings themselves, but to the influence of others they encountered in space. Others who encouraged and misled the Groundlings out of jealousy and hatred. That these evil others were the Blynthians."

"We have never conversed of this openly beyond our seas."

"I realize that. And what I have to reveal to you is that for all this time, you have been wrong."

Tentacles waved and an uproar broke out, until the Head Delegate clashed his own claw hooks together with such a smack that it quieted the Song Pai.

The Delegate spoke now with added gravity and menace. "From this point on, human, if you speak without truth or proof, your life is forfeit. Do you realize this?"

"Respectfully, I do. I assure you that I am just as prepared to die as you are."

The Song Pai changed color and Entara inferred this was a move from outright hostility to guarded admiration. Fearlessness could never be entirely negative to them.

"What is an angelic being, Delegate? It is more than a creature of goodness, a creature of innocence, a creature with regard for the sacred, even a creature accomplishing the divine mission of providing for the advancement and generation of the species. It is a creature that has reached beyond all that is material, all that is physical, one that has passed into an existence that is purely spiritual, without the need for all the machines and technologies that were their legacy for you. Do you not admit, Wise One, that the

Groundlings sought to dematerialize themselves completely? That they sought to leave their bodies behind to achieve an immortal and ethereal existence? One that would never end?"

Slushy murmurs once again spread among the cephalopods. The Head Delegate reassured and quieted them with a swerving movement of his body. "You have indeed gone far in discovering that which is only entrusted to the most experienced, the most worthy in our seas. So why do you blaspheme by saying we are wrong to blame the treachery of the Blynthians? For they must have known that the transcendence sought by the Groundlings could only be temporary and illusory."

"Yes, Wise One. Truly the Groundlings found a way, through their cleverness, to project their intelligence away from their bodies, leaving them in dormancy. It involved altering their genes and abandoning the path of generation. They were willing to make that sacrifice in their quest to become immortal. How they must have reveled in their new consciousness, free from any material! When they extended this wonderful privilege to everyone on the planet, it must have felt like paradise, and they must have exalted for a time. Too long. Because they were shocked to find out it was one thing to leave physical existence and another to come back. Because organic intelligence ultimately must be reconnected with the organic body or it will dissipate and dissolve. How they must have suffered in those final instants as they sought to return to the physical, before their intelligence winked out of existence, leaving barely a trace. Nothing was left but a race of cadavers, carrion to the scavengers of Song Pa."

"And how much the perfidious Blynthians must have rejoiced to see their rivals destroyed," loudly added the Delegate. "How their unholy laughter must have filled the cosmos."

"Only lamentations, Delegate. For what you do not know yet is that the Blynthians actually did speak to the Groundlings about transcendence, but it was to warn them, rather than to encourage them."

"What! Heed what lies you tell, human, for they will be your last." Already the Delegate was brandishing his own claw hooks to strike.

"You mentioned truth and proof."

Trevor's objection stopped the tentacles in mid-motion. "How can you prove such a wild suggestion?"

"As I said before, Wise One, learned scholars on other worlds knew of what was transpiring even as it happened. In my pilgrimage, I have found recorded testimony in four places, and one of them is on Song Pa itself, so you can easily check it. The other three are on worlds where archive keepers are prepared right now to attest to what I state. I will give you their coordinates and you can verify it yourself. You will see that the revelations of forgotten documents will at last allow you to be able to fully comprehend inscriptions on Song Pa that your elders have long debated."

There was a reverent pause among the Song Pai as the message sank in. "This could change everything," the Delegate slowly admitted.

"The evil ones you sought to punish in just warfare have become the would-be benefactors of your Ancient Ones. If only the Groundlings had listened. I am sure your race will not repeat their mistakes."

The Delegate turned to Entara and said, "Honorable ally, please lead the courageous human to a safe and hospitable place. We people of the sea have much to discuss and investigate."

8

Ayan'we had been dozing and dreaming of eating Earth fruit with her friend Amanda Pedersen-Klein when her multi-sensorial alarm activated, buzzing, vibrating, flashing a strobe, and emitting an acrid odor, so that a Forlani could not avoid being roused immediately by a multiple assault indicating danger. She hopped up and saw that the location indicator showed the great conference hall. She motioned to Leli and Pulanate, who had approached when they heard and smelled her warning, to follow her and the three of them sped down the corridors of the station. When they reached the hall, they saw that other security forces had begun to assemble: some Blastöo, Ramatoulaye and a few Phiddians, a Thil. They clustered around a team of Robotic Guild guardians who seemed to be in charge of the scene. Ayan'we spotted at once the cause for concern – a layer of some suspicious substance had been applied around the base of the Blynthian tubes and various unfamiliar devices that were stuck into it.

The Guild commander KC moved over to her. "I have just been explaining that an explosive mining material, Uk-12, has been used to make a bomb at the base of the tubes. We discovered it during a patrol a short while ago and found no other bombs in the hall."

"And those things are detonators, I suppose?" queried Ayan'we, pointing at the objects protruding from the gooey Uk-12.

Ramatoulaye stepped up and answered before the robot could. "I recognize them. Unfortunately. They are an advanced model just put into service in our military."

Ayan'we was puzzled. "Haven't you taken steps to disarm the devices?"

Ramatoulaye shook her head. "Impossible. This monstrosity contains secondary anti-personnel measures that will kill anything that approaches, organic or mechanical."

It figured. The Phiddians were held by other species to be miserable soldiers, but perhaps because of that, they excelled at designing all manner of traps that could remotely destroy the enemies they were unable to defeat in person.

"That was our conclusion, too," added KC. "My guardians have cordoned off the area scanned by the detonators and it covers that half of the hall. We have no experience with this technology and are communicating with Guild bases to get ideas about how to approach and disarm. Frankly, we have no answers yet."

"It all seems overly contrived and elaborate," mused Ayan'we. "Why not just blow up the tubes before leaving?"

"It is more clever than you realize." The voice was that of Kee'ad of Tionar, who had arrived during the conversation. "If the tubes were destroyed, we could start replacing them right away. As it is, the whole conference hall is rendered useless until further notice."

Ramatoulaye was equally mystified. "But if the goal was to stop any settlement between the Blynthians and the Song Pai, as is now rumored, couldn't all delegates simply communicate electronically?"

"Indeed, no," interjected the Kael security chief, who alit next to them after inspecting the situation from above. "You see, the Song Pai, like several other delegations here, will only agree to abide by a diplomatic treaty approved *in the presence*. There must be physical proximity and acknowledgment for the terms to be binding, both on them and on others."

"Yes," Tionar added. "This is in effect a very elegant means of preventing a treaty from being ratified. No doubt the perpetrators count on provoking the start of hostilities right away, before the bomb can be disarmed. And who knows how long it will take to disarm this thing?"

"I see," Ramatoulaye agreed. "We Phiddians ourselves cannot disarm these devices except by sacrificing assets such as suicide dummies for several days to wear down the defensive power supply. And it would be a tremendous risk to allow a fail-safe detonation of the exposed Uk-12. It could destroy not only the entire hall, but a good part of the station, forcing evacuation. It seems we are stymied."

The Kael was scratching his wing, as they do when in deep thought. "Perhaps we could employ a buffer shield that would absorb much of the explosive shock? Those tubes are quite strong, able to withstand Blynthian atmospheric pressure, so if we could deaden the blast by, say 80 %, wouldn't that solve the problem?"

"That's not a bad idea. If we could cover the UK-12 to prevent air from reaching it for a few milliseconds, that would also make it possible to detonate inside the station. But how could we get close enough to install the buffer material?"

Ayan'we had also been deep in thought, but suddenly she remembered something. "Tell me, what would this buffer shield be composed of?"

"What we use," the Kael answered, "is a viscous liquid that sets into a colloidal foam with layers of dead air in between. Simple enough to make with ordinary chemicals, but as my Phiddian colleague points out, how could we approach to set it up?"

"A viscous liquid, is it?   I just may know someone who can help." Ayan'we stepped back a bit and whispered into her communicator.   Then she nodded to the others, "He's on the way."

Less than three minutes later, Isshel burst through the doors of the hall, running at full tilt – not bad for a Forlani male. A few seconds later, he was followed by a Kholod carrying several boxes and sprinting along on his webbed lower limbs at a pace almost equaling Isshel. So unlike their usual menial shuffle. Ayan'we rapidly explained the problem to the artist.

"Certainly. My stasis projection equipment can move up to several thousand litres of liquid through the air and place it around those bombs in a matter of a few minutes."

"Brilliant!"   applauded   Tionar,   touching Ayan'we's hand in respect.   "It won't set off the antipersonnel devices because it is neither mechanical nor organic, just a cloud of inert foam. I'll bet even the Phiddian weapons makers haven't thought of that scenario."   Ramatoulaye   and   the   Kael   sent messengers off to obtain the required chemicals and they returned to say that luckily most of them had already been mixed and only a single titration was necessary to produce five thousand litres of buffering compound. Ten ship minutes later, just as Isshel was finished assembling his apparatus, relays of Kholods began appearing with heavy containers of the stuff.

Under Isshel's skillful direction, columns of buffering compound were soon floating into the air and across the hall to settle over the Uk-12 and the detonators. A great blob of foam engulfed the base of the tubes to a height of several meters, until the Kael waved a wing to indicate the quantity was sufficient. Then he timed it mentally while it set, finally announcing it should be ready.

At that point the Guild chief stepped forward and warned, "You organics should now retire behind the protective barriers my units have set in place. We will take it from here."

One of the mechanical guardians began inching forward bit by bit, and all at once there was a muffled popping sound as the Uk-12 and the detonators exploded together. Success. The tubes did not crack at all. The "suicide" robot raised a limb to assure his comrades that he had not been harmed by the detonator pulse that, without the foam, would have fried him as quickly as it would a being of flesh and blood. There was whooping and whistling and flapping in celebration from the various security details who had watched. Ayan'we was about to give some orders to Lila and Pulanate when a tracked guardian who had been examining the floor of the hall near the side door rolled up and told them, "Chief, delegates, there is something over here that you should perhaps examine."

They walked to the area the tracked unit had been scrutinizing and saw nothing. A mechanical arm pointed to a place on the floor and informed them, "Organic perspiration has been found in a trail from here to the exit.   My chemical analysis counterpart is working on it now."

A very compact, circular mechanoid with about twenty limbs reported, "It is Phiddian. Most likely the result of hasty flight."

Ramatoulaye looked shocked, "Are you sure it's not from me or one of my aides who have been assisting in the disarming?"

"Negative. Volatilization rates verify the deposit was left here about five ship minutes before our routine patrol arrived, long before your presence. It was another Phiddian."

Ayan'we glanced at Ramatoulaye, who murmured, "Fianni!" and rushed away with the rest of the Phiddian contingent.

The crowd dispersed as Kholods began to clean up the debris of bombs and foam. Isshel, after accepting a round of congratulations, started to take apart his machinery and pack it. Ayan'we turned to Leli and Pulanate and said, "I will help Isshel in his packing."

Pulanate understood and took Leli's hand, giving one finger a little pinch. A Forlani signal. "Then if you don't need us right now, Cluster Leader, we will go compose our report so that you will not be delayed in checking it." The two left discreetly as Ayan'we bent to assist the male and whispered, "There are some things I want you to know."

She passed him some tubing. "I'm very pleased with the discreet way you've handled things since our incident."

"You deserve no less. I suppose that's true of me, too. I really would have had some terrible explaining to do if we had gone farther. Both to the Brotherhood and to my wives. Oh, slime, I probably would have had to appear before your matriline, as well, and that would have shamed me for life."

"Well, I thought I'd better tell you I've decided to talk about it with Mother. If I don't, I think it would be even more awkward in the long run. I'm confident we can trust her, though."

"Yes, of course. You have every right to do so. If we can't trust Entara-para-pa, who could we possibly trust? Should she decide something else needs to be done, I will abide by her judgment, no matter what the consequences."

"Even if it costs you your standing in the Brotherhood?"

"If it must be, it will be."

Ayan'we reflected for a minute. "You realize we'll still have to be together for the voyage away from Varess. Peace or war, there's no altering that."

"Yes, I thought about that, too. I've decided to launch a new project to keep me busy for the waking section of the trip home. That should make it a little easier."

"Good. I'm sure I can think of something on my end so that we won't be bumping into each other too much. You know, even if we had let go of ourselves and mated, I wouldn't feel that you had dishonored me in any way.   It was a surprise to both of us. Unavoidable, I guess. Do you feel that way?"

"Much the same. I think you're a wonderful person, but remember, I have already made commitments that I would have been breaking. Not so much on account of unfaithfulness as far as my wives are concerned. They might not even have objected. Neither has ever said anything about being jealous of a possible third wife. It's that all the lines would be scandalized because of my individual fault. I have to admit, sooner or later, that shame would have worn away at personal affection I felt for you."

"I hadn't come to that conclusion yet, but you're right. Mother is involved in some great projects for our whole society.   She's sure to encounter some opposition, and a scandal involving me would be truly harmful."

"Ayan'we, if you want, I am willing to break off all contact with you. If that would help you stay free of problems. Look, you may decide to get..."

"Let's not go that far right now. We can be cordial for the rest of the assignment and leave open the chance of communicating again some time in the future if we feel we need to." Ayan'we knew that Isshel had been about to broach the subject of an upcoming marriage for her, and that was one topic she was certainly not prepared to delve into with anybody at this point. Except, she mused, maybe Amanda. Somehow she might understand.

In a special quadruped passenger compartment of the Blynthian ship, a certain Garanian was growing bored. He had been concealed there ever since his previous interview with the wormlike creatures in the deserted great hall. They assured him that it was safer than staying in the medical isolation ward any longer. The Blynthians had to smuggle him aboard through an external hatch after disguising him as a member of an interspecies hull maintenance crew. Once he was inside, his exosuit had been occupied by a "squishy" hologram that walked it back onto the station and promptly disappeared. The operation had been timed to coincide with the departure of some supply freighters to suggest that he had departed already into deep space. The dinosaurian flexed his claws on hands and feet and admitted that his weird hosts seemed to be well schooled in the game of interplanetary intrigue. Tashto had always found the tubes of the Blynthians unnerving, standing tall like some kind of cyclopean monuments in the rooms of Transfer Varess they frequented. Even humans and other aliens who had traveled frequently offworld and encountered other unusual species often found interaction with the Blynthians to be a surreal, difficult experience.   A compartment portal opened and Torghh emerged, precisely on time. He had been summoned to attend the next interview and had had no trouble coming straight through the atmosphere and pressure of the Blynthian ship. A circle in the ceiling widened and a Blynthian tube came down to the floor. Together, they walked up to it and Tashto pressed a small green button on the panel on the side. As he gave a soft hiss to relax himself, he watched as one of the worms leisurely undulated its way down the glass tube to meet them.

You have returned to us, Tashto of Garan Prime, the screen said. **What do you seek from us this time?**

Doctor Torghh answered for Tashto. "He seeks asylum on your homeworld. Please grant him an audience to plead his case."

This is a very unusual request. Tashto is surely aware that we Blynthians very rarely grant asylum to offworlders. I must summon others to act as a committee to determine the approval of your request.

The Blynthian made a series of sharp buzzing sounds that Tashto could barely discern through the glass. Three other Blynthians leisurely swam down into other tubes that lowered into the room and began to communicate with the first one through rapid zips. After a couple of minutes, the Blynthians became silent again, and another text appeared on the first screen.

Please explain to us why you seek asylum on our world, Tashto.

Tashto took a deep breath as he prepared to explain his flight. He could feel his neck feathers rising out of nervousness but made a conscious effort to push them back down. Then he began to explain his plight to the Blynthians. "I cannot return to my homeworld. I have committed a grievous crime against my government, in the interests of galactic peace and the liberty of another being. By doing so, I became an enemy of the state and would be murdered if I returned to Garan Prime or tried to seek shelter in most other places. The Garanian Secret Service is so efficient that it would be able to exterminate me on most planets, but the homeworld of the Blynthians is off-limits even to them."

What crime did you commit that was so severe that you are now an outlaw to the Garanians?

"I saved Doctor Torghh from captivity, working with the Forlani Ayan'we and Torghh's colleague Rack. This thwarted the Garanian government's objective to disrupt the peace conference on Transfer Varess. I was originally assigned by my superiors on Garan Prime to guarantee the failure of those negotiations, so their interest in liquidating me is as much about a desire for vengeance as it is to prevent me from disseminating information on their methods and goals."

Doctor Torghh, can you verify the truth of what Tashto says?

"As far as I can tell, he speaks the truth," Torghh said. "However, I was in sleep mode at the time of my recovery, so I cannot detail exactly how my rescue occurred. Only Tashto can tell you that. I can tell you that he has been helpful to Rack and me since the moment he defected from his service to the Garanian government."

Tashto, what do you have to offer the Blynthians?

"I have a tremendous amount of intel..."

Although that is useful, there is no guarantee of the truth of such information. Sometimes a spy or refugee may lie about having valuable information to obtain a guarantee of safety. We require from you a physical commodity as proof of your goodwill to us. Please bring us the most advanced technological equipment you have, so we may consider your request.

Tashto felt an odd sense of regret as he realized what he had to give up to obtain his safety. The pulse rifle was a wondrous, powerful weapon, its specifications and manufacturing process a secret to all the rivals of the Garanians, especially the hated Song Pai. Some tiny loyalist Garanian core in the back of his brain remained disgusted with the thought of relinquishing its secrets to the Blynthians even now.

Forcing his instinct and trained behaviors down with the full strength of his rational mind, Tashto opened his backpack and put the pulse rifle on a table in front of the Blynthians' tubes.

He watched as two small drones flew down from the metal casing that connected the Blynthians' tubes to the ceiling. The two drones hovered over the pulse rifle, scanning it with their beady red electronic eyes as they softly whirred. Then, as suddenly as they had first emerged, the two drones quickly flitted back into the metal casing they had come from.

Your offering is exceptionally interesting... and accepted. You are hereby granted permanent asylum by the Blynthians.

Tashto had no emotional energy left for a yell of triumph or tears of joy. He only released a calming sigh to commemorate his success in one of the most unorthodox negotiations of his life.

The next station day, when the debris from the bombs had been cleared from the great hall, all the delegations were abuzz with anticipation of a breakthrough in the peace talks. Rumors swirled around the lounges and common areas and soon confirmed that all the delegation ships that had been making ready for departure in case of war had stood down, including the Song Pai. The only exception was one human dispatch vessel that had warped out in the middle of the station night, taking some of their representatives. Without breaking confidence with her cephalopod allies, Entara had hinted to the Rokol, the Kael, and the Talinians that a change of attitude might be taking place if the right encouragements could be offered.

Thus, when the next session came to order, the Kael ambassador rose, opened his wings to full span, folded them again, and began, "I wish to address my esteemed counterparts from Song Pa, brave now as they have been in the past, and always ready to hear words of honor. Because no one here doubts the might of these warriors or their desire to fling themselves into battle, I am sure that they will be willing to hear a modest proposition in the cause of justice. There is nothing more fitting to assure honor as tribute. So we offer as tribute to Song Pa our watery moon of Elceph, suitable for their colonization, should they see fit to make a small delay in their immediate military plans for the next zonal cycle."

Before the Song Pai could respond, Tionar lit his light to speak and added that in recognition of this well-deserved arrangement, his people could not add any real territory fit for the cephalopods, but they felt that a cession of photon mining rights in their system was an addition not unworthy of consideration.

Then the Song Pai head delegate rose to his full height and, flashing a glorious red and blue, began to burble in his idiom, as the translators rendered, "Worthy, very worthy tribute for any race these offers. Happy and flattering words to hear. Yet, accept we cannot, for to accept tribute in anticipation of a battle that will not be given would make us too unworthy of these marvelous things.   Let the Kael keep their beautiful moon and the Newts their rich photons. Learning has happened.   Understanding has happened.   From this time forward, the Song Pai are unwilling to make war on the Blynthians.   Their righteousness had been hidden from us, like a pearl in a cloud of muddy water.   Now we know, and this wisdom makes everyone better.   The Blynthians are worshipful, as we are, of the Great Generation, as are our allies the Rokol and the Forlani.   These we do not kill, nor do we consider it fitting to die by their actions. If our older words made you think otherwise, chase them away.   A new current of clarity flows across all these reefs."

The Blynthians buzzed in response.   "We welcome alliance with the Song Pai.   We invite you to fight beside us and for us, as you do with other allies. However, an alliance must be sealed, so we insist that you accept this."   A hologram of a great water world studded with islands appeared in the middle of the hall. "A planet unknown to all your races, lying within the restricted part of our realm.   Absolutely suited to the physiological needs of the Song Pai, as our advisor has certified."   Torghh rose and made a universally recognized nod of approval.

The translators continued, "With it comes an unhindered corridor of access through our space.

Sovereign henceforth to Song Pa. We and others will only enter with your permission. Your access to the native creatures of this world is complete. Engineer it, exploit it as you will. We only ask that you accept a team of Weh advisors who will alert you to any environmental dangers for the native species."

"We accept this honor."

"There is more! It is not right to ask you to reject the possibility to die and to guarantee your seed will pass on. There will be another corridor, leading in the far direction. There you will find a new enemy, a cunning and ruthless civilization that threatens the peace in that sector. They will never back away from your challenge. I add that they will actually test your courage as none have done before. Do you also accept this honor?"

The Song Pai had already given respectful gestures and color changes at the first part of the offer, but at the mention of a military challenge, there was an enthusiastic waving of tentacles and clacking of claw blades. "Let this be a treaty! In the presence, we affirm this. All must remember. A new alliance and a new glory."

There was general jubilation around the room, manifested in a dozen different ways by the various races. Even the humans eventually rose to join the Blastöo in their dancing, despite the fact that half their chairs were now empty. Ayan'we caught Entara's attention and pointed to the empty chair of the dour Anthony Wilson. Finally the celebration started to calm down and signal lights began to go on as other races quickly moved to add clauses to the Zonal Treaty before the adjournment. Entara awaited her turn and the Forlani clauses were approved instantly. Everyone seemed to be getting what they wanted now that the prospect of war was gone. A Garanian, some kin of Tashto as Ayan'we recalled, had taken his place in their delegation. The reptilian (what was his name, Bashon?) had clabbered together a hasty trade deal with the Phiddians, arms for gems, that would give the leaders on Garan Prime a consolation for the failure of their military plans and the apparent defection of his cousin, so he gave a toothy grim of satisfaction when it was approved. It took a couple more station hours before the last of the worlds finished their wish lists and the conference was declared at an end.

Ayan'we had just begun to hope that the end of the conference would give her a few minutes to be alone with Entara and talk about her near-mating with Isshel when two Song Pai approached and texted that their head delegate wished to meet with Entara one more time before immediate departure. Ayan'we was miffed, but accompanied her mother and the cephalopods, signaling to Leli, Pulanate, and two others to follow them. The group had turned a corner in a corridor near the Song Pai ship when a voice called out behind them, "Halt or you die! Turn around and face me, you scum!"

It was Fianni, all alone and armed with a formidable-looking sidearm.   The closer of the two Song Pai focused a couple of eyes on her and ever so slowly extended a claw hook to swing at the Phiddian, happy to have a chance for death in combat in the middle of the boring peace fest that the conference had become.   Ayan'we held up a hand and commanded, "No. Wait." She inched toward Entara to try to get between her and the attacker. The other Forlani were doing likewise. *This is absurd. We're all trying to see who will die first. Can't help it.*

Entara softly asked, "Fianni, why are you doing this? We mean you no harm."

"That's right," Ayan'we interrupted.   "Listen, Fianni, we know what you've been going through. We know about the miscarriage. And the infection. We feel your pain. We can help you."

"Help me?" Fianni seemed confused and lowered the weapon just a little. "Pain? What do you know about pain? You can still feel pleasure. You can feel it all each time a child slides out of you into this rotten universe. Over and over again. Not me. Not any more." Suddenly there was anger again. "And now he's gone, gone with the antidote. There's no hope."

"There's always hope," Entara assured her.

"It's all your fault. Everything I tried, you ruined. You and that brat of yours."

"We can restore you. Make you whole. Torghh and Rack, they can do it."

"No, you don't understand. I'm Phiddian. They will never allow me to be restored. I am a traitor. They will leave me this way forever. It's torture! I can't stand it!"

Entara pleaded, "No, you can come with us. Back to Forlan. We'll give you asylum, amnesty."

"Yes, I'm sure you will. Always one step ahead of me. I'm sick of you having your way. Sick of you. I'll kill you!"

It all happened in the wink of a human eye. Lila anticipated the flash of the weapon and covered Ayan'we's body with her own. Pulanate leapt forward to take the blow herself, but she was too late. The blow hit Lila with immense force in the back and crumpled her. By the time it hit, the assassin's weapon arm had been lopped off in one sweep of a Song Pai tentacle hook. "Hah!" said the Song Pai guard, slapping a patch over the bloody stump to stop the traumatic bleeding. He burbled something to his comrades that meant, "Wish I could play with this one for a good long while, but orders are orders. Has to be in condition to squeal."

Entara slowly stepped up to Fianni, who was writhing on the floor and tearing at the patch. She wanted to bleed out. "Oh, this is so useless, Fianni. I was telling the truth." She tried to replace the patch, but Fianni pawed at her with the other arm.

"No. Leave me, I know what I'm doing. I want it." The Phiddian looked up Entara with a glazed expression. "Sorry. It will be... ohhh!"

"Who did this to you, Fianni, I know it wasn't really you. Who hurt you?"

Ayan'we was standing next to them now and had a horrible thought. *No, it couldn't be! Did we let ourselves be tricked?* "Fianni, was it the Garanians? Was it Tashto?"

"Not him. Not him. Humans. Anthony." There was a final spasm. "Ericaaa."

The Forlani heard Pulanate call out them, "Leaders, please come now." The Phiddian was dead. Now it was time to tend to their own beloved. Ayan'we bent over Lila's collapsed body. "Don't worry, Lila. Well done. We'll heal you."

"Ah! It hurts like hell!" yelled Lila.

On the scene in a flash, Torghh had rushed up to her with syringe in mechanical hand. "This sedative will take away your pain."

"No! Not yet!"

Surprised, Torghh retorted, "Well, if you don't want to be free of pain, I'll just do a little diagnosis." He turned Lila onto her side while he examined her back.

"Yiiii!" shouted Lila, wriggling in pain.

"Let us give you something," pleaded Ayan'we.

"Not yet, Cluster Leader. I need to feel this. Ah! It's good. This will remind me."

"Remind you of what?"

"That I really don't have to envy you at all from now on. This should have been yours. Ahhh!"

"Envy? Me? Why? You just risked your life for me."

"Don't ask. Don't need to know. OOOh! Too complicated."

Pulanatae shook her head to discourage Ayan'we from probing further.

Torghh, who had been passing several sensors over Lila's back, pronounced. "Damaged spine. Needs surgery. Rack, have the duplicator start on a Forlani eleventh vertebra, standard plus .763 millimeters. Type C closure. And get the lab to prepare for a stem cell culture. We may need to add a little tissue work. Now, officer," he said directly to Lila, "Are you at last ready for sedation? In any case, you have no choice. I'm the physician," he added, plunging the syringe into her neck.

It began to take effect immediately. Ayan'we turned to speak with another guard. Lila pulled Pulanate close enough to whisper, "Can you stay beside me? Don't tell Ayan'we, but I'm getting a little scared."

"I won't leave you."

Torghh was not looking at them, but of course his vibro-sensors picked up every hushed word. He spoke to Rack in machine language. "Scared!" with a signal that passed for a snort among members of the Robotic Guild. "Organisms! What do you think of that, assistant? Why it's nothing more than simple back surgery. Apprentice work! I could do it with only infrared and one grasper. Nothing elegant like replacing a Weh eyepod."

"Indeed, main unit. Ordinary for you. Why even I..."

"Easy, Rack, Just because you performed a successful resuscitation, don't get cocky. Still, I admit it was good work. Neatly done. You deserve an upgrade to senior medical assistant. Who knows, perhaps a little training is in order and you can qualify soon as an auxiliary surgeon. Easy stuff at first, naturally, closing up after intrusive operations. Then perhaps something not too demanding like Coriolan vascular replacement. I have complete confidence in you."

Rack seemed alarmed. "Will that mean you will be sending me off and replacing me?"

"Of course not! Don't be daft. It takes a lot of time to adapt to an assistant. You can do it while I'm on a rotation close to a training center."

"Thank you so much, main unit."

"That's all right, Rack. Don't get maudlin."

Ayan'we escorted her mother to the Song Pai meeting and then caught up with the medical staff taking Lila's immobilized body to the operating room. By the time Torghh and Rack were done, Entara's meeting was over and she had gone back to the

Forlani ship to start procedures for their return. Ayan'we reported to her right away.

"Mother, our doctor friends were completely succesful."

"I had been hoping for that. The fact that Leli was in so much pain was actually a good sign, because if her spine had been completely broken, she would not have felt much."

"That's exactly what they said. They were able to start operating right away, without waiting for tissue to be grown, because the Weh had an extensive tissue bank in their hospital ship and sent some over right away.   They had to splice some into the spinal column.   Lila also has two new vertebrae that they fabricated specially for her after scanning in the adjoining ones and the pieces that had been fractured. Torghh even asked Rack to do the closing up, because he has now been promoted somehow and will go on to train as a full-fledged surgeon."

"That's wonderful. Will Lila be able to return to duty in the security force?"

"Torghh said she will need several months of rehabilitation, but it appears likely she will. In any case, she'll be ready to come back with us on the ship."

"We'll take very good care of her and she'll have plenty of rest." Entara gave her daughter a knowing look. "And so will you. You can now be assured that this big assignment has worked out well for you. I know the official part is not as important to you as the fact that you could protect Quatilla and me. This has been a strain, though, hasn't it? I've noticed that these past days you've seemed a little bit more distracted, unlike your usual ready-for-anything self."

"More than you know, Mother." Ayan'we turned away for a moment to ask herself if she were prepared to talk about her incident with Isshel, took a deep breath, and turned back to face Entara.   "There's something more I have to tell you. It involves our male colleague. You see, I found I could confide in Isshel. He is unusually open and considerate for a male. Perhaps I got to trust him a bit too far, to become dependent on him.   I needed someone to listen sometimes and didn't want to burden you, especially with what happened to little sister. I went to get his opinions, to let out some of my anxieties. I didn't mean for anything to happen.   I suppose I had underestimated my own dread, my relief that there was someone who understood right away." She paused, remembering the scene. "At any rate, somehow things went a little too far. I was completely shocked. For one thing, I hadn't thought enough about Isshel, what he must be feeling. He had developed something that went – how can I say – beyond sympathy for me. Mother, we both lost control and almost wound up mating."

"Well."   Entara leaned back and blinked her eyes a few times. She was assessing the situation. Ayan'we expected a stern but very controlled reprimand. What she got was something else. Entara let out a brief laugh. "Firstborn, you're not the only one to be surprised. I don't know why I should be, because as I myself have repeatedly hinted, it's high time you come to grips with all the aspects of being a woman. I can't expect you to stay my girl wonder forever. So, what did you do, did you have to fight him off?"

"That's just it, Mother, I couldn't. I went into the premating trance. Without herbs, without concentration, without anything. It just happened naturally and I was unable to control it. I was going limp and starting to submit. Did you ever hear of that happening? Did it ever happen to you?"

"No, I can't say it ever happened to me. Before my first mating, I took advantage of every herb and every concentration exercise in the book and was terribly happy that they worked. I might have gone crazy if I had to confront the pain without that. But, you know, it's not unheard of. There are stories in the matriline of women who went into a trance voluntarily or not, sometimes under extraordinary conditions during the times of troubles, and also without an external crisis, totally unexpected. We will have to consult the matrons of the mahäme to find if they know of any precedents among our ancestors." Entara's face grew wrinkled with puzzlement. "But Ayan'we, if you couldn't resist, what did happen?"

"Fortunately, by some miracle, Isshel was able to preserve a shred of self control. In the middle of the mating rage, he grabbed a blade and stabbed himself deep in the thigh to distract his feelings. I was so grateful, because when I regained normal consciousness, I realized that I wouldn't have been capable of doing anything, and it would have put us both in such a bind."

"Whew! That was lucky. I don't think I know another male of any species who could do that. So that's why he was limping around for a few days. He gave the guards a cock-and-bull story about breaking some glassware during an experiment. This gets more and more uncanny. What I want to know now, daughter, is how are you feeling about this?"

"I am frightened, naturally. But mostly confused. Deeply, deeply confused. I don't know if it will make me more inclined to become a mother or not. It's almost as if there's another self inside of me that I never suspected and I don't know what to make of it. On the one hand, I'm sooo glad things worked out as they did, and on the other, there's this sort of a phantom me that I can't just turn on or off."

Entara touched her shoulder and smiled, "If you're waiting for me to give you an easy answer, I can't. I've always known that there were facets to you that were totally beyond my influence and this proves it beyond a doubt. It's something you'll have to work out for yourself." She took Ayan'we's chin in her hand and pointed it toward her. "You remember this, firstborn – whatever you decide or whatever happens, I will be here to help you and support you, regardless of what people may say, regardless of the matriline, whatever it costs."

"Thank you, mom." Ayan'we cheered up a little. "You know, it seems illogical, but I think there may be somebody else that can help me, too. For some reason, I think I want to talk this over with Amanda. All of a sudden, I really want to see her. It's not that you aren't enough. You're my mother, my flesh and blood. But Amanda's young, like me. I know people might expect me to listen to the judgment of Ishan and Tolowe, my own biological sisters. But there's this closeness, I don't know, I can't explain it well. I was actually dreaming of being with Amanda lately. Do you think that's too wild?"

Entara grew serious. "No way. Remember, I have dreams, too. Amanda is the human child of Klein and nothing about that relationship would surprise me. I've seen that for a long time."

"Do you think I can get a leave to visit them on Earth once we return to Forlan?"

Entara rested her chin on her fist and reflected for several moments. "Perhaps we don't have to wait that long. We will pass not too far from Tau Ceti Anchorage on the way back. I have plenipotentiary powers for this delegation. If I were to decide that the ramifications of the Zonal Treaty require me to gather information about the resettlement project on Earth, I can send anyone I wish, even if it means suspending their responsibilities on Forlan for a while. At Tau Ceti, you could get a ride to Earth almost immediately. Let's see how that works. Now we both need a sound sleep."

Just as Entara and her daughters were turning in, Erica emerged from a troubled "night" of tossing and turning. Glancing at the station clock, she was shocked to find it was hours later than she anticipated. A communicator alarm was flashing on her desk. Surprised, she answered and heard a recorded message that told her to report immediately to Robotic Guild security.

This is not good. Are they rounding us up? Have they found out something? Must talk with Anthony. Her signals to him went unanswered. She called the human delegation central. She gasped as she learned Anthony was no longer on Varess and had been reassigned to an unreachable location. Trying Chester, she was told he was too busy to speak with her. *This is really awful. What to do? Get to the safe room quick!*

She rushed to pick up a few vital tools of the trade. Her limbs seemed like rubber, impeding her movements. *What the hell is going on? Did someone slip me a drug? Did they get in here and break into my fridge? All the spy traps were intact. Unless... oh, no.* That human safe room might not be as safe as she thought. Anthony's absence and Chester's unwillingness to help suggested that maybe they were setting her up. But for what? She tore open the door to her compartment only to find half a dozen Phiddian security with their sharpened quoits at the ready. She considered trying to break through and run, but the light glinting off those razor-sharp edges stopped her. *No use losing an arm or a leg. Maybe I can talk my way out of whatever it is.*

Ramatoulaye stepped forward and spat out, "Erica Duquesne, you are under station arrest for treason and other offenses. Make no resistance." One of the Phiddians stepped behind her and attached something low between her shoulders in the most difficult spot on the back to reach. An immobilizer or worse. They placed her hands into a kind of double mitten that prevented her from removing it. Phiddian cuffs.

"Are you forgetting I have diplomatic immunity from your Phiddian laws? My delegation will be informed immediately of this outrage."

"Your delegation has just waived your diplomatic rights and is considering its own charges against you. We have asserted our jurisdiction and will be interrogating you about certain matters along with our colleagues from the Guild."

"I have done nothing against Phiddi."

"There is the little matter of several illegal Phiddian operatives, now deceased, that you seem to have had contact with. Delegate Macdougal is preparing to turn over certain documents. That will do for beginners.   Save your protests for the official hearing."

They got down to interrogating her right away. No physical torture or sensory bombardment, as she might expect on Earth or its colonies. In fact, she had a comfortable chair, an unopened bottle of water and a sparkling clean glass, and both human and Phiddian legal counsel. The hearing room was softly lit and perfectly air conditioned for human beings, though her Phiddian questioners were more heavily swathed in clothes than usual and the robots obviously didn't care what the temperature was. Presently, Ayan'we and the old Talinian delegate took seats in the back of the room to observe.

Erica was astonished that they confronted her right away with a vast array of evidence. They definitely had the goods on her, delivered and thoroughly explained by one of Chester's aides that she had always taken for an obedient and clumsy toady. There were bogus recordings of her meeting with the Gropers Four well before the abduction of Quatilla and video of her during an interview with Tashto discussing the equipment used to nab Torghh. There was also a stack of documents she had never seen or heard about alleging her contact with a variety of nefarious alien organizations. *They're not only giving them real secret evidence they collected to set me up for the fall. They're actually fabricating stuff to add to the guilt. They're making it impossible for me to defend myself and discrediting any accusations I can make against them. Why? Why? Why?*

She was about to find out. Ramatoulaye and KC announced the interrogation was officially ended. Erica had of course denied everything and refused to admit anything, but couldn't make much headway with the third rule of human intelligence – making counter-accusations – since the material assembled against her had been so new and overwhelming. She was prepared to get up and leave when the interrogators dismissed the lawyers and told her to sit down again. Puzzled, she complied. KC explained that while the formal hearing was over, they were giving Erica the chance to mitigate an eventual sentence by cooperating with the investigation of a related intelligence matter.

"What can you tell us about a message you sent several days ago through coded channels, a message that might have been labeled Mu?"

"You should be aware that I am not authorized to speak about any coded messages that were sent by anyone."

"We realize that, but it appears that this particular communication involved military details that may constitute acts of war banned by, among other agreements, the treaties just ratified." Ramatoulaye smiled and added, "Does that help jog your memory? You must know that this matter could reach far beyond normal criminal matters and nullify any considerations of diplomatic or ordinary military service, placing you in the category of a spy plotting against the defense of Phiddi and other worlds. Don't you have anything to say for yourself?"

"I send many messages as part of my job and frankly can't remember anything called Mu or anything else in code, for that matter. But tell me this: if this supposed message was in a secret code, how is it that you can charge it involves military matters? I suspect you are simply lying to get me to admit to guilt."

KC focused sensors on her and responded, "I don't think we will do any harm in sharing with you something that will soon be made known to all delegations and has already been shared with other choice connections. Our Kael visitors are unusually proficient in codes and managed to intercept and almost completely decipher this Message Mu. They maintain that it concerns the mobilization, dispatch and coordination of human military resources from various points in the zone to certain points in space in such a way as to attack a certain location. A raid, a coup, a war, call it what you will. Responses are under way as we speak. There may certainly be loss of life, civilian as well as military, if hostilities break out. You might stand to be condemned both as a spy and a war criminal."

For a second, Erica considered spilling everything. After all, there was very little room for her to bargain and nothing much left to lose. She was going to be the scapegoat, no matter what transpired.

It was only some shred of pride or defiance that prevented her from owning up to the conspiracies that she was really involved with. Silence was the one comfort and the one negotiating chip she had left. The interrogators did not berate her or try to break her down. They just confined her to her quarters, now rendered totally inescapable, and invited her to use the communicator if she changed her mind about talking at any time at all.

As Erica left the hearing room, she felt a melancholy disconnect with the world around her, a sense of inevitability about her downfall. She harbored no desire to hear the disposition of her case tomorrow, so assured was she of an eventual guilty verdict. She could not even bother to torture herself with the faint hope of exoneration. The evidence presented against her had proved far too deep and damning for even the most dimwitted of jurors or judges to believe in her innocence. She slowly began to follow her security detail back to her room with a weary gait that would have reminded an observer of sleepwalking, but she heard a sudden yell from someone calling to her that shocked her out of her torpor. She turned around and saw Ayan'we rushing up to her.

"So, you've come to dance on my grave. Did you enjoy watching them rip me apart back in that courtroom? I hope you did, because that's the last you'll ever see of me," Erica said.

"I'm not here to take pleasure in your suffering. The only question I have for you is – why are you so willing to inflict suffering on others for the sake of your own advancemen?"

"You really don't know us humans very well, do you? Doesn't a Forlani ever feel a desire to conquer the world, to gain authority and status above others? Or do all of you just spend your entire lives in these matrilines, content with whatever fate society has predetermined for you?"

"We're far more familiar with the selfishness of ambitious individuals than you think," Ayan'we said, remembering Tays'she's schemes. "You remind me of someone I knew once back on Forlan."

"And what did these Forlani accomplish?" Erica snarled, quickly becoming disgusted with the whole Forlani race. "Did they ever gain a position of authority in a major corporation? Did the board ever tell them that they'd be remembered forever if they gave their life for the advancement of their company's interest? How does your species feel about those people that your corporations work to the bone and throw away once the best part of their career is over?"

"We have no corporations. Most Forlani do not believe that the only objective in their life should be the accumulation of status and wealth. We believe that living our life to honor the mahäme is the highest glory of existence, and to believe differently is selfish, wasteful. However, many of us fail to live up to these ideals."

"What about you? Haven't you ever felt like gaining power and authority over the rest of them? What have those egalitarian ideals done for *you* or your career?"

"For now, recovering Doctor Torghh and my sister is enough of an achievement for me. I am sure it will be looked on favorably on Forlan, and perhaps I will be promoted to a position of greater authority. Perhaps another Forlani will be chosen instead. Either way, as long as I continue to perform well, I will be allowed to continue in my career of pursuing knowledge, and that's the life I truly value."

"Ah, so it's *your* career now. I've done my research on your species. Forlani women are supposed to value the status of motherhood above all else. Your own mother, Entara, always seemed to me to think that way. But you...you don't seem in any hurry to leave that career of yours behind."

"What exactly are you implying?"

"You're more like me than you realize, you arrogant little alien. For all your talk about sisterhood and matrilines, you're an aberrant member of your species. You destroyed the career and the life of a woman who was more your sister than anyone back on Forlan, and for what? So you can get a pat on the back and some damn alien Girl Scout merit badge? The only thing life brings us is endless struggle, and you'll find out soon enough that it's no different for you."

"Your life is endless struggle because you chose it to be so. You wanted that position in Hyperion and believed that it was worth anything – even ruining a peace conference and sparking an interplanetary war. And after being so willing to condemn untold millions to misery and death, now you beg for sympathy? You truly have no shame."

"Shame? No one has ever gotten a damn thing from shame! I believed in achievement and the advancement of the human race! You destroyed all my good work for the sake of a chunk of silicon and a bunch of xenophobic lizards who'd sooner kill you than talk to you! I'm the evil one in your eyes because I opposed that?! You Forlani will be a bunch of arrogant assholes to the day your planet's sun finally dies. If you don't heed my words your species deserves the miserable fate it will no doubt receive."

"I'd rather the Forlani not follow you down that dark path of yours. Your aggression has brought you nothing but isolation and sadness. I don't think you can even be reasoned with anymore. You've become so lost in self-absorption. Goodbye, Erica Duquesne. Take pride in the life you have lived if you can," Ayan'we said.

"Get lost," Erica snarled as Ayan'we walked away from her. "Crow in triumph, you miserable failure of a Forlani woman, for ruining my life! See what it gets you! Damn you, Ayan'we!"

Erica stared at Ayan'we's face as she left. There was no visible emotion, no sadness or anxiety reflected in her red Forlani eyes or purple facial muscles as she walked away.

Erica felt powerless, her authority and influence dissolved in the acrid ruins of her life. Perhaps that inability to rattle Ayan'we was a reflection of her own inevitable downfall. *Is this the end of a woman who once felt so confident that she could challenge the universe to advance her own career?* Erica pondered.

After the guards removed the mitten cuffs from her hands, Erica slowly walked back into the small personal room she had been allowed during her time on Transfer Varess.   She was still shocked at how quickly the end had come for her. During the inquest, the remaining Hyperion employees had been all too willing to turn on her, revealing her role in the scheme to abduct Doctor Torghh. Even Anthony—the one who was supposedly outside the company officially—had been all too willing to reveal the painstaking details of that scheme, and to fabricate more, before he unceremoniously left. This was the true face of Hyperion, the company she had sacrificed so much for—cowardly rats that would run and squeal at the first sign of danger, glorified mercenaries with no ideals of loyalty or honor. Officially the future would start to become clearer tomorrow, but Erica was absolutely certain that it would be a little longer before judges put voice to it. *Thank God I can still enjoy a few moments of privacy*, she thought.

Her tiny chamber, so much smaller than the office suite on Earth that she used to work in, was decidedly the worse for wear after the authorities had been through it. Clothes had been haphazardly tossed on the bed and papers left strewn across the desk, signs that investigators had been searching for evidence pertaining to the investigation. It mattered little to her at this point; they already possessed more than enough evidence to put her away for the rest of her life, if there was to be a life. Erica still felt depressed as she looked at the disheveled room, its disorder connected in her mind to the ruin of her career. She noticed that the answering machine on the telephone was flashing red, indicating that someone had sent her a message while she had been under interrogation. She sat down on the chair beside it and slowly pressed the button, dreading the news she suspected she would hear.

"Erica Duquesne", the electronic voice said in a flat, lifeless drone, "this message is to inform you that your employment with the Hyperion Corporation is immediately terminated. Your conduct has been deemed inappropriate of the standards expected of employees of this corporation, and you are not recommended for any financial aid or assistance in the trial or any legal matters thereafter. Your severance package will be forfeited according to the terms stipulated in your contract. You are no longer allowed on any properties or building owned or administered by the Hyperion Corporation. If you have any further problems, please text us and expect a response in no less than two Earth weeks."

That was it. Years of climbing the steep mountain that was the Hyperion corporate hierarchy all ended in an impersonal phone call by an automated voice system while she was away. The company was too cheap and craven to even bother sending her a written notice. There would be no mention of all she had accomplished for the company in her years of service, nor would there ever be a mention that the mission on Transfer Varess had been the idea of her superiors. She had only the loneliness of punishment and failure to look forward to.

Inside the desk she had brought with her from Earth—one of the few personal possessions she had been able to fit into her chamber—there was a small, locked compartment, only a few inches wide. Erica straightened a paper clip and pushed it into the lock, slowly and deliberately turning the clip in the mechanism until she heard a soft click. She watched as a small, bright yellow pill rolled out into her hand. This nondescript pill, which could have been almost any type of medication, was in fact Erica's personal poison capsule, and her only remaining avenue of escape from the miserable wreckage of her existence.

She quickly popped the pill into her mouth, her throat tingling with the anticipation of death as the capsule slid downward. *I wonder what old Bill Hollingsworth was thinking when he died,* she thought. *Did he realize how pointless it was to give your entire life to Hyperion? Did he have regrets that there was so little freedom from corporate demands and dictates in his life? Maybe I'll see you again soon,* she thought as she waited alone for the darkness to come over her.

9

The crowds at Transfer Varess had begun to diminish as the visiting dignitaries started to crowd into the ships departing for their home worlds. There was a solemn, almost melancholy ambience to the station that reminded Torghh of an old nature documentary on honeybee colony collapse he had casually viewed in between his work cycles one day. Torghh was struck by one particular image from that film: the empty, barren passages of the dead colony, free of the noise and buzzing of the bees that had once dwelt there. Transfer Varess had not truly reached this desiccated state; various maintenance drones and Powls still whirred and skittered through its hallways, and a relatively small crew of Phiddians stayed on to operate the higher functions of the station. Yet Torghh couldn't help but be reminded of the empty beehive, and had a sense of finality to his stay on the station; Transfer Varess, too, was now an empty thing of the past to him, a place of dark memories and disturbing experiences.

"What are your plans now?" Rack asked Torghh, breaking his state of tranquil melancholy. Rack had come across to Torghh as being overly anxious, as if he wanted to leave Transfer Varess quickly and be done with the place, putting it out of his mind as rapidly as possible. Torghh could not understand why Rack was so quick to leave the station; why not linger on the memories and experiences a few moments longer, sift through the data in search of some potential solutions to problems not yet encountered? But he did not question his colleague, for such respect had been earned from his rescue that he no longer believed it productive to doubt his motives.

"I have informed the Guild of your accomplishments here on Transfer Varess. They have taken note of your performance and recommended that I offer you a position working with me on my next assignment. Perhaps you would be interested in this task?"

"I am always interested in new opportunities, however I would like to know what this next assignment is before I agree to accept it," Rack said. *Excellent*, Torghh thought. *He isn't so anxious to leave that he lost his curiosity about the nature of his work yet. Perhaps, even after the strife he endured on Transfer Varess, he can succeed at the new task the Robotic Guild has given me.*

"The Guild has ordered me to go the planet Corlatis to deal with a severe outbreak of disease. A recent, highly virulent plague has emerged from one of the planet's major cities and has begun to occur on all major continents. The planet has sent forth a request for as many skilled doctors and geneticists as it can get to deal with the outbreak, and the Guild has recommend my assistance there to help. I need an impeccable colleague with superior focus to assist me in dealing with this disease."

"This plague sounds somewhat familiar," said Rack. "Recently, Earth had a severe disease outbreak which killed much of its population and has left the planet in a precarious state. Could this outbreak be related to the one on Earth?"

"There is some suspicion of this − the area where the plague originated was one where goods traded from other planets were stored, but the pathogen itself is poorly understood. While we are on Corlatis, I would like you to conduct research on the pestilence and its genetic properties. You could be an invaluable resource in understanding the nature of the spread and how it can be contained."

"I believe that the genetic research and microbiology required for this assignment will be incredibly difficult. Why do you believe me a superior choice for this assignment to other members of the Robotics Guild?"

"Because you told me of the battle inside your mind, the struggle with the thing you called Emm. Such a thing was so disturbing, so counterintuitive to the nature of our duties as Guild members, that the average Guild robot would have been driven to illogical confusion and been forced to shut down at least temporarily as an act of mercy. To have struggled through such a terrible experience and maintained your grip on reality is a sign that I can rely on you more than any of my other colleagues in the Guild. Perhaps it also indicates that you are innovative and clever enough to find a solution to this dangerous problem as well."

"I accept this assignment that you have recommended me for," Rack said. "But before we go to Corlatis, I must tell you that something has been troubling me."

So, he finally decides to tell me why he was so anxious. Better I learn the reason now than later, Torghh thought. "Please tell me what you have been thinking about before we leave for Corlatis. I want you to be at your peak mental focus once we get there."

"Although Tashto helped me save you, I remain concerned that his life could still be at risk even with the steps we have taken to aid him in escaping Garan Prime. We know so little of the Blynthians that their motives and their true nature remain obscure to us. What if the Blynthians believed that selling Tashto back to his old masters on Garan Prime would be of greater benefit than trying to harbor him? Or if he were to become involved in some intrigue on the Blynthian home world and have his refugee status revoked by the Blynthian government? There are so many potential dangers for him, and so little we can do now."

"And because there is little we can do now, we must put Tashto out of our minds for the time being and trust that he can take care of himself. The Guild and all the other planetary powers have little sway over the Blynthians. Tashto must be prepared to face a world where he has few natural allies and only the barest minimum of tolerance and goodwill from the Blynthians. He knows the risks, and has accepted them. As have you in accepting this assignment with me."

"Certainly," Rack agreed. Torghh could not detect any sense of emotional conflict in Rack's voice; it was a perfect monotone. Not unusual, since Guild robots typically conveyed emotions subtly through their actions and behavioral patterns rather than the vocal tones so common in organic beings. Torghh could still not help but wonder if Rack concealed some lingering hesitancy, some angst deep within his cybernetic mind from his experience with Emm. He hoped he had made the right decision in entrusting this great responsibility to his colleague.

In the Forlani quarters, Ayan'we did not feel like the same person she was when she embarked several months ago for the trip to Varess. Then, she was full of confidence and felt she had no need to worry about her own values or to doubt the success of the peace conference.   In the intervening weeks, she had recognized how thin a thread the fate of billions of beings hung from.   Moreover, she had come to see how rapidly her own set of assurances could be thrown into disarray, not only by the manipulations of others, but by the limitations of her own naiveté.   Only now was she beginning to let herself feel the full desolation of what might have happened to Quatilla and Torghh. The wasted lives of Fianni and Erica Duquesne stood before her like messy disasters that she would have done anything to save. She sensed subtle invasions of pure hatred scurrying through her mind like prowling carnivores in the night, finally understanding that they were directed at Anthony Wilson and the other nameless humans and Phiddians who had tried so hard to deceive or injure her and her mother. She often thought of the exiled Garanian Tashto who had sprung up to aid them, ripping himself away from all that he had been brought up with, and who seemed doomed henceforth to a life of drifting between the stars, as if he were a forlorn planetoid or a piece of space debris.   And all the time there was the experience of Isshel, renewing itself again and again in her imagination and provoking a thousand "what if?"s. Could she ever have accepted a future in his household with those other wives and their children and then – good heavens! – with children of her own all around her, to care for and to become the proxies for her own far-flung dreams? Her mind swirled like a cyclone in the wilderness, throwing pieces of lives and places into a spaceborne confusion.

Entara noticed her daughter's state of confusion. "What's on your mind, firstborn?"

"I was wondering whether those two new Phiddian contacts who helped kidnap Quatilla will receive a suitable punishment. Have you had any word?"

"In fact, I've just finished recording a message asking their leadership to reduce their penalty."

"Mother, are you out... Why?"

"The Phiddian high justice proposed completely desexing those two accomplices. Wouldn't you agree that seems like a rather barbarous punishment, especially for Phiddians?"

"Ugh! Still, they probably deserve it."

"I suppose so. But it would not produce any kind of restitution."

"So what did you recommend?"

"First, that they be confined in perpetuity to the home planet of Phiddia so they couldn't provoke any more mischief off-planet."

"What else?"

"That they be permanently supervised by our houses there and that they be required to turn over to a responsible house matron a regular sum of credits to be directed to our mahäme to compensate for the trouble they have caused."

Ayan'we rubbed her left earlobe thoughtfully. "Hmm, that's not at all dumb. They'll have to continue strengthening us instead of weakening us. Punishment by opposites. What if the Phiddians don't go along with it?"

"I hinted that we might have to close our houses there."

"Hooo! That will hit them where it hurts. Entara of the Nine has once again proven her wisdom. You'll deserve a lot of kudos for that when you get home."

"Thank you." Entara paused and looked her daughter in the eyes. "Just what do you mean 'you'? Aren't you planning to go back with the rest of us?"

"Not right away. This thing with Isshel still has me shaken up. Before I get back to normalcy, I need to touch base with some things that are important to me. I also want to go back to Domremy and visit Klein's monument again before I go spend some time with Amanda on Earth. I'm sure I can hitch on as a flight officer on some ship headed in that direction."

"No need. I already wanted to see the monument myself and to talk in person with some of our Dissenter friends. To be honest, I just wanted to walk a bit on the prairie, too, remembering old times. The Song Pai bought this ship for the Forlani people and paid for the Blastöo training crew. You can log more instruction with them. Maybe even qualify for an interstellar navigation license. Then we'll drop you off at Tau Ceti so you can take a shorter leg to Earth. But now, let's get ready to attend the goodbye ceremonies."

"Yes, I especially have to thank KC and Ramatoulaye. I wish I could have had time to get to know that one better. Ramatoulaye showed me that many of the negative stereotypes of Phiddians are untrue."

"Their ways are certainly strange and their politics can be tricky, but I think we can develop more understanding and find things in common."

Many of their off world friends had already gathered in the Great Hall when the Forlani arrived. Not everyone, though, because both the Blynthians and the Song Pai had sped off earlier to bring the treaty details to their councils. The Blynthian tubes stood empty and silent – no more weird zipping noises or cloudy undulations behind the glass. Everyone understood the Song Pai absence, too, since their only collective manifestations seemed to be of a military nature and they were considerate enough not to want to spoil the festive, peaceful atmosphere of the departure party. Each of the remaining delegations had something planned. The Coriolans indulged their love of gambling with a comical lottery that gave out jokes and jests to the other species. The Kael soared around the ceiling in an aerial ballet that allowed them to spread their wings at last and show the others a bit of the magic of leading an airborne life.   The Thil performed a famous comedy of theirs called "The Child that Gave Birth to Her Mother," which was so strange that no one knew if they were laughing at the proper time; however, the Thil seemed quite satisfied with the reception, so they must have done something right. The Talinians brought out long reedy instruments and performed a suite of happy music, with an obbligato by old Tionar himself.   No one knew what to expect from the stumpy little Rokol, but it turned out they had an intricate geometric "march" with surprising changes of rhythm that was meant to represent the serendipity of the Varess proceedings.   The Phiddians, more restrained in their eroticism than usual, had literally covered their bodies with every jewel they could beg, borrow, or buy at the station to make a Gem Parade that stunned everyone present with its magnificence.

When it came time for the Forlani to make their contribution, it was naturally in the form of song, with the entire Security Cluster acting as a chorus to first perform "The Ripening of Red Berries," a peace song recalling the end of the Time of Troubles and the beginning of the matriarchies. Next Leli, still confined to a hover couch, was ushered forward to give a solo of "Turn My Steps Toward Stafford," one of Entara's best-known and most optimistic melodies. Isshel acted as the master of ceremonies for the Forlani, since males never sing under any circumstances. He delighted the whole audience by saying that Entara had accepted his invitation to sing, but all were shocked to hear that instead of a love song or a playful harmony, she would offer a dirge, "Sun Through the Swollen Clouds," in sympathy for those who had suffered or died during the weeks on Varess. As the pure, minor key notes floated through the hall, Ayan'we thought of the Phiddians and their Powl pawns, Erica and the vanished humans, of Tashto journeying farther and farther into the cosmos, of the unknown creature whose blood had been shed in the rescue of Quatilla, and especially of the wasted existence of Fianni.

At the conclusion of the music, as if her thoughts materialized, she saw Ramatoulaye walking toward her with another Phiddian, the consort of Fianni she had met back at the Love Court. The consort held out a dazzling polished stone with highlights of gold and green and urged Ayan'we to take it.

"Blazhin, wouldn't that be inappropriate? No one deserves riches or tribute for what happened to your friend, least of all me. I couldn't possibly..."

Ramatoulaye bent toward her and whispered discreetly, "I'm afraid it would be a kind of insult if you did not. Please take it."

"Yes, please accept," added the consort. "The gem has been collected, worn, and displayed. For us, it represents a continuation of the spirit of Fianni and shows that you have no hard feelings. Gems are almost eternal and incorruptible, as memories should be."

"In that case, I am pleased to accept. I want you to know that I have no bitterness toward Fianni and wish that things could have been otherwise."

"Yes, that was obvious in your mother's lovely song." Blazhin's eyes lowered. "What happened to my loved one was atrocious. The destruction of pleasure is against all civilizations. My partner could not have acted otherwise, deranged by this hideous disfigurement of the body and mind. For Fianni, death was a release."

"Yes," nodded Ayan'we. "I understood that in the last moments."

"Now you have made me happy," exclaimed the consort with a beaming expression. "This is the first success of the funeral."

"You see, Ayan'we, our friend here has just bestowed the first gem of many, many more that will be distributed during Fianni's obsequies," Ramatoulaye explained. "All the gems must be shared out, and Fianni had a huge and famous hoard amassed during a career of giving and attending fabulous exchange parties."

"Exchange parties?" Ayan'we mused. "Are they anything like what the humans called potlatch, an old custom almost forgotten."

"I believe so," responded Blazhin. "I have read of such things. My partner was respected throughout our worlds for generous giving and receiving of both gems and affection, so it is only fitting that I perpetuate these feelings by making a remarkable bestowal."

"Won't you hold onto anything yourself as a keepsake ?"

"That would be a rude and disrespectful gesture, preempting the growing magnificence of Fianni's fame. Besides, each Phiddian who receives a Fianni gem will hasten to offer me something equally spectacular in return. I assure you, it will be difficult to manage all the precious jewels I will receive and then to re-bestow them. It will probably keep me busy for the rest of my life. But now I must make some arrangements and I will leave you to say goodbye to each other."

When Blazhin had walked off, Ramatoulaye gave Ayan'we a wide smile of approval. "Congratulations, Cluster Leader, you handled that in a remarkably smooth and compassionate way. Not all aliens can grasp the significance of our 'potlatch' exchanges. So many assume they are just superficial demonstrations of wealth and grandeur. I could tell you immediately tuned in to the emotional importance of that gift."

"Thank you." Ayan'we paused, raising her eyebrows in puzzlement. "I just wish I had something to give you as a going away present. I didn't even think about it with all that's been happening."

"Don't be concerned. I have nothing personal for you either. That wouldn't be proper exchange, at least for Phiddians. You have already given me much to think about and to discuss with my relatives."

"Yes. That's right. With no war, there will be no convoy duty for you and you can meet with your loved ones again."

"I have already signaled them when to expect me. It is a great relief to me that you won't have to decide who to sacrifice in a hex interceptor operation. Doesn't that clear your spirit?"

"It should, if I were really thinking properly. But, Ramatoulaye, I have other personal concerns that have left me emotionally dizzy. I feel more confused than when I was a hapless schoolgirl. I confess to you that I almost mated while on this mission. Do you know what that means to us?"

"Yes, yes," drawled the Phiddian. "I have read about that in databanks. So you, like me, must struggle with sexual confusion, frustrations, and the deferral of pleasure. You are young, but I've had to fight that demon for fifty years. You will face challenges, oh, how many challenges! Yet, you are also strong. I'm sure you will overcome all the difficulties the universe throws at you. I will remember you in my devotions and ask all my relatives to do likewise. Together, our spirits will have a mighty power."

"Thank you, my friend. How about a hug before we depart?" They threw their arms around each other and squeezed so hard and so long that Ramatoulaye suddenly exclaimed, "My goodness, I can feel you have two heartbeats! Wait till I tell my parents about that!

"And I will sing about our friendship when I am back at the mahäme with my sisters and my near-sisters. Take good care of yourself, Ramatoulaye. I will try to stay in touch, but I am headed for Domremy, which does not have very active communications, and then Earth, which has even less. You will hear from me, though, I promise."

Ayan'we was walking away when she heard a different voice. "Cluster Leader Ayan'we, may I have a moment of your time?" She heard the call over her shoulder, coming from a translator, along with a burbled string of expressions that hinted to her that Tionar wanted to talk. The Newt approached slowly on his hind legs, a procedure that required special skill for his watery race. It gave him a stately air that was accentuated by his unusual height, fully seven feet, not counting his temporarily idle tail. "I have been speaking with your mother, the Delegate, and I hear you are planning to travel to Tau Ceti Anchorage on the way to Earth."

"Yes, friend Tionar. I want to spend some time with Amanda Pedersen, a human female who is the daughter of Klein. We became close during Klein's funeral ceremonies on Domremy several years ago. I still have not been able to arrange passage from Tau Ceti to Earth, but I suppose I can hitch a ride from the anchorage."

"It so happens I also wish to visit Earth to inspect the colonies our people are setting up in the deltas they have been granted in exchange for their post-plague rebuilding work. I was hoping that I could accompany you Forlani as far as Tau Ceti. From there, it would be my honor to provide passage for you to Earth along with a party of us Talinians. We already have arrangements on a Blynthian shuttle that is bringing down supplies."

"I would enjoy your company very much. Unfortunately, I am not authorized to make an offer myself. That is my mother's bailiwick. Should I ask her?"

"I already have and she has agreed. I wouldn't dream of embarking without also asking you. I am getting to be an old mud Newt now and I don't want to impose. This will be my last interstellar trip. After my return to Talini, my goal is to return to my fief of Tionar and relax with relatives, descendants and neighbors, swap old stories, and play games of skill as long as I draw breath."

"Then we will be especially privileged to be your last fellow travelers. There are many things I want to ask you. Your advice can give me such a boost, not just in my career, but in my emotional life, as well."

"An old fossil like me advising a dynamic young being full of energy and potential! I find that amusing. Of course, if there is anything useful I can share with you, I will be glad to do it And by the way, since I will be the only one of my race on your new ship, please be completely informal and just call me Kee'ad. There will no longer be a possibility of confusion with the four other Kee'ads in our delegation. Obviously a very common name. That's why we have to use place names like Tionar in their place."

"Very well, from now on we'll be what Amanda called buddies."

The crew of eighteen Blastöo hired by the Song Pai before they left Varess had been working at a breakneck pace on the former human spacecraft that had served as the Forlani quarters during the conference. Nevertheless, they were behind schedule in bringing the outdated ship up to their exacting standards. The Song Pai had left them a Kholod laborer who helped by finding a few of his kind to help with heavy work. They would have also hired some Powls, but were afraid of offending the Forlani, who had such a harrowing experience the last time the tick-like technicians had been admitted into their domain.

The Blastöo leader who was to serve as Ship's Master once they were under way arranged a conversation to that he could report to Entara on their progress. The delegate and her cluster leader met him on the bridge of the vessel, which they had seldom visited before. Even so, the changes made by the workers were unmistakable. Control consoles had been completely redesigned for both the Blastöo and the Forlani they were preparing to train in celestial navigation and operation. Blastöo could use all six of their limbs on controls once they were ensconced in the oddly shaped seats that had extra space for the stubby hind parts that they often used as a built-in stool.   The other positions, designed for quasi-marsupials with only two fully-digited limbs, were far less compact.   There was no race in the Zone more ideally adapted to piloting space vehicles than the Blastöo.   With characteristics of both reptiles and amphibians, as well as some genetic material otherwise mainly found in insects, they could stay on uninterrupted watch without rest longer than any competitors.   Their complex eyes had a field of vision only exceeded by the Song Pai and their sensitivity to magnetism actually made many of the usual gauges and indicators quite superfluous to them.   They required little water and only simple protein cakes for the lengthiest voyages.

"You can appreciate how much work there has been to do," the Ship's Master explained.   "When you assume command as captain, we want to make sure everything is totally operational, though there may still be a few superficial details to see to."

"I thoroughly approve, but you must realize that I am in no position to give navigational commands," Entara pointed out.   "I will be a captain in name only."

"No problem at all.   We are quite used to a system of Ship's Masters.   I will handle the minutiae. Of course, the choice of destination and overall traveling protocols will be entirely yours.   I will be content to be a very well-paid factotum and all my colleagues will be very happy to perform all the usual tasks."

"Have you worked out how to lay out the training schedule?" Ayan'we inquired.

"As I understand it, your people are used to a shift of about six station hours. Our instructors will adapt entirely to that, while the rest of our crew will follow their usual rotation of fifteen station hours. I foresee no difficulties. This is because we have brought this craft up to date. Those humans! The original was typical of their impractical priorities – over-armed and under-powered. I don't understand how they get anywhere with their sub-par sensor arrays. Your Song Pai benefactors wisely provided us with credits to obtain the best modern equipment. Thirty percent better in all categories and a full eighty percent more efficient at life support. You will not be uncomfortable. No bothersome, inconvenient icing. Above all, your trainees will be qualified on appropriate equipment."

It was two full station days before the Kholods finished loading all the supplies and spare parts so that the ship could leave. One of the last details was that an exterior team had to remove the human markings on the hull, covering the old numbers and the name *HCAF557Mayakovsky* with the new designation *FFF001Bountiful.* Ayan'we watched attentively as the Ship's Master, who insisted on being called simply Groth, pushed away from Transfer Varess and set a course for Domremy.   Since the station was in interstellar space, well clear of any solar system, the navigation was easy – just right for the Forlani trainees who were picking up the rudiments of operating a vessel of this size, destined to carry a mixture of passengers and freight.   Those who, like Ayan'we, had flight experience in hex interceptors limited to intra-system patrols, had a lot to learn.

Before long, the Forlani were rotating in their six-hour shifts and making test runs on a simulators the Blastöo had rigged up for them. Then, one by one, they were given the opportunity to work beside the pilots at the real controls, under the watchful dark eyes of Groth and his colleagues.   Most made rapid progress. Even Lila, recovering from the injuries she suffered from the blast from Fianni that she took to shield Entara, finally joined them. As they neared the Domremy system, about half-way to Tau Ceti, the pilot crew on the bridge was all-Forlani, except for a single Blastöo officer to supervise training. One Forlan week into the voyage, Entara met Ayan'we as she was finishing her shift.

"Come along, firstborn. Kee'ad has asked us to wait with him for some important news affecting our destination at Tau Ceti." The two Forlani walked down the central corridor of the ship to Kee'ad's apartments, which had been hastily fitted with both pool and dry areas to accommodate his amphibian lifestyle. Ayan'we noticed that no other members of the cluster were with them, which suggested that this was a confidential matter.

"Welcome, welcome," said the old Newt through his translator. "We are about to hear something quite secret that I have tapped into through a protected link done by the Talinian intelligence services. It involves that complicated coded message sent by the unfortunate Erica Duquesne, Coded Message Mu. As you know, Kaels decrypted the message and determined it referred to a military deployment of human vessels to a point close to the anchorage."

"What my daughter does not know," added Entara, "Is that an interspecies expeditionary force was rapidly organized to try to block the human force. We estimated that the human goal was to retake control of that valuable anchorage."

"Ah, yes," Ayan'we mused. "Very plausible. It has been administered by an intrazonal authority ever since the plague broke down all human political control, hasn't it?"

"Quite true," nodded Kee'ad. "At present, the authority comprises a triumvirate of Phiddian, Blastöo, and Coriolan directors."

"Where did you find enough military vessels to confront the humans? Given the current instability about the Song Pai and the Blynthians, most planets would have grouped their fleets close to home, I suspect."

"Right again, my daughter. As I understand it, it was quite a stretch to cobble together a squadron anywhere near Tau Ceti. They could only assemble a half dozen ships of different types."

"I can tell you exactly," noted Kee'ad. "We are patched into the com section of a Coriolan cruiser that is the flagship. Other than that, there are two Thil corvettes that were returning from a tour of duty on the Zetan frontier, a Phiddian armed cargo ship that was in port, and a Blastöo mine layer."

"I see. Now I guess there is nothing to do but wait and hope the commanders don't lose their heads."

They settled down to nibble a few treats and listen to the odd music of Talinian sea pipes. After a few minutes, Ayan'we got nervous and needed to talk. "Tell me, Kee'ad, were you surprised by the concessions the Blynthians offered to the Song Pai? I had no idea Blynthians were facing hostilities we didn't know about."

"Yes and no," drawled the Newt. "There had been rumors picked up by our workers here and there in the zone. Naturally, we didn't get anywhere near the area where the new Song Pai world lies, deep in the heart of closed Blynthian space. You can imagine, though, that details tend to pile up – a military vessel hurrying from a border base, a larger than expected purchase of weapons materials, a decrease in patrols along a peaceful frontier. So far the Song Pai aren't telling much about whatever they are learning from the Blynthians. We'll find out more later."

Entara chimed in with some diplomatic expertise. "Personally, I think the offer of an undeveloped water world was a stroke of genius. I believe the Song Pai were in desperate need of a place to expand their population."

"No doubt about that," agreed Kee'ad. "That I can confirm with total assurance, based on observations of our construction crews on Song Pa. You're aware that since the discovery of the prion disorder than claimed Klein's life, there are no more human indentured servants on that planet and they depend more than ever on our teams, since we are immune. My people report that despite the attrition of combat casualties among immature Song Pai, the population had reached its maximum based on food supply. Their hatcheries have become so efficient at caring for hatchlings that the total population reached a ceiling. Consequently, they were forced to delay defrosting sperm and eggs of dead warriors. That is the very gist of Song Pai values. Further delays would soon strain their social order. Now they can continue to breed and maintain the reward for their warrior mentality, at least for the foreseeable future. But wait, here comes some com traffic from Tau Ceti..."

"Commodore Zelaran of the Coriolan fleet reporting from Point Intercept off the Tau Ceti Anchorage. Sensors detect a group of twelve... no, more... fifteen human military vessels decelerating from light speed on the expected heading. I am leaving the channel open so that authorized listeners can monitor our hails and conversations. Please adjust your translators for both Coriolan and Human Trade English." A pause of several seconds. Then Zeleran began issuing orders to the crew. "All squadron ships, assume configuration alpha, power all shields, prepare to arm weapons on my command. Stand by." Another pause. "Hail the human fleet." The Coriolan went on to greet the human ships with a polite but firm inquiry as to their purpose.

A reply sounded clearly over the link. "Rear Admiral Yu Xi-huang of Human Expeditionary Force Mu on board the battleship *Big E Fortune*. Our mission is to peacefully insure operations at Anchorage Tau Ceti, according to existing mandates. You must disperse and vacate our approach lanes or we will be forced to engage."

"You must be aware, Admiral, that the recent Treaties of Varess have altered previous mandates and licenses. The presence of a military deployment by your species, its fleets or corporations is expressly forbidden and we must enforce those treaties."

"The alleged treaties are not part of our mission. They will not affect our rules of engagement. Stand down immediately. We are arming weapons."

The Commodore immediately ordered the allied squadron to do likewise.

"Coriolan, you are risking annihilation. Do as commanded."

"Oh, I don't think so. We are confident of our abilities."

"You have only six ships. A couple of lousy Thil corvettes, other rag-tag vessels you found somewhere. Apparently the Petrusians, Kael and Rokol who've infested the Anchorage didn't even have any military craft to reinforce you. I give your own cruiser credit for being a fit ship, but you cannot win. We will not spare you if we open fire."

"Then you have undoubtedly noticed that those Thil vessels are fresh from the Zetan frontier. They are used to dealing with much tougher customers than you. And our Blastöo pals have an empty hold. Do you take the implications of a mine layer with an empty hold? There's a lot more between you and Tau Ceti than just this squadron. Maybe you've also heard of what kind of tricks the Phiddians are famous for. Did I mention that they provided the mines?"

"Are you trying to bluff us, Zeleran? This is your last chance."

"Ha, ha!" scoffed the Commodore in a coati-like chuckle. "You are aware that we Coriolans love nothing better than gambling. And we are not easy marks. Me, I like the odds. Are you sure your sensors can tell you everything? How do you know I'm not patched into a certain Song Pai Carrier Number Nine? Six hundred interceptor pilots hot to breed and die. When will they arrive? That's for you to find out. I know your game of poker and have won many times. I'll stay with this hand. Your move."

A long silence. "Comlink disconnected. The human ships have powered down weapons and shields and have begun jumping to trans-light velocity on a course towards Epsilon Eridani. We are likewise powering down but will stay on station. Over and out."

Ayan'we, who had been listening with clenched claws, retracted them and glanced at Entara, who seemed to have been equally concerned, and at the impassive Kee'ad, who had never flinched.

"Whew! That was tense. That Zeleran is a cool-headed character."

"I wouldn't want to have to face the Commodore in a game of poker," said Entara.

"Friend Kee'ad, was there really a Song Pai carrier on the way?"

"On the one hand, one might think that the Song Pai are already deploying to their new Blynthian corridor. On the other hand, are the Song Pai ever ready to pass up a chance to fight? Who knows? Obviously the humans of Force Mu were not prepared to take that chance."

The trio separated, as Entara headed for the communication shack and Ayan'we strolled back to get some rest in the sleeping area. On the way, she nearly bumped into Isshel. The male had also not been watching where he was going, absorbed in deep thought. The two stared awkwardly at each other for a second before blurting "Good day" at the same time. That caused them both to smile.

Finally the female decided to break the ice. "It's nice to see you again, Isshel. You've certainly been holding to your intention of diving into your work."

"I imagine you've been busy, too.   Another of the cluster told me you've already had your hands on the controls."

"Correct.   And how's your new project coming along?"

"With difficulty.   It's taken a different turn than what I foresaw.   Would it bother you too much to come take a quick look at it?   You can bring along others if you'd prefer not to be alone with me."

"That won't be necessary.   We're both adults. Besides, I now know I can trust you farther than I would any other male.   Lead the way."

They made their way to the studio Isshel had prepared in one of the compartments.   He made a point of leaving the door wide open.   As Ayan'we passed through it and adjusted her eyes to unusually dim light, she was shocked to discover not one of the artist's previous intricate liquid creations, but a flat rectangular tableau smeared with discordant pigments in a chaotic design.

"This is such a departure from the work I've seen before! Why have you changed medium?"

Isshel's face formed the straight-lipped, rigid frown of the Forlani.   Ayan'we was almost convinced he was going to shudder. "I tried for days, for days, but the stasis equipment just refused to produce what I wanted.   Then I realized I didn't know what I wanted. My mind is troubled somehow."

"By what happened to us?"

"No.   At least I don't think so.   I've been preoccupied with what to do when I get back to Forlan."

"Your family?"

"No.   I'll be happy to see them, of course, to settle into the comfort of their attention and respect, to get caught up on all the little news of daily life. In fact, I long to just plunge into domestic tranquility and never come out.   What bothers me has to do with the Brotherhood.   I think that's what has been inspiring these dark visions in my work. I hadn't worked with tableaux and pigments for the longest time and suddenly it seems the only way to express my inner feelings."

"Has there been some big disruption in the Brotherhood?" Ayan'we had to stretch her imagination to picture the aesthetically obsessed males getting stirred up over anything more significant than the necessity of including diagonals in a three-dimensional composition.

"Nothing major. I've only had a few contacts with friends scattered here and there and only bits and pieces of political news. It appears the big synod meeting did not produce any progress. In fact, all they did was to reaffirm the most ultra-conservative ideas in an even more block-headed manner. All our hopes for an end to gelding the less talented and abolition of the *dobutu* serfdom seem more hopeless than ever."

"So why should you be more pessimistic if nothing changed?"

"The changes are so subtle. I sense a breakdown of interaction, a radicalization within the Brotherhood and perhaps even between them and the matrilines. It seems un-Forlani, dangerous." He sighed and added, "I only hope Entara-para-pa's presence will re-establish security and dialogue. Someone needs to still the new and strident voices that are coming forward."

"I'm sure she will have the wisdom to put everything right. Don't worry. You'll see that as soon as she sets foot on the planet again, females and males will rally to her. Don't lose hope." Even as Ayan'we said these encouraging phrases, there was a disquieting murmur somewhere in her mind that wondered if she could be wrong, if perhaps she had made a mistake in heading for Earth instead of staying by her mother's side. But in another instant, she shrugged it off as excessive caution, an after-effect of the turmoil on Varess. Especially when she saw that her words had brightened Isshel's mood, she congratulated herself on saying the right thing. After urging him once more to return to his stasis sculptures, she took her leave and walked away toward a well-earned rest.

When she awoke, Ayan'we realized that she had slept much longer than she intended. A glance at the ship's indicators in the compartment told her that *Bountiful* had already entered the Domremy system and would soon be in orbit around the planet. Chiding herself for turning off the shift change alarms and notices before she collapsed, she hurried to stuff clothing and a few gifts into a duffle before racing to the shuttle bay. Fortunately, she did not have to pack much, because she knew the maximal window for the second leg to Tau Ceti was only two planet days away and their visit would be all too brief. In the spanking new shuttle the Blastöo had substituted for the pre-plague human model, She and Entara, along with a bleary-eyed Trevor, who had been in space sleep the entire way from Varess, descended blissfully to the tawny surface of Domremy, where Peebo and half his family were awaiting them at a nearly deserted landing area outside Stafford Station. After many embraces, they drove them by thallop-drawn wagon to the homestead and regaled them with fresh delicacies from their orchards and gardens. Ayan'we gorged herself on some red things called raspberries that she had never tasted before, much to the amusement of the hosts. As evening fell, Dissenters assembled to speak with them late into the night, including a fellow named Luis who had once been a close friend of Klein during his mankiller days and another named Barber John who brought them a sachet with a lock of Klein's hair that he had snipped during Klein's recuperation from the horrendous wounds received on Song Pa. A couple of Forlani from a local house joined them, including one who had been a student of Klein's in the pleasure class at the mahäme and later served as a messenger to him. Stories were told until no one could keep their eyes open any longer.

All too soon, the travelers had to rouse themselves, since Peebo had arranged to take them by blimp to the southern continent to see the memorial and visit the research center where Klein spent his last days. Entara was delighted to learn it was the "original" Domremy blimp, the airship Klein had followed to the Middendorf Hills during his trek through the uncharted grasslands after his duel with Aleksandrov. Ayan'we tried to imagine what her mother was thinking as she stared out the window while the blimp guided along, watching the sea of reeds as though she might spot a hairy Klein and his pack thallops still trudging along. When Ayan'we herself looked out the window, she gave a yip of surprise upon spotting a group of giant grasshopper-like beings bounding along. The Locals could spring up almost as high as the blimp as they migrated through the savanna. "Look, mom! I wonder if of any of those actually linked up telepathically with Klein?"

"You know what, my dear? I wouldn't be surprised if one of them even grew in Klein's body when he donated himself as a host.   In a way, they could claim to be his children."

That made Ayan'we think of Amanda, who had insisted that Ayan'we was as much Klein's adopted daughter as she was his biological offspring.   When the blimp passed over a narrow strait of salt water and eventually landed on the southern continent, Peebo's son Mel was there to greet them, as was Dr. Patak, the scientist who had supervised Klein's experimental communications with the Locals and the genetic engineering project to restore Domremy's original ecology as it had existed before Hyperion Corporation attempted to terraform the planet.   They guided Entara and Ayan'we through all the units in the experiment station, which had developed a great deal since Klein's funeral.   The pippos that Klein once tended had bred so successfully that dozens had been released into the wild and only a few remained as test animals.   Besides those pig-hippos that formerly roamed the plains in great numbers, the Dissenter scientists had restored six other animal species to the southern continent, as well as over fifty plant species that were thriving in many locations.   They were still working on their biggest project, an attempt to revive the sheep-like creatures who had once served as hosts for the infantile Locals.   Recent discoveries of new DNA in a cave north of the Middendorfs held out hope that a viable, fertile clone could soon be created.   When Entara and Ayan'we were offered the chance for a telepathic communication session with Locals, they both accepted without hesitation.   Soon insectoid feelers were tickling their inner ears and the session began. The Forlani gasped as they began to visualize images of Klein himself in his earliest contacts with the one he called Stumpy and later with other Locals in the research center. Their race had widely shared these memories with each other and now happily bestowed them on those Klein had loved. In return, they would bring impressions of Forlan to share with their relatives.

As the suns set, the Dissenters brought the Forlani to the stone memorial that stood some distance from the center and set out mats and blankets so that the females could lie under the stars as Ayan'we had once done with Amanda, and the daughter could point out to her mother, as she and her friends had with the human girl, the location in the sky of Amanda's Star. With Klein's likenesses moving in their dreams, they slept under the caresses of a warm Domremy wind. In the morning, Mel and Patak drove them hastily to the landing area where their *Bountiful* shuttle would alight. Ayan'we was startled to see the figure of Trevor already at the site. She had assumed he would stay on Domremy with his closest associates.

When she asked him if he would accompany them to Tau Ceti, he replied, "Sure thing, Cluster Leader! I have made a complete report of all my wanderings and discoveries to the Circle here on this world. Now I am on the way to Tomakio to share everything with them."

Ayan'we remembered that Tomakio was the other planet chiefly inhabited by Dissenter farmers. It made perfect sense. "Where will you go after that? Off into some new corner of the Zone or even beyond?"

"Most likely not. I will rendezvous on Tomakio with a lady named Indira who is to carry on my work once she is up to date on the trail of the spiritual substrate. As for myself, I plan to stay on Tomakio and devote myself to farming and social issues. My quest is complete and I plan to 'quit while I am ahead,' as they used to say on Earth. Sharing the news of the ancient inhabitants of Song Pa with the present species is a pretty good crowning achievement. I doubt whether I could ever get such an opportunity again for an act that is meaningful and satisfying. What do you think?"

"You are right," nodded Ayan'we. As she glanced at her mother, she added, "Later, when we are under way, I'd like to talk to you again about something."

"I understand," he winked. "I will be available."

On the second leg to Tau Ceti, the transport ship began to seem quiet and drab to Ayan'we compared to the bustling, noisy Transfer Varess space station in the days of the conference. Other than the occasional meal in the mess area, she had little opportunity to discuss things with her fellow travelers. Even during lunch they seemed too absorbed with training and work duties, or distracted by writing messages to their mahäme friends on their tablets, to care about anything else. Ayan'we now missed the electric atmosphere of Varess – that undeniable tension of rival species attempting to understand their adversary's political maneuvering, the feeling of openness that came from a rare place of galactic interaction with multiple life forms forced to work together, the sense of intrigue as she worked to unravel a shadowy conspiracy of humans and Garanians. After the next couple of days, she had given up on her attempts to seek stimulation with her fellow passengers and spent most of her hours in her small personal chamber, meticulously recording the events that took place on the space station. She had been calmly going about her routine until the telescreen began making a soft beeping noise.

Ayan'we swiftly pressed the small red button on the telescreen, her reflexes sharpened almost to the point where she could hit the button quicker than thought. The tension from Transfer Varess had never completely left her mind, even during the languid interlude on this transport ship, and she was still incredibly alert to the slightest sign of irregularity or danger. As the screen quickly turned on, Ayan'we's eyes were confronted with a distorted, wavy image that seemed to lag and audio that was choppy. She could just make out Amanda's face in the blurry, pixelated image.

"Sorry. Conditions – faulty here on Earth. Infrastruc – still primitive. Can't wait to see you here in Germany," the fuzzy image of Amanda said. The audio feed was so bad that an alien with poor knowledge of the English language would have had great difficulty interpreting what Amanda was trying to say. Luckily, Ayan'we had been extensively exposed to the language, both from her time in the Academy and her conversations with Klein, and could fill in the gaps and understand the basic sentence structure of Amanda's conversation.

"What's going on there?" said Ayan'we. "Why is your video feed in such bad condition? I thought Earth's reconstruction had more advanced infrastructure by now!"

"Looters came last week. Guild unit drove .... ff. New system – set up with spare parts, low quality. Still... bugs in it. Wait, try .... is. Better?"

"Is there a war going on down there? Who are these people?"

"Call themselves – Blood Riders. They started showing up in the American Midwest at the time the national government collapsed, now they're appearing here in Europe. Claim they're legi... government, but they murder and steal as much as they can. I'm ur... worried about my mother back in North America. We... tell you about it all when you come."

"I'll try to help. I have a lot to discuss with you."

"… conference?"

"Yes, that, but other things more important, too. At least to me. And I need to tell you about the visions I saw of Klein."

"Visions? Oh, I want…"

The video feed abruptly cut off before Amanda finished her sentence. A sense of foreboding fell over Ayan'we, the more she thought about Amanda and her mother menaced by these Blood Riders. She instantly missed the sense of dull ennui that had pervaded her mind only minutes earlier. She also realized that among the motivations behind the Hyperion Corporation's conspiracy on Transfer Varess, she had neglected the most likely of them all – a last, desperate grab at extending their power beyond their deteriorating home world. She had become all too familiar with Hyperion's executives and their methods of operation. Confronting that huge human institution, if noxious and dangerous, was at least somewhat predictable. What type of human opposition would she encounter on an Earth defined not only by its tremendously powerful megacorporations, but by tumult, violence, and chaos?

Ayan'we began to type the first paragraph of her synopsis into the computer. *I had no belief that the negotiations on Transfer Varess would be simple and without difficulty, but a shadowy conspiracy emerged that made the negotiations on the station more dangerous and tense than I possibly could have imagined. The following report details both the conspiracy and its likely motivations and the potential political fallout from its failure on Earth, which has already become destabilized.*

Ayan'we considered the tone of her report. Perhaps it would seem a bit melodramatic at first to her superiors. They would likely see things her way, though. Some events deserved a bit of dramatic flair in the narration, recommended governmental styles be damned!

When she was done with the report, Ayan'we still felt she had something to do. Talk with Entara? No, the one she needed to see was Trevor. She found the wizened black man enjoying a cup of warm beverage in the mess area. No one else was around.

"Trevor," she began, sliding into a seat opposite him, "It's time I had that little talk with you."

"Sure. What's on your mind?"

"I'm on my way to discuss my personal life with my friend Amanda down on Earth. But with you I need to find out about something that points in a completely opposite direction. Listen, you've gone farther through the galaxy than almost anyone else I know, searching for traces of this thing you call the spiritual substrate. You've uncovered so much. But tell me this. Do you believe there's any such thing as a soul? That is, is there anything beyond this organic life of ours?"

"Now, that's an awfully big question. Can I ask what brings you to it? I thought you Forlani did not believe in an afterlife."

"Not like humans. It holds no importance in our ceremonies. Our songs are as close as we get to a life after death. That's how we perpetuate ourselves. In a way, we live on through the matriline. Yet it's not separate from our physical lives."

"So, why the uncertainty?"

"On Domremy, you know we visited the research center. There were Locals there. They shared telepathy with us through their touch. Trevor, the images they shared mainly featured Klein. It was a direct contact with his life. They will pass it on amongst them forever if they can. I envy that. I long so to be able to connect with him and the things that have been. Is there any chance of that? Is there any 'me' aside from the cells in this body of mine? I suppose if I were a conventional female like my sibs, I wouldn't be so concerned. But you know that I've always considered myself a weird Forlani."

"You are indeed special, Ayan'we. I do understand how you've been shaken up by the telepathic experience. I've done it myself with different motives. To answer your original question, I do believe in soul. Not because I am a member of the Circle, for as you may know, there is no orthodoxy of beliefs in our fellowship. So I believe it based on my private mind, as your consciousness is distinct from that of your younger sisters, or even Entara's. Hard to explain by rationalism alone. Soul, yes, I have a sense of soul. I sense you do, as well."

"You sense it in me?"

"Yes, I do. Maybe it's connected with the idea of fate. Almost all organisms comprehend that. I sense soul in you. I'll tell you something else. No matter how much fate played a role in what happened on Varess, I sense that your soul will somehow grow on Earth. You must open yourself to that. Be mindful of it. Please remember that."

Ayan'we reached into her sash and touched the jewel Fianni's consort had bestowed on her. She could not see it, but through her fingers it somehow seemed to glow. "You're right. I will remember."

In the spacious transport on the way to Planet Blyn, a large chamber lit up and three worm tubes descended from the ceiling, filled with foggy gas, and soon contained the segmented bodies of the creatures recognized at the conference as Blynthian delegates. A pink light suddenly illuminated the wall facing them. It scintillated so much that the delegates could not see whatever was behind it.

"You summoned us, supervisors?" zipped the leader in their inscrutable language.

"It is time," droned a synthesized voice they could understand. "You have performed your assignment admirably and deserve to be rewarded as planned."

"Yes, we feel we have been successful. The treaties reflect the major conditions you specified. Moreover, no one suspects a thing."

"We have closely monitored the state of mind of all the races involved. You are right. The security of our identity has been preserved. We will soon be able to view the deployment of Song Pai forces to the sector we seek to protect."

"We were very careful to ensure that the humans, the Phiddians, and the Garanians did not obtain any unbalanced advantages from the agreements. The chance of them getting involved in large scale violence is very small."

From the pink lights came a welcome assurance. "Indeed, the human raid at Tau Ceti has been foiled without loss of life."

"What about this Garanian individual we are bringing back? What are your plans for him?"

"Bring him to the first planetfall and turn him over to Command 51. They will deal with him. We foresee a use for him and some of his kind to whom we have granted asylum."

"So do you consider our mission completed?" asked a second worm.

"Return to your world and enjoy all that has been promised to you, with some considerable bonuses that will delight you even more. Separate and share your experiences with others that you trust. We will certainly have further chores for you in the future.

You deserve the respect of our Blynthian domain and are hereby awarded honorary citizenship. Congratulations and good voyage."

The wall darkened, the tubes slid back into the ceiling, and the ship was soon engulfed in the expanses of space beyond the Zone, far beyond the outposts that the most curious travelers, like Ayan'we and Trevor, had ever visited.

ABOUT THE AUTHOR

James F. Gaines and John M. Gaines have been writing science fiction together for several years as a father-son team under the collective name J. M. R. Gaines, besides publishing some pieces individually. Living in Fredericksburg, Virginia, close to the nation's capital makes them yearn for other worlds. In the Forlani Saga they have created, alien life forms are a central concern, not just for their physical appearance, but because of an interest in how separate evolutions in vastly different environments could cause widely varying psychologies, social forms, languages, and mental outlooks. In alien contact situations, these differences offer unending possibilities as sources of either cooperation or conflict.

Before there was *Spy Station*, there was *Life Sentence,* the sweeping story that introduced Klein, Entara, Ayan'we, Torghh, Trevor, and a host of other characters.

Here's what one reviewer on Amazon say about the first novel of the Forlani Saga:

Great Oak Lover Gives Five Stars
"This is an eventful, wide-ranging, indeed universe-ranging, sci-fi novel, with a large cast of characters representing a number of different species. Klein, the complex protagonist--violent and vengeful, but also sensitive and loving--knits them all together through his often involuntary travels. By the end, he has become, in spite of himself, a movingly heroic figure. But the crowning achievement of the book is perhaps its vivid creation of aliens and their cultures. The aliens include the Locals, big, bug-like creatures who use humans as hosts for their larvae (but turn out to be something quite other than Hollywood monsters); the cephalopodan and disgustingly scatological Song Pai, and the furry, tailed, and seductive Forlani. The last species, in particular, is presented in persuasive detail, from their matrilineal culture to the biological and emotional aspects of their sexuality. The authors' rich imaginations draw the reader in, but so do their considerations of such themes as moral aspiration and time's passage. All in all, a novel with something for every sci-fi fan, and for every reader who enjoys an interesting story."

400 J. M. R. Gaines

www.ingramcontent.com/pod-product-compliance
Lightning Source LLC
Chambersburg PA
CBHW060143260626
47160CB00001B/97